NEW MONEY

ALSO BY LORRAINE ZAGO ROSENTHAL

Other Words for Love

NEW MONEY

A Novel

Lorraine Zago Rosenthal

Thomas Dunne Books
St. Martin's Press ⚏ New York

THOMAS DUNNE BOOKS.
An imprint of St. Martin's Press.

NEW MONEY. Copyright © 2013 by Lorraine Zago Rosenthal. All rights reserved. Printed in the United States of America. For information, address St. Martin's Press, 175 Fifth Avenue, New York, N.Y. 10010.

www.thomasdunnebooks.com
www.stmartins.com

Library of Congress Cataloging-in-Publication Data

Rosenthal, Lorraine Zago.
    New money : a novel / Lorraine Zago Rosenthal. — 1st ed.
        p. cm.
    ISBN 978-1-250-02535-7 (hardcover)
    ISBN 978-1-250-02534-0 (e-book)
    1. Upper class—Fiction.   2. Wealth—Fiction.   I. Title.
    PS3618.O8423N49 2013
    813'.6—dc23   2013013484

St. Martin's Press books may be purchased for educational, business, or promotional use. For information on bulk purchases, please contact Macmillan Corporate and Premium Sales Department at 1-800-221-7945, extension 5442, or write specialmarkets@macmillan.com.

First Edition: September 2013

10 9 8 7 6 5 4 3 2 1

Acknowledgments

I would like to express my sincerest gratitude to my stellar agent, Elizabeth Evans; my talented editors, Brendan Deneen and Margaret Sutherland Brown; and everyone at St. Martin's Press who contributed to this novel. I also want to thank my husband, who has always supported me and my work.

New Money

One

I stopped short. My cart filled with books in plastic covers screeched against waxed tiles. Had the South Carolina heat melted my brain? Was I hallucinating and hearing things? I must have been, because someone could *not* have just called me that.

My head snapped toward three teenage boys sitting at a row of computers under a skylight as the blazing July sun streamed through the glass and onto their hair. I'd seen them before and knew they went to Charleston High. I hadn't been a student there for six years, but it seemed like yesterday.

"*What* did you say?" I asked in a stern voice.

One of the boys shrank into his seat. His hair was dark and his eyes were blue, and he reminded me of someone. "I wanted to know what time the library closes tonight," he answered.

"And how did you address me when you asked that question?"

"Library Lady," he said meekly.

So I *hadn't* imagined it. They obviously saw me as one of those dateless women who dress in costumes for Renaissance Festivals and knit sweaters for cats and fret about the possibility of their lady parts rotting if they don't get some use soon.

I almost fell over. Except for the Renaissance Festivals and the cat thing, that *was* me.

"Dear Lord," I muttered through my fingers, wishing I hadn't twisted my hair into a bun that morning. I'd forgotten that a pulled-tight bun was part of the official Library Lady uniform.

The dark-haired boy's friends laughed at him. "Don't let her use that tone with you," one of them said, shooting me a condescending smirk. He had dark-blond hair like mine, a Confederate flag tattooed on his wrist, and a supersized Coke in a cup beside his keyboard. Cokes weren't permitted in the library. I usually hated enforcing that rule and all the other ridiculous, nitpicky, uptight regulations. But I didn't mind now.

"Get rid of that," I said. "No drinks allowed in the library."

He sneered. "Don't tell me what to do. You're not even a real librarian."

It was bad enough that I hated my job. I didn't need criticism from some snarky teenager. "How would *you* know that, smartass?" I asked. I'd been told since I was old enough to talk that swearing was unladylike and ungodly and rude and crude and I should never do it. But that rule often felt suffocating, and cusswords were sometimes just necessary to describe certain people.

Blondie pointed to my blouse. "Well, it's right there."

How embarrassing. I'd forgotten about the laminated name tag pinned to my shirt that outed me as a lowly library assistant. My job title shouldn't have slipped my mind, since the genuine librarians never let me forget it.

I tried to maintain dignity. "So you can read," I said, lifting my chin. "How shocking."

Blondie's face fell. I supposed he was the bullying type who was used to dishing out crap but didn't enjoy the taste of it. "I'll bet reading is all you ever do," he said. "I'll bet you curl up with a book every night because it's just so lonely in your bed."

Damn that little bastard. Why did so many guys believe the

theory that any woman who has a brain and values quality literature can't possibly attract a man? And why did this theory have to be right when applied to me? Not that it had always been that way.

"Hey," the dark-haired boy said sharply. "Cut it out."

I stared as mid-afternoon sunlight beamed down on him. He was handsome and sturdy, with big arms and a strong jaw and *Charleston High Football* printed across his shirt. I'd had a boyfriend like him once—a boyfriend named Jamie with sapphire eyes and a gleaming smile. His breath had always smelled like Original Mint Scope. But things had ended between us two years ago. We'd wanted different things. And now he was getting everything he wanted, while I shelved books and got harassed by teenagers.

"I'm sorry," said the dark-haired kid. It was probably meant as an apology for the entire group even though the other boys had gone back to the Internet and didn't seem the least bit remorseful. "I didn't mean to insult you with that Library Lady thing, ma'am."

What nerve. *"Ma'am"* was for mothers, grandmothers, and decrepit spinster aunts whose biggest thrill was church on Sunday. "Don't call me *that,* either," I said. "Do you know I was a cheerleader at Charleston High? I dated a quarterback, but that doesn't mean I was an airhead. I was on the honor roll all four years. I wanted to be a writer and travel everywhere, and I will if I ever get the chance. This job is just temporary. So don't make assumptions about people and put ugly labels on them. You have no idea how much that can mess with a person's self-image."

He looked at me with a bewildered stare as the other guys dissolved into a fit of laughter. I'd gone from Library Lady to Crazy Library Bitch. I'd always hoped people saw me as Sexy Librarian, but who was I kidding? I'd been neglecting myself. I didn't have time to blow-dry my hair and devote the time to makeup application like I used to. These days, all I did was a rush job on my mascara during my morning ride to the library and I spent so many working hours under fluorescent lights that my skin had turned deathly pale. I was exhausted and disheveled, but this wasn't the real me. Checking out books and nagging teenagers to shut off cell phones hadn't been my plan. It had just . . . happened.

"I didn't know what else to call you," the dark-haired boy said. "I couldn't read your name tag from here. I'm sorry."

Another apology. He was about sixteen and I was twenty-four, and he'd probably been taught to respect his elders and to call women ma'am. It was the southern way. I'd been taught good manners, too. I'd just been pushed far enough today to forget them.

"You can call me Savannah. And the library closes at six. If you came in just to use the Internet, you've got a half-hour limit," I said, and then pointed my finger at Blondie. "I told you to get rid of that Coke."

He kept his eyes on the computer screen. "Don't you think you're wasting your life enforcing meaningless rules that nobody cares about?"

Every single day.

"It isn't a meaningless rule," I said, walking around the table to stand beside him while he tapped at his keyboard and ignored me. "Cokes can spill, and they can wreck books and computers. You wouldn't want to be responsible for that, would you? So throw it away."

He stared at sports scores. "Go screw yourself. You've probably had a lot of practice."

I wanted to crack his jaw, but instead I casually skimmed my hand across the top of his cup, tipping it over. Coke and ice cubes splashed across the keyboard, dripped down the table, and soaked his crotch.

He jumped out of his seat, brushing ice off the front of his shorts as his friends laughed at him. "What the hell do you think you're doing?" he shouted in my face.

Showing you who I really am. "Don't raise your voice in the library, young man. Bad things happen when you break the rules."

I walked away, leaving him cussing behind me while I savored feeling good about myself. That was an unusual thing lately. I glanced over my shoulder and saw him complaining to my boss—a card-carrying Library Lady who had a mop of frizzy gray hair, a lazy left eye, and a failed relationship with Jenny Craig.

I sped up to flee the crime scene. The past few minutes had given me a throbbing headache and I needed peace and quiet, so I pushed my cart to a secluded corner with shelves marked *Adult Fiction,* where I jammed novels into tight spaces.

I remembered an old dream of seeing my name on a cover and my words on pages. *A novel by Savannah Morgan*—that's what I used to doodle in the margins of my notebooks while my mind wandered during biology and algebra. Back then, I didn't know that Charleston High was so far from the real world. I didn't know that dreams don't come true, happy endings only exist in fiction, romance never lasts, and all the fantasies that authors put into girls' impressionable heads amount to nothing but lies and deception and unrealistic expectations.

I was tempted to shred every page of *Pride and Prejudice* that I held in my hand.

"Savannah," said a monotone voice behind me.

I put the book on a shelf, turned around, and looked at my boss. She smelled like coffee and always had a piece of hard candy in her mouth.

"Some boy told me you threw a Coke on him," she said. "Is this true?"

I touched my head. There was my man-repellant bun. I yanked out the elastic band, and my hair flowed over my shoulders and down my back. It had been flaxen when I was younger, but over the past few years it had turned into a shade that Mom called golden wheat. She had a name for everybody's hair color. She was a beautician and she worked out of our house, which we'd been struggling to keep.

"No way," I said indignantly, trying to figure out if my boss was looking directly at me. Her wayward eye drifted so much that I was never sure. "I told him several times that having a Coke in the library is a violation of our rules, but he wouldn't listen. He spilled it himself."

She crossed her arms over her torpedo-sized boobs. She seemed doubtful, which was no surprise. She was always on my back about something, and I never met her standards even though most of what I did was brainless labor.

I didn't care—or at least, that's what I always told myself. I just needed a paycheck, although a little gratitude and encouragement would have been nice once in a while.

She slurped her candy. "You don't have proof of that."

"No," I said, "but you should believe me anyway."

The candy cracked between her molars. "Actually," she said, "I don't. So I'm putting you on probation for the next ninety days. I'll keep a close watch on you and see if there's any improvement."

Could I be degraded any further? I wiped my hand across my sweaty, aching forehead.

"You do that," I said, "and I'll quit right now."

I meant it. But I hoped she'd cave. My knees shook beneath my skirt as I thought about everything Mom and I could lose if I stopped bringing home a check.

She shrugged. "Go ahead. I'm not changing my mind."

"I'm not, either," I said as I unpinned my name tag. I tossed it onto the novels in my cart, where it skidded, dropped to the floor, and landed on her practical shoes.

. . .

Tina Brandt pulled her car to the curb. It was a white BMW convertible that had been a gift from her father for her last birthday, and she'd covered the bumper with stickers that said things like *Dixie Chick* and *Keep Calm and Get Your Diamond On.*

I opened the door and slid onto the front seat. The car smelled like a cross between the inside of Victoria's Secret and an ashtray. A Marlboro Light dangled from Tina's mouth, which was smeared with a hot-pink lip-plumping gloss. She didn't need to plump anything, though. She also didn't have to wear so much liner around her big green eyes, clip extensions into her wavy brown hair, or keep the push-up bra industry in business. She was even more beautiful without all the fakeness, but she didn't seem to think so. Not that she'd ever say it out loud—even to me, her best friend since kindergarten.

I snatched the cigarette from her lips and flicked it out the window. I wished she'd stop smoking, because I didn't want cancer to take Tina from me like it had stolen her mother when we were in fifth grade. The only proper female guidance she'd gotten since then was from me and Mom, but she rarely took our advice.

I pointed my finger at her. "Give up that nasty habit or I'll tell your daddy that you haven't really quit."

She stared at me for a moment. "Jeez," she said. She'd been raised in a no-cuss zone like I had, and we both believed that uttering *Jesus Christ* or *God Almighty* might get us struck by lightning. *Jesus* was one word we couldn't say out loud unless it was in the sacred sense. "What's *your* problem?"

I let out a heavy sigh and leaned into the cushy leather seat. "Sorry. I had a bad day."

This wasn't news to Tina. She was used to hearing about my bad days. "Well," she said, "maybe this will cheer you up: It's over with the latest."

She meant her latest boyfriend. There'd been so many since

we were kids that I couldn't keep track. She didn't hide them from me like she tried to keep them from everyone else—especially her father. She'd spent years crawling down the trellis outside her bedroom window so she could meet guys waiting in cars. She'd started that when we were fourteen, and she still had to sneak out at night because she still lived at home.

She knew I didn't care for the latest. I didn't care for any of her men. And I wished she wouldn't give herself away so easily and so often. "I'm sorry to hear that," I said, which was only half a lie. I wasn't sorry she'd broken up with that waste of air, but I felt bad that she hadn't once had a boyfriend who was decent to her. "How did it happen?"

She grabbed her cell phone from the dashboard and showed me a text message that said

I don't want you. I don't need you. I never gave a shit about you.

My heart sank. Tina had a knack for finding the meanest and most worthless men in Charleston. She met most of them at the country club where her father played golf and her stepmother organized ladies' luncheons, and the latest had crossed her path while she was answering phones at Mr. Brandt's accounting firm downtown. He'd given her the job the autumn after she dragged herself home from Davidson College in North Carolina, where she'd been accepted only because Mr. Brandt was a friend of the Dean. Her performance in high school hadn't been anywhere near good enough to get her into such a prestigious college, and she'd promised not to let anybody down.

But she did. Just like in high school, she didn't live up to her potential. She blew off studying in favor of her football-player boyfriend and all-night parties, and her abysmal GPA got her kicked out after one year. When she came back, she seemed even more disappointed than Mr. Brandt did. Then she whiled away the summer doing nothing but frequenting The Spa at Charleston Place and tanning beside her pool. *Sugar,* her stepmother, Crystal, had said, *just because you're not college material doesn't mean I'll let you do nothing but loaf around my house like a useless socialite.*

"Tina," I began, ready to say something encouraging and sympathetic about how the latest wasn't worthy of her, but she cut me off.

"Who cares," she said with her deep, throaty laugh that sounded like it belonged to a much older woman. She tossed her phone onto the dash and turned up the radio to blast her favorite Dierks Bentley song. "I was fixin' to dump him anyway. He was below average where it counts."

She drove away from the curb and sped down the street with a stiff smile and a clenched jaw. Tina always pretended that nothing bothered her, but I wasn't fooled.

"Thanks for leaving work early to pick me up," I said.

She pressed a button on the dashboard to open the roof. "It was no problem. Daddy never puts up a fuss if I leave before five or take a day off. So why'd you want to cut out early today?"

"I have to apply for a new job . . . at the mall," I said, forcing the words from my throat. I felt like hurling myself out of the car.

Tina glanced at me as she swerved to avoid an armadillo splattered across the road. She didn't care for critter guts on her brand-new tires. "Did you get fired? If they fired you, you could sue. You do a good job . . . you're always filling in for everyone, and—"

"I didn't get fired. I quit. And I don't want to talk about it."

She stopped at a red light and lifted her naturally high-arched eyebrows. "Okay," she said. "But don't you think you should take a break for a little while? You could use some time off. And you can always ask my daddy for a job."

I shook my head. Her *daddy* was the last person I'd ask for anything, but I couldn't tell her that. "I don't want to bother him. I can't take time off, either. I need money."

Tina had a constant cash flow, but unlike most of the girls I'd grown up with, she'd never been snooty about the fact that I didn't. She nodded, the light changed, and she hit the gas. "You mean you need money to get your car fixed? Don't worry about that . . . I'll take you anywhere you want to go."

"I know. I appreciate it, but I'm not going to keep imposing on you. I need my own car, and I also need to help Mom. Business has been slow . . . the bills are piling up."

Tina drove me to an upscale outdoor mall where I handed in applications at Sephora and Banana Republic and eight other stores before catching up with her at the bridal shop where we'd planned to meet. She was leaning against its front window and twirling her hair.

"Maybe I should apply here," I said, peeking in the window. Tina was covering part of it, and all I could see was half of a mannequin dressed in a white organza gown.

She shook her head. "I don't think that's a good idea."

I kept trying to look into the store, but she blocked me. "Why isn't it a good idea? And what are you doing?" I asked impatiently. "Get out of the way."

She folded her arms over her low-cut blouse and didn't move. "Forget this place, Savannah. It's filled with snobby women like Crystal. You don't want to work here." She draped an arm around my shoulders, shoved my head down so I was staring at cement, and led me away.

The smell of her mango perfume was suffocating in the heat, and I wasn't in the mood for whatever game she was playing. I disconnected myself from her and headed back to the store.

She tried to stop me, but it was too late. I stared through the bridal shop's window at a pretty redhead admiring her reflection in a full-length mirror. She wore a flowing wedding dress, and her mother and a saleslady beamed at her. She looked like a princess. Cinderella. Somebody's dream.

I swallowed. This was why Tina had tried to keep me away.

She was beside me. "It doesn't matter. It isn't what you wanted."

That's what I'd thought two years ago, when Jamie bought a diamond ring and asked me to marry him. He was in law school at the University of South Carolina then. He'd wanted to tie the knot when he graduated, buy us a house in a fancy area nearby called Mount Pleasant—where Tina lived—and have babies together, in his own words, *ASAP*.

Only that wasn't what I wanted. I wanted to go places, see things, and write award-winning novels that would fly off bookstore shelves. I'd thought that none of those things would happen if I became what he expected: a stay-at-home mom who ate lunch with attorneys' wives and spent her free time getting massages and manicures.

It had been so hard to end it. But he just wouldn't wait, and I couldn't blame him. I knew how it felt to want things. The problem was that lately I'd been thinking that everything I wanted was never going to happen. I'd been wondering if I'd made a terrible mistake.

"I didn't know they were getting married so soon," I said, my voice raw and tight. But I should have known. Jamie had graduated recently. Maybe I'd been blocking it out.

I'd heard about the engagement a while back. The bride was a girl from my high school class who'd been on the cheerleading squad with me and Tina, but Jamie was a year ahead of us and had barely known her then. Now she worked as a paralegal at a law office downtown and the rumor was that they'd hooked up when he clerked there.

"Yeah," Tina said. "I heard about it last week."

I turned away from the window. "Thanks for not telling me."

She smiled. The bells on the bridal's shop door jangled, the door swung open, and there was the redhead with the saleslady calling after her, nervously warning against stepping outside because the sidewalk would dirty her hem.

The bride went by two first names. She'd been one of those pageant contestants with a pushy mother who'd dressed her up in high heels and a thick layer of makeup like a six-year-old prostitute. She'd also been my nemesis from eighth through eleventh grade. Now she gave me a phony smile and spoke in a sugary voice as she lingered in the doorway.

"Savannah, are you stalking me?" she asked.

"Don't flatter yourself, Eva Lee," I said.

"*Seriously,*" Tina added. "Savannah has better things to do."

Sure, I thought. *I have better things to do, like resume my desperate search for a minimum-wage job while this empty-headed debutante gets ready to marry the only guy I've ever loved.*

"Of course she does," Eva Lee said in her saccharine tone, moving her steel-blue eyes from the run in my panty hose to my smeared mascara. She'd always been so calm and cool and polite, like a shady version of Melanie Hamilton Wilkes from *Gone with the Wind.* And it killed me to think that she and Jamie were going to make the most beautiful children.

It had been bad enough imagining them together at the law firm. She'd probably batted her false eyelashes in his direction and pretended to drop pens so she could bend over in tight skirts to pick them up. Maybe she'd offered to help out when he was working late for the sole purpose of tempting him to nail her on a desk covered with pleadings and contracts.

"Are you still working at the library?" she asked.

"No," Tina answered for me. "Savannah's pursuing better opportunities."

Eva Lee touched the string of pearls around her graceful neck. "Like what?"

My mouth opened, but nothing came out. I just stared at the cute spattering of freckles across her delicate nose and her bee-stung lips. I couldn't even hate her, because this was my fault. She hadn't stolen Jamie from me. I'd let him go.

Tina hiked up her blouse to stop her satin bra from sticking out. "None of your business, Cinderslutta. You can put on that well-bred, Miss Priss act all you want, but we've known you long enough to see what's behind it. So spare us the phony conversation."

Eva Lee cocked an eyebrow. She was still touching her pearls, and the massive, marquise-cut diamond on her left hand glinted beneath the sun and practically singed my retinas. It wasn't the ring that I hadn't taken from Jamie. This one was an upgrade. Maybe he thought *she* was, too.

"I've known you for a long time, too, Tina," said Eva Lee, completely unmoved. "Do you still sneak out of your daddy's house after dark like an oversexed alley cat?"

All the color drained from Tina's bronzed skin. She didn't talk about her late-night doings with anybody except me, yet it hadn't kept word from trickling out. But even when we were whispering, she always held back. She tried to turn things romantic when I knew they weren't. Her stories always ended before they got too personal, like when a couple kisses in a movie and the screen goes dark just as they open a bedroom door. But when Tina had a few drinks in her, the stark truth flowed from her mouth.

Eva Lee shifted her eyes from Tina to me and widened her fake smile. "I'm sure I'll see you around, Savannah."

I was sure she would. I was sure we'd run into each other for the rest of our lives.

When she was gone, I sighed and my shoulders slumped, and Tina put her arm around me as we headed toward the BMW.

"Jeez," she said. "What a snotty B."

"There won't be any hellfire and damnation if you swear, Tina. And I know Eva Lee's a bitch. She's been that way since junior high. But she's smart . . . unlike me."

Tina stopped walking and looked into my face. "You're *very* smart. You've got a college degree in English literature. And the stories you write are some of the best I've ever read."

Tina had been my unofficial editor since we were kids. She was the only person I trusted not to snicker and criticize first drafts straight off the printer. For years, I'd been pacing nervously in the hallway outside her bedroom while she curled up on her window seat with my work and her Sharpie, writing things like *Beautiful imagery* and *I'm not clear about why the aunt doesn't get along with the sister.* I just wished she'd used her smarts at Davidson.

She looked at me more closely. "If you're thinking about Jamie, it's only because the right guy hasn't come along yet. You just have to get back out there and meet someone else. I mean . . . Jamie's the only guy you've ever slept with."

I rolled my eyes. "Say it a little louder, Tina. Somebody across the street didn't hear."

She covered her mouth to smother her husky laugh. "You have a lot to offer," she said, bending her elbow around mine. "Don't forget it."

I'd forgotten it a while ago. But I was lucky that I had her to remind me.

Two

"Want to come over?" Tina asked as we drove away. "Daddy has a business dinner at The Wentworth Mansion tonight, and Stepzilla is eating at Magnolias with some of her friends. I'm sure they'll guzzle chardonnay for hours and she won't be back until late."

Magnolias was a restaurant on East Bay Street, and Stepzilla was Tina's name for Crystal, who was only nine years older than we were and had become the second Mrs. Brandt at the age of twenty, just eight months after Tina's mother was buried inside a pink casket under a dogwood tree.

I nodded, and soon we were in Tina's curving driveway that led to a two-story brick home with black shutters and towering white columns that framed the front door. It overlooked Charleston Harbor, where Mr. Brandt kept his boat docked at the marina.

Then we were inside the five-bedroom, six-bathroom house that had been gutted and redecorated after Crystal returned from her European honeymoon. The colors were warm, the furniture was elegant, and the living room was filled with welcoming wing chairs. But there wasn't a trace of the first Mrs. Brandt except a faded photo that Tina kept in her bedroom.

We looked up from where we stood in the foyer to see Raylene—Tina's ten-year-old sister—rushing down a palatial staircase in a white dress embroidered with cherry blossoms. Her blond tresses bounced around her face as her dour babysitter lady trailed behind. Raylene hit the last step and jumped onto the shellacked wood floor.

"Raylene," said the babysitter, "well-bred young ladies don't jump in the house."

"Sometimes they do," Tina said, reaching into her purse for a few crisp bills. "Thank you for your time. It's a lovely evening . . . you're free to enjoy it."

The babysitter took the money and left, and I closed the door behind her as Raylene wrapped her arms around Tina's narrow waist. I'd always thought it would be sweet to have a sister who'd do that sort of thing.

Tina sifted Raylene's hair through her fingers. "What do you want for dinner?"

She flashed a gap-toothed smile. "Fried chicken and cheese spread on Ritz crackers."

Tina's upbringing of debutante balls had done nothing to reduce her affection for down-home cooking and junk-food appetizers, which she'd been devouring at my house for years with no effect on her curvaceously trim figure. She was good at making those things herself, and she'd also won lots of blue ribbons for her cupcakes and cookies at church bake-offs.

"Make the spread with pimento cheese and chopped pecans like you always do," I said as we went into the spacious, airy kitchen that had French doors with a view of the pool in the yard and the palm trees that surrounded the harbor. Tina was organizing ingredients when we heard the front door open, keys jangle, and high heels tap against the wood floor.

Crystal stood in the doorway. She had big blond hair and breast implants, and she'd once won a Faith Hill look-alike contest. She always pretended not to notice when much younger guys ogled her on the street and whispered that she was the hottest MILF in Mount Pleasant.

"What happened to your dinner at Magnolias?" Tina asked.

"It's been rescheduled," Crystal said, parting her lips into a bleached, toothy smile as she walked toward us and then closed a button on Tina's blouse. "You must've gotten dressed in the dark this morning, sugar. You don't want to give your half sister a bad example, do you?"

Sugar. That's what Crystal called Tina when she was putting her down. Crystal also loved to point out that Raylene was Tina's half sister, even though neither of them saw it that way.

"Tina isn't a bad example, Crystal," I said, eyeing the saline-filled balloons on her chest.

She turned toward me. "Your mama raised you better than to stick your nose into family business. And when will you learn to call me Mrs. Brandt?"

I shrugged. "We're so close in age that I just don't think it's proper."

She ignored me and looked at the cheese and the crackers and the raw chicken legs spread out on the countertop. "Tina, I've told you to stop buying that redneck food."

Tina put her hand on her hip. "I'd think it would make you feel like you're right back at home in North Charleston. And I'll buy whatever I want with my own money."

Crystal laughed. "You don't have your own money. Every cent in your wallet comes straight from your daddy's pocket, and don't you forget it. Now throw that trash in the wastebasket where it belongs. I don't want it stinking up my house."

"It's *my* house, too," Tina said. "It was mine when you were living in a double-wide."

I kept quiet, stuck somewhere between smiling and wincing at Tina's reference to the trailer in which Crystal had grown up and which she hadn't escaped until she met Mr. Brandt.

"As you constantly remind me," Crystal said while we heard the front door open and close and footsteps in the foyer. "But this house isn't yours, sugar. It belongs to me and your daddy. Since you ruined the chance he gave you to get an education, the only way you'll ever have your own home is if you find a husband who'll buy you one. You're certainly past due to walk down the aisle."

"If this was 1955," I said. "I think the female species has evolved since then."

"You go on justifying if it makes you feel good about yourself," Crystal said with the same patronizing smile I'd gotten from my neighbors when they found out that Jamie had proposed to Eva Lee. "When I was your age, I was celebrating my fourth wedding anniversary and Raylene was a year old. But I'm sure everything will happen soon enough for both of you. Tell me, Tina . . . how's that nice boy you've been seeing?"

Tina's lips tightened. Then Mr. Sawyer Brandt, CPA, was in the kitchen, dressed in an expensive suit. He was a handsome man in his fifties with chestnut hair who looked as if the water-cooler at his office had a direct line to the fountain of youth.

"My meeting was canceled," he said in his thick Charleston accent as Raylene sprang into his arms. He laughed and hugged her while Tina watched like she missed being ten.

"I'll be in my room," she said, storming out of the kitchen.

Mr. Brandt moved his eyes between me and Crystal while Tina's feet pounded against the stairs. "What happened?" he asked.

Crystal shook her head. "Same old thing. You know how your daughter is."

I gave her a dirty look and went upstairs, where I opened

Tina's bedroom door. She was on her window seat with her knees pulled to her chest and a Marlboro Light in her mouth, blowing smoke from her nose and through the open window.

She turned toward me. "Don't say anything. I *need* this."

I supposed I might pick up a nervous habit, too, if I'd been forced to live with Crystal for the past thirteen years. I probably would've been convicted of murder by now, some form of slow poisoning like antifreeze in her chardonnay. So I just shut the door and walked into the room, which had vanilla walls, a king-size bed with a brass frame, a desk, and two oak dressers. The walk-in closet was crammed with the dresses Tina had worn to country-club parties and black-tie galas, including her own debutante ball at the Island House—a grand southern mansion set against the Stono River. Her room was a beautiful prison cell kept clean by a maid who visited every Wednesday morning like a magical fairy for sloppy girls.

"Your mother was so pretty," I said, admiring her photo on the dresser. "She passed her looks on to you."

Tina crushed her cigarette in an ashtray adorned with a painted-on sunset and *Love from Myrtle Beach*. She'd picked it up when we drove there for Labor Day weekend last year. "I only wish she could come back and pass Crystal right out into the street."

"I know. But you don't *have* to put up with Crystal. You can leave whenever you want, Tina."

She snorted. "And go *where*? I hate to admit it, but she's right about a few things. I don't make enough money for my own place, she'd never let Daddy buy me one or pay my rent, and one disastrous year in college won't help me find a better job. The only way out is to get married . . . and the chances of that are bleak."

I plopped down across from her. "That isn't the *only* way. You can take care of yourself."

She laughed. "What a nice idea. But that's all it is."

I sighed. Tina was smarter than people thought. She was smarter than *she* thought, too. She loved to read—and not just the celebrity gossip blogs that had become a second addiction. She was always checking novels out of the library, and she recognized good literature when she saw it. And before her mother died, Tina had gotten high grades and won spelling bees and illustrated stories that I wrote on construction paper and bound with yarn. Two of them were on a shelf above her desk. I sprang up and slipped them out from between fashion magazines, then sat opposite her again and smiled as I flipped through the pages.

"Remember this?" I asked, holding up a picture.

"Yeah," she said wistfully as she touched a flower she'd drawn in yellow crayon.

"Remember the time in ninth grade when Eva Lee stole one of my stories out of my knapsack and posted it online?" I said, cringing as I remembered that my classmates had written the cruelest comments and laughed so loudly about it in the cafeteria that I locked myself in a bathroom stall and cried. "You stood up for me. You told them off. You said it didn't make sense for them to criticize my story when it was just as good as the soap operas all the girls watched."

"It was *better* than any soap opera," Tina said.

I smiled, remembering her going ballistic on those kids. "You always defended me . . . you were my friend even though I didn't live in Mount Pleasant and I didn't have designer clothes and a big house like most everyone else."

"Of course I did. You were nicer and more interesting than any of *them*."

I touched her hand. "You can do more than answer phones, Tina. You're not stuck here."

She sighed and popped open the button on her shirt that

Crystal had closed. "Well," she said after gazing out at the harbor for a moment, "now that you mention it . . . there *is* an accounting assistant job open at work."

I perked up. "And you *do* have some connections there," I said with a wink.

She twisted a lock of hair around her finger. "I guess I could ask Daddy."

I jumped out of my seat before she could change her mind. She hid her ashtray behind the curtain and I dashed into the hall and headed for the staircase, where Mr. Brandt was walking up the steps and loosening his tie. "Tina wants to ask you something," I said.

He gave me a skeptical glance as he followed me into the bedroom, where he sniffed the air and frowned. "You better not be smoking again, Tina Mae Brandt."

She stared at him. I didn't mind him getting on her back about the cigarettes, but she couldn't stand up to him no matter what. She'd mouth off to anybody except him.

"No, sir," she replied.

"Mr. Brandt," I said, and he turned his head toward me. There wasn't a line on his face except for the wrinkles that creased into the corners of his eyes whenever he smiled. He wasn't smiling now, though. He rarely did when I was around. I'd always gotten the feeling that he'd rather Tina be best friends with a shrinking violet who shared her zip code. "Tina mentioned there's an accounting assistant position open at your firm, and we were wondering if you'd consider her."

He squinted in my direction. "*We* were wondering?" he said. "*You're* usually the one who's wondering. You've got quite a talent for pushing my daughter into places she doesn't belong. Do you think I've forgotten the time you pressured her into applying for the editor-in-chief position at the school newspaper?"

"That was nine years ago," I reminded him. "And she would've been brilliant if she'd been given a chance. People were just too ignorant to see her as anything but a cheerleader."

He slid off his tie. "And as I predicted, that endeavor ended in disappointment. You're always putting crazy ideas in Tina's head."

I stared at the carpet. "You won't let her have *any* ideas."

"I beg your pardon?" he said indignantly, like I was a sassy teenager.

"Daddy," Tina broke in, "*this* isn't a crazy idea. I want a better job so I can make enough money to get my own place."

He scratched his head. "And why would you want to do that?"

"Because," Tina said, "I'm twenty-four . . . and I can't deal with your wife anymore."

Mr. Brandt stared at her as he wrapped his tie around his hand. Then he strode across the room and sat on the window seat. "Bunny," he said gently, and it worried me. *Sugar* and *bunny* always preceded bad things. "You're much better off at home than out on your own. This is one of the best houses in Mount Pleasant. I bought you a new car. I take good care of you, don't I?"

She nodded. "But I should take care of myself."

"Why? Because Savannah says so?" he said, stuffing his tie into his pocket. "Now I know you don't really want to be an accounting assistant. You'd be hidden away in the back of the office, buried in facts and figures. The job is for a dull, serious, meticulous type who's good with math. That's not you, bunny. You belong right out front where you can shine. I want everybody to see what a pretty daughter I have." He leaned across the space between them and kissed her forehead. "Now forget this foolishness before you carve worry lines into that gorgeous face."

I couldn't stand it. Ever since Tina came home from Davidson, it seemed like Mr. Brandt had lost all faith in her. *The Dean let you into that school as a favor to me,* he'd said that summer. *Do you know what an embarrassment this is?*

I supposed he thought that keeping her chained to the reception desk would prevent any more embarrassment. But I wanted her to argue. I wanted her to tell him to give her another chance. I wanted her to show him that she could do more than manage a multiline phone system and frost cupcakes. Instead she just twisted her mouth into a pout and stared at the sparkling water in the distance.

Tina was quiet while she drove me home. The top was down, our hair swirled around our heads, and I didn't speak up until she tuned the radio to a country music station. "Your father's wrong," I finally said.

Tina's eyes were hidden behind sunglasses with rhinestone frames. She tapped her French manicure against the steering wheel as she stopped in front of my house, which was in a neighborhood without a harbor view or curving driveways. The homes were small and one-story, with chipped paint and carports and broken-down Buicks on concrete blocks.

"My father's a smart man, Savannah. He graduated from Duke."

She'd told me this a thousand times. "That doesn't mean he can't make a mistake."

She raised an eyebrow. "You're always criticizing him, and he doesn't deserve it."

"Tina," I said tiredly, "I know your father's been generous to you . . . but he also wants to keep you locked up. The accounting assistant job is for somebody who's good with math? You could be good with math if you tried. *That's not you, bunny.* He treats you like you're twelve years old. He's holding you back, and you're letting him. What he's doing isn't right."

She drew in her lower lip. "Well," she said, "how would *you* know how a father's supposed to act? You've never had one."

I swallowed. "Don't change the subject. And it's just deliberately mean of you to bring that up. It has *nothing* to do with this."

She yanked off her sunglasses and flung them onto the dashboard. "It has *everything* to do with this. Maybe you wish you didn't have to worry about paying bills and finding a job. Maybe you're jealous."

I winced, staring at the only flaw on her face—a chicken-pox scar at the edge of her left eye. I'd heard the same sort of thing before from Mount Pleasant girls, but never from her. That made it hurt so much more, especially because it was partly true. Still, it wasn't the reason I'd pushed her to stop being so helpless.

I tossed my hair. "What a petty way to get back at me for telling you the truth."

"If I'm so petty," she said, "then maybe you should get the hell out of my car."

I faked a gasp as I opened the door, slid off the seat, and stepped onto the sidewalk. "Oh, my," I said, slamming the door shut. "Tina Brandt said the *h* word. What's next? Are you going to replace *fudge* and *shoot* and *b* with the real thing? But don't worry . . . if you start talking with a grown-up's mouth, I promise not to tell your daddy."

Tina hit the gas. The BMW screeched and left tire tracks on the road as she drove toward the setting sun. I watched until I couldn't see the car anymore, and then I turned and walked a few feet from the curb to the house I shared with Mom. It had two bedrooms, one bathroom, and an American flag out front.

I stepped across creaky wooden slats on the front porch, passing my old bicycle propped up in the corner. It was pink with a personalized license plate—*Savannah* in iridescent letters—and I'd worn out its tires from riding around town all through junior high. It was rusty now and I kept telling Mom to get rid of it, but she was sentimental about that thing. I supposed this was because it had come from her aunt Primrose—an eccentric widow with money whom I'd never met. She'd moved way out to Arizona before I was born, but she never failed to send me a gift each Christmas when I was a kid. *Aunt Primrose has a good heart,* Mom always said with a smile as she watched me unwrap those presents every year.

"Savannah?" Mom called from inside.

I opened the screen door and walked into the living room. The whole house smelled like a perm. Our plaid furniture was battered and the paint on the walls was faded, but we kept the place neat and clean and there were fresh flowers in a vase on the coffee table. Mom grew them in the backyard.

"Hi, darlin'," she said as I passed the room where she was styling a woman's hair.

It was a small spare bedroom that Mom had begun using as a beauty salon when I was a baby so she could keep one eye on her customers and the other on me. Her business had supported us for years without help from anyone—including my father, whoever he was. Mom had said she didn't know—that when she was young she'd done things she wasn't proud of—and the paternal possibilities weren't worth thinking about. But that hadn't stopped me from wondering.

I gave her a listless wave. Mom was forty-five and in phenomenal shape from Pilates and Zumba DVDs. Her body was taller and curvier than mine. She'd passed her honey-brown eyes along to me, and she spent a half hour every morning turning her long auburn hair into a mass of spiral curls. She was also diligent about her skin. She stayed out of the sun and moisturized daily, and the only wrinkles on her face were three thin horizontal lines across her forehead that creased deeper as she stared at me.

"What's wrong?" she asked.

Everything, I thought. But I was too worn-out to explain. "I had a fight with Tina."

"About what?" she asked as she finished blow-drying her customer's hair.

I couldn't tell her. The father issue always lingered like an ugly wart on somebody's nose that nobody dared to mention. So I just shrugged.

Mom unplugged the blow-dryer. "Well," she said, "whatever it is . . . I'm sure you two will work it out. You always do."

That was true. I'd had lots of arguments and estrangements with Tina, but they'd never lasted long. I wasn't sure about this one, though. She'd never said anything that had cut so deep.

"I'm going to take a shower," I said, and Mom nodded while she combed and teased.

I went into the bathroom, which had weak water pressure and chipped tiles the color of pistachio ice cream. When I came out in my robe with wet hair hanging down my back, Mom's customer was gone and she was sitting on our porch swing.

"The mailman brought you something," she called through the screen door. "It's on the kitchen table. It has to be good news . . . we're due for some."

I rushed to the kitchen and tore open a manila envelope from a literary magazine. A few months ago, I sent in a short story that I'd worked on for weeks, and I was sure it could make me a published author. I hoped it would be the start of something big. But when I tore open the envelope, I felt so incredibly small. The magazine had returned my story with *I'm afraid this simply isn't something we'd like to pursue* written in red ink.

"Are they going to publish your story?" Mom shouted from the porch.

I shoved it in the trash. Then I lugged myself outside and sat beside her on the swing. The sun was nearly gone, and the sky looked like it was on fire above the houses across the street.

"Not exactly," I said. My voice was as raw as it had been when I was staring at Eva Lee, and I couldn't have been more depressed. "They didn't want it . . . just like all the other stories I've sent in."

She scoffed. "Is that so? Well, if brains were leather, those people couldn't saddle a flea."

A weak smile spread across my lips. Mom had a collection of hokey southern-style insults and an accent as thick as Paula Deen's. She always did her best to cheer me up, even though it was hopeless right now.

"Mom," I said, deciding to spit out my bad news quickly, "I quit my job."

She turned her head toward me. I'd thought my impulsive decision might flare her temper, but she kept a straight face and pushed a wisp of damp hair away from my eyes.

"Why'd you do that?" she asked, and after I explained she nodded and stared at the orange sky. "I'm proud of you for quitting. Like I've always told you . . . you should never stay anyplace where you don't feel comfortable and you aren't appreciated. You're better than that."

"Thanks," I said, relieved. "But what about the bills? It might take me a while to find an equally boring, dead-end, soul-killing job."

Mom laughed and set her eyes on mine. "We'll get by. We always have."

That was yet another truth. I tried to relax and think of positive things, but my mind was crammed with negativity. "Mom," I said after a while, "Jamie's getting married soon."

She nodded again. "I've heard."

So she'd kept it a secret, too. "Do you think I should've accepted his proposal?"

"Of course I don't, Savannah. Why do you ask that?"

"Because," I said, "I thought that if I married him, I'd be giving everything up. But since I made that decision, I haven't gotten a single thing I want. I don't think I'll ever be a writer. Maybe I should've been more realistic."

Mom shook her head. "What you're saying is that you should've settled. But you wouldn't be happy if you had. And your dreams aren't unrealistic. Maybe they just aren't in Charleston."

I knew what was coming next. She was going to say that I was intelligent, attractive, and talented and I deserved so much more than anything I could find around here. I loved her for thinking so, but I was tired of hearing it.

"I know there might be better jobs and more opportunities in other places, Mom . . . but I'm not going. I can't leave you here alone."

She raised an auburn eyebrow. "Is that *really* why you can't go?"

"Absolutely," I said. "What else would it be?"

"Oh, I don't know . . . maybe you're afraid the world is filled with people like the ones at those magazines."

Her maternal radar was precise. She could always find what I was trying to hide. She seemed to know I didn't want to jet off somewhere, only to fail and come crawling back to Charleston, where I'd have to paste a smile on my face whenever I ran into Jamie and Eva Lee walking arm in arm with their stunning children and say, *Oh, things just didn't work out and it's all for the best.*

The phone rang. I grabbed the excuse to escape. I sprang from the swing, pushed open the screen door, and plucked the receiver off the kitchen wall. "Morgan residence," I said in a hoity-toity voice, thinking Tina was at the other end with the most sincere apology ever.

"Is this Savannah Morgan, Joan Morgan's daughter?"

That wasn't Tina. There was no southern drawl. This lady spoke with an upper-crusty lilt.

"Yes," I said, clearing my throat.

"I'm Mercedes Rawlings Stark. I'm an attorney in New York, and I'm calling about Edward Stone."

Edward Stone. That name sounded familiar. I was sure I'd heard it on TV. "You must have the wrong number. Nobody here knows an Edward Stone," I said, and then the screen door slammed. I looked up to find Mom standing against it. Her body was stiff, and all the color had drained from her face.

I stared at her. What was the matter? And what was that Yankee saying?

". . . to fly you up here. I have some important things to discuss with you."

It had been such a rough, hideous, endless day, and now I had to concoct a polite way to get this misguided woman off the phone so I could find out what was going on with Mom.

"I'm sorry, ma'am. You've got the wrong person."

"No, I don't. You're the right person, Savannah. And Edward Stone was your father," she said quickly. "I apologize for telling you this way . . . but you have to understand why I'm contacting you. He was in a fatal car accident, and there are matters relating to his death that we need to discuss face-to-face."

Father. Accident. Death. Was I really hearing this? My ears were ringing. My eyes shot toward Mom. "Edward Stone was my father," I said slowly, like that would help it make sense, but it didn't. "He was in a fatal car accident."

"Correct," said Mercedes Rawlings Stark as Mom clutched one hand to her heart and clamped the other over her mouth. "I know this is quite a shock, so I'll give you my phone number and time to think. But as I said . . . I need you to come to New York as soon as possible."

I grabbed a pen and scribbled a number with a 212 area code on the back of a Sally Beauty Supply receipt. Then I hung up the phone and looked at Mom, who was crossing the room. She plunked herself down on the couch and stared at her flowers. And then I knew. She was so limp and dazed that everything I'd heard on the phone *had* to be true.

I repeated it all as she kept her focus on a yellow jessamine. "Mom," I said, and she finally looked at me. The lines in her forehead had gone even deeper. "This is for real, isn't it?"

She exhaled a ragged sigh and leaned into the plaid cushions. "Yes," she said. "It is."

I wasn't sure whether to scream or cry or throw something that would shatter against the wall. "Why didn't you tell me? Why did you pretend you didn't know who my father was?"

Mom rubbed her temples. "It's a long and complicated story, Savannah."

The receipt with the phone number was in my hand, and it crinkled as I clenched my fist. "Is it so long and complicated that you had to hide it? I thought we told each other everything. I thought there were no secrets between us."

Tears sprang into her eyes. That was rare. I was really hurting her. I almost apologized, but I couldn't because she'd hurt me, too. I'd been deprived of so many things because of her—like someone to put me on his strong shoulders at the local carnival when I was little, father-daughter dances at Charleston High, and a man to shake Jamie's hand when he used to come to my door. Not having a father had made me believe I'd been born with some flaw that deemed me unworthy of the T-shirts that girls like Eva Lee had proudly worn—the ones with *Daddy's Girl* printed between two glittery hearts.

But I *did* have a father. He'd been in New York all along. And now he was gone.

"There aren't any secrets between us," Mom said, her voice soft and raspy, "except this."

I let out a harsh laugh. She was about to cry and so was I, but

I held it back. "Well . . . it's a pretty big one, don't you think?" I said sarcastically.

Mom sniffed and composed herself. "Calm down," she said. Her voice was back to normal. "Let me explain."

Calm down? I couldn't calm down. I didn't want to hear what she had to say and that felt strange, because we didn't fight much. We'd always been so close. At least, that's what I'd thought.

"Don't bother," I said, and headed for my room, but Mom caught up to me in a few strides. She grasped my arm and spun me around.

"Remember what I told you before," she said as her fingers dug into my flesh, "about not staying anyplace where you're uncomfortable and not appreciated? Well, that's exactly how I felt about New York. I wasn't going to let Edward Stone turn me into something I wasn't. And I couldn't fit in with a bunch of stuck-up, judgmental people who'd never accept me. I've always told you not to settle . . . and I didn't want to."

The room was spinning, and whatever she'd just said was only a jumble of words. "What are you talking about? I don't understand."

"I know you don't," she said, and pointed to the couch. "But I want you to. So sit down and let me tell you everything."

I jerked my arm away. "It's too late. I wouldn't believe a word you said, anyway. I'll find everything I need to know in New York."

Mom's spiral curls had wilted around her face. But she absorbed my venom like she deserved it and then put her hands on her hips. "Don't talk crazy. You're not going anywhere."

I glared at her. "Why shouldn't I? I thought you wanted me to leave Charleston. You've been bugging me about it for the past two years."

"Yes," she said, "but I didn't want you to do it *this* way or to go *there*. Anything having to do with Edward Stone is the *last* thing I want for you."

I didn't care what she wanted. She'd never asked what I wanted when it came to that man. She'd never even told me that he existed, and it was my right to know.

"Well," I said, "we don't always get what we want, do we?"

She called my name as I stormed across the carpet and into my room, where I locked the door behind me. I paid her no attention, even when she banged on the door and threatened to take it off the hinges, which she'd done all by herself when I was in tenth grade.

She'd cut her hand on a screwdriver then. I didn't want her to do the same now, but I couldn't let her in. Maybe I needed to leave this room and this house and South Carolina for good. Maybe this was the push I needed, as painful as it was. So I dragged my barely used suitcase out of my closet and called Mercedes Rawlings Stark.

"If you'd like to book that flight for me," I said, "I'm *so* ready to go."

Three

The next morning, I buckled my seat belt and stared through a window at the tarmac. Mercedes Rawlings Stark had booked me on Tuesday's earliest flight to New York City out of Charleston International, and I hadn't let Mom drive me to the airport even though she'd wanted to. *At least let me give you a ride,* she'd said, but I'd refused. I'd taken a cab, leaving her standing on our porch in her nightgown and slippers as she gave me a limp goodbye wave.

I blinked that image away. I had enough to worry about—my fight with Tina, New York, Edward Stone, and the stewardess who was demonstrating how to properly use an oxygen mask and a flotation device. The middle-aged man in a tan business suit sitting in the aisle seat beside me listened intently, but I didn't.

The possibility of needing an oxygen mask or a flotation device made me nervous. It made my stomach churn and my palms sweat. I'd only left South Carolina and been on a plane once before—when the Charleston High cheerleading squad attended a competition in Lehigh Acres, Florida—and that flight had

been filled with bumpy air, a sharp drop in altitude, and screaming teenage girls. The memory of it made me bite my nails,
which Tina had always considered the vilest of habits.

Get yourself together, Savannah, I heard my own voice say. *That
flight was in high school. You're a grown-up now. You can handle this.
You can handle all of it.*

Right. Sure. Of course I could. I took my fingers out of my
mouth and pulled my cell phone from my pocket, thinking I
should text Tina to let her know where I was and what was going on. I wanted to unload the whole Edward Stone mess, but
then I remembered I couldn't. She was mad at me. I was mad at
her. *Maybe you're jealous,* she'd said. But that didn't make me miss
her any less.

I glanced at my phone and saw a new text from Mom: *Please
have the courtesy of letting your mother know when you land. And come
back as soon as this nonsense is out of your system.*

"You'll have to shut that off," said the stewardess. She'd finished her presentation and was beside me. "We're about to de-
part."

The flight was drama-free until the plane approached John F.
Kennedy Airport. Then it descended through a mass of thick
clouds that made everything shake. I dug my nails into my thighs
until I heard my voice again. *Get yourself together, Savannah.*

I took the final sip from a tiny bottle of orange juice the
stewardess had given me with an equally stingy bag of pretzels.
I'd skipped dinner last night and hadn't eaten breakfast this morning, and my stomach growled so loudly that I was sure the man
beside me heard it.

"First time in New York?" he asked.

Was it *that* obvious? I thought I looked professional. Stylish.
Sophisticated. I wore a pin-striped black pants suit and a pink
satin tank top that I'd bought for my interview at the library two
years ago. And I'd set my alarm clock to go off extra early this

morning so I could put on makeup and wash, blow-dry, and add some bounce to my hair with hot rollers. It hung down my back and was similar to Crystal's. Even though she got on my nerves, her style attracted enough attention to be worth copying.

I was sure my ensemble was appropriate for a 10 A.M. meeting with Mercedes Rawlings Stark at the law firm of Patterson, Simmons & Gold. *I'll send a driver to pick you up at JFK. We're in the Condé Nast Building,* she'd said casually, like its location was common knowledge.

I glanced at the man beside me. He was fifty-something, and he had thick gray hair and a deep line in each of his cheeks. "Yes, sir," I said. "It's my first time here for sure."

He smiled. The plane cleared the clouds and sailed through still air. I looked out the window, where I saw water, a bridge, and rows of brick apartment buildings.

"This is Queens," he said with a tinge of scorn. "Manhattan is much better."

The plane hit the runway. I turned my eyes toward him. "Is it? Why's that?"

He shrugged a shoulder beneath his suit and I glanced at the briefcase tucked halfway under the seat in front of him. There was a luggage tag attached to it with a business card inside.

"The boroughs are for . . . ," he began, moving his eyes around as if he was searching for words, ". . . average people," he said in a whisper and with a wink, leaning too close to me. "I'm sure a stunning girl like you isn't one of *them.*"

I nearly gagged from the smell of pretzels on his breath. I'd thought he was a friendly older man trying to welcome a newcomer to the city, but I changed my mind. I edged away from him until my back was against the window. "I *am* one of them. So you should be more careful what you say . . . you never know who might be listening."

He let out a chuckle. "I didn't mean to get you riled up,

sweetheart. But you're awfully pretty that way. And your accent is as cute as you are."

What a dirty lech. He was even wearing a wedding ring. "Don't call me sweetheart," I said as the plane headed toward the gate. The stewardess instructed all of us to keep our seat belts fastened, but I couldn't. I wanted to bolt out of there.

"Then what should I call you?" he went on. "I'll bet you've got an adorable southern name like Georgia or Mary Lou."

I wished that weren't true as I struggled to unlatch my seat belt. I was an intelligent person. I had a college degree. So why couldn't I open this thing? But I finally did when the plane stopped at the gate. Everybody turned on cell phones and iPods, sprang up, and opened overhead compartments to get their bags. I wanted to do the same, but this jerk had me trapped.

"Listen," he said in a syrupy voice, "I didn't mean to get off on the wrong foot. You're a New York virgin, and I'd love to educate you."

He did *not* just call me that. "There is *nothing*," I said, "that you could possibly teach me. Now please get out of my way before I stop being polite."

He smirked like my seething anger was a turn-on. "You're a feisty one. But you don't know it all, honey. Let me take you out tonight, and I'll show you a few things."

I knew precisely what he wanted to show me. I shook my head, but he didn't give up. He put his fingers on my knee and squeezed.

You can handle this. I shoved his hand off my knee, snatched up his briefcase, and yanked the business card out of its holder. *"Leland Barry . . . Professor of Economics at Columbia University,"* I read, and moved my eyes from the card to his face. His smile had disappeared. "I hope you don't treat your female students the way you've treated me. I'm sure the Dean at Columbia wouldn't be happy to hear about it. And neither would your wife."

I stuffed the card in my purse. He grabbed his briefcase and glanced around, checking to see if anybody had heard. Then he smoothed his suit and looked at me. "I don't know who you think you are," he muttered before blending into the crowd that headed toward the exit.

I don't know who you think you are. Well, apparently I was the product of Edward Stone and Joan Morgan, but I had no idea who he was and I knew less about her than I'd ever imagined.

Mercedes Rawlings Stark had said that a driver would meet me at the baggage claim. By the time I found it, the only suitcase left on the conveyor was mine and the driver who was supposed to meet me wasn't there. I wheeled my suitcase toward a row of chairs, where I plopped down and checked my phone. *I would appreciate confirmation that you've arrived*, Mom had texted. *I hope New York hasn't already made you lose your manners.*

I couldn't deal with her right now. I snapped the phone shut and slumped into my seat as I watched people picking up luggage and hugging whoever had come to meet them. And then I checked my watch. It was almost eleven, I was late for my meeting, and I decided to catch one of the cabs waiting by the curb outside JFK. I slung my purse and my carry-on over my shoulder and wheeled my suitcase toward a set of automatic doors, but I stopped when I heard footsteps rushing my way.

"Ms. Morgan?"

A young man in a black suit was standing to my left. He wasn't very tall. He had a slight build, reddish-brown hair, and dark-brown eyes. He couldn't have been much older than me.

"Sorry I'm late," he said in a nervous voice, breathing like he'd run a mile.

"It's okay," I told him.

He seemed surprised that I hadn't thrown a hissy fit. "I just have to bring the car around. It'll only take a minute." He grabbed my suitcase and hurried off, and a few minutes later I was standing outside the airport in muggy heat while he loaded the rest of my luggage into the trunk of a fancy black sedan that looked as if it was polished daily.

He opened the rear door, and I slid onto black leather. Then he slipped into the front, shut the door, and veered between cabs and shuttle buses as he drove away from the airport. Soon we were on a crowded street, passing those brick apartment buildings I'd seen from the plane.

I stared at everything whizzing by—the graffiti on the concrete barriers at the side of the road; the old two-family houses with air conditioners sticking out of their windows; the blue-and-orange license plates everywhere. I supposed this was Queens like Professor Pervert had told me, but it didn't seem common. It had a pulse, a buzz in the air, a feeling that everyone had somewhere to go and something to do. It was different from Charleston mornings, where things moved slowly and birds chirped in trees strewn with Spanish moss. There wasn't any moss here, and instead of birds I heard car horns blaring and the radio that the driver had on low volume. "WCBS News time," it said, "is eleven ten."

"Oh," I said when we passed a huge plot of land crowded with gravestones of different shapes and sizes. "That's Calvary Cemetery, isn't it?"

"Excuse me?" the driver said with surprise in his voice. I wasn't sure if it was because I was completely wrong, or if being a tour guide wasn't part of his job description, or if he just hadn't expected me to talk. But I wasn't about to pretend I was at a wake and keep my mouth glued shut for the whole ride.

"I just asked if that was Calvary Cemetery," I said, watching it disappear in the rearview mirror.

"Yeah," he said as he drove through an underpass, "it is."

"So I was right," I said excitedly, leaning toward him from my seat. "I recognized it from *The Godfather* . . . the part with

Don Corleone's funeral. I've read that a lot of real-life mobsters are buried there . . . and some actors and Civil War soldiers, too."

"I know," he said flatly, and turned up the radio.

I sank back into my seat. Wasn't there one friendly person in this city? I gave up on talking and stared out the tinted window until Manhattan appeared in the distance. Then I perked up and admired the skyline and its buildings that were shiny silver against the pale-blue sky.

"It's so beautiful," I said, mostly to myself.

We were crossing a bridge, and the car rattled on metal grates. The driver glanced over his shoulder. "What is?" he asked.

"That," I said, pressing my finger on the window. It looked as if I were touching the spire on top of the Empire State Building. "It's so much bigger than in pictures."

"Oh. I've lived here a few years now . . . I don't pay much attention to it anymore."

I couldn't imagine not paying attention to such a thing. I edged forward, watching his key chain dangle from the ignition. It had a plastic circle with a photo of a little red-haired girl inside. "Where are you from?" I asked, deciding to give him another shot at polite conversation. From the way he'd been acting, I got the feeling he was used to driving around stiffs who focused on their iPhones and pretended the car was on autopilot.

"Upstate," he said, then told me that he lived on Staten Island now but didn't say anything else, so I tried to think of another topic as he drove along.

"Is that your daughter?" I asked, nodding toward his key chain.

We were in Manhattan. The streets were crowded and he swerved through traffic, coming so close to cabs and cars that my stomach felt like it might lurch right out of me.

He nodded when he stopped for a red light. "She's six . . . and she's the reason I was late picking you up. She skinned her knee on the stoop at our apartment building, and it took a while to get her cleaned up . . . and Ms. Stark will cut my head off for keeping you waiting."

The light changed. He started driving again, past sidewalks jammed with people and massive buildings made of glass and steel. "She won't," I said. "I'll tell her it was my fault."

He shook his head. "I can't let you do that, Ms. Morgan."

"You have no say in it. And you should call me Savannah. What's *your* name?"

There was a traffic jam in front of us—a bus, a taxi, a lady poking her head out of a Porsche while she leaned on its horn. "Tony Hughes," he said as he stopped behind her.

I stuck out my hand. "It's nice to meet you, Tony Hughes."

He took my palm in his, giving me a puzzled stare that made me think I was as different to him as New York was to me.

Before he left me at 4 Times Square, Tony said he'd keep my bags in his trunk and Ms. Stark would let him know when he should come back to pick me up. I got out of the car and stood on the sidewalk, taking everything in—the noise and the lights and the bicycle messengers zooming by. Skyscrapers loomed above me, and I was surrounded by giant billboards advertising Broadway shows and designer underwear modeled by well-endowed men with oil-slicked skin.

I stayed frozen until a UPS driver carrying an armful of packages and heading toward the Condé Nast Building grumbled that I was blocking the service entrance. So I went into the lobby, which had a scalloped ceiling and a glossy floor. Then I dashed into a crowded elevator and rode it to Patterson, Simmons & Gold LLP.

The office was sleek and modern, like something out of an *Architectural Digest* I'd skimmed at the library. A brunette who was attractive enough to be an actress sat behind a silver desk, answering the phone with the firm name and *good afternoon*.

Was it afternoon already? I was *so* late. I waited for the girl to get off the phone, but it kept ringing and she didn't even glance up, so I walked toward a wall a few feet away. It had built-in shelves covered with glass vases in different colors. The prettiest was red and in the shape of a flame, and I couldn't resist running my finger over the smooth, cool glass.

"Can I help you?"

I spun around, my fingertip still on the glass. The receptionist was staring at me, and my heart jumped when I felt the vase tipping forward. *Oh, God. Oh, no. Oh, please don't break.*

I grabbed it before it hit the floor. I put it back on the shelf and then held my hand to my chest, thinking I'd escaped a coronary and a bill for whatever outrageous sum that thing was probably worth. "Well," I said with a nervous laugh, "that was embarrassing."

I was hoping for a comforting response—something like *It could have happened to anyone* or *Don't give it a second thought*—but that didn't happen. All I got was a blank stare.

I cleared my throat. Her phone rang again. She picked it up, listened for a moment, and then turned toward me. "Are you Savannah Morgan?" she asked.

"Yes," I said.

Her eyes glided from my strappy sandals to my bouncy hair like I was something that wasn't worth buying. She told whoever was on the other end of the phone that I was here, and a minute later I was sitting inside a corner office with floor-to-ceiling windows, a wide desk, and framed diplomas from Ivy League schools.

Mercedes Rawlings Stark was across from me and behind the desk, swiveling in a brown leather chair. I guessed she was close to sixty, but I doubted anyone else would. She was statuesque and well-put-together with her beige wrap dress, her blond bob, and a three-strand necklace made of black-and-white beads.

"You can call me Mercedes," she said as I sat down, like this was some sort of honor. "And you're late. Didn't Tony didn't arrive at JFK on time?"

"He did, but . . . I got lost in the airport. Sorry to keep you waiting."

She pulled a pair of glasses from a drawer. "Let's focus on the reason you're here: As I mentioned on the phone, Edward Stone was your father, and—"

"Please don't go so fast. Tell me who he is."

She put on her glasses and peered at me over the Gucci frames. "Didn't your mother fill you in on *anything*? And if not, didn't you look up Edward online?"

Mom had never told me a thing about Edward Stone, and when she wanted to I wouldn't let her. And I'd always avoided trying to figure out who people were by searching the Internet, which seemed to me like a squalid space where the gutless let out thoughts they wouldn't dare speak, emboldened by invisibility via an anonymous ID. I'd gone through that when Eva Lee posted my short story online, so I didn't trust any source of information or opinion that couldn't look me in the eye.

"She didn't . . . and I didn't," I said. "I've heard his name mentioned in the media, but I never paid much attention. I never had a reason to. But now I want to know the truth about him, and I'm asking you to give it to me."

Mercedes took off her glasses, tossed them onto a legal pad, and leaned back into her chair. "Edward Stone," she began, "was the founder, Chairman, and CEO of Stone News Corporation. He owned newspapers, magazines, and television news channels all over the world." She twisted her computer monitor around to show me a Web site titled Stone News. "I'm sure you've seen this before."

Of course. But I'd never known it had anything to do with me. I hadn't imagined my father was so important, so accomplished, so insanely successful. Mom had led me to think I'd been cooked up in the back of a Chevy.

I was stunned. Dazed. Speechless. I stared at the computer screen, watching the Web site fade into wavy lines until Mercedes snapped her fingers in my face.

"Please don't pass out in my office," she said. "I hate dramatic scenes."

I broke out of my trance. I was sweating under my suit and close to throwing up, but I wasn't going to give this ill-mannered lawyer the impression that southern women are crybabies who faint and swoon. Hadn't she seen *Steel Magnolias?*

"I never pass out. And what you're saying is that Edward Stone—"

"—was a billionaire," she said, "and he's left a big chunk of his empire to you."

Everything was getting blurry. "You mean I'm supposed to run the corporation?"

She laughed in the most stuck-up way. "Don't be absurd. Edward's legitimate children will head Stone News and deal with its current problems."

I ignored her superior tone, and I didn't spend time wondering about the corporation's problems, whatever they were. *Legitimate children* had my attention.

"There are other kids?" I asked.

She nodded. "Just two . . . Ned and Caroline. Edward had them with his ex- and only wife, Virginia . . . and you were also conceived during their marriage. Edward went to South Carolina with one of his news crews to investigate a case of political corruption in Charleston, and he came across Joan in a local bar. She was gullible enough to believe he was single."

I hadn't known any of that. And even though I was angry with Mom, I wouldn't stand for anybody putting her down. "My mother isn't gullible . . . and don't you dare criticize her. She's a sweet and kind and wonderful lady."

Mercedes kept her eyes on me as she calmly reached for her glasses. "Well," she said in a less abrasive tone, "Edward felt the same way."

What was *this*? Why did she sound human all of a sudden?

She sighed, leaned back into her chair, and smoothed her bob. "Listen," she began. "I should tell you that I'm a friend of Virginia's."

No wonder she'd been so testy. "Oh," was all I could say.

"I was Edward's friend, too," she went on, "and as much as I loathe unfaithful men—and regardless of how irritating it is to be in the middle of this—I have to admit I understand his reasons for getting involved with your mother."

I blinked. Mercedes was just full of surprises. "What were those?" I asked.

She took off her glasses again and rubbed the space between her eyes. "I hate to disparage Virginia. She's always been lovely to me. But I saw what went on behind the scenes with her and Edward."

She paused. I leaned forward. "Go on," I said.

"Your father was a self-made man," Mercedes told me. "He came from nothing—a poor family in Pennsylvania—and he met Virginia at a social function when he was on scholarship at Yale and dreaming of making a name for himself. They fell in love, sure, but I always wondered if Virginia's pedigree wasn't part of the appeal for Edward. Then his career took off and cash flowed in . . . he and Virginia rushed into starting a family, and everything happened so quickly. I'm not sure either one of them knew what they were getting themselves into until it was too late. It took quite a while for Virginia to really get to know who Edward was . . . and vice versa."

That sounded sort of tragic. "And who *is* Virginia?"

"She's part of a family that made its money long ago in shipping and railroads. Her mother died in a skiing accident when Virginia was three years old. She's a Sarah Lawrence graduate, a Daughter of the American Revolution, and a very popular socialite," Mercedes said, lacing her fingers together on her desk. "She's quite different from your mother . . . and I'm not just talking about her background. Edward wasn't a serial philanderer, and Joan was the only woman special enough to make him stray from his wife. He thought Joan was very . . . real. *Genuine,* he said."

I stared across the desk at Mercedes. This was so much to absorb.

"Edward told me Joan has a lot of character." Mercedes said. "I suppose that's true . . . or she would've snatched up his offer."

My forehead scrunched. "What offer?"

"Well," she said, "when Edward found out that Joan was pregnant with you, he asked her to move to New York. He wanted to buy her an apartment here in Manhattan. He wanted to take care of you both . . . he hoped to be a father to you and continue his relationship with Joan."

I was starting to piece things together. "Continue his relationship," I echoed. "I don't suppose that involved divorcing Virginia and marrying my mother?"

Mercedes shook her head. "And that is *exactly* why Joan stayed in Charleston."

I was sure that was true. And Edward had been right—Mom *was* genuine, and she *did* have character. She'd never accept being a married man's mistress.

"Joan was furious with Edward for not telling her that he was married until he absolutely had to," Mercedes went on. "Honestly, I don't think she would've wanted him to divorce Virginia even if he'd offered. *You have children,* she said. *I'm no home wrecker.*"

That sounded like Mom. And after hearing all this, I wanted to slap myself for running out on her. "But why *didn't* he offer?" I asked. "If he was unhappy with Virginia, why wouldn't he just divorce her?"

"He did that last year," Mercedes said. "But when the children were young, he didn't leave her for the same reason Joan wouldn't have let him. He didn't want to hurt his kids."

"Oh," I said, glancing down at my hands.

"Don't conclude that he gave no thought to you," Mercedes said. "He would've loved to have a relationship with you, Savannah . . . but he thought that after all these years, you might not want to see him . . . and that contacting you would've caused trouble between you and Joan. And when you were a child, he felt he had to respect Joan's insistence on raising you without any help from him." She smoothed her skirt across her lap. "Frankly, I have a lot of respect for her because of that, too. She never took a dime . . . so Edward resorted to sending you Christmas gifts under some silly alias. What was it?" she said, moving her eyes around the ceiling. "Aunt Patty or Paulina or . . ."

My eyes widened. "Aunt *Primrose*?"

"Oh, *God,*" Mercedes said. "That's worse than I thought. But he *did* have a crazy sense of humor."

My mind raced with fond memories of presents like that pink bicycle with the monogrammed license plate. It had magically shown up outside our door—covered in shiny red paper—and Mom had sat on our porch swing, smiling while I gleefully tore the paper to shreds.

"Those gifts were all Joan would take," Mercedes said. "But they weren't enough for Edward. And that's why you're here."

I tilted my head. "Pardon me?"

She cleared her throat and leafed through papers in a manila folder. "These are the details of your new arrangement: Edward has left you an apartment he owned here in the city, and your inheritance has been deposited into a trust fund. You'll receive ten thousand dollars every week this year, fifty thousand dollars weekly next year, and one hundred thousand each week for the year after that. In the fourth year, your weekly income will go up to two hundred and fifty thousand, and it will continue to increase from there."

The numbers seemed impossible. Just yesterday I was hoping to get a job at the mall for minimum wage and worrying that Mom and I would lose our house.

"But," Mercedes said, rapping a pen on her folder, "there *is* a stipulation."

Of course there was. I waited for her to wake me up from this crazy dream.

"You'll have to stay in New York and work at Stone News," she said. "It doesn't matter what position you take . . . I'm not sure what you're qualified for. Did you finish high school?"

I had to stay in New York and work at an international news corporation. Was that the only catch? It sounded more like something I'd fantasized about while toiling at the library.

I nodded, thinking that her burst of niceness had worn off. "I also have all my own teeth. And none of my relatives sell moonshine or married their first cousins."

"Good to know," she said as she swiveled in her chair. "But I'm being serious."

"I have a bachelor's degree in English from the College of Charleston."

"How'd you manage that?" she asked, eyeing me skeptically. "Tuition wise, I mean."

"I had a full scholarship."

Her eyebrows shot upward. *"Really,"* she said. "Just like Edward. I'm sure he would've been proud."

That was a sweet thing to say, and I wondered if she was some sort of a schizophrenic. She dished out kind words and cruel comments at equal rates. "Thanks," I said. "But getting back to my *arrangement* . . . you've told me what's been left for me, but what about the other kids? Do they get weekly checks and new apartments, too?"

"Their situations will be different," she said, closing her folder. "You'll be starting at Stone News from the ground up . . . and as I mentioned, Ned and Caroline have executive positions."

"That doesn't seem fair," I said as I crossed my legs.

"They don't think so, either. But Edward did. You'll get all the money you didn't have during the past twenty-four years, but they'll have to *earn* theirs. He left them nothing."

Maybe I shouldn't have complained. "Why not?"

She shrugged. "Edward thought it would be good for them . . . in the long run, that is. I've explained this to Ned and Caroline, but it hasn't helped. They're beyond irate."

"I can imagine."

Mercedes adjusted her necklace. "I know it might seem harsh . . . but Edward truly did this with the best intentions. He changed his will recently and intended to explain his plans to them . . . but of course, he thought he'd have more time." She cleared her throat and picked up a business card that she handed to me over her desk. "You're expected here at nine thirty tomorrow morning to begin work."

I looked at the card. *Stone News Corporation,* it read. *Avenue of the Americas.*

"But before then," she said, "lose the drugstore makeup. Green eyeliner and pink glitter lipstick will get you nowhere. Neither will your hair."

I rubbed my lips together and touched my head. "There's

nothing wrong with my hair," I said, baffled by her criticism. I'd taken my cues from the hottest MILF in Mount Pleasant.

"You look like you just stumbled off the stage at the Miss Corncob pageant. Hack off a few inches and ditch the hairspray. And buy yourself a decent outfit."

There she was, going schizo again. "For your information, I've never been in a pageant . . . and this *is* a decent outfit."

Mercedes scrunched up her nose like she'd sniffed sour milk. "The suit is from an outlet mall and the shoes cost nineteen ninety-nine at Payless."

"How'd you know *that*? Do horrid manners come with psychic powers?"

She shrugged. "The fabric is cheap. And there's a price tag on the bottom of your shoe."

I lifted my foot to check while she picked up her phone and told the receptionist to have Tony meet me outside in five minutes and drive me to my apartment. Then I ripped off the tag and stuck it in my purse before she looked at me again.

"You sure do speak your mind, don't you?" I said.

"We have that in common," she replied with a wry smile. "Welcome to New York."

Four

I was alone in the elevator as it whisked me away from Patterson, Simmons & Gold. I kept thinking it all must be a joke and I'd wake up and be on the creaky porch at home, listening to Mom gossip with a customer while she highlighted hair.

I was still here, though. I slid my phone out of my purse when the doors opened, and then I leaned against a wall in the lobby while I read a new text from Mom: *You owe me a call.*

I sure did. I shouldn't have left Charleston in such a huff. I should have listened to Mom last night. *I've always told you not to settle . . .* , she'd said. *And I didn't want to.* Now I understood what she meant and I was sorry for judging. I didn't blame her for not wanting to be a married man's mistress, to spend her life as second best. Maybe hiding the truth had been Mom's way of protecting us, but I didn't need to be protected anymore. And I wasn't going to run.

I had to call Mom, and I was just about to when I saw the black car in front of the building. I dropped the phone into my purse and walked out to the sidewalk, where Tony scrambled from the front seat and opened the back door.

"You don't have to do that," I said. "It's gentlemanly of you, but my arms aren't broken."

He smiled. "So we're going to the Upper West Side?" he asked when we were in the car and he maneuvered through traffic. "Fifteen Central Park West . . . that's what Ms. Stark said, right?"

I shrugged. "Your guess is as good as mine."

He looked at me in the rearview mirror. "Are you okay?"

"I'm . . . not sure," I said. "I was wondering . . . do you only work for the law firm?"

He shook his head. "The car service tells me where to go . . . I drive for the firm pretty often, but I mainly work for Stone News."

"Oh," I said, hoping for some inside information. "Did you know Edward Stone?"

Tony nodded. "I drove him once in a while. Coincidentally, he died at Lenox Hill . . . the hospital where my wife is a nurse," he said as he turned a corner. "I was lucky I wasn't driving him that night."

"What do you mean?"

We were stuck in yet another traffic jam. Tony honked his horn at a taxi that cut in front of us, and then he turned toward me. "From what I've heard . . . a car came out of nowhere and slammed into Mr. Stone's car, shoved it into another lane, and he and the driver got hit head-on by a truck. Nobody knows what happened to the car that hit them . . . it took off so fast that none of the witnesses read the plate . . . and of course Mr. Stone and the chauffeur are dead. They've been saying on TV that it might've been a drunk driver . . . but considering what's been going on, who knows?"

We started moving again, and I remembered Mercedes mentioning the Stone News Corporation's *current problems.* "What's been going on?" I asked. "I haven't heard."

"Well," he said, "up in Putnam County, there's this lake . . . Kolenya, it's called . . . I've never been there, but I guess it used to be popular with the locals. Anyway, several people in the area have gotten sick over the past few years—"

"What kind of sick?" I asked.

"Cancer," he said, and I cringed, thinking about Tina's mother's chemo and how she'd wasted away to nothing but a skeleton in a bed with an oxygen mask on her face. "A few of them died . . . kids, even . . . and their families blamed this big company called Amicus Worldwide that has a plant a couple of miles away. Allegedly, chemicals from the plant leaked into a nearby stream that fed into the lake and that's why everybody got sick."

"How awful," I said, imagining a summer day with sunshine and kids floating around with inner tubes, completely clueless that they were playing in poison.

Tony stopped at a red light. "What's even worse is that Amicus supposedly knew what was going on but didn't do anything about it. They deny any responsibility, but that's what companies always do to avoid lawsuits."

I nodded. "But what does any of this have to do with Edward?"

The light turned green, and he drove ahead. "They claim he sat on the story. Before this whole thing broke open, some of the victims went to Stone News, asking for an investigation. Mr. Stone promised there'd be one, but it never happened. Everybody got sick of waiting and talked to other news organizations . . . and that's when it all came out. Like I said, Amicus hasn't been convicted of anything . . . but people aren't happy with Mr. Stone for keeping quiet."

"Why would he?" I asked. "Other than it being the right thing to do, he had everything to gain from exposing that story."

"I know . . . it doesn't make sense. And he had no connection to Amicus. According to the news, he didn't even own stock in the company. That's why the whole mess is under investigation." Tony reached into the glove compartment, pulled out an iPhone, and handed it to me. "It's all over the Internet if you want to check it out."

He was right. Hatred of Edward Stone and Stone News was everywhere, splattered like sludge on Web sites and blogs. I wouldn't normally read this sort of thing, but I couldn't help it now. I also couldn't stop staring at Edward's photos. He was handsome and looked much younger than his fifty-seven years. He had a square jaw, a deep cleft in his chin, and dark eyes. And I finally knew for sure where my blond hair had come from.

Tony looked at me over his shoulder. "I'm not sure if he was guilty of anything, but I'd be surprised if he was. I didn't know him well, of course . . . but he was very nice to me. He was a friendly guy . . . . really thoughtful and generous. He even sent flowers when my grandmother died. How many rich people would care enough to do that?" He parked in front of a soaring tower and twisted around. "Did you ever meet Mr. Stone?"

"No," I said, "but he was my father."

Tony said he was sorry at least five times as he lifted my bags out of the car in front of 15 Central Park West, but I told him that apologies weren't necessary.

"Ms. Stark wouldn't like that I blabbed all this," he said.

"Why?" I asked. "It's public knowledge."

"But *you* didn't know about it. My big mouth could cost me my job," he said as we stood on the sidewalk and a hot wind tousled his auburn hair.

I shook my head. "Not because of *me* it won't."

He didn't seem sure of that. But he nodded, got into the car, and drove away. Then I leaned against the building with my luggage at my feet and took out my cell phone to call Mom.

"Savannah," she said in a voice tinged with anger and panic and relief. "Are you okay?"

My $19.99 shoes pinched my toes. I slumped down and sat on my suitcase. "I think so," I said. "And I know there was never an Aunt Primrose."

I heard nothing. Then there was a long sigh. "Whoever you've been talking to sure has done some research."

"It was Edward's lawyer," I said as I watched a woman walk by, pushing a Pomeranian in a baby carriage. "But she didn't have to do any research, because he told her everything. She knows what happened between you and Edward. Now *I* do, too."

Mom was quiet again. I waited for her to say something as a town car pulled to the curb in front of the building. A doorman in a black suit with gold trim rushed toward it to greet whoever was inside.

"And I guess you're angry with me for keeping you from Edward and everything he could've given you . . . other than the Christmas gifts," she said finally.

I looked at someone getting out of the car at the curb—a tall, handsome man with designer shades who carried a gym bag and looked like a top-level executive returning from his workout on a day off. I supposed this building was filled with big-deal people like him, that this whole city was, and I couldn't help but wonder what it would have been like to grow up as the daughter of one of them.

"I don't know how I feel about that," I said. "But I understand why you chose not to be with him."

She exhaled a relieved breath. "Then get on the next flight home, Savannah."

After what I'd been through since last night, the predictability of home was tempting. But it was also miles from perfect. For so long, I'd wanted to do something that mattered, but it would never happen if I went back to Charleston and spent my days as a Library Lady or a clothes-store cashier while I lived in fear of bumping into Jamie and Eva Lee.

"I can't," I said after some thought. Then I let Mom in on everything—the apartment, the job, the money, and its stipulations. I also mentioned what I'd heard and read about what Edward had allegedly done. "I'm not going to run from this."

"It wouldn't be *running*," Mom insisted. "You shouldn't be *there* . . . in that *city*, with those *people* . . . especially with this scandal going on. I don't want you there."

"But I want *you* here, Mom. Move to New York, and I'll take care of you."

She scoffed. "Where have I heard *that* before? I didn't want to live off Edward's money then, and I don't want to now. The answer is no. I just want you back at home."

My heart deflated. I needed her to stand by me. And how could I live inside a big, fancy building while she stayed in our dumpy little house?

"Well," I said, "*my* answer is no, too. I'm not leaving here. But if you won't come, and if what that lawyer told me about the inheritance turns out to be true, I'll send money for your bills and put more aside until I have enough to buy you a gorgeous car and a brand-new house in Mount Pleasant. You won't have to do hair anymore."

"I'm not giving up my job. I can't sit around watching *Keeping Up with the Kardashians* all day."

I should've known. "I'm going to support you anyway. And I wish you'd do the same for me."

She let out a sigh. "Savannah," she said, "*keep your life free from the love of money.* . . ."

I rolled my eyes. "Why are you quoting scripture? You're not even religious."

"*. . . and be content with what you have.* That's what I believe, and it's one of the reasons I never took a cent from Edward Stone. Don't let money sway you."

I looked at an army of ants inside a jagged sidewalk crack. "It's not just the money, Mom. This is an opportunity . . . for both of us. I don't know why you can't understand that."

"Well," she said after a moment, "then I suppose we're done talking."

The connection crackled and died. I felt cold in the heat, and everything suddenly looked like it was underwater. I sniffed, wiped my eyes, and stood up. I wasn't exactly sure if what I was doing was right, but I had to find out for myself.

I pulled my suitcase into the lobby, which had frosted-glass lighting fixtures and a sleek floor made of ebony marble. I heard the screech of wheels against the floor, which made the lady at the concierge desk shoot me a disapproving stare. I'd probably left scratches and scuffs, but I was too exhausted and embarrassed to check.

"I'm Savannah Morgan," I said. "I'm supposed to move into an apartment here."

Not a single line creased into her face when she smiled. She had the smooth, shiny complexion that comes from needles at a plastic surgeon's office. "Edward Stone's daughter," she said. "I've been expecting you. Let me show you your new home."

She brought me to an apartment on the eleventh floor and led me through each fully furnished and decorated room. I was so bowled over by how spacious and classy everything was that nothing she said about the building's limestone architecture or its fitness center or the seventy-five-foot pool really sunk in.

When she left, I wandered around in a state of shock. Or maybe it was ecstasy. The apartment was twice the size of my house and just as beautiful as Tina's. It had two full bathrooms and an office with built-in shelves and a computer on a glass-topped desk. I'd been inside so many places like this in Mount Pleasant, but I never imagined I'd live in one—especially in New York. I never expected to have a sunlight-drenched living room painted the color of lemon cake batter, a big kitchen stocked with state-of-the-art appliances, and two pale-blue bedrooms that had windows with spectacular views of Central Park.

I lingered outside one of the rooms, my eyes on a king-size canopy bed draped in white fabric. I walked across the hardwood floor, sat on a plush comforter tucked into the mattress, and looked at the phone on the night table beside me, wishing I could share this with Mom and Tina.

But I couldn't. And I was drained. I needed to rest for a few minutes. So I slipped out of my blazer, dropped my shoes onto the floor, and leaned back into what had to be the softest and most luxurious bed in all of New York City.

Somebody was banging on the door. I opened my eyes, which wasn't easy because my lashes were crusted shut with mascara. *Never go to sleep without washing off your makeup,* Mom had always said. *It's a critical rule of femininity.*

I hadn't planned to break a cardinal Womanhood Law. I hadn't expected to fall asleep. I'd just wanted to relax for a while, and now what time was it? I flipped over and squinted at a clock radio on the night table. Its glowing red letters said *7:02 A.M.*

Had I really slept since yesterday afternoon? I lifted my head, looking at morning sunlight and glittery pink lipstick on the white pillow. I was in desperate need of Listerine, and my fingers stuck in a knot when I combed them through my hair. I wanted to brush my teeth, wash my face, and change out of yesterday's clothes, but whoever was banging on the door wouldn't give up. It wasn't a dainty, civil knock, either. It was loud and testy and demanding.

I dragged myself out of bed and through the living room, where I opened the door.

"Did you even lock up last night?" asked a man standing in the hallway.

I'd forgotten to, but that was none of his business. "Say what?"

"You heard me," he replied as I stared at him. He was tall and handsome with dark, wavy hair, olive-green eyes, a square jaw, and a cleft chin. I guessed he was about thirty-three, and he wore a slick gray suit with a tie made of indigo silk that was pierced with a diamond pin.

There was a petite woman beside him who seemed to be around thirty. Her irises were the same shade of green as his, she wore cat's-eye glasses, and she was dressed in ripped jeans and a ratty T-shirt with *The United States: Created by geniuses and run by morons* printed across her chest. Her hair was dyed as black as shoe polish, and it was cut into a messy shag that reached her shoulders.

"You can't sleep with your door unlocked, even in a building like this," the man went on, brushing past me and into the apartment. He sat on the seashell-shaped couch, stretched out his long legs, and undid a button on his blazer. "You're not in Tennessee anymore."

"I'm not from Tennessee," I shot back, wondering if every southern state was the same to anybody who lived above the Mason-Dixon Line. My mouth was parched and my voice came out raspy and I was confused and jittery, but I tried not to let it show. "And who are *you*? You're acting like you own this place."

"We do," said the woman as she walked by me and took a seat on the couch. "Or at least . . . our father did. I'm sure you can imagine our surprise when we heard about *you*."

They had to be the *legitimate* children—Ned and Caroline. I studied them as I stood by the door. Other than their eyes, nothing about them was the same. I wouldn't have suspected they were brother and sister, since he looked as if he'd stepped off a *GQ* cover and she resembled a grungy rocker chick. But they both had the same accent as Mercedes Rawlings Stark.

"Are you planning to stand there all day?" Ned asked. "Or are you going to sit down and talk to us like a nice little hostess?"

I leaned against the door to shut it. "*Hostess* implies I asked y'all to come here . . . but I didn't," I said, striding across the room to sit in a chair opposite the couch. "And just so you know, people with manners don't show up uninvited at other people's homes at seven in the morning. They also don't barge in without properly introducing themselves."

Caroline propped her elbow against the torn denim on her knee and leaned her face on her palm. I was close enough to see the pockmarks in her cheeks and the dark kohl smudged around her eyes. "I'm Caroline Stone," she said wearily in a nasal voice. "My brother is Edward Stone, Junior. He goes by *Ned*. And we know you're Savannah Morgan. Funny how we'd never heard of you until our father died . . . and now here you are, living rent-free in one of his apartments and stealing his money."

"I'm not *stealing*," I said as I dug my nails into the cushion on my chair. I moved my eyes between Caroline and Ned, who was rubbing his cleft chin. "And I understand my existence is a shock. I really do sympathize with how you feel. This whole thing is a surprise for me, too. I never knew until a few days ago that Edward was my father."

"How convenient," she said.

I'd meant it when I said I sympathized. They'd just lost a parent, and I could only imagine how it must have hurt for some strange girl to come out of nowhere and take what Caroline and Ned thought belonged only to them. So I ignored Caroline's snottiness and kept trying to be polite."Look," I said. "We can be cordial, can't we?"

"No," Caroline said dryly. "We can't."

I sighed. "Like I said, I understand. I know you're both upset—"

"Try homicidal," she cut in.

"—and I really don't blame you. Edward's lawyer told me all about the will."

Caroline rolled her eyes. "*Did* she? How considerate of her to share our misfortune with a total stranger. So I guess you know that although Ned and I have full control of Stone News and the paycheck that comes with it, we've otherwise been completely disinherited. Our father left us no money. No real estate. He didn't even cover Ned's golf club dues for Shinnecock Hills in Southampton. And I used to have an apartment this size, courtesy of Dad. Except it was downtown and trendier," she said, glancing around like she wasn't particularly impressed. "But it was sold . . . and the money went into *your* trust fund."

I cringed. I felt so guilty that I could barely look at her, so I glanced at the marble fireplace across the room. "Oh," was all I could say before shifting my eyes toward her again. Her hands were balled into fists, and she and Ned were giving me hateful stares. I wasn't sure whether I should hate them back or keep feeling sorry for them, but I decided to try to make them feel better by putting a positive spin on things. "I know none of this seems right. But you're lucky you had a father for so many years . . . that's more important than money, and it's also more than I've ever had."

Caroline laughed and turned toward Ned. "She's delusional."

"More like ignorant. But she never met him. She doesn't know any better," he replied, and then looked at me as he twisted the thick silver ring on his left hand. "Let me enlighten you, Savannah: You didn't miss out on anything when it comes to Edward Stone."

"Based on what he's done to us through his will," Caroline said, "we've concluded that we didn't know him at all . . . especially since he's also been accused of something that's beyond unethical."

I nodded. "So I've read."

"Oh," Caroline said. "You actually learned how to do that in Tennessee?"

"South Carolina," I corrected her. "And just because you're angry with Edward doesn't mean you have to be so—"

"Then you know," Ned interrupted, "that Stone News has been dealing with some serious problems. But what you might not be aware of is that these problems could be related to Dad's death. We don't know for a fact . . . but it's possible that what happened to him wasn't an accident. The police have initiated a full investigation."

I smoothed my tangled hair. "That's a good idea."

"Here's another good idea," Caroline said, adjusting her glasses. "Leave town."

I looked at the pricey furniture and the oak floors that had been polished to a glimmering shine. "I'm not going anywhere, Caroline. I like it here."

Ned hunched toward me from his seat on the couch. "You like the apartment and all the money coming your way. But are those things worth your life?"

I had a vision of being shot through the head and rolled up in a carpet that would be dropped into the Hudson River or the East River or wherever the corpses of inconvenient people got dumped.

"Are you threatening me?" I asked.

"My, aren't we dramatic."

"What my brother means," Caroline said, "is that someone could've intentionally killed Dad. That person is on the loose, and Dad's death might not have been enough revenge. Husbands have lost wives; mothers have buried children . . . there's a lot of anger out there. Any member of the Stone family could be next on this person's hit list . . . including you."

"You're paranoid," I said, wavering between laughter and a

panic attack. I wondered if Edward knew *he* might be on a hit list and this was why he changed his will. Maybe he didn't expect to have as much time as Mercedes thought.

"We have every right to be. This mess with Amicus Worldwide gave Dad enemies," Ned added. His hand moved from his wedding band to his Rolex, which he tightened around his wrist. "Unfortunately, Caroline and I are stuck here because we have to run Stone News . . . but you're free to leave. If you go back to South Carolina, anybody who hated Dad will never know you exist. If you stay here, you'll be walking around with a bull's-eye on your back."

I shook my head. "You want to get rid of me. You know if I leave New York, my inheritance is gone."

"We only want what's best for you, Savannah," Caroline said. "We're trying to protect you. You *are* our half sister, after all."

She was so phony. I would've welcomed the two of them as kin if they weren't such sleazy schemers. They had no idea how much I'd longed for siblings. I'd spent years wishing for a protective big brother or a sister to share my room and giggle and whisper with until we fell asleep.

I couldn't let myself waste another second being disappointed. And I didn't want to hear more talk about Edward Stone's enemies and their thirst for vengeance. So I stood up, headed for the door, and held it open.

"Thanks for the information," I said. "I hope y'all have a nice day."

"I *knew* it," Caroline said to Ned like I wasn't there. "I knew all she cared about was money. She's greedy enough to risk getting tortured or raped or murdered just so she can live an easy life off a stranger's hard work."

"He might've been a stranger," I said, feeling angry heat rise from my neck to my forehead, "but he was as much my father as he was yours. And you know a lot more about having an easy life than I do. I wonder if that's why Edward didn't leave you any money. Maybe he thought it would do you some good to find out what the real world is like. Maybe he thought having to *earn* a living would make you a better person."

She bolted off the couch and clomped across the floor in her black hiking boots. I'd never seen anybody wear those ghastly things in July. Then she got so close to me that my back was against the door and her nose was an inch from mine.

"You don't know *anything* about *my* father," she said as a foamy bead of spit sprang from her mouth and landed on my cheek. "All he was to you was a fucking sperm donor. And if you stay in New York, it'll be the biggest mistake you've ever made . . . trust me."

My heart was thumping beneath my pink satin shirt. She stared at me like she was waiting for me to cower and cry and book the first available flight back to Charleston.

"I *don't* trust you, Caroline. Sorry to disappoint, but I'm staying."

She stormed off. Ned had been watching from the couch; he sauntered toward me as I wiped Caroline's spit from my face with the back of my hand.

"My sister," he said, raking his fingers through his wavy hair, "is a smart girl. She went to Harvard. She used to work for a public interest group, and she loved that job even though it didn't pay much. Of course, money didn't matter when Dad was alive . . . he subsidized everything to ease his guilt."

"Guilt?" I said, confused. "About what?"

Ned ignored me. "Now that things have changed," he continued, "Caroline has to pay her own rent. She won't be able to travel as much as she used to, and she has to give up her job to work at Stone News. I've worked there since I finished my MBA, albeit in a much less time-consuming position. Still, I'm used to this industry . . . but it'll be a rough adjustment for her."

I supposed that was true. And even though most of Earth's population has to pay rent and doesn't get to travel much I still felt bad for Caroline. But it would have been easier to show her some compassion if she weren't—as Tina would say—such a snotty B. "That was Edward's decision," I said, "not mine."

Ned towered over me. His shoulders were broad and his features had turned stern and sharp. "Like I said . . . Caroline's smart. You should take her advice and go back to the shithole you crawled out of. Nobody wants you here, Savannah. We can make your life quite difficult."

He said the last sentence in a calm, ominous way that sent an icy shiver down my spine.

"I'm not going anywhere, Ned. I deserve to be here as much as you do."

He stared at me for a moment before taking a step back and adjusting the diamond pin stuck through his silk tie. "That's your choice. But if you think Caroline's bad, you better stay out of my mother's way. She wasn't pleased to find out that you exist. In fact, she was goddamned furious. Can you imagine how it feels for a woman of the finest breeding to learn that her husband had a bastard kid with some slutty backwoods beautician?"

I wanted to yank the pin out of his tie and use it to slice his throat. "Don't you *ever* disrespect my mother," I said, standing on my tiptoes to get up in his face. "And get out of my apartment. Too bad Edward didn't leave one for you."

"Is that supposed to sting?" he asked, giving me a smarmy smile. "I don't need an apartment, Savannah. My wife is loaded. We live in a lovely brownstone on East Seventieth that she inherited from her aunt before we were married. I'm partial to that side of town anyway."

He walked out with a sickeningly self-assured swagger. I slammed the door behind him and collapsed into a heap on the glossy floor, where I stayed until I heard another knock. Even though this one was mannerly, I thought Ned and Caroline might be back for a second round of mind games. But it was just the doorman I'd seen downstairs.

"Package for Ms. Savannah Morgan," he said.

I grabbed my purse so I could give him a tip, and then I took the delivery from him. It was just a thin envelope. "Thank you," I said, slipping him a five.

He gave the money back. "That isn't necessary. The messenger who dropped off the envelope wanted me to tell you this: Ms. Stark said you have unlimited access to the car service, courtesy of Stone News. Tony Hughes will be your personal driver. His direct number is in the envelope."

So was a check for ten thousand dollars, made out to me. I discovered this after the doorman left and I opened the envelope as I stood like a statue in the middle of the living room, trying to figure out whether this was a nightmare or a dream.

Five

I couldn't stand around. The Stone News Corporation was waiting.

I dashed into my bedroom and flipped on the clock radio as I stripped off my clothes and listened to a traffic report warning about road construction on the Cross Bronx Expressway and an accident inside the Holland Tunnel. After that, I went to the master bathroom and stepped into the shower, which was so much better than the one at home. This shower was made of tiny silver squares that sparkled beneath recessed lighting, and the water cascaded in a firm stream from a metal circle in the ceiling.

An hour later, my hair was done and my makeup was on and I was dressed in a suit I'd taken from my suitcase and wished I had time to iron. Then I called Tony, who pulled to the curb in front of my building while I waited on the sidewalk. He jumped out and headed toward the back door, but I got in his way before he could touch the handle.

"Mind if I sit in front?" I asked. "This isn't *Driving Miss Daisy.*"

He smirked and opened the front door. "At least let me do

this. You shouldn't stop me from doing my job right, especially since we'll be seeing a lot of each other from now on. Ms. Stark said I'll be driving you to and from work every day."

I gave in and got into the car, and Tony sat in the driver's seat beside me.

"When do you get off work?" I asked when he sped away from the curb. "I'm not sure what time I'll leave the office every day, and I don't want to call and bother you while you're not on the clock."

He shook his head. "It's no bother. You'd be doing me a favor, actually. After six on weeknights and anytime during the weekend is overtime pay . . . so feel free to call whenever. I'll probably be in the city anyway, driving some of the service's other clients."

"Oh," I said, glancing at the picture of his daughter as it dangled from the ignition. "But don't your wife and daughter want you at home at night and during the weekend?"

He turned a corner. "Sure. But they also know I don't want them living in a cramped apartment for the rest of their lives. We're saving for a house."

I nodded. "I'm sure the sacrifice will be worth it, then."

"*I* think so. I'd like to get a little place out in Nassau County where my daughter can have her own yard. And fortunately, my mother lives down the hall in our building, so we have a baby-sitter on call twenty-four/seven." He stopped abruptly, like he was breaking Chauffeur Etiquette by talking about himself. "So . . . what will you do at Stone News?"

I shrugged. "I'm not sure, but they must have something set up for me. Before we head that way, though . . . would you mind taking me to any bank that'll let me open an account?" I said, and a few minutes later I was inside Chase Manhattan with my check while Tony waited in the car.

"I'd like to open a checking account and a savings account,"

I told a woman behind a desk as I sat opposite her and explained how she should divide my money into each account. "I'll take the rest in cash . . . thousand-dollar bills, please."

Her tired eyes rose above her bifocals. "Thousand-dollar bills haven't been printed since 1945, dear."

"Is that so?" I said, trying not to sound as stupid as I felt. "Hundreds will be fine, then."

The money was inside my purse when Tony stopped the car in front of a massive skyscraper near Rockefeller Center that had a ticker spelling out the latest news in red neon letters. *Headlines from Stone News,* I read as I stared through the window at people rushing through revolving doors with *Stone News Corporation* carved into a plaque above them. There was also a line of protesters on the curb, chanting and holding signs that said *Stone News Kills.*

"What floor is it on?" I asked, my eyes gliding up and down the building.

"*Every* floor," Tony said. "Don't be nervous, Savannah. You'll be fine."

I grabbed my purse and a folder that held my résumé, which I'd printed in my office at the apartment because I thought it might be needed for my employment records. I clasped the folder tightly to my chest, trying to slow my heart.

"Who's nervous?" I said as I slipped out of the car. "See you at five."

I closed the door, and he drove away. I lingered on the sidewalk, listening to the protesters and the voice in my head. *You can handle this. You can handle all of it.*

I took a deep breath and marched past the picket line, through the revolving doors, and into the lobby, where I wondered if every woman who worked at a front desk in Manhattan moonlighted as an actress or a model. The glamorous girl in front of me looked that way, with her ash-blond hair and delicate features. She answered a phone while a hulking security guard stood behind her with his arms folded across his chest.

I waited until she hung up. "Excuse me," I began. "I . . ."

She didn't make eye contact. She took another three calls and then turned her attention to a man who'd cut in front of me.

"I was here first," I said, but I was invisible. She answered the man's questions and two more calls before she finally deigned to look in my direction.

"Now what can I do for you?" she asked.

"Forgive me for bothering you," I said as sarcastically as I could, "but I'm starting my first day of work here, and I don't know where to go."

She breathed a long sigh. "You're working in which division? Who's your supervisor?"

The only people I knew at this company were Ned and Caroline, but I wanted to steer clear of them. "I have no idea. Somebody's expecting me, though. Can you please call whoever's in charge and say Savannah Morgan is here?"

"Just a minute," she said, and took another call.

I checked my watch. It was after nine, and how unprofessional would it look if I was late on my first day? I kept trying to talk to the receptionist, but she pretended I wasn't there until I slammed my hand on her desk and raised my voice. "Can you take a two-minute recess from whatever is so important and call whoever's in charge of hiring people to let him or her know I'm here?"

She glanced at the security guard. He stepped forward, and then his massive hand was clamped around my arm and he was hauling me across the lobby.

"Get your paws off me!" I screeched as he shoved me through the revolving doors and onto the crowded sidewalk, where I lost my grip on my folder and my résumé fell out and drifted to the ground. "You're clearly abusing steroids, sir. You're also making a mistake. I'm Edward Stone's daughter."

"Caroline Stone is the only daughter I know about," he said, "and you're not her."

My sleeve was wrinkled from all the manhandling. I smoothed it while I tried to catch my breath. "I'm his *other* daughter . . . from South Carolina."

"Right," he said slowly, and pointed to the street. "Take a cab to Bellevue. Maybe they can help you there. Just don't trespass in this building again or you'll find your ass in jail."

He went back inside and I glanced at my résumé being trampled by a pair of stiletto heels. I crouched down to rescue it, but someone else was faster. She grabbed the crinkled paper, looked at it, and handed it back to me.

"So you're Savannah."

We were squatting on the cement. I took the résumé, straightened up, and she did, too.

"I heard what you were saying to the security guard," she said as I looked at the shiny copper hair skimming her shoulders and her deep-set eyes that were the same shade of brown as mine. She seemed to be nearing her mid-thirties. She stood a few inches taller than me and was svelte and chic in a beige jacket with a matching skirt. "I'm so sorry about the confusion . . . my husband should've let the receptionist know you were coming."

"Your husband?" I asked.

"Ned Stone," she said as my stomach dropped and I feared I'd been lured into a trap by Lucifer's bride. And of course Ned hadn't let the receptionist know I was coming. It was probably part of his twisted plot to sabotage me. Or maybe he thought I'd run back to Charleston by now. "I'm Katherine . . . but everybody calls me Kitty. You haven't met Ned yet, have you?"

"I sure have. He and Caroline made a surprise appearance at my apartment this morning."

She cringed. "I didn't know that. I assume they didn't behave themselves?"

"You assume correctly," I said.

She stared at me for a moment. "I apologize again, Savannah. Ned and Caroline don't have much experience with things not going their way, and your sudden appearance has brought out the worst in them. But don't take it personally . . . it really has nothing to do with you. It's just the idea that Edward had more generosity toward a child he never knew than the ones he raised . . . it's been devastating for them. You can understand that, can't you?"

"Yes, I can. It's already crossed my mind. But it doesn't mean they can treat me like a . . ."

I stopped. She grinned. "A redheaded stepchild?" she said. "I agree. But I think they'll come around eventually. As for me, I'm thrilled to have a new sister-in-law . . . especially such a beautiful one," she said, her eyes moving around my face. "You resemble Edward, you know. You have his hair."

She seemed too kind and sincere to be from the dark side. *My wife is loaded,* Ned had told me. Maybe he put on a nice-guy act to keep her fortune around. "Thanks for the compliment," I said. "I've seen a picture of Edward online. Ned has his chin."

"And his jawline . . . but that's where the resemblance ends. Ned looks like his mother, and Caroline . . . well, she's an original. Of all the kids, I think you favor Edward the most. Anyway . . . I hope nothing else you've seen on the Web about Stone News scared you too much. There's a lot of mudslinging going on," she said, glancing over her shoulder at the protesters on the curb, "and the Internet can be a real sewer."

"I don't scare that easily," I said, which was almost true.

"I'm happy to hear it. And I'm even happier that you're mixing some new life into the gene pool. Now let's go and get you started in the family business."

Kitty hooked her arm around my elbow and led me into the lobby, where we stopped at the front desk. The receptionist and the security guard stared at me, and I stared right back.

"I realize you two were uninformed this morning," Kitty said. "You should've been told about Ms. Morgan's arrival. You also should've checked with somebody upstairs before you tossed her out into the street. She's part of the Stone family now, and you'll treat her with all the respect you give the rest of us. Understand?"

Damn straight. I'm part of the Stone family. I deserve to be treated with respect. Maybe you should've investigated my lineage before you got uppity with me, Bitchy Receptionist Chick.

I didn't say any of that, of course. But I didn't need to. The chagrined look on the security guard's face and the irritated way the receptionist nodded at Kitty was enough for me.

"I'm glad that's settled," Kitty said, tightening her grip around my elbow. She guided me toward an elevator, we darted inside, and it raced upward. I smiled to myself, relieved that at least one living member of the Stone family wanted me around.

Kitty gave me a tour of what she said was the corporate division of Stone News. The lobby looked like a living room, with lavish couches, elegant lamps, and an oil-color portrait of Edward Stone. She led me down halls with offices and cubicles, introducing me to secretaries and people with titles like GM and FCO, and then we were standing in front of a closed door that had a placard engraved with *Edward Stone, Jr., Chairman & Chief Executive Officer.*

"What's he doing?" Kitty asked a dowdy secretary who sat across from the door.

"Talking to your college buddy," she said.

Kitty twisted the knob. "Sorry to interrupt," she said when the door opened into an office that could have doubled as an apartment. Ned sat leisurely at a wide desk in a stuffed leather chair while a woman who was blonder and even more glamorous than the receptionist downstairs sat opposite him. "It's been a while, Darcelle. We're due for lunch."

"We sure are. You should come up here more often," Darcelle said, springing from her chair to give Kitty a hug. "You're as gorgeous as ever. And tan, too. Have you spent much time at your parents' house in the Hamptons this summer? Or have you been too busy jetting off to the islands in your dad's plane?"

"Neither," Kitty said. "The magazine's struggling, so I'm needed here."

"I have no doubt that an editor with your talent can whip it into shape."

"You're a sweetie," Kitty replied, and then moved her eyes between Darcelle and me. "Darcelle Conrad . . . I'd like you to meet Savannah Morgan, Edward's daughter. I'm sure Ned has mentioned her."

He looked out the window. Darcelle's forehead creased. "No," she answered, and quickly broke the awkward silence by giving me a firm handshake and a dazzling smile. "But it's nice to meet you. Do you live in New York?"

"I just moved here," I said.

"That's so exciting. And what do you do?"

I glanced at Kitty, who snapped her head in Ned's direction. He was still focused on the window and a foam rubber ball he'd snatched from his desk and was squeezing in his fist.

"That's what we came up here to find out," Kitty said. "Edward wanted Savannah to work at Stone News, and I'm sure Ned has made plans for her."

"I work in the newsroom," Darcelle told me. "There might be some openings, and—"

"There *aren't,*" Ned cut in, tossing the ball toward a bookshelf. It landed beside a photograph of him in a tux and Kitty in a wedding gown. "Speaking of the newsroom . . . aren't you needed down there, Darcelle? Your show can't start without its anchorwoman."

"The boss has spoken," she said brightly before dashing into the hallway.

Kitty stayed beside me. "Ned," she started, "do you have a position ready for Savannah?"

He plucked a silver pen from a drawer and twirled it between his fingers. "I do not," he said, staring at me with eyes that had frozen into olive-green ice. "The company doesn't have anything to offer at the moment . . . unless she wants to work in the mailroom."

Kitty bristled. "I think you can find your sister a better job than sorting envelopes."

He dropped the pen onto the desk, tossed his wavy hair, and leaned forward. "Caroline's my only sister, and she's starting here tomorrow. As for Savannah . . . I'll be happy to employ her as a mail clerk. It's that or nothing. She can decide for herself."

Kitty slung her arm around my shoulders. "Do you mind waiting outside for a minute?" she asked, sounding embarrassed as she led me toward the door that she closed when I was in the hallway. I stood there and listened to her voice through the wood.

"Stop being such an asshole," she said. "You know very well that how your father left his money isn't her fault . . . and even though it's been hard on you and Caroline, you have to stop trying to punish Savannah for it."

"If I wanted to punish her," he said, "I'd find something more painful than the mailroom."

"Stop it, Ned. This isn't who you are . . . you're a much better man than you're leading her to believe. Now if *you* won't give her a decent position, *I* will. I fired my assistant last week, so I'll let Savannah have the job."

He chuckled like this was a crazy idea. "You can't put her in a position she isn't qualified for. Being an editor's assistant requires a college degree and skills you don't acquire from handing out fries at McDonald's or whatever she did before. It would be unethical to take nepotism so far that we hire an uneducated hillbilly at one of our magazines."

My blood heated up. I wasn't surprised that he saw me as an ignorant scrap of nothing, but that didn't make me any less angry. This was exactly the type of job I'd always wanted, and I wouldn't let anybody keep it from me, especially Ned Stone. So I opened the office door and burst inside, where I slapped my crinkled résumé down on his big mahogany desk.

He was still in his chair, and he didn't move. All he did was glide his eyes over the résumé and then shift them back to me. He kept his face straight, but there was a trace of annoyance in it, like I'd beaten him at a critical move during a chess game.

After Kitty graciously offered me the job and I enthusiastically accepted, she brought me to a lower floor that was decorated in a more modern and less formal style than the corporate division of Stone News. The furniture was made of shiny metal and sparkling glass, and the magazine's title was splashed in purple paint across a white wall.

"As you can see," Kitty said as we waltzed past the reception desk, "it's called *Femme*."

Really? Really? *Really?* I'd been a fan of that magazine since it started a few years ago. It was edgy and witty and smart and fun, and when I read it on my porch swing I never imagined I'd get to be a part of it. But I couldn't jump up and down and giggle and squeal like a goofball. "Oh," I said coolly. "I think I've seen it around."

Kitty led me to her spacious office, where she settled behind a desk and I sat across from her while she told me about the magazine—that it mixed stories such as "How to Choose a Red Lipstick That Won't Make You Look like a Bordello Madam" with "Ten Ways to Outwit the Office Psycho" and "Keep Your Hands off My Birth Control, Uptight White Man."

"We're online and in hard copy," Kitty said, showing me *Femme* on a Web site and in glossy print. "As you might know, our articles focus on what interests women: politics, entertainment, fashion, relationships, and sex. We also have a literary feature . . . we run short fiction written by readers."

"Oh," I said again. "I'm a fiction writer. Well . . . I want to be, anyway."

"Employees aren't exempt from consideration, so you're more than welcome to submit your work . . . directly to me, of course," she said, giving me a wink, "to avoid pesky delays."

Did I see cartoon butterflies and bluebirds landing on her shoulders? Who was piping Disney music into the vents? Kitty was like a fairy godmother inside a swirl of glitter.

"You should make time for your aspirations," she went on, "but I have to warn you . . . you'll be busy here. My last assistant left a lot of work, and our social media sites are in desperate need of updating." She wriggled out of her jacket. "You know, I've never had an assistant who was truly interested in this job. Every one of them wanted to be something else . . . a singer, a dancer, an *actress*. . . ." She rolled her eyes. "I'm really happy that you're a writer. You came along at just the right time."

"So did you," I said.

After that, Kitty gave me a rundown of my job duties, which included handling her schedule, monitoring reporters' progress on articles, doing research whenever necessary, and maintaining *Femme*'s social media sites.

"I'll have an intern show you how to access and update the sites," Kitty said as she balanced a pencil between her fingers. "It's not the most exciting part of your job . . . and frankly, none of it is particularly enthralling . . . but it's a start."

I nodded more enthusiastically than I'd intended. Everything about the job was fine with me. I was just happy to be there.

Then Kitty brought me to my designated cubicle, where I spent almost two hours filling out employment forms and reading the employee manual. Just as I finished, Kitty came back and said it was time for lunch and she wanted to take me out as a celebration of my first day.

I followed her into an elevator, through the lobby downstairs, past the protesters who clearly didn't believe in a lunch break, and inside a taxi that drove us to Fifth Avenue and a restaurant that was airy and sunny and crowded with professional-looking people. I ordered a salad, and the waitress promptly corrected my pronunciation.

"*Fro-mage de chè-vre salade,*" she said, enunciating each syllable like I was slow-witted.

Fromage was cheese . . . of some sort. And way too risky.

I glanced at the menu again. "What's this?" I asked as I pointed to an item that I didn't dare try to say.

"*Pen-ne fun-ghi tar-tu-fo,*" she told me in her I'm-better-than-you way. "It's—"

"Pasta with mushrooms," Kitty cut in, shoving her menu at the waitress. "I'll have the endive-and-pear salad. And you can spare us the foreign language lessons."

The waitress left. I looked across the table at Kitty. "I'm used to fried chicken and she-crab soup," I said. "I've only eaten fancy food at debutante balls, so this is fairly new to me."

She sipped her ginger ale. "I love fried chicken. And *this,*" she said, glancing around the restaurant, "is just boring people being pretentious because putting other people down makes them feel important. Don't let it bother you."

Later, we were on Fifth Avenue again, where we decided to walk back to work. We strolled past a street lined with stores, and my eyes lingered on a baby doll in a frilly tulle dress inside FAO Schwarz's front window.

"A friend of mine has a six-year-old daughter," I said. "I wonder if she'd like that doll."

Kitty smiled. "Buy it for her. Your new boss won't mind if you're a few minutes late."

I went in, swept past salespeople jumping up and down on giant piano keys to play "Chopsticks," and returned with the doll inside a bright-pink shopping bag. "I hope I'm right about this gift. I don't have much experience with children," I said as we headed toward the office. "Do you have any kids?"

Kitty's face dimmed. I wanted to kick myself. I shouldn't have asked; it was a personal question, and she probably would have already mentioned her children if she had any.

"No," she said, staring straight ahead. "Three rounds of IVF and I'm still *childless,* as my mother-in-law so eloquently puts it."

"I'm sorry. I didn't mean to pry—"

She held up her hand. "It's okay. I'd rather you hear the truth from me instead of gossip from the rest of the family. I've given up on fertility treatments for now . . . I've had enough of the nausea and the mood swings and the endless disappointment. I'll try again when I feel ready, but my focus is making the magazine a success. *Femme* is my baby at the moment."

"You'll make it a success for sure," I said. "And I hope I can help."

She turned toward me and smiled. "As do I . . . that's why I hired you."

We went back to Stone News, where I spent some time on the phone, scheduling Kitty's meetings and figuring out how to record them in her online calendar. When that was done, I headed to the ladies' room and almost slammed into somebody when I rounded a corner.

"You must be Kitty's new assistant."

"Yes," I said, looking at a pretty young girl with a dark-brown bob and a tiny waist.

"My name's Ainsley Greenleaf. I've heard all about you."

"Is that right?" I said as she grabbed my hand and shook it.

"Uh-huh. Word travels fast at Stone News."

I wrenched out of her crushing grip. "Do you work here?"

"I'm an intern," she said so proudly that her brown eyes sparkled. "I'm going into my freshman year at Purdue. Well, I'm not *officially* an intern because you can't be one until your junior year. Or is it senior year? Anyway, my dad was a close friend of Edward Stone's so Ned made me an unofficial intern. I do everything the real interns do, though. I'm a mass communications major . . . I want to work as an investigative TV news reporter or become a journalist who covers wars. I haven't made up my mind yet."

I was dizzy from the information avalanche. She reminded me of a cheerleader on my squad at Charleston High who'd been voted Miss Effervescent.

"I float," she said. "I go where I'm needed. Sometimes I'm in the corporate division, sometimes the newsroom, and sometimes I come down here and assist the assistants. Do you need help with anything? I can handle whatever task you throw at me. Just let me have it."

Her enthusiasm was exhausting. "I have nothing to throw right now. But thanks."

Then she was gone and I went back to work, e-mailing reporters about the status of their articles-in-progress until Kitty popped her head into my cubicle. She was holding her purse, and her blazer was draped over her arm.

"It's five o'clock," she said. "No overtime on your first day."

I glanced at my lengthy to-do list. "But I've got all this work, and—"

"There's a big city out there, Savannah. Don't waste a beautiful summer night sitting behind your desk. I'm sure you've got better things to do, right?"

How sad it was to be in the most exciting place on the globe and have nothing to do and nobody to do anything with. "Of course," I said, pushing my chair away from my desk like I couldn't wait to hit the town.

She smiled and left, I called Tony, and he said he'd be there in a few minutes. I picked up my FAO Schwarz bag, went downstairs, and walked through the revolving doors and out to the street, where the gang of protesters from this morning had dwindled to six. One of them—a fiftyish man with a graying goatee who wore a Mets baseball cap backward—came up to me when I was standing a few feet away from him, waiting for my ride.

"You work there?" he asked, nodding toward Stone News.

"It's my first day," I said as I noticed a birthmark on his face—a reddish-purple stain between his eyebrows that was shaped remarkably like Spain on a map.

He spit into the gutter. "Make it your last. Stone News is the Evil Empire. They don't report the news . . . they cover it up to protect their interests. Do you want to be part of a company that looks the other way when innocent people are being put in the ground?" Spit bubbled at the corner of his mouth, and he stood so close to me that I could smell tobacco and sweat. I didn't know what to say—nothing had been proven, and it made no sense that Edward would protect a company that was putting an entire community in danger. What was there to gain except a bad reputation? "You'd be wise to rethink where you get your paycheck," he added.

Tony pulled up in the black sedan. The man walked away, I slid into the car next to Tony, and we headed into rush-hour traffic. "The temperature," the radio said, "is eighty-nine degrees."

"This is a tip," I said, putting the FAO Schwarz bag in the backseat.

"I can't accept gifts, Savannah. It's company policy that drivers aren't allowed to—"

"Your daughter has nothing to do with your company policy. The gift's meant for her, so hush up and take it."

A bus nearly grazed the car. Tony punched his horn, and then he was quiet for a moment as he navigated through a crowded street. "Thank you," he said finally.

"You're welcome. By the way, what's your daughter's name?"

"Marjorie," he said. "It's old-fashioned, but it's my mother's name and I thought she deserved to have a grandchild named after her. She's earned it."

Tony turned a corner. I started thinking about dinner and eating it by myself, which I wasn't used to. Mom had always been across the table, and whenever she wasn't I'd had Jamie or Tina passing the okra or the ketchup. I considered asking Tony if he'd like to join me, but that quickly fizzled. It wasn't proper to invite a married man to dinner, even if all I wanted was company.

"What's your favorite restaurant in Manhattan?" I asked.

Tony combed his fingers through his hair. "I usually eat at Subway or Burger King," he said with a laugh. "I'm not into those fancy, overpriced places with tiny portions where you leave as hungry as you came. But for my last wedding anniversary, I took my wife to a nice restaurant on East Forty-sixth. It's perfect for a meat-and-potatoes type like me."

I asked Tony to take me to East 46th, where I got out of the car. He drove away, and I passed a man who sat slumped on a bench outside the restaurant. He looked like an old sea captain, with a fuzzy white beard, a grizzled face, and soiled clothes that were too heavy for July. He said hello to people on their way into the restaurant—men in sharp suits, women who wore simple black dresses. They kept their eyes straight ahead, pretending they couldn't see or smell him.

"What a pretty lady," he said to me.

"Thank you, sir," I replied.

I went into the restaurant, which had red leather booths, lit candles on tables, and black-and-white autographed photographs of celebrities covering the walls.

"How many?" asked an attractive hostess.

"Just one," I said.

She looked at me like I was as tragic as that homeless man outside. She asked me to follow her, and then I was sitting alone in a booth with filet mignon and a baked potato. When the bill came, it floored me even though I could afford it.

"How come a potato is fifty cents at the Piggly Wiggly in South Carolina and it's more than eight dollars here?" I jokingly asked my waiter.

"At the . . . where?" he said with a straight face.

I shrank into my seat. "Never mind. Can you please wrap this up?" I asked, pushing half of my steak to the edge of my plate.

The waiter came back a few minutes later with a mini shopping bag. I tossed some cash into it and reached over to an empty table to swipe a set of silverware, which I tucked into the bag for that man on the bench. I wasn't going to let him eat filet mignon with his fingers.

I unlocked the door and walked into my apartment. It was nearly dark, and long shadows streamed through the windows and covered the furniture. I left my purse on the coffee table, flipped on the lights, and wished I weren't alone. I wished things were back to normal with Mom and Tina. But they weren't, so I consoled myself with the pint of chocolate ice cream I'd picked up on the way home. I ate it straight from the container while watching TV on the couch. Then I pulled my cell phone from my purse and decided to text Mom. *I'm okay,* I wrote. *Just wanted to let you know.*

Good, she texted back a minute later.

One word was better than nothing. I was still looking at the message when my phone vibrated in my palm. *Tina Mae Brandt,* the caller ID said.

"I decided to be the one to give in," she told me after I answered. Her Dixie drawl sounded like home. "Since you're stubborn and thickheaded."

I laughed. "Yeah, like you don't know about being either of those things. But I'm not as bad as you think. I actually considered calling and apologizing for the other night. I still stand by what I said, but I didn't mean to upset you . . . so I'm sorry."

She paused. I heard crickets in the background, and I wondered if she was on her window seat, exhaling smoke into the muggy Charleston air.

"I accept your apology," Tina said after a moment. "And I'm sorry for what *I* said, too. It was a really low blow. But I've heard that your paternal status has changed since then."

I sat up straight, hoping the news hadn't spread all over town. "How'd you know?"

"Your mother told me everything. She wants me to convince you to come home."

That figured. "Well . . . before you give it a try, let me tell you my side of the story," I said, and rested my feet on the coffee table while I told her about the job and the money and gave her every detail about the apartment.

"Jeez," she said with a gasp. "It sounds like a fairy tale. It seems perfect."

"Nothing's perfect."

"True," she said slowly. "I'm sorry about what happened to your father, Savannah. You must feel like you lost him twice."

Every so often, she'd open her mouth and the wisest words

would fly out. "That's *exactly* how I feel. Now I'll never get a chance to know him, or to find out who he really was," I said before spilling out every single thing that had happened since I left Charleston. She got all outraged when I mentioned I'd been ambushed this morning and I might be—as Caroline had said—on a lunatic's hit list.

"Treachery and deception is all it amounts to," Tina said assuredly. "Those two weasels are trying to mess with your head . . . so don't let them."

I smiled into the phone, grateful that part of Team Savannah was back. "Come up for a visit, Tina. There's plenty of room for you in this apartment, and it's in a great location . . . Fifteen Central Park West. Maybe you'll like it enough to stay."

She paused once more. I heard the crickets again. "I can't leave Raylene," she said, and I couldn't blame her. If I had a little sister, I'd have a hard time leaving her, too. "Daddy wouldn't pay for my plane ticket, anyway . . . and I've already blown my latest paycheck on the sweetest pair of Badgley Mischkas."

I wasn't surprised about the shoes, and I agreed with what she'd said about Mr. Brandt. He was a pushover when Tina wanted a car or jewelry or clothes. But he'd slam that checkbook shut if what she wanted had anything to do with me.

"I can pay for your ticket," I told her.

"He wouldn't go for *that*, either," she said, and wisely changed the subject. "So are you happy there, Savannah?"

"Not really," I said.

"I didn't think so. I can hear it in your voice. And I'd like to tell you to come back . . . but that'd be selfish, wouldn't it?"

"I guess so," I agreed, gazing through the window at the dark sky above the forest of trees in Central Park as Tina filled me in on the latest Charleston gossip. There were stars in the sky, and it was hard to believe they were the same ones I saw from my porch at home. Home felt so far away.

Six

Tony picked me up the next morning. "Marjorie loved the doll," he said when I sat beside him and he drove toward Stone News. "She made this for you."

He handed me a piece of construction paper covered with *Thank You* in crayon scribble.

"That's the best thank-you card anybody's ever given me," I said as my heart swelled. "It'll be displayed prominently on my refrigerator."

Tony smiled. I carefully folded the paper and slipped it inside my purse, and soon I was at work. The protesters were outside as usual, and I found out that Kitty had a stomach bug and was taking the day off. But there was plenty to keep me busy. I was in the middle of some online research when my phone rang and I grabbed the receiver without checking the caller ID.

"Savannah Morgan," I said, still focused on my monitor.

"Edward Stone, Junior. I need you in conference room C on the fiftieth floor."

He hung up. I stared at the phone, wondering what he could possibly need me for and wishing I didn't have to obey his orders. But there was no choice if I wanted to keep my job, so I went upstairs to the corporate division and found conference room C.

I knocked on the door, heard Ned's voice telling me to come in, and found him sitting at the head of a long glass table. Men and women in suits were to his left and his right, and there was a platter in the center of the table filled with discarded muffin wrappers and banana peels.

"My secretary left due to a family emergency," he said, barely looking at me as he thumbed through a document in front of him, "and as you're not assisting Kitty today, you can fill in. Clear this mess and bring us more coffee."

He shifted his attention to everyone sitting around the table and started talking business while I stood there, completely humiliated. He wanted me to wait on him like I was his scullery maid, and I felt lower than a soot-faced urchin in a Dickens novel.

"I'm . . . ," I began, but my voice cracked.

Ned and everybody else looked at me like I had a lot of nerve to interrupt.

"I beg your pardon?" he said.

I cleared my throat and started again. "I'm not your secretary. Somebody else can clear the—"

"I asked *you* to do it. I know you're new to the corporate world, but that isn't an excuse for not respecting authority. Don't forget, Savannah . . . *I'm* your boss."

He said the last sentence in a half-smug, half-joking way that made a woman sitting beside him lift her hand to her lips to stifle a laugh. I glanced around, thinking there were too many people here. I couldn't cause an ugly scene, and that was probably what he'd been counting on. And I could tell how much Ned *loved* being my boss.

He tapped his silver pen on the table and stared at me. "Some-time today would be nice."

My throat tightened and my fists clenched. I felt like spitting in his face. But instead I forced myself to walk toward the table, where I collected coffee cups and other breakfast remnants that I placed on a tray and carried across the room. I balanced it on one hand while I struggled to open the door with the other. Then Ned left his seat, stood beside me, and turned the knob.

"I take my coffee black," he said. "Please get that right."

I stormed into the hall in search of a kitchen, but the office was a maze of cubicles filled with people who seemed annoyed by my three aimless laps around the floor. I passed a corner of-fice where Caroline was sitting behind a desk, staring bitterly at a maintenance man hanging her Harvard diploma on a wall. Nobody asked if I needed help, even when two cups slipped off my tray and landed on the carpet. They didn't break, but cold coffee splashed onto a cubicle and the secretary inside rolled her eyes while she typed on a keyboard at warp speed.

"Do you have any paper towels?" I asked her.

"In the kitchen," she said with her eyes on her computer screen.

"And where exactly *is* that?"

"I'll show you," said a bubbly voice. It came from Ainsley, who was suddenly next to me. She wore a button-down blouse and a short plaid skirt, and she smelled like she'd been doused with baby powder. She led me to the kitchen, where I slammed cups into the sink.

"What's wrong?" she asked from behind me.

"Nothing," I heard Ned say. "She's just pouting because I expect her to pull her weight."

I spun around. He was in the doorway. "That's not true. I *want* to work."

He walked slowly toward me. "Then what's the problem? You're above serving coffee?"

"No," I said, crossing my arms, "I'm above serving coffee to *you.*"

He was in front of me now, standing too close and invading my personal space. "When I tell you to do something, I don't want any back talk . . . especially in the presence of my employees. I'm in charge here, and you'll do as I say or I'll show you the door. Now get the job done. Such a menial task shouldn't take so much time."

He turned and left. I flung open cabinets, searching for clean cups and muttering to myself about what a bully and a pompous ass he was until Ainsley squeezed my shoulder.

"He's a little grumpy in the morning. He doesn't mean it," she said with a sympathetic smile. Then she showed me where the cups were and volunteered to help me serve the coffee, and I thought that blessings often come from the most unexpected places.

For lunch, I bought a hot dog from a vendor's cart and finished it as I headed to Fifth Avenue, where I walked through Louis Vuitton's revolving doors and admired purses inside a glass case while a salesgirl trailed me like I was a shoplifter.

"You know they sell the same purses on the street for twenty dollars," I said with a grin.

Her lips shrank. "Those are knockoffs. They're trash. And they're illegal."

Nobody around here seemed to get my attempts at humor. I pointed to the case and slipped my wallet out of my purse. "I'll take two," I said.

One was for me. I brought the other to the post office, where I packed it inside a box along with a check that I sent to Mom. I was heading for the door when I felt my phone vibrating inside my purse, and I answered it as I hit the sidewalk and the humid air.

"Hey," Tina said. "What are you doing?"

I leaned against a brick wall. The sky was cloudy, and everything was covered in an ashen haze—the buildings, the cars parked on the street, a pay phone that stood out like an ancient relic. "I'm on my lunch break," I answered.

"Remember when I'd pick you up from the library and we'd eat lunch at the Hominy Grill?"

That was one of my favorite Charleston restaurants. It was in an old house with red shingles and the slogan *Grits are Good for You*. Tina mentioned it wistfully, as if we hadn't been there in years.

"We did that two weeks ago," I said.

She exhaled a lengthy sigh. "I know . . . it just seems longer."

That was so true. We talked for a while and then I went back to work, where I walked through the lobby and into a crowded elevator. The doors were sliding shut when Darcelle Conrad slipped through them and squeezed her slim figure into a narrow space beside me. Her tresses were bleached so blond that they had the fake shininess of a Barbie's hair, and she was close enough for me to see a millimeter of dark roots growing into her part.

"Hi, Savannah," she said. "I hear you're working for my old college roommate. Is she here today?"

I shook my head. "She's out sick. Do you want me to give her a message?"

She smiled. "Just tell Kitty I hope she feels better real soon."

We said good-bye after the elevator reached my floor. I strolled past the reception desk, headed down the hall, and stopped in front of my cubicle when I spotted Ainsley in my chair.

"Jeezle Pete," she said, holding her hand to her chest. "I didn't hear you coming."

"And I've never heard anybody say *Jeezle Pete*."

She giggled. "It's a Midwest thing. I'm from Indiana. Actually, I'm from New York, but my parents got divorced when

I was a baby and Dad stayed here, but Mom took me back to Indianapolis. I'm visiting him for the summer. Oh, and *Jeezle Pete* is a nicer way of referring to Jesus Christ," she said, whispering the last two words.

"That's what I figured," I said with a wink.

"Anyway," she went on, "Kitty asked me to show you how to access *Femme*'s social media sites when I had a chance, and now I do. But I should give your seat back, shouldn't I? It was wrong of me to sit here without permission."

"It's fine," I said. "I don't mind if—"

There was no time to finish because she sprang up, dashed over to an empty cubicle, and returned wheeling a chair that she put next to mine. Then we sat side by side, she gave me log-in IDs, and she asked me to create a password.

"Jessamine," was the first word that came to mind.

"Oh," she said as her dark bob bounced around her face. It was as shiny as a mink coat. "The state flower of South Carolina. I learned all the state flowers in school. Now let's see if I can remember the rest," she went on, and I hoped she wasn't planning to recite all fifty. "The peony is the flower of Indiana, and for New York it's the rose, and then of course Iowa is—"

"Just as dull as this conversation," said Caroline, who'd materialized like a vampire and was standing beside my desk in a frumpy brown suit and clunky shoes. "Don't put Savannah to sleep with your inane babbling."

"Ainsley isn't babbling," I said. "She was telling me some interesting facts about—"

"Please," Caroline said. She took off her cat's-eye glasses and pinched the bridge of her nose. "You were just about to nod off."

Maybe. But she didn't have to say it. "Do you want something?" I asked.

"Hmm," she said as she put her glasses back on and folded her arms. "I want you to get the hell out of my father's building . . .

but since it seems that your stupidity is exceeded only by your tenacity, I'll settle for Ainsley going to the corporate division. Ned has some work for her."

"On my way," Ainsley said, then bolted out of her chair and sprinted down the hall toward the elevators while I swiveled in my seat to face Caroline.

"You could be more patient with her," I said. "She's a kid."

Caroline rolled her eyes and leaned her back against a calendar that was tacked to my cubicle wall. "She's a rah-rah class president on acid. And she's not nearly as stupid as she seems. She was also an excuse for me to come down here and tell you that if you cop an attitude with my brother again, I'll make you extremely fucking sorry."

The fluorescent lights were merciless. I saw every dent in Caroline's face—the deep ridge by her mouth, the purplish indentations across her jaw. "He told me you were smart," I said. "If you really are, then I can't imagine you agree with the way he's treating me."

She touched the scraggly ends of her hair. "*I* can't imagine," she said, "why you presume to know what I think about *anything.* And if you don't care for my family, then maybe you should run along home to your own."

"That's not going to happen. There's so much to keep me here. Look at all this work," I said, glancing at my cluttered desk.

"Oh," Caroline said lightly, "don't worry about *that.* You can be replaced with any bubblehead from a shitty college that nobody's ever heard of."

My toes clenched inside my shoes. She really knew how to needle a person, but I did my best to stay calm. "We can't all go to Harvard. But isn't it funny that our degrees have ended us up in the exact same place?"

"Not the *exact* same place, Savannah. I'm up *there,*" she said, pointing to the ceiling, "and you're all the way down *here* where you don't matter to Stone News in the slightest."

I pretended that didn't bother me. "Well," I said, "at least I don't hate my job and I come to work with a smile on my face. Hold that scowl long enough and it'll stick."

Her mouth shriveled and turned white. "Don't be too confident about keeping your job. Kitty's fired scads of assistants for screwing up . . . and you're no better than they are."

"You're right, Caroline. I was raised to believe I'm no better than anyone . . . and no one is better than me. But you're wrong about the job. I'm *not* going to screw it up."

"We'll see," she said with a smug smile before vanishing down the hall.

I stayed late that night since Kitty wasn't there to make me leave at a civilized hour. Her stomach virus kept her at home for the rest of the week, and I worked overtime every day because as long as Ned and Caroline kept clear of me I was happier at the office than at my apartment. All those rooms felt empty and still and much too quiet.

Then it was Friday. The office had emptied out and the cleaning staff was vacuuming when I decided to leave. I called Tony to pick me up, and I was walking through the lobby when my phone vibrated in my pocket. I pulled it out, flipped it open, and heard Mom's voice.

"Thanks for the fancy bag . . . and for the money. I won't use either, but it was sweet of you anyway."

"You should use *both*," I said. "And I don't want what's happened to change anything between us. I know you don't want me to be here, but—"

"You're right . . . I don't. So let's leave it at that and drop the subject."

I sighed, we said good-bye and hung up, and a few minutes

later I was walking past the anti-Stone protesters on the curb. Then I got into the front seat of the black sedan, where Tony lowered the volume on a Yankee game and pulled into traffic just as my phone vibrated again and someone started talking before I could say hello.

"What in God's name do you think you're doing?"

It was a man whose accent was southern, but I couldn't figure out who he was or why he sounded so angry. "Pardon me?" I said, glancing at the caller ID. *Sawyer Brandt,* I read, which was still confusing. I'd known that man for nineteen years and he'd never once called me.

"No, I *won't* pardon you. You convinced my daughter to secretly charge a plane ticket on the credit card I gave her and run to New York without consulting me."

Had she really? "Mr. Brandt," I said, "I had nothing to do with it. I didn't know Tina was coming up here. I asked her to, but she—"

"Don't lie," he said. "Of course you had something to do with it. She'd never do such a thing on her own."

He had no idea that Tina could be secretive and crafty and devious, but that was her fault. All these years, he'd thought she was fast asleep in her bed when she was wide awake in someone else's.

"She shouldn't have done it this way," I said. "But maybe she couldn't find another."

"Don't psychoanalyze the situation. Just tell my daughter to call me when she gets there."

A few minutes later, I found out that Tina was already here and in front of my building, sitting on a pile of designer suitcases in a lime-green sundress like a queen in exile from a foreign land.

I flung open the car door, rushed toward her, and gave her a hug as I savored her Victoria's-Secret-and-cigarette smell. I'd never been so happy to see her big emerald eyes, her clip-on hair extensions, and her lips smeared with that stupid plumping gloss.

Seven

Tony loaded Tina's bags onto a luggage cart the concierge had let us borrow. He pushed it into an elevator and offered to bring everything upstairs.

"That isn't necessary," I told him.

"But it sure is nice," Tina said, giving him a coquettish wink.

The elevator took us to the eleventh floor, where Tony wheeled the cart into the hallway and walked ahead of us toward my apartment while Tina kept her eyes on him like she was a lioness and he was a hunk of raw meat that had just been tossed into her cage.

"Don't even *think* about it," I said. "He's married. And he has a daughter."

She puckered her lips into a pout. "That figures. He's sweet looking . . . and the best guys are always taken," she said with a mischievous glint in her eyes. "But he works for you, which means he has to obey your every command and we can make him do *anything* we want."

That type of talk worried me. I knew she'd never make a serious play for a married man, but she sure would flirt with one.

"Why'd you bring so much stuff?" I asked to distract her, nodding toward all the luggage on the cart.

"What do you mean? That's just a few weeks' wardrobe."

Of course it was. How silly of me. "So you don't mind leaving Raylene?"

Tina shook her head. "I discussed everything with her, and she told me to come."

"Well . . . I always knew she was a smart kid."

We reached my apartment, and I opened the door and showed her around while Tony unloaded her bags in the guest bedroom.

"It's beautiful," she said, leaning her elbows against the marble countertop in my kitchen.

I pulled a chair from the table and sat down, glancing at Marjorie's thank-you note on my refrigerator. "I'm glad you like it . . . and that you came. But I'm *not* happy about the way you got here. Your father called and yelled at me."

She frowned. "Sorry about that. You wanted me to stand up to him, though."

"Standing up to someone doesn't mean being sneaky and deceitful, Tina."

She sighed and sat on the windowsill. "I didn't know how else to do it."

"That's what I told him. Call him back and do the same."

She turned her head to stare at Central Park. "He shouldn't be upset . . . this is just a vacation."

I wanted more than that. I'd been doing my best to face this city alone, but it would be so much easier with Tina around. "It doesn't have to be. You can stay here for good."

She looked puzzled. "I might be able to convince Daddy to finance a few weeks . . . but he won't do more than that."

I got out of my chair and sat beside her. "You don't need him to. I can try to get you a job at Stone News so you can take care of yourself. Isn't that what you want?"

She shifted her gaze to her French manicure. "I guess. But first I need to relax," she said, studying the immaculate white tips on her nails. "This has been an unbelievably exhausting day."

I stared at her. Dark hollows were seeping through the makeup below her eyes. "I'm sure it must have been. Have you eaten anything?"

"Not since breakfast," she said, and perked up in her seat. "And I'm starving . . . so can we go to a diner? I know it's stereotypical, but whenever I see movies set in this city, people are always eating in diners. I want a pastrami sandwich on rye bread and a big old hunk of cheesecake. That's New York–ish, isn't it?"

I smiled. Manhattan was going to be so much more fun with Tina in it.

I walked into the kitchen the next morning, wearing shorts and a T-shirt and rubbing the sleep from my eyes. The room smelled like toasted bagels and Tina's mango perfume.

"I woke up early and bought breakfast at a deli down the street," she told me.

That was thoughtful. I thanked her as I pulled out a chair and sat down across from her, looking at fruit salad and doughnuts and glasses filled with juice.

She took a sip from her glass and looked at me above the rim. "I called Daddy. We had a long talk . . . and he understands why I want to stay here."

Seriously? That seemed to have come too easily.

Tina reached for a bagel, stood up, and shoved it into the toaster. "I've always told you he's a smart man. He finally realized I need to be on my own, and he's agreed to support me until I find a job." She glanced at me over her shoulder. "Wipe the shock off your face. And hurry up and eat your breakfast. As fabulous as this apartment is, I don't want to spend a Saturday in it when Manhattan's right outside. Oh, and I made a reservation for dinner tonight at Le Bernardin," she said, popping her bagel out of the toaster and onto a plate before she sat across from me again. "I've been dying to go there ever since Eva Lee came here on a family vacation. She bragged about that restaurant for two weeks straight. And today . . . I want to go shopping on Fifth Avenue. Eva Lee did *that,* too."

Soon we were strolling by archaic churches and Fendi and Chanel as double-decker tour buses drove up and down the street. We browsed at Saks and I bought us matching Gucci purses that we swung from our wrists while we strolled along, stopping to pick up souvenirs to send to Raylene. I also bought Chanel sunglasses and wide-brimmed hats for both of us because it was blindingly sunny outside. Our glasses had violet-tinted lenses and oversized frames, and Tina said they made us look like celebrity twins dodging the paparazzi.

We wandered the streets for a while and ended up on West 57th. Tina complained about being hungry just as a thunderstorm sprang up, so we ducked into The Russian Tea Room, where they were serving royal high tea. A hostess told us that reservations were required, but a spot miraculously opened up after I slipped her some cash. She seated us at a round table, and a waiter brought us glasses of champagne.

"It's so beautiful," Tina said giddily, glancing around.

I nodded, noticing a woman at a nearby table staring at our hats. I supposed she didn't know it was improper for men to wear hats indoors, but it was appropriate for ladies. Those were the rules in Charleston, at least.

I ignored her and admired the mirrored walls and a tree-shaped sculpture with what looked like glass Easter eggs dangling from its branches. Everything was so bright and colorful that it seemed as if we'd crawled inside a kaleidoscope.

The waiter came back with a plate of tiny sandwiches on white bread with the crusts cut off, miniature cupcakes, and crackers covered in caviar. Tina and I hadn't known what to order, so we'd asked him to bring whatever was most delicious— but this wasn't what we'd had in mind.

"Caviar?" Tina said, eyeing it like it was a squashed armadillo on the street at home.

"Crystal had it on the menu at your debutante ball," I reminded her.

"That doesn't mean I *ate* it, Savannah."

I hadn't, either, but it was time to get adventurous. "We should give it a try," I said as the waiter filled our cups with tea.

I was hoping she'd go first, and she did. She picked up a cracker, bit into it, and then her face scrunched up and she spit a mess into her napkin.

"It tastes like rotten fish bait," she said.

As if she'd ever tasted fish bait. I kicked her under the table as the waiter sighed.

"Shrimp salad with rémoulade, smoked sturgeon with dill and sour cream, and artichoke with sun-dried tomato goat cheese," he said, pointing to the sandwiches. "Enjoy."

He left. Tina sank into her red velvet chair, and we stared at each other.

My eyes scanned the table. "I don't know about sturgeon or goat cheese. But cupcakes and champagne are a good combination," I said, swiping my finger against chocolate frosting.

Tina perked up and a smile crept across her puffy lips. "To cupcakes and champagne and nothing but good things ahead of us," she said as she lifted her glass and held it over the table to clink with mine. It sounded as hopeful as a toast on New Year's Eve.

Another storm blew into the city at dinnertime. Tina was in her bedroom, where she'd unpacked her bags and was ironing a white lace dress from Lilly Pulitzer as she faced a half-open window and I passed the doorway.

"Tina," I said, rushing in to slam the window shut. "It's pouring."

She shrugged. "I just wanted to feel the air. It's so different here."

I sat on the bed, sinking into the soft comforter. "I know," I said, looking at a pile of dresses beside me. She seemed to have planned for every possible occasion. "Mind if I borrow one for tonight? I didn't bring much from home, and I haven't had a chance to buy new clothes."

"Take whatever you want."

She'd always been generous, letting me choose from her closet like it was Tina's Boutique, where everything was free. She'd even let me borrow a dress when I went to her debutante ball—a strapless number with a satin bodice, full skirted and covered with flowers made of rhinestones, in a shade of pink called lipstick rose. For some reason, she'd brought it along with her.

This time I chose a navy-blue tunic dress with crocheted sleeves. Tina slipped into her lace dress, and then we were outside, where I tried to hail a cab.

"Why are we standing out here in this disgusting humidity?" Tina asked. "We don't need a cab, do we? I thought Tony was always at our service."

He is. But that's an awfully tight dress you're wearing and I don't want you sticking your assets in his married face. "Not always," I lied, and a few minutes later we were in the back of a taxi that took us to West 51st and Le Bernardin, which was chic and elegant and had soft lighting and gigantic flower arrangements.

"Well," Tina said, tossing her napkin onto the table after we'd finished dinner and split a slice of cake. "Eva Lee does have good taste when it comes to *some* things."

I agreed, thinking that food in fancy restaurants tasted so much better when I had somebody to share it with. "So what do you want to do now?"

"Dance," she said.

We asked the hostess for a club recommendation and gave the address to a cabdriver who dropped us off all the way down on Orchard Street. The club wasn't crowded at first, but as the night went on it got crammed with guys and girls who guzzled drinks from glowing glasses and rubbed up against each other under strobe lights on a jam-packed dance floor like they were in a techno-music rapture.

We danced by ourselves for a while, and then we went to the bar where Tina downed three Manhattans and five vodka shots while I sipped Sex on the Beach and ignored the lustful stares of two overly tanned guys who had hair that was stiff with gel. It wasn't long before they made their move, asking the standard questions about where we were from and what we did for a living, as if they cared and weren't just trying to get us under their sheets.

"We're from the Bronx," said the guy who'd sidled up to me. He kept trying to look down my dress and up Tina's. He oozed sliminess and his friend was even worse, but Tina was too drunk to catch on. She let her guy stand between her legs as she sat on a barstool and smoked a Marlboro Light until a bartender slid an ashtray in her direction and said the club was smoke-free. She shrugged, crushed her cigarette, and went on flirting.

"You should be more like your friend," my guy said after he'd given up on enticing me and I was gazing at the dance floor with a bored stare. "She's a good time."

The last sentence made me mad. "Don't talk about her like that," I said, glancing in Tina's direction. All I saw was an empty stool.

He jerked his thumb toward the back of the club. "They're in the men's room."

I panicked. Tina made such poor decisions when she was drunk. I jumped off my seat and shoved through the crowd until I reached the bathroom, where I opened the door and found her bolting from a stall with the other guy from the Bronx staggering after her. He was bent over with veins bulging out of his neck and his hands clutching his crotch. I caught Tina's arm and yanked her from the bathroom into a dim, private alcove. Her whole body was quivering.

"I just wanted him to kiss me," she said. "I miss kissing so much. My last boyfriend always went straight for the golden ticket."

Booze never failed to bring out her secrets. "You deserve better than everybody you've dated, Tina. And for future reference, any guy who wants to fool around with you in a men's room isn't Mr. Right." I glanced down and saw that her dress was hiked to the tops of her thighs. "Are you okay?" I asked nervously, imagining he'd tried to force a good time out of her.

She yanked the dress toward her knees and tightened her jaw. "Of course I am. Like I said, I was just going to make out with him . . . he was the only one who thought that buying me one lousy shot entitled him to a horizontal jog. But nothing happened. He stopped being so pushy when I jammed my knee into his baby maker."

I guided her out of the club, where she sat on the curb while I tried to hail a cab under the crescent moon. But every passing taxi was filled or driven by someone who wasn't in the mood to stop. Or maybe I just needed lessons in taxi hailing, since I was terrible at it.

I pulled out my phone and clutched it in my palm, figuring out how to get home. We were way too far from the apartment to walk—especially in heels. I didn't even know where to find the nearest subway station, and I hated to call Tony. *After six on weeknights and anytime during the weekend is overtime pay . . . so feel free to call whenever,* he'd said, and I reminded myself of that as I dialed his number. I hoped he might be in the area anyway, getting overtime pay from another annoying night-owl client.

"Hello?" he answered.

He wasn't in Manhattan. His voice was muffled and sleepy,

and I shouldn't have called. I almost hung up, but then I remembered that caller ID would expose me. I also remembered that he wanted a little house in Nassau County.

"I'm sorry, Tony. I know it's late, but—"

"No," he said through a yawn. "It's okay, Savannah. Where are you?"

I told him, and he said he'd be here soon. Then I sat beside Tina and waited, watching a woman sleeping in an alley across the street. There was a shopping cart beside her filled with stuffed garbage bags.

"That makes me so sad," Tina said, inhaling a ragged breath.

I took some money out of my wallet, dodged cars as I crossed the street, and tucked the cash into a coffee can beside the woman's feet. Then I sat next to Tina again and we waited for Tony, who eventually pulled up in the sedan, got out, and looked down at Tina.

"Need some help?" he asked.

She held her wrist in the air. He took it and helped her into the car, where she collapsed onto her back and hogged the whole seat. I sat in front, and Tony turned on the radio when he pulled away from the curb. "WCBS News time," it said, "is one fifty."

He glanced in the rearview mirror at Tina, who'd fallen asleep. "Is your friend okay?"

I shrugged as we whizzed past lit-up skyscrapers and sidewalks crowded with people even during this ungodly hour. Everything was amazingly alive and I wanted to feel it, so I pressed a button to lower my window and let the electrified air sweep across my face. "You know something? I just found out before I moved here that I'm Edward Stone's daughter. Until then, I had no idea who my father was."

I kept my eyes on neon signs while Tony drove through Times Square. He was quiet, and I wondered if the one drink I'd finished at the club had made me too gabby.

"I've never met my father, either," he said after a while. "My mother raised me alone."

I shut the window and turned toward him. He really was sweet looking like Tina had said—wholesome and boyish and clean. "Mine too," I told him.

"So we have something in common," he said. "I think I've mentioned that Mom takes care of Marjorie when Allison—my wife—and I are working. She did a great job raising me . . . but I promised myself a long time ago that no kid of mine would know what it feels like not to have a father around."

I nodded slowly. "Then your daughter's a very lucky girl."

Soon we were back at my building, and Tina was still spread out on the backseat. I shook her shoulders to wake her while Tony waited on the curb, but it didn't work. And he couldn't leave with a plastered girl in the car.

"I'll bring her upstairs," he said.

He carried her into my apartment like she was a bride on her wedding night, and then he put her on the bed in her room. Her eyes flickered open, and she squinted at him through a strip of moonlight that glimmered against his face.

"Aw," she said, splaying her palm on his cheek, "I knew you were sweet."

He moved her hand away and rested it on the mattress before he walked out. I followed him, closed the door behind me, and we went into the living room, where I took my wallet out of my purse so I could give him a well-deserved tip. I stuck a hundred-dollar bill in his hand.

"I can't take this," he said.

"Sure you can. You've earned it."

He gave the money back and left the apartment after saying good night. I watched from the window as he drove off in the shiny sedan, wishing that Tina hadn't been right when she said, *The best guys are always taken.* She needed a sweet guy like him.

Eight

Tina and I slept late the next day. When we woke up, we went to a diner where she sat across from me, devouring a stack of pancakes. "Tell me," she said, "what happened after we got into the car last night. I don't remember a thing."

"You passed out, Tony carried you to your bedroom, and then he left."

"Carried me to my bedroom," she said slowly, then licked her lips like every word was made of sugar. "I'll have to get sloshed around that boy more often."

I shook my head. "No, you won't. Do yourself a favor and forget him."

But she didn't forget. On Monday morning, when I was sitting beside him in the sedan and he was just about to take off, there was a tap on my tinted window. I rolled it down, and Tina stuck her hand inside to dangle a brown paper bag in front of my face.

"I made your lunch," she said, and I took it from her while she leaned forward, pressing her cleavage against the window frame and giving Tony a coy smile. "Did you know there's an off-Broadway show called *Tony n' Tina's Wedding*?" she asked. "I saw a commercial on TV."

I hit a button to close the window. Tina waved from the sidewalk as Tony drove us away.

Then I was at my desk at work and Kitty walked into my cubicle, looking like an Ann Taylor ad in her mocha jersey dress and single-strand pearls. Her hair was shiny and her skin glowed, and she held an envelope in her hand.

"You must be feeling better," I said.

She leaned against the wall and tapped the envelope against her thigh. "I am. And it seems as if a gang of elves slaved all night to get your work done."

"Well," I said sheepishly, "that was me."

She smiled. "You shouldn't push yourself so hard . . . but I appreciate it. You're really doing well."

I thanked her and wondered if she knew how much her praise meant. This was my second full-time job, but it was the first to make me feel like I wasn't squandering my limited time on earth. "Kitty," I said, "my best friend moved here from Charleston, and she needs a job. You've already done so much for me and I don't mean to be pushy, but do you think there's any way . . ."

She shook her head. "I'm sorry, Savannah. It was hard enough convincing Ned to let *you* in the door. I don't think he'll even let your friend have the mailroom position."

I nodded, silently cussing that man. "Oh," was all I could say.

Kitty broke the awkward silence by moving on. "Anyway . . . I'm sure you put in a lot of overtime last week, but I want you out of here at five tonight. You have somewhere to be."

She gave me the envelope she'd been holding. It was lined with foil and held an invitation printed in raised gold letters on thick paper.

Please join us for Stone News Corporation's Annual Gala at The New York Public Library, I read. *8:30 p.m. at 455 Fifth Avenue.*

I glanced at Kitty. "What should I wear?"

"A simple black dress always works. And since I can't help get your friend a job, the least I can do is let her be your plus one," she said. "I suppose I should tell you that part of tonight will be devoted to honoring Ned as the company's new Chairman and CEO."

I nodded, stifling all the biting and sarcastic things I wanted to blurt out.

"I know he's treated you badly," Kitty said, "but try not to hate him too much. He isn't as awful as he seems. My mother-in-law, however, is another story. She'll be at the party . . . unfortunately."

I leaned back in my chair. "*Unfortunately* is right. From what I've heard, she'll be unhappy to see me."

"Well," Kitty said, "Virginia Barlow Stone has been unhappy to see *me* since my first date with her son. But I do my best to ignore that frosty bitch . . . and you should, too."

I nodded and got back to work. The day went by quickly, and soon I was inside my apartment, where I plopped into a chair at my kitchen table. Tina sat beside me while I gave her a wrap-up of my conversation with Kitty.

"I'm so sorry I can't get you a job," I said. "Ned is impossible."

A flash of disappointment crossed her face but quickly vanished. She shrugged, stood up, and walked across the kitchen to the windowsill where she'd left her new Gucci bag. She unzipped it and pulled out a pack of Marlboros, staring through the window like she was far away. Then she blinked, glanced at me, and gave me a guilty smile. "You don't mind, do you?" she said. "I'll blow the smoke outside like I do at home. I promise not to let this beautiful apartment reek of cigarettes."

"You *better* promise," I said, taking in the clean scent of fresh paint and new carpet.

She crossed her heart and opened the window before she lit up. "Anyway," she said, "don't worry about Ned. I'll just find another receptionist job."

I watched her exhale smoke through the screen until I couldn't stand it anymore. I joined her by the window and yanked the Marlboro from between her fingers. "This is bad for you. And so is answering phones. I want you to do something better."

She snatched the cigarette back and let out a harsh laugh. "What exactly am I qualified for, Savannah?"

I sighed. "Stop being so negative. You're qualified for plenty of things . . . we just have to narrow them down. But let's not worry about it right now," I said, grabbing the cigarette again. I walked over to the counter and crushed the Marlboro on a plate. "We're going to a party."

There was a dress in Tina's closet that I'd completely forgotten. Maybe I'd made myself forget because I'd borrowed it for one of Jamie's law school events and we'd broken up the next week. I stared at it until Tina came into the room with a toothbrush in her mouth and wet hair dangling over her shoulders.

"I remember when you wore that dress. Little did you know you'd put it on again for something more important," she said before she spun around and left, leaving a trail of mango-scented air behind her.

I took the dress out of the closet and brought it to my room. Then I hot-rolled my hair, put on my green eyeliner and my glittery lipstick, and slipped into the dress, which met just half of Manhattan's fashion code. The color was right, but the style was far from simple. It was a mermaid silhouette with a high-cut, ruffled slit in front and a sweetheart bustline that hiked up my chest. And the bodice was covered with rhinestones that sparkled in the lamplight when I checked myself out in a full-length mirror.

"Every guy at the party will want to take you home and sop you up with a biscuit," Tina said from behind me.

I chuckled. She was in my bedroom doorway, wearing a dress that had a halter top and was made of faux silk the color of a tangerine. A few minutes later, her hips swayed beneath the dress as she sashayed ahead of me toward the car, where Tony was holding the back door open. I didn't correct him this time; sitting in the back felt almost okay if I wasn't the only passenger.

"You ladies look lovely," he said.

"Your mama raised such a polite boy," Tina told him, ducking into the car.

I sat beside her, Tony took off, and eventually he stopped at Fifth Avenue and 42nd Street, where Tina and I peered through the tinted windows at formally dressed men and women holding hands while they climbed broad steps toward a grand building that had arched doorways and tall columns. At each end of the steps was a marble lion that seemed to be on guard duty.

"Don't they look proud," I said.

"You mean the lions?" Tony asked, and I nodded. "Their names are Patience and Fortitude. Mayor La Guardia named them during the 1930s because he thought those were the qualities New Yorkers would need to get through the Depression. But originally they were called Leo Astor and Leo Lenox, after John Jacob Astor and James Lenox . . . they donated money to build the library."

Tina and I stared at him. His cheeks reddened.

"Sorry, girls. I didn't mean to force you into a history class."

"No need to apologize for being interesting," Tina said. "How'd you know all that?"

He shrugged. "I read. There's not much else to do while I'm waiting for people to come out of parties."

She ran her finger along her halter top. "That sounds awfully lonely. I wish you could come in with us."

"I do, too," I said, "but he can't. And we have to go."

Tony said he couldn't park in front of the library, so he was going to grab dinner. I told him I'd call when we were ready to leave, and then he drove away while Tina and I climbed the steps toward the library, which was lit up and looked like a castle against the dark sky. We grasped our beaded clutch purses with one hand and raised our hems with the other, trying not to make idiots of ourselves by tripping over our dresses in front of the photographers who were snapping pictures of people who seemed to be big deals.

We breezed past them and into the library, where we were stopped by a man who asked our names and gave us a table assignment in a room called Astor Hall.

Tina nudged me. "Tony really does know his stuff."

We weaved through the crowd toward Astor Hall, and she kept poking my ribs and pointing and whispering well-known names into my ear. There were actors and football players and female models who were six feet tall and had legs that went on forever. The men were in black suits, and as far as I was concerned, the women's dresses were much too plain for such a glitzy party.

"Are these ladies going to a funeral?" I asked Tina.

She laughed as we stepped into a massive space with a ceiling so high that I had to strain my neck to see it. The room was made of ivory marble, and a giant lantern hung above the base of a sweeping staircase. There were flickering candles and vases bursting with white orchids, the tables were covered with silver cloth, and a band in a corner played classic jazz.

We wandered around and took glasses of champagne from a waiter who was carrying them on a tray. I was halfway through mine and Tina had already downed hers when we passed two men who seemed to be in their late thirties and looked like they were ready to pounce on something. One of them had a video camera, and the other caught my elbow as I walked by. I lost my grip on my champagne and dribbled some on the floor.

"You're Savannah Stone," he said.

"Morgan," I corrected him.

He snapped his fingers at the other guy, who turned on his camera and a blinding light that made me squint. "I'm Fabian Spader," he said, flashing a press badge. "I have a blog called *Nocturnal* . . . I'm sure you've heard of it."

What he seemed most sure of was himself. He had a confident air about him, eyes the color of pewter, and a pointy chin. He was what Mom would call a strawberry blond, and he paid way too much attention to his hair. It was longish and layered, and he kept touching it. I wondered if he spent an hour blow-drying like a girl. And he wasn't dressed right. His outfit was informal and thrown together—jeans and a blazer and a shirt with the first few buttons undone.

"I read that blog all the time," Tina told him.

"Never heard of it," I said.

He blinked. "Then I'll bring you up to speed. I cover the social scene. Every morning, I write about what Manhattan celebs did the night before. I write about what they do during the day, too . . . but *Nocturnal* has such a snappy ring to it."

"O-kay," I said slowly, "and what does this have to do with me?"

"You're part of the game now, Scarlett O'Hara. How does it feel to be the newest member of one of this city's most prominent families?"

Word travels fast at Stone News. Ainsley was right. "Who says I am?"

"It's the latest buzz. So it must've been quite a shock to learn that you're Edward Stone's long-lost daughter. Do you have any thoughts about his death? Such a tragedy . . . and everyone's speculating that it wasn't an accident."

A drop of sweat slid down the crease in my back. One minute I was anonymous, and the next I was the topic of buzz, being hounded by a pushy gossipmonger who was probably dying for a dopey quote he could spread all over the Internet and a video that would replay endlessly to make me look like a ditz. And I didn't want to be part of a game.

"No comment," I said.

We walked away and he followed us, but we managed to lose him in the crowd. Then we plucked hors d'oeuvres from trays and I finished my champagne and three glasses of wine that went right through me. I asked Tina if she needed to join me in the bathroom, but she shook her head.

"You've guzzled more of the devil's water tonight than I have," she said.

She strode toward the bar as I rushed to the ladies' room, which was empty inside. I locked myself in a stall, and I was still there when I heard the door open, heels tapping against the floor, and a nasal voice with an upper-class accent.

"Please stop tormenting me, Mother."

"I'm just trying to help you, Caroline."

It had to be Caroline Stone and her mother, Virginia Barlow Stone, who'd allegedly been *goddamned furious* when she found out that I existed. I pressed my ear to the stall door, straining to hear over a running faucet.

"*Help* me?" Caroline said. "Am I really *that* pitiful?"

Virginia had the same accent as her children. "I'm in no mood for your histrionics. All I said is that I know of a good dermatologist who can—"

"Sand down my hideous skin so my scars won't embarrass you?"

Virginia sighed. "You couldn't help that you had acne when you were a teenager . . . but there are things you can do to improve yourself now. I'll be happy to pay for it."

"That's *all* you're happy to pay for. Daddy gave you a fortune in the divorce, and if you'd share it with me and Ned, we wouldn't have to work at Stone News. I'd rather slit my wrists than sit at a desk all day. It's draining the life out of me."

"More drama," Virginia said tiredly. "You're better off working there than at that useless public interest whatever–it–is you've wasted your time on since you graduated from Harvard. And how your father left things with you and Ned isn't my fault. I had no control over him."

"That doesn't mean you can't help me financially, Mother."

"I might if you'd abide by my wishes, Caroline. Stop being so distant and secretive."

The water stopped running. The room got quiet.

"So," Virginia said, "should I schedule you an appointment with the doctor?"

Caroline snorted. "Looks are all that matters to you."

"They should matter to *you*, too. How are you ever going to find a husband? Glasses and combat boots and that raccoon makeup you insist on wearing will keep you single forever. And this potato sack you've chosen tonight isn't exactly fashion forward. I want grandchildren someday, you know. It seems I'll never get them from that barren wasteland your brother married. All she cares about is her vulgar magazine."

Kitty hadn't been joking. Virginia *was* a frosty bitch. Now I understood what Mercedes Rawlings Stark had meant when she said Virginia was different from Mom. And I didn't want to feel sorry for Caroline, but I really did.

There was nothing after that except footsteps and the bathroom door clicking shut. I came out of the stall, rounded a corner that led to the faucets, and stopped when I saw a woman looking in a mirror and touching up her lipstick. She moved to the edge of the counter.

"Forgive me," she said. "I don't mean to be in your way."

It was Virginia. I crept toward her and turned on the water, watching from the corners of my eyes as she brushed her long dark wavy hair and freshened up the makeup that flattered her heart-shaped lips and her olive-green eyes.

Her dress was made of muted-gray silk, and her necklace dripped diamonds. She had to be in her mid-fifties but could pass for much younger, with her slim figure and her skin that was as pale and sleek as the marble inside Astor Hall.

"The magazine isn't vulgar," I muttered, staring at my hands while I washed them.

Virginia turned toward me. "I beg your pardon?"

I turned off the faucet, dried my hands, and shifted my eyes toward her. She didn't have that phony, plastic look I'd seen all over Manhattan. Her beauty was real.

"You were talking about *Femme*," I said, "and about Kitty."

She took a step back. "Excuse me . . . do I know you?"

I braced myself for an earthquake. "I'm Savannah Morgan."

She seemed to stop breathing for a second. Her eyes moved around my face and lingered on my hair. "Well," she began after a moment, "I . . . I didn't . . ." Her voice quivered and cracked, and I stared at her as she awkwardly adjusted her dress. Then her jaw hardened and so did her voice. "I didn't know you were eavesdropping on my private conversation."

"I didn't mean to. But like I said, the magazine isn't vulgar . . . and Kitty's a good person. We're working together now."

"So I've heard," she said, raising her chin, "although I doubt you've been around her long enough to know what kind of person she really is."

"I know you shouldn't judge her because she can't give you what you want. It's not the only thing she has to offer."

Virginia's mouth fell open. "That's your opinion, and it means *nothing*."

She spit the words at me. For a minute there, I'd felt as sorry for her as for Caroline. It couldn't have been easy to see her husband's betrayal in the flesh. But I didn't pity her now, since she was looking at me like I was something she'd stepped on in the street.

She narrowed her eyes, denting two vertical lines between them. I was close enough to see that Kitty had been right—Ned really did look like Virginia. They had similar features, and hers turned stern and sharp the way his had when he was at my apartment.

"You have nerve to even *speak* to me," she said in a hiss. "I can't believe your gall to show up here tonight. But I suspect people of your class are clueless about proper decorum. And I wonder if you have any idea of how much trouble you've caused my family."

I was sweating. My knees shook. But I wouldn't give her the satisfaction of knowing it.

"You can blame your late husband for that," I said. "I had no control over him, either."

Her cleavage heaved beneath her dress, but the rest of her didn't flinch. She reached for her purse, slung it over her wrist, and headed for the door. Her hand was on the knob when she stopped and looked at me over her shoulder.

"You know something, Savannah?" she said in an eerily calm voice. "Of all the places we could've met . . . it's quite fitting that I found you beside a toilet."

Nine

⤫

I stormed toward the bar. A few people were milling around it and Tina was there in her slinky dress, chatting with one of the twentysomething bartenders. He was a blond while the other one had dark hair, and they both wore black pants and matching shirts with white ties. She turned in my direction when I snagged the stool beside her and dropped my purse onto the bar.

"What's wrong with you?" she said. "I'm waiting for steam to shoot out of your ears."

I didn't want to talk about it. I'd tell her later. I refused to let Virginia Stone ruin tonight.

"Nothing," I said, and then the dark-haired guy looked at me. "What's your name, sir?"

"Alex," he answered.

"I'm Savannah. And I'd like a stiff drink, please."

He made an old-fashioned. I tossed it back and ordered a Long Island iced tea that I swallowed while Tina giggled as she talked to the blond. The cocktail hour was ending, the bar was clearing out, and everybody started to fill the tables. But Tina seemed hungrier for what was behind the bar. She stayed put and so did I, making sure she didn't get into trouble and watching Alex polish champagne flutes.

I tipped the remnants of my drink toward him. "Can you give me another one?"

"I think you've had enough," he said.

I slammed down my glass. "That isn't up to *you*."

"But it's a good suggestion," I heard Kitty say, and I spun around on my stool to face her. She wore a simple burgundy dress, her hair was pinned up, and copper ringlets fell around her cheeks. "I understand you had a run-in with my mother-in-law, so I'm not surprised you're trying to forget it with booze." She leaned closer to me. "If I took a drink whenever she got on my nerves, I'd be in rehab right now. Trust me . . . she isn't worth it. So tell me everything, Savannah. I want the dirt."

"What did *she* say?" I asked.

"You started an argument with her over nothing."

"That isn't what happened," I said, deciding to keep the truth to myself because Virginia wasn't worth upsetting Kitty. "But we shouldn't waste this beautiful party talking about it. You haven't even met my best friend yet."

I grabbed a strap on Tina's dress to yank her away from the blond. I introduced her to Kitty, and afterward Kitty said we should join everyone for dinner because the salads were being served. Then she walked off and I watched her settle down at a table toward the front of the room. Ned was beside her, and he looked deceptively dapper in an ebony suit with a garnet tie. His mother sat opposite and so did Caroline, who kept tugging at her plain beige dress like it was squelching her circulation while Virginia yukked it up with some VIP.

I turned back to the bar, where Alex was stacking glasses. "You were right," I said, "and I was rude. Somebody made me mad, so I snapped at you . . . and I'm sorry."

"Apology accepted," he said in a voice that was deep and

velvety. His hair was thick and nearly black, and he had full lips that stayed slightly parted when he stopped talking.

"Can I have a Coke?" I asked.

He nodded, filled a glass with ice, and held it under a tap. "I heard your conversation with Kitty. Mrs. Stone's made me mad, too . . . so I get it."

"You know her?" I said as he slid the glass toward me.

"Only as an employee . . . I've worked at a few of the family's parties here in the city and out on the island. Kitty's a sweetheart, I haven't figured out the daughter yet, and Mrs. Stone's charming . . . until you step out of line. I felt her wrath when I was five minutes late to work for her birthday party last year because I got stuck in traffic on the LIE."

"How long have you worked for her?" I asked.

He leaned his arms on the bar. His biceps nearly burst through his sleeves. "Since I graduated from college four years ago . . . that shows how much a BFA is worth. I should've listened to my dad and joined his plumbing business."

I glanced at the stool beside me; Tina was gone and so was the blond, who had ducked out on his job and left all the work to his partner.

I sighed and turned back to Alex. "I know what you mean . . . I graduated two years ago, and I just recently found the kind of job I want," I said, feeling a pinch of guilt for skipping ahead in the employment line because of my new connections. "What did you major in?"

"Creative writing," he said, "with a minor in acting."

"You could be an actor. You're handsome enough."

I felt my face flush. I was worse than Tina. And I got so loose lipped whenever there were a few drinks in me.

He smiled shyly. "What did *you* major in?"

"English lit," I said, grabbing a napkin to dab my sweaty neck. "I wanted to be a writer, and . . . I'm still trying. I moved here from South Carolina and started working as an editorial assistant for a magazine at Stone News. Kitty's my boss."

"And she told you to come to dinner," said a jarring voice that made me look over my shoulder. Ned was looming above me with a piercing stare that he shifted to Alex. "Please excuse Savannah. She doesn't know it's improper to seduce the help."

He wrapped his hand around my arm and yanked me off the stool. I skidded on the floor.

"Let go of me or I'll slap your face," I said, but he just tightened his grip, pressing his fingers so deep into my flesh that they struck bone.

"Hey," Alex said sharply. "What do you think you're doing?"

"Get back to work," Ned told him, "unless you want to lose your job."

"You'll lose your teeth if you don't take your hands off her."

I hadn't noticed until now that Alex's eyes were even lighter than Jamie's. They reminded me of my trip to Lehigh Acres and the crystal-blue swimming pools that Floridians had in their backyards.

"I can handle this," I told him. "Don't worry."

But he did look worried when I glanced back as Ned practically dragged me toward the other side of the room. I yanked my arm free and sneered at him.

"You will *not* fire Alex," I said, "and you will never touch me again."

"Don't whine. You wouldn't want to embarrass yourself. Remember . . . the press is here."

I looked at the opposite end of the hall, where Fabian Spader seemed to be itching for something scandalous to happen. "Screw the press," I said, "and screw you. You've already embarrassed me. But that was your goal, right?"

"My goal," he said, "was to teach you a lesson. Your identity has been leaked, and now that everyone knows who you are, I have to make sure you don't disgrace my family's name. We do *not* fraternize with bartenders, and neither will you."

I scoffed, studying his square jaw and his cleft chin and those frigid eyes. "I'll do whatever I want. I guess you're used to ordering people around, but you're not in charge of *me*."

"Lower your voice. That southern-spitfire act might work in Charleston, but not here."

I didn't lower anything. "And I wasn't trying to *seduce* Alex. We were just talking."

"Just talking," Ned echoed doubtfully, looking me up and down. He reached into his pocket, slid out his wallet, and pressed a wad of crisp bills into my hand. "Do me a favor and buy some respectable clothes. You're spilling out of that dress."

I didn't glance at my sweetheart bodice to check. I just let the cash slip from my hands and drift to his expensive shoes.

He shook his head. "You should have more respect for money, Savannah. You never know when it might be gone for good. Oh, and that friend of yours . . . don't bring her around again. She's outside, acting like a slut."

He stuffed the wallet into his pocket and stepped on hundred-dollar bills as he walked off with a cocky swagger. I headed out of the library, where I stood at the entrance and saw Tina and the blond bartender kissing on the lower steps. The air had cooled down, the moon was shining, and stars twinkled in the night sky. She leaned her forehead against his cheek as he took off his jacket and spread it across her shoulders.

I turned around, went back into the library, and found Fabian Spader standing near the entrance to Astor Hall. He held out Ned's money.

"You dropped something," he said.

"Keep it," I replied as I glimpsed his half-open shirt when I tried to walk past.

He actually did keep it. He stuck the cash in his pocket and blocked my way. "I saw you arguing with Ned. Tell me about it."

I exhaled a frustrated sigh. "I know you're doing your job, but I can't tell you anything. So if you'll excuse me, I have to get back to the party."

He caught my wrist. "You know," he said, "the only reason Virginia gives me access to her inner circle is that I gush about her on my blog. But it's getting boring . . . and you can spice things up. Now tell me what happened with Ned."

I peeled his fingers off my skin. "Button your shirt. This is a formal function."

He laughed. "You think I give a fuck? I stopped playing by these people's rules a long time ago."

I lifted an eyebrow. "What's *that* supposed to mean?"

"I'll show you mine if you show me yours. A secret for a secret is a fair trade. Come on . . . you couldn't possibly want to protect a scumbag like Ned Stone."

How intriguing. I'd thought that if Ned had been crafty enough to get Kitty to marry him, then he must have had the entire city under his spell. But maybe not. "Why would you call him that? Let me guess . . . because it takes one to know one?"

"Touché," Fabian said, leaning his back against ivory marble. "I have my reasons, but you shouldn't worry your pretty little Confederate head about them. And I don't like to be kept waiting. Hurry up and talk."

"You don't like to be kept waiting? Well, I don't like to be bossed around. So get lost."

I strode into Astor Hall. He trailed behind me. "I don't appreciate your tone, little girl. Ask anyone . . . they'll say you'd be better off to stay on my good side. Get snippy with me again and

I'll have to . . . what do they call it down south? 'I'll have to take you out to the woodshed.'"

I spun around with my hands on my hips. "What did you just say?"

He snickered. "I meant that figuratively."

"Stay away from me," I said, jabbing my finger toward his pointy chin, "or I'll tell Kitty what you've been up to. She'll have you tossed into the street where you belong."

He stroked his hair. "Kitty has no power, love. Ned thinks he does, but the truth is Virginia rules the Stone family. And she's not a fan of *yours.*"

I whirled around, and I ignored him as he followed me. I was heading toward my table when I crashed into Alex. Until that second, I hadn't realized how tall he was.

"Is everything okay?" he asked, moving his eyes between me and Fabian.

"Just making a living," Fabian said lightly as he patted Alex's shoulder.

Alex shoved his hand away. "I know how you make your living. You're a lowlife parasite who intimidates people into giving you your next story. You smear them all over the Internet and ruin their lives just because you think you can."

Fabian let out a short laugh. "I don't *think* I can. I *know* it."

"You're not going to do it to *her.* Take your vendetta elsewhere and back off."

"My goodness," Fabian said, crossing his arms and tilting his head, "are we grouchy tonight, Alex? Maybe you're jealous because I'm a raging success and you're a struggling nobody."

Alex squinted at him. "You don't know anything about me."

"You're wrong, handsome," Fabian said with an amused smile. "Your ex-girlfriend from East Eightieth has a big mouth, and she likes to use it." He focused on the zipper in Alex's pants. "But of course . . . you know that."

Alex shook his head and took a step forward. "Get the hell out of here before I—"

Fabian backed up. "Take it easy. I just meant she talks a lot. And she told me you're an aspiring actor-slash-writer. But what you *really* are is nothing but a bartender with dreams that won't come true."

He gave us a satisfied smirk before striding to the other side of the hall. I looked at Alex, thinking that even though I could take care of myself, it was nice to be rescued. It gave me hope that chivalry hadn't really gone the way of parasols and hoop skirts. But I wished his good deed hadn't gotten him slammed.

I touched Alex's sleeve. "Don't listen to him. *Aspiring* means you're on your way . . . not that you'll never get there," I said, and remembered something that Kitty had told me. "He's just a pretentious jerk who wants to put you down because it makes him feel important. He has no idea what you can do. People hardly ever do."

He stared at me as I studied the strong angles of his face. "Are you speaking from experience?"

"Oh," I said, glancing at candles and orchids and waiters clearing empty plates from the dinner I'd missed. "Let's just say I've had my share of rejection. I'm used to getting my work sent back with comments that indicate utter apathy or stress my general lack of talent."

His smile showed his flawless teeth. "I've been through that, too, but I prefer the apathy to the mockery. *You write with a boundless lack of grace*—that was my latest rejection. It isn't enough to turn your work down. They have to insult you, too . . . and in such vivid detail."

I laughed. It was amazing that pain could turn funny when shared with somebody who'd felt the same thing. "Anyway," I said, "thanks for helping me with Fabian. I couldn't get rid of that creep."

"You're welcome, but it happened accidentally. I was trying to find you so I could give this back. You left it on the bar," he said, holding up my beaded purse.

I took it, thanked him again, and asked "What did you mean about Fabian's vendetta?"

"Well," Alex said in a low voice, "word on the street is that he comes from a rich family . . . and when he was a teenager, his parents lost everything to some crook who was supposed to be investing their money but was stealing it. They got dumped by their high-class friends, and Fabian's been clawing his way back up ever since. He's done well . . . and he doesn't mind taking down anybody who gets in his way. I guess trashing high society is his revenge."

"What a gentleman," I said.

"Speaking of gentlemen," Alex went on, "another reason I was looking for you was to make sure you were okay after what happened with Ned. Who is he to you, anyway? I know you work for Stone News, but—"

"It's a long story," I said, shifting my gaze toward the bar. Nobody was behind it and a line of guests was growing. "I owe you another apology . . . this one's for getting you in trouble with Ned. You should go back to work before it happens again . . . I don't want you to lose your job because of me."

"I don't care about Ned. And we don't even know each other's last names," he said as he stuck his hand into the space between us. "I'm Alex Adair."

"I'm Savannah Morgan," I said, feeling goose bumps burst on my arms when our palms met and he gave me a handshake that was firm yet gentle. "It's good to meet another writer."

"You'll find a lot of them in New York. But I've never asked one out before."

The last time I'd been asked out by a guy who made butter-flies whirl inside my stomach was a lifetime ago, when I was a high school freshman with flaxen hair and pom-poms in my locker. Until now, Jamie was the only man who'd been able to make me feel that way.

"I think we have a lot in common," Alex said when I didn't answer. He didn't know I was too giddy to talk, and he seemed to believe he still needed to sell me on the idea of a date. "I mean . . . with the writing and all. So . . . would you like to get together sometime?"

I looked to my right. There was a silver-haired man with a microphone at the far side of the hall, giving a speech that commemorated Edward Stone and welcomed his son as the new Chairman and CEO. Ned smiled, Kitty lovingly rubbed his back, and Virginia and Caroline beamed at Ned like he was worth a million times more than the diamonds that glimmered around his mother's neck.

"Yes," I said. "I'd love to."

I wasn't bothered that Virginia had turned up her regal nose at me. It made no difference that Ned had been his usual condescending self. I'd almost forgotten about Fabian and his threat of a virtual beat-down. All that mattered was that Alex had my phone number and I was cutting into a luscious hunk of red velvet cake that a waitress had put in front of me when I finally made it to my table. There was nothing better than going directly to dessert.

The seats at the table were full except the ones to my left and my right. One was meant for Tina, and I wasn't sure about the other. I'd popped my head outside again a few minutes ago and seen her and the bartender eating giant pretzels on the library's steps, so I knew she was safe and I could relax.

Then my cake was gone and I couldn't stop thinking about the untouched glass of red wine and the slice of key lime pie on the plate beside mine. I grabbed the glass and quickly drank the wine, but it wasn't enough. Whoever had abandoned that dessert probably wasn't coming back, and wasting food was such a sin. So I leaned over with my fork and scooped up a bite, and it was sliding down my throat when a woman who had been glancing at me from across the table took Tina's empty seat.

"You must be Edward Stone's new daughter," she said.

She was attractive, probably in her early fifties, with straight hair the color of caramel that hung just above her shoulders. Her figure was slim beneath a dark-blue dress, and she wore an antique wedding band.

"You resemble him so much," she said, moving her dark eyes around my face.

"Are you a reporter or a blogger or something?" I asked.

She blinked and shook her head. "No, I knew your father through my work . . . he was a very good friend to me, and I respected him tremendously."

"Really? I think you're in the minority."

She put her hand on my wrist. "Savannah," she said, which was odd, since I hadn't told her my name. Then again, gossip seemed to spread so quickly around here that I supposed I shouldn't be surprised. "Edward was as flawed as the rest of us, but he was still a good man. So don't let secondhand opinions tarnish your view of him. He deserves better than that."

She was leaning in close and delving into my business, and it made me uncomfortable. "Excuse me," I said, "how'd you say you knew him?"

She edged backward, crossed her shapely legs, and smiled. "Everybody knew him. He was a supporter of mine . . . it's not always easy for women in politics, and he did what he could to smooth my way." She stood up. "So when you think about him . . . remember things like that."

She walked away just as a tall man in a black suit slipped into the chair beside me. He was holding a Scotch glass in one hand and jamming a cell phone into his pocket with the other.

"I didn't know there were mice in Astor Hall," he said with a laugh, eyeing the pie and empty wineglass.

That woman had stolen my attention from the dessert I'd ravaged. "I missed dinner," I said.

He laughed again, but not in a mean way. My eyes shifted to his face, which was slightly older than Alex's, a little more rugged but equally handsome. He had tan skin and straight, shiny hair that skimmed his forehead. It was golden wheat like mine, and his eyes were the most interesting shade of hazel. The iris was jade, and flecks of amber rimmed his pupils. He smiled, and two deep dimples sprang into his cheeks.

"Here," he said, sliding his plate toward me. "I can't let you go hungry." His voice was as deep as Alex's, and he smelled of cologne and Scotch and a trace of cinnamon. "It's my own fault, anyway. It was impolite of me to skip out on the party to take a business call." He slung his arm over the back of his chair and his sleeve rode up, exposing a Cartier watch.

"What's your business?" I asked.

"Real estate development," he said, and nothing else. Judging by his suit and his watch, I suspected he didn't design mobile home parks, but I admired that he hadn't said so. "I'm Jackson Lucas," he told me, extending his hand. "But my friends call me Jack."

I pressed my palm into his. "Savannah Morgan . . . I hope you haven't heard of me yet," I said, feeling the heat of Fabian's stare from across the room.

He raised an eyebrow. "I've been away on business for the past few weeks, so I'm out of the loop. What would I have heard?"

A hand touched my shoulder; I turned around and there was Alex, rescuing me for the second time. He said his shift was over, he was heading home, and he'd call me soon.

"Hey, Jack," Alex said, "nice to see you."

Jack was pulling a tin of cinnamon Altoids from inside his jacket. "You too," he answered, and then Alex left and Jack looked at me. "You know him?"

"We met tonight," I said, detecting a touch of concern in Jack's voice. "Why?"

He shrugged and popped an Altoid into his mouth. "Just something I heard. I only know Alex from Virginia Stone's parties . . . I don't like to spread gossip and I'm not even sure it's true, so let's forget it. Now tell me, Savannah . . . what's a nice southern girl like you doing in this city of wickedness and vice?"

I laughed and hiccupped and wished I hadn't downed that last glass of wine.

"Working," I said. "I just moved up here and started at a magazine. I'm also a writer."

He kept his eyes on me like he was actually interested in what I had to say. Except for Alex, Jack was the only person besides Mom and Tina who'd done that in forever.

I hiccupped again. "Damn it to hell," I couldn't help but say. I threw my napkin down, looked at Jack, and exploded with honesty. "Can you believe this? Sitting here at a formal event in an almost-new dress, hiccupping like a disgusting pig. I must be making you sick."

He laughed as he pushed his hair back. It was blondest around his forehead. "Hardly," he said, "and the last thing you are is disgusting. But I can solve your problem." He reached across the table for a crystal bowl filled with sugar cubes and handed it to me. "Take one and let it dissolve under your tongue."

I didn't think he meant that to sound sexy, but it did. I followed his advice, and soon the sugar was gone and so were my hiccups. "I'm impressed, Jack. I'm also glad you didn't suggest my mother's remedy from when I was a kid. She forced me to drink a shot of lemon juice."

"Aw," he said. "I wouldn't do that to you."

Why did every word out of his mouth make me sweat? Maybe it was because his voice was so outrageously smooth. I grabbed a napkin and dried my forehead as the band started playing a slow song and couples left the tables to dance. Jack asked if I wanted to join them, but it had been so long since I'd danced with a man that when we were standing in the center of Astor Hall I couldn't remember what to do. Which hand was supposed to go where?

I froze. He gingerly took my left palm and put it on his right shoulder, where his suit felt soft beneath my fingertips. Then he slipped his hand around my waist, rested it on my back, and we swayed to the piano and the saxophone while other couples swerved around us.

"How old are you, Savannah?" he asked.

"Twenty-four," I said. "And you're—"

"A senior citizen compared to you. I turned thirty-one last month."

I laughed. "Then you're far from collecting Social Security. You're young, Jack."

He smiled, creasing his dimples into his cheeks. "I work so much that it doesn't always feel that way. I inherited my father's business after he died unexpectedly last year . . . I'd been working for him since college, but I never thought I'd have to run things so soon."

"That must be tough," I said, glancing over Jack's shoulder at Ned dancing with Kitty. He didn't seem pleased with me, but I couldn't figure out what I'd done wrong this time. I wasn't dancing with a bartender. Were suave businessmen off-limits, too? It didn't matter, though. I couldn't have cared less what he thought, and I'd never follow his rules. Ned turned his back on me and I shifted my gaze to Jack.

"I'm sure you miss your father," I said.

Jack shrugged. "I always have."

There was sadness in his voice that I understood. I wanted to find out exactly what he meant, but I couldn't be that nosy. "Well," I said, "my father died unexpectedly, too. We actually never met . . . but that doesn't mean I didn't miss him. Still, it's probably not as rough for me as it is for you."

"Maybe," he said gently, "it's even worse."

I nodded, we kept dancing, and his strong hand against the curve of my back made my heart thump through the rhinestones on my dress. It also made me wonder what was wrong with me. I'd been so attracted to Alex just a little while ago—and that hadn't changed—but now I felt just as drawn to Jack. They were so different, and yet they somehow made me feel the same way.

"Have you been enjoying New York since you moved here from . . . ?"

"South Carolina," I said. "And I have . . . for the most part. My best friend came up, too, and we've been doing all the touristy stuff . . . restaurants, shopping, dancing at a nightclub. We went to The Russian Tea Room once, but we only had cupcakes and champagne."

He grinned, and I blushed. It seemed like all it took to charm him was me being me.

We danced until the band stopped playing, and then the party was over and he walked me out of Astor Hall. The front entrance was crowded with noisy departing guests, and he led me to a secluded corner where he took my hands in his.

"I don't mean to be forward," he said, "but I really want to see you again."

I'd spent years without a drop of romance, and suddenly two gorgeous guys wanted to see me again. It didn't seem right to have given my number to Alex and to now be forking it over to Jack, but I couldn't help myself. I had to stop thinking like a small-town church lady. There was no ring on my finger, I was single and free, and I had every right to date two guys. People did it all the time, especially sophisticated women who lived in a city like this. I'd waited so long for something exciting to happen, and now that it had I couldn't let it slip away.

Jack put his cool palm on my bare shoulder as he gave me a good-night kiss on my cheek. It sent a current of electricity through me and made sparks burst in my fingertips, and I wished I could keep his hand and his lips where they were for the rest of the night. But it was time to go.

The kiss prickled on my skin after he walked out of the library and disappeared into the crowd that was filing into limos and glossy sports cars on the street. I trailed slowly behind, feeling like I was floating above the library's steps. Tina was down on the sidewalk in her tangerine dress, standing between Patience and Fortitude and waving at me. I waved back, my mind stuck on Alex's blue eyes and Jack's cinnamon-and-Scotch scent as I headed toward Fifth Avenue in the warm midnight air.

Ten

I squinted at the computer screen in my home office while I sipped tomato juice. It was daybreak, the room was dim, and the light from the monitor pinched my pupils.

"You need a shot of Tabasco in that."

I turned toward the doorway, where Tina stood in shorts and a violet top. "I doubt it would help," I said, pressing my palm above my eyes. "This headache's fixin' to split my skull. It woke me up an hour ago."

"You never could hold your liquor," she said with a grin as she strode across the room and plopped onto a couch. "You were walking on a slant when we left the party last night."

"That had more to do with the men than the alcohol."

She grabbed a cushion and hugged it in her lap. Her mascara was smudged around her eyes because she'd gone to sleep in full makeup. Her mother hadn't been around long enough to fill her in on all the Lady Laws. "So which one do you prefer?"

I'd gushed about Alex and Jack when we came home last night, and Tina had done her share of gushing, too. She'd told me that her bartender's name was Kyle, he was from Brooklyn, and he was a grad student at some city college here in Manhattan. He'd taken her number and promised to call, and I hoped he would. I hoped he'd be good enough for her.

"Too early to tell," I answered, rubbing my bare foot across the hardwood floor.

"Give them both a try," she said with her husky laugh. "It's been two years since Jamie, and I don't know how you've lasted without—"

"*Enough,* Tina," I said, shooting her a warning glance.

She giggled and shoved the cushion behind her head. "You're reading *Nocturnal*? That's not like you."

"I know," I said, turning toward the monitor and a Web site that had a midnight-blue background covered with blinking silver stars. "I wanted to make sure I hadn't been smeared, but Fabian Spader's latest entry just raves about the party last night:

> *The ageless Virginia Barlow Stone was radiant while she watched her brilliant and handsome son, Edward Stone, Jr., take the reins at Stone News."*

I faked a gag. "He's so full of crap. He would've destroyed both of them if I'd given him the ammunition."

"So he didn't mention you at all?"

I scanned the screen and then looked back at Tina, who was examining a lock of her hair. "I've been spared. I thought he might butcher me, but I'm relieved he didn't. I don't want my name all over the Internet . . . I like being a nobody."

She tore apart a split end and flicked it into the air. "You've *never* been a nobody."

I smiled. Then I stood up, walked toward the door, and stopped on my way out. "Tina," I said. "Check online for a job. Find something that matters to you. And make sure that from now on, you wash off your makeup before going to bed. Your skin's much too pretty to ruin."

"Mind if we stop at Starbucks?" I asked a few hours later as Tony drove away from my building. "I need lots of coffee."

He gave me a wry grin. "Maybe you shouldn't stay out so late on weeknights."

"I doubt I'll take that friendly advice," I answered with a laugh. "And we *are* friends now, aren't we?"

"My boss wouldn't want us to be. Drivers aren't allowed to fraternize with clients."

Why was everybody around here so hung up on this type of person keeping away from that type of person? It reminded me of the novels I'd read about Victorian England and all that upstairs/downstairs garbage. "I'm not big on rules," I said, "especially stupid ones that try to keep me from people I like. So let's just say we're friends, okay?"

He moved his eyes toward me. The early-morning sunlight brought out the fading freckles on his cheeks. "Okay," he said.

He brought me to Starbucks and then dropped me off at work. The usual gang of protesters was out front, walking in a circle with their *Stone News Kills* signs. I dashed by them and went inside, where Ned ignored me in the elevator and I waved to Kitty as I passed her office and headed toward my desk with a cup of dark roast. I stayed there all day without even a bathroom break, doing research for Kitty and typing up memos summarizing my findings until six thirty, when words started blurring together. Then I gathered up my papers, brought them to Kitty's empty office, and put them on her desk. When I went back to mine, I found Caroline sitting in my chair.

"Remember what I told you about watching your attitude

with my brother?" she said. "That goes for my mother, too. She let me in on what happened in the bathroom last night."

I leaned against the wall. "She's your mother . . . so I don't blame you for defending her. But I heard her say some horrible things."

Caroline's thin upper lip twitched. "Like what?"

She was probably praying I hadn't heard everything, and I didn't have the heart to tell her I had. Just because I was surrounded by rats didn't mean I was going to become one.

"Like her opinion of Kitty," I said. "I know you don't want me to presume what you're thinking . . . but I doubt you believe Kitty's worthless if she can't have a baby."

Caroline stood up. "Shockingly," she said after a moment, "you're right."

She walked past me, bumped into my shoulder, and didn't apologize. I reclaimed my seat and logged off my computer, and then my cell vibrated on my desk. I answered it and someone said, "Hey, Savannah . . . remember me?"

The voice had to belong to Alex or Jack, but it was so deep and smooth that it could have been either. "Can you give me a hint?" I asked without checking the caller ID.

"I cured your hiccups last night."

"Jackson Lucas," I said, feeling the sizzle of his kiss on my cheek. "How are you?"

"Hungry," he replied. "Want to join me for dinner?"

He invited me to a restaurant called Masa in the Time Warner Center, I agreed to meet him there at seven thirty, and then Tony drove me toward Columbus Circle while I refreshed my makeup.

"Do you have a business meeting?" he asked.

"I have a date," I said, and I hadn't uttered those words for so long that they made my stomach twist. "Since we're officially friends, I should probably explain why I sound like a teenager."

I told Tony about Jamie and Eva Lee, the dreary existence I'd been living for the past two years, and my handful of miserable dates. He was quiet after I stopped talking, and I wondered if I shouldn't have run my mouth off. I had a habit of doing that around him.

"Well," he said finally, "I'd be nervous, too, if I had to get into the dating scene. I actually have no experience with it . . . I met Allison when we were in seventh grade, and we've been together ever since. I haven't shown you her picture, have I?" He pulled a battered wallet from his pocket, handed it to me, and I opened it and looked at a wedding photo of Tony with a girl who was the image of Marjorie.

"She's so pretty," I said, examining the picture. Tony's face was fuller and his hair was longer, and I wouldn't have been surprised if he'd walked down the aisle before he was old enough to order a drink. "That's such a sweet story, too . . . not many people get to marry their seventh-grade girlfriend. Like I told you before, I could've married my high school boyfriend, but . . . I didn't."

Why did I bring that up again? I cleared my throat and dabbed illuminizer onto my cheekbones.

"Well," Tony said after a pause, "whoever your date is . . . he should be honored to go out with a nice girl like you. And he better not pull anything funny . . . I know some leg breakers on Staten Island."

I laughed. Maybe that was why I told Tony everything. It felt like he was the brother I'd always wished for.

Soon I was inside the Time Warner Center, a massive complex that could have been called Shopper's Orgasmic Dream—a gigantic chi-chi mall overflowing with stores. I rode one of the many escalators to Masa, where I peeked inside and saw serene, understated Japanese décor and touristy-looking people being turned away for not having reservations.

I supposed they didn't know better, but I hoped Jack did as I stood outside the door, slipped my cell from my purse, and called Tina to let her know why I wouldn't be home for dinner.

"Is it the bartender or the rich guy?" she asked.

"The rich guy," I whispered. "Not that his money matters . . . I have my own."

"No kidding. Another ten grand showed up at the front door this afternoon," she said, and I made a mental note to stop at Chase Manhattan, stash a few thousand in Mom's account, and send her a big check. "Anyway," Tina went on, "I'd say I won't expect you home tonight . . . but I know you too well."

"Yeah . . . you do. I'd never spend the night with a first date," I said, and realized I was insulting her only after the words were out of my mouth.

She laughed it off. "Never say never. A man like him might change your mind. He could *bewitch* you."

"I doubt it."

"Well," she said, "just don't forget your birth control pill today."

I'd been taking the Pill since high school, when Mom had made sure to get me on it. And I still swallowed it every morning even though I had no reason to. It was best to be prepared in case a reason came along.

"I never forget *that*. And I'll see you later, Tina," I said, put my phone away, and felt a hand on my shoulder. I spun around and Jack was standing there, looking dashing in a sleek suit. He smelled like spicy cologne and a cinnamon Altoid that he must have had earlier, and just being near him made everything under my clothes ridiculously warm.

"Hi," I said, and it came out sultrier than I'd planned. But that was a good thing.

He squeezed my arm and kissed my cheek. "Hi," he said back in the smoothest voice.

"Did you happen to make a reservation?" I asked. "We need one."

He shook his head. "We don't," he said, resting his hand on my back to guide me into the dimly lit restaurant. A pretty hostess gave him a smile, greeted him as "Mr. Lucas," and led us through a windowless room to a table with a view of sushi chefs in action.

"Your usual spot," she said, winking at Jack before she walked away.

This was impressive. My last date had taken me to a sports bar where he'd gotten drunk on beer and pulled out a coupon for half-price onion rings when the bill arrived. "Well," I said as we sat down, "what a lovely restaurant. It's nice to know a VIP."

Jack's lips spread into a grin. His teeth weren't perfect like Alex's—they were crowded close together in his mouth—but his smile was still charming. "I'm just a regular guy, Savannah. And this *is* a great restaurant. But I have to admit," he said, lowering his voice like he was sharing a dark secret, "Nobu is my favorite place for Japanese food . . . and I go there a lot, even though it's not as trendy as it used to be."

I almost laughed. He was so far from being a regular guy, and his trendiness concern was adorable. "I wouldn't know the difference. I've never eaten Japanese food before," I said, glancing around at other tables. "Why doesn't anyone have a menu?"

"There isn't one. We're subject to the chef's whims."

He said that lightly, like it was amusing and exciting. But it made me nervous. And when the food came, I stared at plates filled with seafood that I couldn't name.

"Sorry," I said, hoping Jack wouldn't think I was crass and ignorant and ungrateful. "This is all so fancy, but . . . I guess I'm used to common, American food. My favorite restaurant in Charleston is the Hominy Grill."

"The Hominy Grill," he said with a smile. "And what's on the menu there?"

"Oh, you know . . . simple things like fried chicken and shrimp Creole. Personally, I'm addicted to the grits."

"I've never actually had grits," Jack said as he sipped sake. "Maybe you can introduce me to them sometime. But for now . . . a new experience is waiting for you right here."

I got the point. I was holding on to grits because I feared bluefin tuna tartare and fried fugu. But I shouldn't have been so narrow-minded, because everything turned out to be interesting and delicious and excitingly new.

"Tell me more about yourself," Jack said when we were finished with dinner and eating grapefruit granité. "You haven't given much away about what brought you to New York. I know you're a writer and you're working at a magazine, but—"

"That's all there is to it," I said. I didn't want to spoil tonight with talk of Virginia and Ned and Caroline and my illegitimate birth. "Have you lived here your whole life?"

He nodded, circling the rim of a teacup with his finger. "The Upper East Side, the Hamptons . . . same monotonous routine for thirty-one long years. But now," he said staring at me as his blondish-brown hair skimmed his brow, "I'm looking for something unique."

Jack paid the bill at Masa with a thick wad of cash he took out of a leather wallet that looked ready to burst. Then we rode in a taxi to a jazz club inside an old building all the way down on Murray Street. It had a bar, brick walls, and a singer with a dulcet voice. Her face was sweaty and strained while she sang about something tragic and lost that tied my stomach in knots.

Jack bent toward me as we sat at a small table in the back. "Do you like it?"

I nodded, slipping out of my blazer. The singer switched to a happier tune and Jack ordered a single malt, neat. I kept away from the booze because I was still recovering from the previous night, and I'd just asked the waitress for a virgin piña colada when a guy in a suit came by and spoke to Jack. Jack introduced me, and he had to do it more than five times because men and women kept stopping at our table to shake Jack's hand or to give him a hug or a kiss or a slap on the back. The proud way he showed me off to everyone and the envious looks I got from lots of ladies made me feel like something special. And the music reminded me of the glamorous F. Scott Fitzgerald novels I'd read in high school. I felt like I was sitting next to Jay Gatsby.

A woman stopped at the table. She was gracefully tall and incredibly thin, dressed in jeans and a red halter that showcased her toned arms and her glowing skin. Her side-parted hair was long and black and shiny, and a section of it cascaded over her left eye.

"*Bonsoir,*" she said.

She and Jack started speaking French. I was clueless as to what they were saying, but his curt replies gave me the feeling that he didn't want her around. I wondered why, since she was exotic and exquisite and seemed very friendly.

"Angelique," he said, "this is Savannah."

"Nice to meet you," she said in an enchanting accent. She exchanged a few more words with Jack, and soon she walked away to join a crowded table at the other side of the room.

"Who was *that*?" I asked. "She's stunning."

Jack finished off his scotch. "She's my ex-girlfriend who I asked to marry me a few months ago. I'd already bought a house for us . . . I guess I was too confident about the whole thing. All I ended up with is an overpriced engagement ring."

He slammed down his glass and called the waitress over so he could order another drink. Then he swigged Scotch with one hand and drummed his fingers against his knee with the other as he stared at the stage where the singer was crooning.

I touched the cuff of Jack's crisp white shirt and leaned

toward him. "Just because she turned you down doesn't mean she didn't love you. Maybe it wasn't the right time."

He slowly turned toward me. "How do *you* know?"

"From experience," I said, and told him just a few facts about Jamie.

"Well," he said when I was done, "I think Angelique had other reasons, and our situation was very different . . . but I'm glad you shared yours. I've had the feeling that you were holding something back."

That was true. I hadn't even told him who I really was. "I should be more honest. But my story has some ugly parts that don't belong in a beautiful night like this."

He cupped my chin in his hand. "I'm sorry you've ever had to go through anything ugly."

His thumb moved back and forth across my skin, sending a spark from my feet through my stomach and into my head. "I like the way you speak French," I said.

"And I like the way you speak South Carolina."

I laughed, settled into my chair, listened to the music, and chatted with Jack until I glanced at my watch, shocked that it was after midnight.

"I hate to leave," I said, "but I have to work in the morning."

He nodded, reached into his pocket, and pulled more cash out of his wallet. He tossed the money onto the table, and then we left the club and were back on Murray Street, where the air was strangely still and silent. All I heard was a muffled saxophone and a car alarm screeching in the distance.

"I know you want to get going," Jack said as we stood by the curb to hail a taxi. "But if you don't mind a quick detour, I'd love to show you my home."

A cab stopped. Jack walked toward it, but I stayed where I was, thinking that during the past two years in Charleston I'd never gone to a man's house after a date. I'd been invited, but

I'd known what those guys were expecting and I had no interest in giving it to them, especially after a night of beer and discount onion rings. I wondered if Jack felt entitled to something since he'd spent lots of cash and gotten me into an exclusive restaurant without a reservation. Maybe there was a price for going to the front of the line.

He opened the cab door and turned toward me. "I had the place renovated and decorated . . . but I'm not sure if I got my money's worth. Angelique never saw it, and I need a woman's opinion."

Was that really what he needed? But if it was something else, he could get it from beautiful, lanky women who spoke fluent French. And I didn't want this night to end, so I took a chance and slipped into the cab.

Eleven

The taxi driver took us to a quiet neighborhood on the Upper East Side with elegant four-story brownstone homes and expensive cars lining the street. Then I was inside Jack's house, which had classy furniture, high ceilings, huge windows, and gleaming wood floors. After Jack gave me a full tour, we stood in the hallway on the second level, where he leaned against the spindle railing that framed a curving staircase. He'd taken off his jacket and his tie, unbuttoned the top of his shirt, and rolled up his sleeves.

"It's perfect," I said. "This house is a dream."

He gently latched his fingers around my wrist. "So are you."

I smiled as I studied his straight nose and the crescent-moon dimples that formed at each side of his mouth when he smiled back at me. Without thinking, I lifted my free hand and traced one of them with my finger.

He pulled me close to him, ran his fingers through my hair, and kissed me. I tasted cinnamon and Scotch, and it had been so long since I'd felt soft lips and strong hands that I thought I might dissolve into the carpet.

He started walking, guiding me backward, kissing me all the

way into a room decorated simply, with dark walls and a king-size bed that was neatly made with fresh white linens. Matching pillows were lined up against a headboard covered in black silk, and a lamp in the corner lit the room with a soft, silvery glow. I glanced at everything quickly, then closed my eyes again, wrapped my arms around Jack, and went on kissing as he guided me down to the bed, where my back pressed against the sheets and my hair fanned out across the pillows. It felt cool and soft there and I didn't want this to stop, but I was afraid to keep going. I was rusty. Jamie was all I knew. And I wanted to be sure Jack cared about me before I did something that would make me care too much about him. So I opened my eyes and moved my mouth away from his.

"What's wrong?" he asked as he leaned over me. His eyes were shimmering.

He was gorgeous, and I was embarrassed. He was probably accustomed to women who'd fling their G-strings onto this bed and swing naked from the crystal chandelier downstairs. I doubted he'd ever met a twenty-four-year-old with only one name on her list of conquests. I pushed my hair out of my face and hoped sweat stains weren't spreading all over my shirt.

"I don't want you to think that just because I came here tonight, I'm . . . I mean, I . . ."

I stopped. He stared at me for a moment, like he wasn't used to women holding back. But then he reached for my hand and squeezed my fingers in his. "I understand," he said. "You're a lady. And I'm a gentleman. So we'll get to know each other and take things slow."

That was what I wanted to hear, and it made him even hotter. "Are you sure?" I asked.

"Yeah," he said. "Don't worry, Savannah. I'll be a good boy."

I smiled. He kissed me again, and he was *very* good. He also kept his word to take things slow—his kisses were careful and deep and lingering, and they left me craving what we might do right here in this bed as long as I was sure it wouldn't be a one-time thing.

"Hey," Jack said softly.

My eyes opened. I loved the sound of his breathy voice. I knew we'd been caught up in each other for a while, but I was surprised at how long it had been when I glanced at the clock on his night table. "Hmm?" I said dreamily. My entire body was so relaxed that it was hard to talk.

He smiled down at me. His rapt attention felt like sunshine on my face. "We'd better go downstairs . . . or I might not be able to keep my promise."

I gave him a knowing grin. Jack straightened up, sat at the edge of the bed, and moved his eyes to my hair spread across the pillow. He picked up a section of it and ran it through his fingers, sending a warm quiver through me. "Want to watch TV?" he asked, his voice still low and whispery. "I bought a gigantic flat screen, and I've only turned it on twice."

I laughed. "You spend too much time at the office."

He shifted his eyes back to my face. "Maybe you can help me break that habit. I think you have the power to distract me."

I sat on a leather couch in Jack's living room, listening to a microwave beep in the kitchen. I smelled something burning, and then Jack sat beside me and put a glass bowl filled with popcorn on the coffee table.

I chuckled at the burnt kernels at the bottom of the bowl. "Do you eat out a lot?"

"I eat out or order in every single night. I'm useless in the kitchen."

"Then I admire your effort. I'll have to reciprocate by making you grits for breakfast," I said as I picked out a few kernels of popcorn that had avoided getting scorched and shoved them into my mouth.

He raised an eyebrow. My face went hot and I choked on the popcorn. I'd sounded as if I was planning to spend the night, even though I'd already gone to so much trouble establishing that we weren't going to wake up next to each other in the morning.

"I didn't mean it like *that*," I said between coughs. "I meant . . . if I ever come over for breakfast . . . like on a Sunday . . . then I can . . ."

He headed for the kitchen, came back with a glass of ice water, and stuck it in my hand as he crouched in front of me and reached around to pat my back. "I know what you meant," he said with a beguiled grin while I drank and coughed. "You're cute when you blush."

I leaned into the couch, cleared my throat, and gathered my hair into a knot at the nape of my sweaty neck. "You make me nervous," I admitted.

He got up and sat beside me. "Why's that?"

I pointed to the abstract art on the walls, the fine lamps, the Ferrari key chain on the coffee table. There was even a framed photo of him in climbing gear as he stood on a mountain's snowy peak, surrounded by clouds. "Look at all this stuff. Look at *you*. You speak *French*."

He opened the second button on his shirt, and I tried not to stare at his smooth, tan skin. "It isn't all that impressive. I never even wanted to learn . . . but my mother demanded I start studying when I was six years old. She even used to make me wear a suit for my lessons. It was so fucking humiliating." He held up his hand. "Sorry. Excuse the language."

More proof that he was a gentleman. "Go on," I said.

He snatched a cushion from the couch and shoved it behind his back. "As if the suit wasn't enough agony, the lessons were on Saturday afternoons. For ten years, I had to go to this spooky old apartment in the Village and sit for hours with a sour old lady who'd scream at me and force me to write vocabulary words a hundred times if my pronunciation didn't meet with her approval."

"That's plain evil," I said, my heart aching at the thought.

"I know." He twisted his watch. "Anyway . . . one time I was coming home on the subway after one of her torture sessions . . . I was twelve . . . and I got my ass kicked by a gang of kids from the Bronx who thought it'd be fun to beat up some little wimp in a designer suit and shiny shoes. One of them was a *girl*. Can you imagine?"

I held my hand over my mouth, horrified at the image of a well-dressed blond boy getting punched and kicked and degraded on the floor of a dirty subway car.

"That's terrible," I said. "Did you tell your mother?"

He shrugged. "I just pretended I fell down the steps at the station."

He was still fiddling with his watch, and his eyes were on his wrist. I reached out and smoothed his hair, wanting to ask why he'd pretended. But it just felt like I shouldn't.

"The lessons paid off," I said. "I'm *very* impressed by your French."

He looked at me and smiled. His dimples were so deep. "Hey," he said as he stood up, "want to watch a movie? I've got an extensive collection of old films." He walked to a cabinet beside the TV, opened it, and started reciting titles—*Ghost, Father of the Bride, Sleepless in Seattle*.

I never expected him to have an array of chick flicks. "Those are *yours*?" I asked.

"Yeah," he said sheepishly. "Actually, they belonged to one of my babysitters when I was a kid. She'd bring movies over to watch while my parents were out, and she'd leave them with me afterward. She knew I spent a lot of time in front of the TV." He stopped and raked his hand through his hair. "I'm sorry,

Savannah. I must be boring you. You're probably not into old movies anyway, right?"

He closed the cabinet. I walked over and opened it again. The shelves inside were filled with DVDs and old VHS tapes and I'd never seen *Ghost,* so I slid the tape out and stuck it in his hand. "You're not boring me," I said. "Give me another new experience."

There were footsteps over my head. Water rushed through pipes. I opened my eyes and looked at my purse on the floor, a bowl filled with leftover popcorn, and sunlight streaming through blinds on a bay window.

It took me a second to figure out that I was at Jack's house, stretched out on his couch and covered with a soft flannel blanket. I lifted the blanket, dreading the sight of my underwear or complete and total nudity, but I was still in my pants and my tank top.

Of course I hadn't done anything. I hadn't been drunk last night. And unless I was a poor judge of character, Jack wasn't the type of guy to slip me a Roofie. But my mind was filled with fogginess, and I struggled to remember what had happened after I handed him that movie.

I slung my legs over the couch and sat up just as the water stopped running. I rubbed the blurriness out of my eyes, remembering that *Ghost* had been one of the saddest and most romantic flicks I'd ever seen and I'd bitten my lip to keep from crying. The last thing I remembered was the credits, so I'd probably fallen asleep after that and Jack must have taken off my shoes and covered me with the blanket.

I dashed across the hardwood floor and ducked into a bathroom, where I shut the door behind me and flipped on a light. I avoided the mirror because I didn't need confirmation that I looked like a leftover from last Halloween. I grabbed a Listerine bottle, poured some into my hand, swished it around my mouth, and spit into the sink. Then I cracked open the door and stepped into the living room and crashed right into Jack.

He was dressed in a shorts and a T-shirt that clung to his broad shoulders and his flat stomach. He had a just-out-of-the shower smell—soap and shampoo and shaving cream. His hair was wet and slicked back, and there was a patch of razor burn on his jaw.

I rubbed it gently with one finger to ease the sting. "Thanks for the blanket."

"You're welcome," he said as he pressed his thumb below my eye. He laughed at the black smear that was left across his skin. "Did you work in a coal mine while I was asleep?"

I looked away. His gorgeousness had temporarily made me forget my disastrous state.

He turned my face toward him. "I'm just kidding. The guest bathroom upstairs has soap, towels, a new toothbrush . . . use whatever you want."

I used all of it and then went back downstairs, where Jack was taking a plastic bag from a delivery boy. "Since I don't cook," Jack said, closing the front door, "I ordered breakfast."

I glanced at my watch. It wasn't even seven, so I had time to eat and call Tony to take me across town so I could shower and change before work. But even if I didn't have time, it would have been hard to tear myself away. Jack was smiling at me, the sun flowing through the windows made his hair look like gold, and I sensed that even a rich and handsome guy might get lonely in a big, empty house. So I followed him to the kitchen, which had cherry cabinets and black granite countertops and a double oven that still had an Electrolux sticker on it.

"I should get going," I said when we'd finished eating. "I need to go home and change."

"Where do you live? You haven't told me."

I pushed my chair back and stood up. "Central Park West," I said.

His forehead wrinkled. "Really? That's a nice area."

He was probably wondering how an aspiring writer could afford my address, and part of me felt guilty for keeping the reason a secret. The other part thought it was fun to be a woman of mystery—at least for a while.

I leaned down and kissed his cheek. "Thanks for last night. Let's do it again."

"We will. Can I give you a lift?"

I shook my head. "I'm going to call a friend to pick me up."

We walked to the front door. Jack opened it and circled his arms around me, and I rested my face against the soft cotton that covered his hard chest.

"Want me to wait with you until your ride comes?" he said into my hair.

"Get ready for work. You don't want to be late . . . I've heard your boss is a jerk."

He laughed and kissed the top of my head. I went outside, he shut the door behind me, and I sat at the bottom of eight cement steps while I called Tony.

"I'm on East Seventieth and Park," I told him, squinting to read a street sign at the end of the block. "I'm halfway down on the right . . . it's my date's house. But don't judge me. I slept on his couch, and I swear on twenty Bibles that nothing funny happened."

"No judgment," Tony replied. "And I believe you."

I put the phone away, lifted my face to the warm morning sunshine, and closed my eyes as I rewound everything that had happened last night.

"Savannah," someone said in the distance.

My eyes sprang open. They scanned the block—a wreath made of dried flowers on a door, a woman loading a baby into an Escalade, Kitty standing across the street in a khaki suit.

What was *she* doing here? Why was she giving me that befuddled look? And was that *Ned* coming out of the town house behind her? I gasped, glancing back at the street sign. *We live in a lovely brownstone on East Seventieth,* he'd said.

He and Jack were neighbors? That sort of explained why Ned had shot daggers in my direction when he saw me dancing with Jack inside Astor Hall. But did Ned think he could bar me from *fraternizing* with everybody, including all residents of the Upper East Side?

Ned spotted me. His face clouded over as he stormed past Kitty and across the road. I stood up, put my hands on my hips, and tapped my foot against the step, just waiting.

"Ned, take it easy," Kitty called after him when she paused for the Escalade to go by. "Don't jump to conclusions."

What conclusions? I wondered as Ned's leather loafers hit the curb. He stood in front of me with his cold green eyes fixed on my face and his lips set into a thin, tight line.

"What the hell are you doing at Jack's house?" he asked, looking me up and down. "Your clothes are wrinkled. Is that yesterday's outfit?"

Kitty rushed up behind him and tugged at his blazer. "Ned, don't—"

He shrugged her off. "I asked you a question. You were here all night, weren't you?"

His voice was loud and demanding, and professional-looking people leaving houses were glancing at me like I'd done something slimy. But I hadn't, so I raised my chin and lifted my shoulders.

"That's none of your business," I said as Tony pulled up in the black sedan. "Even though you seem to want to, you can't run my life. I'm allowed to date your neighbor."

"My *neighbor,*" Ned echoed with an indignant laugh. "You know better than that."

Tony got out of the car. "Everything okay?" he called toward me.

"Fine," I said, waving him away. I couldn't let him get mixed up in whatever this was. But he didn't go back into the car. He leaned against it like a bodyguard as the doorknob clicked behind me. I turned around and saw Jack on the top step, half-dressed in gray pants and a fresh white shirt that he hadn't buttoned all the way. A striped tie was in his hand, and he looked more confused than I felt.

"What's going on?" Jack said, glancing between me and Ned and Kitty.

"*You* tell *me*," Ned shot back. "Did you sleep with my sister?"

Now I was the one to laugh. "I'm your *sister*? Since when?" I asked, but Ned ignored me.

"Caroline?" Jack said. "Ned, you know I'd never—"

"Not *Caroline,* for Christ's sake." Ned pointed to me. *"Her."*

Jack's bright-hazel eyes turned dull and wounded, and I could have cried. He must have known he was right when he'd felt I was holding something back. He was probably sorry for telling me about his surly French teacher and the engagement ring that Angelique didn't want.

Ned put his foot on the bottom step. "Oh," he said, the outrage in his voice changing to snotty satisfaction, "I guess Savannah's kept a little secret from you, Jack. Actually, it's a *big* secret, and I'll give it to you straight: She's the product of an affair my father had with a woman in South Carolina. Savannah's come to New York to claim her fortune and stir up trouble."

"That's not true," I said. "*You're* the only troublemaker here."

"I suspect," he went on, "she wanted to hurt me by deceiving my best friend. I have no doubt she was trying to use you. God only knows what sort of perverse plans she had."

"I didn't have plans of any kind," I said. "I didn't know Jack's your best friend."

Ned rolled his eyes. "What you tell me and what I believe are two very different things."

I turned to Jack, who was frozen in his doorway. "I thought . . . ," he said, his voice trailing off. He cleared his throat. "You seemed so taken by everything . . . the house, and . . . I mean . . . was that all an act?"

"Of course not," I said. "It was real, Jack. I wasn't acting."

"You had to be. Nothing I have could impress a Stone."

I'd been wrong about being mysterious. It wasn't fun at all. "You don't understand. I just found out a few weeks ago that I'm Edward's daughter. I'm not really a Stone; I—"

Ned chortled. "That's quite a change of tune. What happened to *I deserve to be here as much as you do?* I guess you're a member of my family only when it works to your benefit?"

My head snapped toward him. "Stop twisting everything."

"You're doing a good job of that on your own."

I looked at Jack again. "I swear I didn't know who you were. My intentions were completely honest."

"Honest?" Ned cut in. "You don't know the meaning of the word. If you did, you wouldn't have kept your identity from Jack. Is your job at Stone News too difficult? Maybe you were ready to quit and decided to look elsewhere for your pot of gold."

"I can handle my job just fine, and I wasn't looking for anything of the sort," I said through clenched teeth before turning toward Jack. "You believe me . . . right?"

He slowly wrapped his tie around his fingers. "After all this . . . I'm not sure."

Blood drained from my head. I felt woozy and ready to explode. Ned smiled, and I was dying to punch him or kick him or claw out those pale, icy eyes.

"Are you happy now?" I shouted. "Is this what you wanted?"

He folded his arms across his blazer. "If you mean I wanted to stop a scammer from ruining my best friend's life, then yes . . . I'm quite happy."

I stared at him, breathing warm air in and out through my

nose. "You're repulsive. You're disgusting. You're a liar and a manipulator and a low-down dirty bastard."

He gave me a patronizing wag of his finger. "That's not a nice way to talk."

"You're making me out to be something I'm not," I shrieked with no regard for the gawking neighbors. "You're trying to ruin everything. You want me to lose my money, my apartment, and now you've—"

"I've what? Ruined your imaginary romance? Stop making a fool of yourself."

That clinched it. Everything turned into a white-hot blur, and I backhanded Ned across his face. I connected with his cheekbone, which seemed to hurt me more than him. My knuckles stung, but he didn't even flinch or blink or back up. A shocked silence filled the air until he laughed and stroked the pinkish stripe I'd left on his skin.

"You should learn to control that temper," he said. "After all your hard work to pull off an Oscar-worthy performance, you don't want Jack to think you aren't a lady, do you?"

I was sure Jack had already changed his mind about that, because he didn't defend me. He didn't say a single word. I supposed it was easier to believe a best friend than a girl who'd hidden her true self and was screeching and assaulting people on his front steps.

I had to get out of there. I headed toward Tony, but Kitty caught my arm.

"Take the day off," she said, and I couldn't tell if she was mad at me for clocking her husband or she was trying to be nice.

"No," Ned bellowed from the stairs. "If she takes today off, she can forget about ever coming back to work at Stone News."

I narrowed my eyes. "Don't worry, Ned. I have no plans to leave Stone News, and after this . . . you can be sure I *never* will."

Twelve

∞

I sat beside Tony as he whisked us away. I gazed blankly through the windshield and rubbed my sore knuckles while I listened to WCBS News radio and tapped my foot against books about the history of New York.

He leaned toward the books when we reached a red light. "Let me get those out of your way."

"Leave them," I said, thinking my battle with Ned had eaten up so much of my time and energy that I couldn't go home to shower and change. "And take me right to work."

Tony paused before pulling my seat belt across me and clicking it into place. "There's no need to bite my head off. Now let me see your hand so I can make sure you didn't break anything."

I held it out and kept my eyes on the windshield while he stretched my fingers, squeezed my bones, and told me to make a fist. "You're okay," he said finally, and then the light turned green and he started driving again.

"How can you be sure?" I asked. "It hurts."

"A friend of mine used to be a cage fighter. I helped him

train and I was in his corner during his matches . . . so I can tell if bones are broken or not."

I was quiet for a moment, thinking he deserved an apology. "I'm sorry for snapping at you, Tony. Certain people have done things this morning to put me in a nasty mood."

He slung one arm over the back of my seat as he steered with his free hand. "So I saw. Wanna talk about it?"

I looked at him. His window was open a crack, and the breeze ruffled his auburn hair.

"Well," I said, "now you know how Edward Stone came to be my father."

"I also know Ned wants to make you feel inferior because of it . . . but you shouldn't. Nobody can control how they're born."

I nodded. This was such an unfortunate truth. "I guess you've met Ned before."

"I've driven him around . . . and Jackson Lucas, too. What were you doing with that guy, anyway? I wouldn't have expected you to be interested in a slick type like him."

I thought about Jack's expensive suits, the way he strolled into Masa without a reservation, the sugar under my tongue. "He might come off that way . . . but he's different when you get to know him."

"And you know him after just one date?"

I sank into my seat. "I was starting to . . . but I'm pretty sure I won't have another chance."

We were both quiet as we listened to a report on the radio about a fatal hit-and-run in the Bronx. I had no right to be so dismal when there were real tragedies happening, but I needed a few minutes to feel sorry for myself.

Tony stopped at another light and gave my shoulder a light shove. "Come on, Savannah," he said cajolingly. "Don't be upset. I get a shady vibe from Jack, to tell you the truth. I doubt he's any better than Ned."

"You're wrong . . . but it doesn't matter. Ned's spoiled everything."

He moved his eyes around my face as he stepped on the gas. "You look tired. You should go home and let Ned shove that damn job. I would've told off so many of my lousy bosses over the past few years if I didn't need a paycheck. But *you* don't need one."

I shook my head. "If I lose my job, I lose my inheritance. That's what he and his sister want."

Tony glanced at me. "Is *that* their game?"

"Yeah . . . and I have no choice but to play. I won't let them disqualify me."

"Good for you," he said, then thought for a moment. "Well . . . it's obvious that Ned's had a lifetime supply of getting exactly what he wants. We should make sure he doesn't get any more."

Tony left me at Stone News, and I texted Tina a truncated account of all the latest developments while I was riding in a crowded elevator that stopped at almost every floor before reaching *Femme*. I sent the message when the doors opened into the lobby, and then I dropped my phone into my purse, headed down the corridor toward my desk, and saw Ainsley walking in my direction.

"Is that yesterday's outfit?" she asked.

I rolled my eyes. "You sound like Ned."

She bounced up and down in her shoes. "Do I really?"

"Oh, Good Lord. Don't make that man your idol, Ainsley. He's an abomination. And if it's his success you admire, remember he didn't get it from hard work."

She tilted her head like she was mulling that over but quickly blew it off. "He's been one hundred percent terrific to me. So do you need any help with your work today?"

"Tons," I said wearily. "But I can do it myself. Thanks for asking, though."

She shrugged and nearly skipped her way down the hall.

I dragged myself to my desk, plopped in my chair, checked out the latest online edition of *Femme*, and chose two catchy articles that I posted on its social media sites: "Twenty Things You Can Do Instead of Sex during a Never-Ending Dry Spell" and "No, I Don't Have My Period . . . You're Just a Prick."

Kitty popped into my cubicle. She rested her back against the wall and twisted her necklace around her fingers. It was a circle made of diamonds—an eternity ring on a thick silver chain.

"Ned was way out of line," she said, "but so were you. You're lucky he didn't call the police. He could've had you arrested for battery, you know."

I imagined myself being cuffed and fingerprinted and shoved into a dank cell, waiting for Tina to bail me out. "That's true. But don't expect me to be grateful to him."

Kitty folded her arms across her blazer. "Savannah," she began in a low, steady voice, "I really like you, and I want to keep helping you. But if you put your hands on my husband one more time, I won't be your friend or even your boss. Understand?"

She sure did know how to stand by her man, even though she'd chosen the wrong one. "I do understand. I'm sorry if what I did upset you . . . and you're right . . . I shouldn't have hit Ned. I've never hit anyone before. But he drove me to it."

"Yes," she said with a sigh, "he did. I apologize for that."

"You should leave the apology to your miserable husband."

Her face fell. I felt bad, but I couldn't pretend Ned was a great guy.

"I'm surprised he and Jack are friends," I went on. "They're *nothing* alike."

Kitty cleared her throat and tossed her hair. "You're wrong about that. They have a lot in common . . . and they were next-door neighbors growing up on Park Avenue. They were both alone a lot as kids, and they just gravitated toward each other."

"Why were they alone?" I asked.

"Because they had career-obsessed fathers and socialite mothers who passed off their kids on high-price nannies," she said simply.

I remembered when Ned told me that Edward had *subsidized everything to ease his guilt* but wouldn't explain what that meant. Now I was pretty sure I knew. And I couldn't imagine being passed off to anyone. Mom had always been around, and she worked at home just to keep me out of day care. I might not have had a lot growing up, but one thing I'd never gone without was her.

"Virginia was bad enough with her frigid parenting and her non-stop social life," Kitty went on. "But from what Ned tells me, Jack's mother was *so* much worse. She spent most of her time pill-popping and ignoring her son. Jack's father cheated on her left and right, but that's another story. She was usually zoned out in her bedroom, and Ned would come out of his apartment and find Jack sitting in the hallway by himself."

"That's horrible," I said, imagining Jack as a cute blond-haired boy on the floor of an empty hallway, just hoping for someone to invite him in.

"Ned's a little older than Jack," Kitty went on. "And Jack got picked on a lot as a kid. Ned looked out for him . . . and they've been friends ever since."

I couldn't picture Ned ever being that considerate, but I was glad he was. "I guess that explains why Jack bought the house across the street from you," I said.

Kitty nodded. "Jack was planning to get married—"

"He told me about that."

"—and he and Ned thought it would be nice to raise their families close by. Things haven't quite worked out that way yet," she said with a forced laugh. "But anyway . . . why didn't you tell Jack who you are?"

"Because it didn't belong on a first date," I said.

She nodded slowly as I swiveled in my chair. "Okay. All

right. I get it. So let's drop the subject for now . . . but I meant what I said. You and Ned have to learn to get along."

Like that would ever happen. "Gorgeous necklace," I said to change the subject.

"Thank you. It's an early birthday gift from my miserable husband."

I gulped. I just couldn't get away from him. "When's your birthday?"

"This weekend," she said. "My parents are hosting a party for me at their summer home in East Hampton . . . on Saturday at seven. I was planning to invite you, and even after what happened this morning, I still hope you'll come. You can bring your friend Tina as your plus one again. It'll be casual attire, so something like a sundress would be fine. And no gifts, please."

I tapped my fingers on my thigh. "I'd like to come, Kitty . . . but I doubt I'm welcome anyplace Ned will be. And he told me not to bring Tina around anymore."

She walked toward the doorway. "Both of you are welcome," she said. "Ned doesn't make *all* the rules."

Later, she gave me a monogrammed invitation printed on ritzy stationery, but I held off on my RSVP. I didn't want to think about the party or Ned or the disappointed look on Jack's face. I focused on my work, and I was feeling proud of myself when Kitty left at five and I'd finished everything on my to-do list. I left a research memo in her office, went back to my cubicle to pick up my purse, and answered the phone when it rang.

"I need you upstairs," said a nasal voice.

My eyes shot toward the caller ID: *Caroline Stone*. "Excuse me?"

"Don't you understand English? *I . . . need . . . you . . . upstairs*," she said slowly, like I was dim-witted. "My assistant had to leave, and there's a mountain of filing to be done."

She had to be kidding. I was ready to pass out. I wanted to go home and nurse my wounds with the most fattening and sugar-filled ice cream available. "Then I guess your assistant will be busy when she returns," I said.

"Or you'll be unemployed. Make up your mind."

I was trapped, and I was sure Caroline loved it. She probably savored and relished and ate it up like candy. "I'm sure what happened with Jackson Lucas this morning has absolutely nothing to do with this."

"Jack," she said musingly. "Oh, yes . . . I believe my brother mentioned you put out for his best friend on your first date."

"Ned's a liar," I said. "And at least I can *get* a first date."

That was harsh. I didn't care. It shut her up, but not for long.

"Your work is waiting," she said. "I'm on my way to Gramercy Tavern, so Ainsley will show you what to do before she leaves for the night. Get it done or don't come back tomorrow."

She slammed down the phone so hard that it made my ear buzz. I kicked the side of my desk and threw my purse onto my chair, wishing there weren't a few other people working overtime, so I could scream and possibly destroy something expensive. Instead I just stomped toward the lobby, where I waited for an elevator while I texted Tina so she'd know I was going to be home late. Then I called Tony to tell him I'd take a cab tonight.

"I'm on my way to Gramercy Tavern," I muttered as I dropped my phone into my purse. I was sure Caroline would stuff her face with fine dining while I ate stale Doritos from the vending machine.

Her office was empty when I went past. So was Ned's, but a lamp on his desk was on and his blazer was draped over his chair. I found Ainsley waiting for me down the hall, and she led me to a conference room that had walls made of mahogany wood and brass lamps in every corner. There was also a long shellacked table covered with stacks of documents.

"Here's our challenge," she said, tucking her bob behind her ears.

I dropped my purse on the floor with a thud. "I object to your word choice."

"Oh, this project isn't so bad. I'll give you a hand."

"No," I said. "I appreciate the offer, but you should leave. It's late."

She checked her watch. "It's only just after five. I don't usually leave before eight. Ned always has something for me to do, and I never refuse because he'll be a valuable reference when I job-hunt after I graduate. He's already promised to say the most glowing things about me. Come on . . . the sooner we get started, the faster we'll finish."

Her positivity was a weird mix of annoying and admirable. She said the documents belonged in a file room two floors below, so we loaded everything into boxes and made multiple trips before we started sticking papers into folders. We'd been slaving for three hours when I noticed that Ainsley's eyes had gone glassy.

"What time did you come to work this morning?" I asked as I stood beside a filing cabinet and she sat on the floor with her legs crossed under her skirt and a folder on her lap.

"Six," she said, carefully placing two metal prongs through a hole-punched contract. "Or maybe five thirty . . . I'm not exactly sure."

I reached down and swiped the folder. "Go home. You've done enough."

She put up a fight, but I pushed her out of the room and onto an elevator. Then I went back to finish the job, which took until ten thirty. By then, my neck ached and I couldn't wait to go home. I'd left my purse in the conference room upstairs, so I rode the elevator to the corporate division and walked past empty offices with open doors and vacuum cleaner lines on the carpets. Ned's door was the only one shut, and there was a strip of light underneath. I got my purse from the conference room and passed his office again on my way back to the elevators. I was a few feet away when I heard a crash.

I backed up and opened Ned's door. A broken lamp was lying on the floor and Darcelle Conrad was on the desk, her blond hair dangling from the edge. Her skirt was pushed to her stomach, her blouse was open, and Ned was on top of her with his shirttails hanging out and the waist of his pants around his knees.

"Jesus Christ," escaped my mouth.

Darcelle's lips were on Ned's. Her eyes opened and her hand sprang to her blouse, which she clutched to cover her naked chest. He looked over his shoulder at me; I spun around and dashed into the corridor, hearing commotion as I hurried away— Darcelle's anxious voice, Ned angrily shushing her, his office door banging shut. I sped up when I heard his footsteps rushing in my direction and turned to find him zipping his pants.

I didn't need to see that. I cringed and shifted my eyes toward the lobby, where a lady pushing a cart filled with cleaning supplies seemed to be getting ready to leave. *Just tell Kitty I hope she feels better real soon,* Darcelle had said when I ran into her in the elevator, and now I knew she was even phonier than her hair.

Ned grabbed my arm and twisted me around. The space between his nose and his mouth glistened with sweat, and his upper lip curled into a sneer. "What the hell are you doing here?"

"Caroline had the bright idea to make me work all night," I said.

"That was *my* idea. But you were supposed to be downstairs."

"Why?" I said. "So I wouldn't know you're screwing your wife's friend?"

His eyes shot toward the woman in the lobby, who was now pressing an elevator button on the wall. Then he shoved me into an empty office with tall windows that overlooked the city. "I guess you think you've got me now, don't you?" he growled as he knocked the door closed with his foot. "Is *that* what you think, Savannah?"

I yanked my arm free and perched my hands on my hips.

"How do you do it?" I asked. "How does a pompous sleaze like you get two beautiful, accomplished women to fall into your trap?"

"I don't know," he said, rubbing his cleft chin. "Maybe it's my good looks and my big—"

"Name? That's what you meant, right? If not, I'll puke on your overpriced shoes."

He took a step back and gave me a smug smile. "Actually, that *isn't* what I meant."

I shook my head and raised my voice. "I was right this morning when I said you were disgusting. You're also an unbelievable hypocrite. You tried to humiliate me at Jack's house when I'd done *nothing,* when all the while you're whoring around on Kitty. You don't even have the decency not to do it right under her nose."

"What I do," he said, drying his upper lip with his sleeve, "is none of your business."

"But it *is* Kitty's business. From the moment I met her, I knew she was too good for you. Thanks for the confirmation."

He smoothed his crinkled shirt. "She loves me," he said.

"She loves a phony version of you that you've tricked her into believing is real. And what do you love about *her,* Ned? Is it just her parents' tax bracket?"

He stared at me. Then he took another step backward to sit leisurely on the edge of a desk. "You think you've got it all figured out. So what's your next move? Are you going to tell Kitty about me and Darcelle?"

"Of course I will. She deserves to know what's going on."

He crossed his long legs at the ankles. "*Is* that what she deserves? Does Kitty deserve to know that one of her oldest friends has been hooking up with her husband? You're probably not aware of this, but my wife and I have been trying to have children . . . with no success."

"I'm aware. She told me about the IVF. But what's that got to do with anything?"

Ned twisted his wedding ring. "It has *everything* to do with it. You don't know what she's endured . . . the hospitals, the let-downs, the nights she couldn't stop crying. She's gone through months of therapy, and she's only started to feel better over the past few weeks. So if you tell her just to spite me, you'll end up sending her right back to the emotional wreck she was. And I don't want that. Do *you*?"

Of course he had to complicate everything. Even worse, he made the tiniest shred of sense. "No," I said. "But I can't let her live a lie. She should know who you really are."

His jaw hardened. "Then tell her. Darcelle and I will say you're making the whole thing up . . . and Kitty won't doubt us."

"Don't count on that," I said. "She seems fair and objective."

"Even so . . . whose word means more? Her husband and her friend's, or somebody she hardly knows? You made your opin-ion of me quite public today, which will be all the more reason for her to think you're lying. She'll think you're trying to get back at me because I stood in the way of your little crush on Jack. Didn't you learn *anything* this morning? He didn't believe you, so why would she?"

I wished I could push him through the window and watch him splatter on the sidewalk fifty floors below. "You're a sick son of a bitch, Ned."

He slid off the desk and straightened up. "Maybe," he said. "But you should give what I told you some serious thought. You've probably got the sense to know I'm right. Despite what you might think based on what you saw here tonight, Kitty and I have a good marriage."

I shook my head. "It only appears that way . . . because of what Kitty *hasn't* seen."

"Savannah," he said, "marriage is more complicated than you seem to realize. And believe it or not, Kitty is very happy with me. So do the right thing and don't try to destroy that."

Thirteen

My apartment was dark, but a blow-dryer was humming in the guest bathroom. I tossed my keys and my purse onto a table, walked down the dim hall, and passed Tina's bedroom. Kyle the bartender was inside, sleeping facedown with his arm hanging off the mattress and his knuckles skimming the floor.

Was the moon full tonight? I was running into sex everywhere. I shook my head, went to Tina's bathroom, and opened the door. She was standing at the counter in a skimpy negligee made of lilac lace, looking in the mirror and styling her hair. The air was steamy from the shower as I shut the door, walked past her, and sat on the edge of the tub.

"A little soon, isn't it?" I asked, jerking my thumb toward her bedroom.

She fingered the silky bow around her narrow waist. "Don't be mad, Savannah. I know this is your apartment, but I didn't think you'd mind if I—"

"It's not that. This is your apartment, too. What I mean is that letting a man into your bed forty-eight hours after meeting him is a bad idea. It's never ended well for you."

She slammed her comb onto the counter. "He's a nice guy. Don't ruin this."

"I'm not ruining anything. I'm being sensible. I don't want you to get used again."

"Nobody ever uses me," she said in her toughest voice, as if that would make it true.

I rubbed my aching neck. "Just take care of yourself, Tina. I worry about you."

She stared at me for a long moment before cinching the bow snugly around her waist. "I know," she said as my eyes moved toward a snuffed-out Marlboro Light in an empty soap dish beside the sink.

I glared at her. "I thought you weren't going to smoke in the apartment."

She let out a nervous giggle. "The bathroom counts?"

"You know it does."

She picked up the soap dish and dumped the cigarette butt into the toilet. "Won't happen again," she said, and quickly changed the subject. "Guess what? I got an interview for a job at a homeless shelter on West Forty-first. It's at eleven thirty tomorrow. Maybe I can convince them that I'd be helpful there. I'm not as useless as everybody thinks."

"*I* don't think you're useless, and you know that. They'd be lucky to have you."

She scrunched her mouth into one corner. "How was your day?" she asked while she absentmindedly organized her makeup. "Did it improve?"

"It got worse," I said, and then she joined me on the bathtub rim, where I told her about what I'd seen in Ned's office and his attempt to manipulate me. "I'm not sure what to do."

"Rat him out to Kitty," Tina said decidedly as she crossed her legs.

"She might not believe me. Ned was right about that."

Tina shrugged one shoulder. "Maybe he wasn't. And if you're her friend, you won't keep this from her. A real friend always tells the truth."

"Yes," I said, "a real friend always does."

She shifted uneasily and said she was going to sleep. She went to her bedroom and I went to mine, where I peeled off my suit and sprawled out on my bed and didn't open my eyes until the next day, when I heard garbage trucks on the street and pots and pans clanging in the kitchen.

"Good morning," Tina said as I stood in the doorway and she scrambled eggs on the stove while Miranda Lambert blared from the radio. Kyle was sitting at the table, all blond hair and tan skin and muscles beneath a shirt that said *Baruch College.* "Want something to eat?"

I nodded, watching her sing with the music and cheerfully add pepper to the eggs like she was a stay-at-home mom jacked up on Prozac. I slid into a chair beside Kyle and leaned toward his ear. "I'm warning you," I whispered, "don't do her wrong."

He edged his chair away from me as Tina glided to the table with a pan in her hands, and then she spooned breakfast onto our plates while I prayed that Kyle wouldn't erase her smile.

I sat at my desk an hour later, trying to read but seeing nothing except Ned and Darcelle devouring each other on that desk. I'd always felt sick at the thought of Jamie and Eva Lee doing the same thing, but that didn't seem as grotesque in comparison. At least they weren't breaking vows.

My phone buzzed. "Savannah," Kitty said through the speaker. "Come in here, please."

My knees were wobbly when I stood up from my chair, but I steeled myself as I walked toward Kitty's office, trying to find the best way to tell her about Ned and convincing myself that I was doing the right thing. I couldn't let her continue to be deceived by a philandering man-whore, could I?

I adjusted the lapels on my blazer and walked through the doorway. Kitty was behind her desk, and on top of it sat a vase filled with peonies.

"Like the flowers?" she asked with a radiant smile. She was in a teal dress, her hair was pinned up, and her deep brown eyes glimmered. "They're from Ned."

He'd gotten to her first, but I should have expected that. "Of course they are," I said flatly. "I mean . . . are they another early birthday gift?"

She shook her head and stroked the diamond circle dangling from her neck. "They're a congratulations present. I scored an interview with a top politician . . . I can't tell you her name because the interview isn't official yet, but trust me . . . it's in the bag. Anyway," she said, leaning back in her chair, "it'll be good for *Femme,* and I'm so happy," she said as I sat opposite her. "You know . . . this time last year, I was a disaster. But now . . ." She looked out her window and smiled at Manhattan. "Everything's gotten better . . . and it's so funny how things change, isn't it?"

I kept my eyes on her while she admired skyscrapers and smokestacks and puffs of white clouds in the blue summer sky. "Yes," I said, "it is."

She looked at me. "Forgive me for babbling. So . . . you're coming to my party, right? It'll be perfect if you're there. You can't ruin perfect."

I left Kitty's office without letting her know about Ned because she was right—I couldn't ruin what she mistook for perfect. But I wanted to kill Ned for backing me into a corner, sticking me in the middle of a sordid mess, and turning me into a con artist. I hadn't lied, but hiding the truth was just as bad and maybe worse.

"Where is he?" I asked Ned's drab secretary five minutes later. She pointed toward the conference room where Ainsley and I had been last night. I marched down the hall, opened the door, and found Ned sitting at the head of the long table like a king, surrounded by dark walls and glowing lamps. His head was bent over a thick document, and he was scrawling notes in its margins with a silver pen.

"Close the door if you're going to throw your usual tantrum," he said without looking up.

I slammed it, marched toward the table, and stood beside him. "I talked to Kitty."

He stopped writing. His shoulders tensed beneath his pin-striped suit. "And?"

I exhaled a heavy breath. "And even though you might be wrong about her not believing me . . . I didn't say anything."

He started scribbling again. "Good girl," he said.

I snatched the pen from his hand, leaving a jagged blue line across a page that looked important and official. "Did anybody ever tell you that you're very patronizing?"

He slid his eyes from the paper to my fingers. "Did anybody ever tell *you* that a Visconti pen isn't a toy?" He reached out and took it back. "Now if you're done reporting that you're learning to do as you're told, you can leave. I have work to do . . . and so do you. Get back to your trivial job or I'll be forced to fire you."

He returned to reading and scribbling. I grabbed his papers.

"I'll never do what you tell me, Ned. This was *my* choice. But just because I saved your sorry ass for Kitty's sake doesn't mean I'll do it again. The decision I made has consequences."

He leaned back in his chair and let out an impatient sigh. "And what exactly are *those*?"

I squared my shoulders. "Get rid of Darcelle. Send her away."

He reached out to yank his papers from my hand. "You're out of your mind," he said.

I sat in a chair beside him. "I'll only keep your filthy secret if the affair stops."

"*Affair?*" he said scornfully. "Christ, you're sappy. It's just a casual arrangement."

Why didn't this surprise me? "That woman has to go," I said. "Stone News has offices all over the world, and I'm sure you can find a job for her elsewhere . . . somewhere far away and dangerous with bad-hair weather. It's what she's earned, don't you think?"

Ned tossed his pen onto the table. "Well," he said, "maybe you *are* a Stone. I'm moderately impressed by your negotiating skills. But the thing is . . . you're out of your league. So run along."

"Okay," I said perkily, springing up from my chair. "I'll just spill everything to Kitty."

He kept quiet as I crossed the room. My hand was on the doorknob when he said, "All right," in a taut voice. "You have a deal, you second-rate extortionist."

I whirled around. "Smart move," I said, walking toward him. I plopped into my seat and rested my feet on the table. "Send Darcelle to the Middle East."

"Don't get carried away. She'll go to Los Angeles."

"Nope," I said. "I want her to leave the United States."

"Come *on*," he said, pushing away from the table. His chair rolled backward and skimmed the wall. "You're not serious, are you?"

"It's the only way I can be sure you won't keep seeing her."

He combed his fingers through his thick hair. "Fine, God damn you. It'll be Paris, then."

"Too glamorous, I'm afraid. Got anything else?"

A crooked vein throbbed in his forehead. "Is Moscow dreary enough?"

"Well," I said, "the frigid air will dry her skin and cause premature aging, and the lack of sunlight might result in chronic depression . . . so I suppose Moscow will have to do."

He rolled his eyes. "Are we done now? Have I satisfied your sadistic tendencies?"

"If I have those . . . it's just additional proof that I've got Stone blood."

"Or maybe it just shows me," Ned replied, grabbing his pen, "that you're a more serious problem than I thought. And the best way to deal with a serious problem is to eliminate it."

He was glaring at me, but I didn't move an inch. I stayed in my seat, swung my feet back to the carpet, and crossed my legs. "Our negotiations aren't over, Ned. Another item on the agenda is that Kitty wants us to get along."

"Yes," he said musingly. "She has this odd obsession with family harmony. Maybe I need to get her some counseling for that."

"Get yourself some first. But for now, think about this: It'd benefit both of us to keep the peace in her presence. Do you agree?"

He twirled his pen slowly between two fingers. "Reluctantly and under duress," he said after some thought. "And now that our business is done, I'd advise you to get out of here before I bash your fucking head in."

I laughed at that threat as he hunched over his document and started reading again. "One more thing," I said, to which he slammed his fist against the table and gave me an irate stare. "If I ever catch you with another woman . . . if I even hear a whisper of gossip about you and any woman who isn't your wife . . . this contract is null and void."

. . .

It was noon and my lunch hour, and I was sitting in the back of a cab heading toward West 41st when my cell rang. I answered it, and Mom's voice was on the other end.

"I haven't heard from you in a while," she said.

I felt terrible. Things had been so crazy and time had sped by so quickly that I hadn't even thought to pick up the phone. "I'm sorry," I said.

"Just because I don't approve of you being in New York doesn't mean I'm not interested in what you're doing. And I worry about you much more than when you were here."

I turned toward the half-open window. The cab was passing vending carts, and the air smelled like sausages and roasted peanuts. "I know . . . and I need your advice more than ever."

"About what?" she asked.

I sighed, twirling my hair as I stared through the window. "Do you think it's wrong to keep a secret from someone if telling the truth might destroy her life?"

"I think I need more information," Mom said, so I gave her the tawdry details while my cab made its way through traffic. "What I think," Mom said when I was finished, "is that you've done everything you can. And even though Ned's lower than dirt, you can't hold him completely responsible. *Do not judge by appearances, but judge with right judgment.*"

She was spouting scripture again. "What does *that* mean?"

"It means he's spent his life in a world where lying and cheating and breaking vows is normal. That boy didn't stand a chance."

Leave it to Mom to get Christian about someone as awful as Ned Stone. But I didn't want to think about him anymore, so I moved on. "I'll be sending you some money today. I'm going to the bank on my way back from lunch."

"Don't send me anything," she said.

"Can't hear you," I lied as the taxi stopped and I shoved a twenty into the driver's hand. I said good-bye to Mom, stepped out of the cab, and walked into the lobby of a six-story building where I waited until Tina came out of an elevator in a sharp tan suit.

"What are you doing here?" she asked, giving me a puzzled stare.

"I just wanted to see how the interview went."

Her puffy lips spread into a smile. "They want me to start tomorrow."

I gleefully clasped my hands together, thinking that good fortune had finally come her way. "Like I said before . . . they'll be lucky to have you. And now I think I should take you somewhere special for lunch to celebrate."

"Do *you* have anything to celebrate?" she asked as we left the building and stepped onto the sidewalk, where a man in a hard hat was breaking up concrete with a jackhammer at the end of the block. It was so loud that Tina had to raise her voice for me to hear. "I mean," she said, "have you liberated Kitty?"

I took in a sharp breath. I'd told Mom about my deal with Ned, but I couldn't bring myself to admit it to anyone else. "I just couldn't do it. And I don't want to talk about it anymore," I said, hailing a cab that brought us to Fifth Avenue and the restaurant where I'd eaten with Kitty. It was as crowded and sunny as it was then, we had the same waitress, and I shook my head when she offered us menus.

"We know what we want," I said. "We'll both have that pasta-with-mushrooms thing."

Tina screwed up her face after the waitress left. "I can order for myself, Savannah. And you *know* I don't like mushrooms."

I sighed, watching as she unbuttoned her blazer. "You *don't* know if you like mushrooms . . . you've never tried them. Expand your horizons. Be open-minded."

She stopped unbuttoning. "What does *that* mean? Am I usually *narrow*-minded?"

"It just means you should try something different. A new experience is waiting for you."

She clicked her tongue against the roof of her mouth. "Where'd you get *that* line from?"

Jack, I thought, but didn't say it. I didn't want to seem unoriginal. My phone rang, and I reached into my purse to grab it just as the waitress returned with ice water and a basket of bread. I looked at the phone and saw a number with a 718 area code and the name *Alex Adair.*

I gasped. "It's the second guy . . . the bartender."

Tina took the lemon wedge off her glass. "Answer it. He can't be worse than the first."

"There's nothing wrong with Jack," I said peevishly. "What happened was Ned's fault."

She sucked on the lemon and shrugged her shoulders. "I wouldn't think too highly of a man who's so easily swayed. It's a bad indication of his character."

I didn't have time to think much about what she'd said because my phone was on its last ring before my voice mail kicked in. I answered it, holding my hand over my ear to block the noise coming from a table beside us filled with chattering businesspeople.

"Savannah," said a deep voice, "this is Alex . . . from the party at the library the other night. I was one of the bartenders . . . you said it'd be okay to call."

His voice was as smooth as Jack's, but he sounded younger and innocent, like a freshly scrubbed schoolboy asking me to a homecoming dance. I couldn't believe he'd think I wouldn't remember him, but I loved that he did.

"I haven't forgotten you, Alex."

"Oh," he said with a dab of surprise. "Well . . . I just wanted to ask if you're free this weekend. I thought we could go out, and maybe we could . . . I don't know—"

He seemed nervous, so I had to cut in and rescue him. "Maybe you could come with me to a party in the Hamptons on Saturday night. It's for Kitty Stone's birthday."

"Kitty Stone?" he said after a pause. "Man, I don't know. I doubt the Stone family would want me there if I wasn't bartending."

The waitress came back with steaming plates that she put on the table. Tina picked up a fork and started poking at her lunch like it was roadkill while I took a deep breath, deciding to learn from my mistakes. I was going to avoid disaster by being honest with Alex from the start.

I let him in on the basic facts of who I was as Tina extracted mushrooms from her pasta. "I'm part of the Stone family," I said after I told Alex everything. "And *I* say you're welcome at the party. So will you go?"

He paused again. "I'm not sure I'll be the right date, Savannah."

"Alex," I said as I remembered Ned's smug smile, "you'll be the *perfect* date."

Fourteen

It was late afternoon on Saturday, and I stood in my bedroom as I slipped into a sundress that I'd bought at Saks. It was strapless, with a full skirt, a smocked back, and a pattern of pink and yellow flowers. I wore a new taupe eye shadow with my glitter lipstick, and my hair tumbled over my shoulders in blondish-brown waves. I brushed it while Tina prepared dinner for Kyle and filled the apartment with the scent of chicken-fried steak.

"Want one?" she asked.

We were in the kitchen. Tina offered me a tray of cheese-smeared Ritz crackers, and I shook my head. Processed appetizers suddenly seemed like poison compared to what was on the menu at Masa and Fifth Avenue lunch spots.

Her forehead creased. "But you love my pimento cheese spread. I even put in chopped pecans . . . just the way you like it."

She shoved the tray at me. I gently pushed it away.

"I don't want that stuff on my new dress," I said.

Her eyes grew big and round. "When did you become such a snob? I've seen you eat Cheez Whiz straight from the can . . .

and one time in high school, you finished a whole plate of deep-fried Twinkies in a single Sunday afternoon. Don't deny it."

Why did she have to remind me of my ugliest moments when I was all glammed up? I'd even bought a wide-brimmed straw hat that was dyed pink and had a yellow flower bursting out of the side. It was in my hand, and I stuck it on my head.

"I'm not in high school anymore," I said, glancing around the kitchen. The garbage can overflowed, eggshells and uncooked elbow noodles covered the countertops, and the stove was splattered with grease. "Are you going to clean up at some point?"

She tapped her shoe against the floor and accidentally crushed a pecan. "I don't give much thought to cleaning, Savannah. You know I had a maid at home. And even if I *had* considered fixing this place up, I wouldn't have had time . . . I've been busy with the shelter and Kyle."

She was so enamored with him that I doubted she'd care I hadn't asked her to be my plus one. And he'd distracted her from Tony, which was a very good thing.

"Whatever," I said. "I'd better get going."

Tina put the tray on the table and looked me up and down. "You don't deserve a compliment right now . . . but the dress suits you well. And the hat is precious."

I felt bad for getting testy even though her slovenly ways and total resistance to change were starting to grate on my nerves. I thanked her, left the apartment, and went downstairs, where I had to wait just a few minutes for Tony to pull up in the sedan.

"Don't you look spiffy," he said after I slipped into the front seat. "Where are we going?"

I adjusted the rim of my hat as I studied my reflection in the windshield. It was cloudy outside, but that wasn't going to make me ditch the most crucial part of my ensemble. "To the Hamptons," I answered, "but first we need to pick up my date."

He raised an eyebrow. "Don't tell me you're back with Jackson Lucas."

I looked at him. His auburn hair was freshly shorn. "I'm not . . . but what if I was?"

"I'd tell you it was a mistake. You don't belong with a guy like that."

"Oh, really? Why's that? Because Jack's worldly and I'm not?" I pointed my finger at Tony. "Let me tell you something . . . in case you haven't noticed, I'm getting more sophisticated every day."

He settled into his seat and slung his arm across the back of mine. "I only meant he's not the right guy for you. And you don't need to be any more sophisticated . . . you're great the way you are."

It was hard to take a compliment when it wasn't the one I wanted. I scrunched up my mouth, folded my arms, and stared at a passing bicyclist. "Thanks," I mumbled.

"So who's the new guy?" Tony asked.

"Nobody you've heard of," I said, and reached into my purse to grab my phone. Then I scrolled through it for an address that Alex had texted. "But you two have something in common . . . he lives on Staten Island."

Tony's GPS led us to a town called South Beach and a modest house with beige shutters and a picture window. It had a maple tree and neatly sculpted hedges that I passed on my way to a front door painted red. I walked up five steps and rang the bell, listening to noise from backyards—a lawn mower, an electric saw, kids laughing and splashing around in a swimming pool.

"Are you sure this is the right address?" Tony called from the car after I'd pushed the bell twice and nobody answered.

I double-checked my phone. "Positive," I said. Then I peeked into the front window at granny décor—antique furniture, an afghan on a couch covered in plastic, and a china cabinet stacked with gold-rimmed plates.

Tony got out of the car, climbed the steps, and stood beside me. "Maybe we should check the yard," he suggested.

"Maybe," I said, hoping Alex hadn't bailed on our date. There was no excuse for a man who'd let a girl buy a new outfit and then take away her reason for wearing it.

We headed toward the yard, which was enclosed by a fence. I heard the buzz of a saw, turned my head, and saw Alex standing on a ladder and cutting branches off a tree. His shirt hung over a lounge chair, his arms were above his head, and his biceps bulged.

"Alex!" Tony shouted from behind me.

I jumped, startled out of my lustful trance. I glanced over my shoulder at Tony, who was smiling and waving. "What's going on?" I asked as Alex turned off the saw and started to climb down the ladder. "You know him?"

"Yeah . . . but I didn't know *you* did. Alex and I are friends . . . neighbors, too. We live in the same apartment building," Tony said, turning his attention from me to Alex, who was walking toward us on the grass. "What are you doing here?" Tony asked. "Did you win some money in Atlantic City and buy a house?"

Alex smiled, and my knees almost buckled. He was close enough for me to see the light spattering of hair across his chest and a fading surgical scar down the center of his washboard abs. "This is my grandmother's place," he said. "She's been in the hospital, and she's coming back tomorrow. I promised not to let the house fall apart while she was gone." His blue eyes shifted between me and Tony. "And what exactly is the connection between you two? I'm baffled."

Tony explained that he was my driver while I tried not to drool. I felt like I was in one of those commercials where a shirtless, hunky construction worker drinks a Coke in full view of sexually frustrated office women and everything happens in sultry slow motion.

"Sorry I'm not dressed, Savannah," Alex said, glancing at the worn-out jeans that hung low on his waist. "I guess I lost track of time . . . I thought you wouldn't be here for a while."

As if he needed to apologize for how he looked. And now that I thought about it, Tony and I actually *were* a little early. Alex invited us to wait inside while he got cleaned up, and a few minutes later Tony and I sat across from each other in the living room as we listened to a shower running down the hall.

Tony shifted in his chair. The plastic covering the cushion squeaked. "I like this," he said. "You and Alex, I mean. I approve of the situation."

I took off my hat, put it on my lap, and combed my fingers through my hair, hoping the humidity hadn't wilted my curls. "That's good to know, Dad. I'm sure Alex will ask you for my hand in marriage very soon."

"Don't crack wise with me, young lady. I'm just saying that Alex is the sort of person I can see you with. He's a good guy. I've known him for a few years . . . he's the cage fighter I mentioned."

"Cage fighter?" I said. "He's a bartender . . . and an aspiring actor and writer."

"He is . . . but he fights on the side. Well, he used to, that is. He stopped about a year ago. Did you notice that scar on his stomach? It's from his last fight. He got kicked so hard that it ruptured his spleen."

I winced. "Is that why he stopped fighting?"

The pipes creaked when the shower shut off. We knew Alex could probably hear us now, so we stopped gossiping. And a few minutes later, he was in the living room, dressed in tan pants and a black polo shirt, smelling of soap and aftershave and a masculine musk that made me want to tear off his shirt and kiss his scar.

"Are you ready?" I asked demurely, clutching my hat.

He nodded, and then I put the hat back on and we sat together in the rear of the sedan while Tony chauffeured us to Windmill Lane in East Hampton and left us at a huge house on a sprawling piece of property that was surrounded by cherry trees and had a curving gravel driveway crammed with expensive cars. The roof was peaked and it had four chimneys, and inside were soaring ceilings and French doors through which I saw a kidney-shaped pool and a big tent set up in the backyard.

"Savannah," Kitty said, weaving through the crowded living room as she headed in my direction. Her red hair had been ironed stick straight, and she wore her eternity-ring necklace with a white sundress. "I'm so glad you came," she said before moving her eyes toward Alex. "But this isn't Tina."

I felt him tense up beside me. "This is Alex," I said. "He's—"

"An amazing bartender," Kitty said, giving him a smile. "Welcome to my party."

We followed her outside and into the tent, where there were twenty tables draped in ivory cloth and a cocktail hour was in full swing. People filled their plates from a buffet and a live band played the kind of music I'd heard at the club on Murray Street with Jack.

Some of the guests were talking to Fabian Spader as he stroked his strawberry-blond hair, and his sidekick photographer snapped pictures of them with a blinding flash. Alex took a glass of wine from a waiter while I sampled caviar on toast and decided that Tina *was* kind of narrow-minded, because it didn't taste all that bad.

Someone tapped my shoulder. I turned around and saw my reflection in cat's-eye glasses.

"What do you think this is?" Caroline asked. "The Kentucky Derby?"

I tried not to let her snarkiness bother me. Someone who chose to pair a denim miniskirt with combat boots and wear them to a birthday party was in no position to criticize.

"Ladies can wear hats indoors," I said. "Gentlemen must take them off."

She rolled her eyes at my etiquette lesson and gave Alex the once-over. "Unwise choice," she said, like he couldn't hear. "Does my brother know?"

I shrugged, thinking about my verbal contract. "Ned won't say a word."

"Oh, *really*? Let's see about that," she said, turning away and swerving through the crowd of guests, most likely searching for Ned so she could tattle on me. I watched as she found him standing in a corner with Virginia.

"What's going on?" Alex asked.

I kept my eyes on Caroline, who whispered in Ned's ear while Virginia gave me a chilly glare. "Nothing," I said, relishing the childish crankiness on Caroline's face when she stormed away from Ned and disappeared into the house, nearly crashing into Ainsley and a silver-haired man who was probably her father. I recognized him as the speaker at the gala who'd commemorated Edward Stone. An attractive woman with long curly brown tresses followed Caroline inside, and I turned toward Alex. "She's rude. Ignore her."

"*You* should, too. I think your hat's adorable. And so are you."

I wanted to say the same, but I didn't. I just smiled, took his hand, and led him to a table where we ate dinner while a singer crooned an Ella Fitzgerald tune as the sun faded from the sky.

"How's the writing coming along?" Alex asked.

It was getting dark, waiters were serving cake, and candlelight flickered against Alex's face. "I've been slacking since I arrived in New York. And you?"

He sat back in his chair. "Another submission was turned

down. I also didn't make it past the first round of an audition for a small part in an independent film. I've been through so much rejection that I'm close to giving up."

"You can't. I felt like that once, too, but everything changed in a second. You never know when things might get better. You just have to hold on until it does," I said, and even though Alex smiled, I felt my cheeks flush. I'd meant what I said, but I sounded as rah-rah as Ainsley. I cleared my throat, a waiter slid slices of cake in front of us, and then I went back to our original topic. "Do you have much time to write?"

He sipped his coffee. "Not as much as I'd like. Work keeps me busy."

"Is that why you quit cage fighting?"

He put his cup down. His whole body stiffened. "How'd you know I used to fight?"

Dishes shattered. A tray rolled along the floor and stopped at my feet. I glanced across the tent, where a waiter was apologizing to a table of guests as he crouched down to the floor. Then a tall man with blondish hair got out of his seat, squatted beside the waiter, and helped him pick up shards of porcelain and forks smeared with vanilla icing. The light in the tent was so dim that it took me a moment to realize the man was Jack, whose eyes connected with mine.

"Savannah," Alex said. "What's wrong?"

I turned toward him, feeling flustered and dizzy and very, very guilty. My pulse shouldn't have been racing for Jack when I was with Alex. Besides, Jack had probably forgotten about me anyway and was back to courting European models.

"Everything's fine," I said, snapping out of my daze. I took off my hat and set it on an empty chair. "You asked how I knew you used to fight, and . . . Tony told me."

Alex's face was straight and serious. "What else did he tell you?"

"Nothing," I said. "Why? Is cage fighting illegal or something?"

He shook his head as his body relaxed into his chair. "It is in New York, which is why I did it in New Jersey. But then I just . . . wasn't interested anymore."

I nodded. "So how'd you get into it in the first place?"

He chuckled. "When your father's an ex-boxer and has three sons who play football and one who aspires to join the drama club and write novels . . . you get pushed into more traditionally masculine activities."

I laughed, too, and a few minutes later I excused myself and went into the house, which was empty except for the catering staff washing dishes in the kitchen. I stuck my head through the doorway to ask for directions to the bathroom, and a pudgy woman at the sink told me it was down the hall and on the left.

The only problem was there were three doors on the left, each made of dark wood with a crystal knob. I opened one, but the bathroom wasn't inside. This room was a study that was faintly lit by the moonlight streaming into the windows. I squinted through the shadows at dark walls and photos on a fireplace mantle, and then I saw a wall made entirely of shelves that contained only leather-bound books.

They seemed to be antiques and I knew I shouldn't snoop, but antique books fascinated me. So I closed the door and crept across the room, where I ran my finger along a row of gilded hardbacks. I had just pulled one out when the door opened and Caroline came in with the brunette who'd followed her into the house during the cocktail hour. They didn't see me.

"I'm tired of hiding," the woman said. "You shouldn't be so afraid of your family."

"My brother knows," Caroline told her.

"But your mother doesn't. You've been hiding us from her since college."

"I don't want to talk about my mother," Caroline said with an exasperated sigh. Then her voice turned low and flirty, and she took the woman's hand in hers. "We came in here to focus on *us* . . . and that's much more interesting, isn't it?"

The book dropped from my hand, falling to the carpet with a thump that made the brown-haired lady turn toward me and let out a startled gasp. I pressed my back against the shelves, wishing I could disappear as Caroline flipped a switch to turn on a light. When she saw me, her eyes widened, then narrowed and finally blazed.

"Get out," she said in a deep growl.

Why did I keep walking in on Stone secrets? I kept my eyes on the carpet as I slipped into the hallway, and I was near the kitchen when I heard clunky footsteps behind me and felt a hand catch my arm. Then Caroline stepped in front of me. Her face was flushed, and her jagged black bangs clung to her sweaty forehead.

"Listen," I said, holding my voice down so everyone in the kitchen wouldn't hear. "It's none of my business or anyone else's. I won't tell a soul."

She spoke in an acrid whisper. "You won't tell . . . if *what*? What are the conditions? That's how it works with you, right? You'll keep this a secret if I do something for you?"

"No," I said. "I don't want you to—"

"Stop playing pure and innocent, Savannah. I know you're blackmailing my brother . . . otherwise he wouldn't stay quiet about your bringing that bartender here. You've clearly castrated Ned, but I don't know what you've got on him. So spare me a sleepless night and tell me the truth. Is he having an affair?"

She'd figured everything out. And she was making me feel

horrible—conniving and vengeful and sly—but I'd concocted that deal with Ned for Kitty's sake, and I was sticking to it.

"I know how to keep a secret," I said. "I'm just not sure why you're keeping yours. These days, nobody cares if—"

She scoffed. "Don't be naïve. People care. In my case, it's the important people."

How are you ever going to find a husband? Virginia had said. I supposed that was why Caroline had to hide in dark rooms, but what I'd seen in one of them would never go further.

"You should sleep well tonight, Caroline," I said, daring to pat her shoulder.

She shrugged me off and took a step back. "What the hell is that supposed to mean?"

I sighed. It was so hard to be decent to that girl. "It means," I said, "you shouldn't worry about anything . . . especially not about me."

She just stared. I turned around and walked away, feeling her eyes on the back of my head. As smart as she was, I was sure she hadn't seen that one coming.

Fifteen

Fabian Spader blocked my way to the tent. "Having a sisterly chat?" he said as he leaned against the door and sipped a cocktail. He was inappropriately dressed as usual, in battered jeans and a mint-green shirt with a striped scarf looped around his neck.

"Is this all you do?" I asked. "Lurk around and eavesdrop on personal conversations?"

"Mostly," he said. "At the moment, however, I'm curious about what you were just discussing. I mean, you can't have anything in common with Caroline. She's homely. Her fashion sense is appalling. And she's such a bookish dullard."

I perched one hand on my hip. "*I* happen to be bookish, too."

He rubbed his pointy chin, sliding his grayish eyes upward from my feet and lingering on my chest. "You hide it well, Savannah. From the way the men around here have been gawking at you, I think they're devising plans to lure you into the backseats of their pricey cars."

"Well," I said, "I don't get into strange men's backseats. And I'm here with a date."

Fabian nodded, stirring his drink. "Yes, I noticed you're

slumming . . . and you're fickle. What happened to Jackson Lucas? You were quite chummy with him at the gala last week, and
he can't seem to take his eyes off you tonight."

He couldn't? I hadn't noticed. I'd been trying so hard to pretend he wasn't here.

"Jack's a delicious subject," Fabian went on when I didn't
answer his question. "He's the sort my readers want to know
about . . . handsome, educated, successful. It's impossible to walk
a block in Manhattan without passing a building he doesn't own."

Jack hadn't told me *that*. He was even more modest than I'd
thought. "He isn't a *subject*," I said. "He's a person."

"Why, of course he is. He's a *fascinating* person. So tell me
what you know about him."

I groaned, feeling like I needed a scalding shower to scrub
Fabian's sleaziness off me. "I don't know anything," I said, "except that you should find another career."

He snickered. "But I'm so good at this one, sweetie. And I
want the two of us to be the very best of friends. I guess I'll have
to think of something to make you fall in love with me."

I scooted past him and into the tent, where his photographer lurched forward and snapped my picture. Blue and yellow
splotches floated across my vision as I made my way back to my
table and plopped into the chair beside Alex.

"I'm sorry for taking so long," I said. "I got caught in a couple of unexpected conversations."

There was a soft tap on my bare shoulder; I twisted around to
find Kitty smiling down at me while she held hands with Ned.
"We're just checking on everyone," she said. "Are you two having a good time?"

"Yeah," Alex replied as Ned and I locked eyes. I'd never seen
him out of a suit before; he was dressed like Alex, in casual pants
and a polo shirt, and he kept staring at me as if he was afraid I'd
make a sudden move. "Thank you for having me."

Kitty jammed her elbow into Ned's ribs. He slowly unlaced his fingers from hers and offered his hand to Alex. "Glad you could come," he said with a stiff smile. "No hard feelings about that misunderstanding at the gala?"

Alex glanced between me and Ned. "All's forgiven . . . as long as Savannah agrees."

"Oh," I said blithely, summoning my best acting skills, "it's forgiven and forgotten."

Kitty's face brightened. "I'm thrilled to hear that. So why don't we make a new beginning to this brother-sister relationship? Give each other a hug and start fresh."

No. No, no, no, no, *no*. I didn't want to hug him. I didn't want to touch him. I could barely stand to breathe the same air. But Kitty was nudging me and everybody at the table was staring, and before I knew it I was standing up and Ned's hulking frame was pressed against me. I had to squelch a gag to keep my dinner down.

"See what you've done?" he whispered into my ear.

"You started it," I said through a frozen grin.

We stepped away from each other, and Kitty clapped her hands like we'd just signed an international peace treaty. I glanced around the tent, where I saw Ainsley talking with her father, Jack looking my way, Fabian eyeing me and typing into his iPhone, and Caroline sitting next to the brunette. Then there was Virginia, who rose from her chair and crossed the floor with the most graceful posture, as if she'd been trained to walk with a book on her head. Her chin was up, her back was straight, and her hips swayed ever so slightly beneath her chic beige dress until she stopped beside Ned.

"What on earth are you doing, dear?" she asked through a fake smile.

"What he *should* be doing," Kitty said. "He's getting along with Savannah."

Virginia's black lashes fluttered as she shifted her eyes toward me. "Well," she said, biting her lip to stifle a laugh while she examined my dress and my date. "That's a matter of opinion." She reached up to smooth Ned's hair. "I think you have more important guests to see."

He walked away with her, and Kitty followed them, glancing at me over her shoulder. She rolled her eyes and smiled.

I dropped into my chair, completely exhausted.

"Are you okay?" Alex asked.

I nodded. "I'm sorry again . . . I didn't mean to expose you to so much drama."

"I don't care," he said with a shrug. "I've learned how to tolerate these people . . . but what about you? Did you really want to make up with Ned?"

"No," I whispered. "I can't stand him."

"Then why'd you do it?"

I shrugged and talked about something else. I'd learned from the Jack disaster that it was better to be honest, and I'd tried to do that so far with Alex. Still, I couldn't tell him why my peace with Ned was just an illusion.

Tony picked us up a half hour later. We sat in the back of the car, where Alex pinched his forehead when we were a block from my building.

"Do you have a headache?" I asked.

"Too much wine," he said with a nod.

I took him inside to give him aspirin while Tony waited in the car, reading one of his library books. Alex turned to me when we were in the elevator and the doors slammed shut.

"This is a real nice place," he said.

"I know. But I didn't do anything to deserve it."

He shrugged. "Maybe you did . . . and you just don't know it."

The doors parted after we reached the eleventh floor. Then we were at my apartment, where I stuck my key into the lock and opened the door. All the lights were on and Tina was slumped on the couch, an ashtray filled with lipstick-stained Marlboro butts and a *People* magazine by her side. She was all gussied up, but her hair was lifeless and her skin was white and wan.

She sniffed and covered the ashtray with her magazine, and I pretended I didn't notice. She looked so sad that I had to forgive her for smoking this time.

"I didn't know you were bringing company home," she said, wiping a damp streak of mascara from her cheek.

"You remember Alex from the gala," I said.

She forced a smile. "You work with Kyle."

Alex nodded and smiled back. "He mentioned you two have been dating."

"Oh," she said with her husky laugh, "that must've been before he stood me up."

I looked at the coffee table and a plate of untouched Ritz crackers covered with pimento cheese. Maybe when I told Kyle not to do Tina wrong I should have threatened death or disfigurement. Maybe he didn't know how rotten it was to let a girl slave over a stove and spend an hour choosing her best outfit for nothing. She was putting on her I-don't-care act, but I didn't buy it. Alex didn't seem to, either, because his smile faded as I took a seat beside Tina.

"I'm sorry," seemed the best thing to say.

"Not even a phone call," she said, and then turned toward Alex, who was standing in the glow of a lamp. "Can you please explain to me why men are such jerks?"

"Well," he said in his smooth voice, "not all of us are. But whenever you get rid of a guy who is, you get closer to somebody who isn't. You're clearing the way."

I wanted to hug him, but I didn't. I also didn't remind Tina that men like Kyle wouldn't hurt her this much if she didn't let them get so close too soon. She made the same mistake constantly and kept expecting a different result, and that infuriated me. But now wasn't the time to bring it up.

"I have so much food in the kitchen," Tina said, and looked at Alex. "I reckon you don't like southern cooking, do you? I'll give you some to take home if you want to give it a try."

His lips parted into a wide smile that brought out the most charming crinkles around his eyes. "I like *all* cooking," he said, and then Tina went into the kitchen and he sat next to me.

"Thanks," I said. "It was sweet of you to tell her that . . . about men, I mean."

He leaned forward, resting his wrists on his knees. "I meant it. I used to tell my little sister the same thing after her high school heartbreaks. Now she's engaged to a great guy."

"So you have a sister . . . and you mentioned three brothers. Is that the whole family?"

"Other than my father," he said. "Mom passed away two years ago. I also have nieces and nephews . . . and everybody's getting together at my grandma's house for a barbecue tomorrow afternoon to welcome her home from the hospital. I'm going to invite Tony and his family, too. It'll be a comedown compared to the Hamptons, but if you'd like to join us . . ."

"It'll be a step up," I said. "I'd be happy to join you."

Someone rapped on the front door; I opened it and found Tony standing in the hallway. He came inside and threw up his arms. "Does it take fifteen minutes to swallow two aspirin?"

We'd been so occupied with Tina that we'd forgotten all about him, not to mention the aspirin. I rushed into the bathroom to get it, and when I came back Tina was standing in the living room, holding aluminum trays covered in foil and gazing at Tony.

"What's the matter with you, Savannah?" she said playfully. "You don't expect Alex to knock those things back dry, do you?"

I supposed not. But now that Kyle wasn't a distraction, leaving her unattended in such close proximity to Tony made me nervous. So I dashed into the kitchen and quickly returned with a Dasani that I gave to Alex along with the aspirin.

"Thanks," he said as I listened to Tina chatting with Tony about what lovely weather we were having. "So can I pick you up at noon tomorrow?" Alex asked, and after I nodded he leaned across the space between us, squeezed my shoulder, and kissed my cheek.

It weakened my knees. "I enjoyed seeing you tonight," I told him.

"And I enjoyed seeing *you,* Tony," Tina said. "I hope it happens again real soon."

He smiled politely as Tina gave Alex the trays. Then the guys left, and I wondered if I was the only one who'd noticed that the smile on Tina's face was much more than polite.

Tina woke me the next morning by shaking my shoulder and shoving an envelope in my face. "Somebody must've slipped this under the door last night," she said, sitting on the edge of my bed as I rubbed my eyes and then tore open the envelope. It held a note card with the initials *FS* printed on the front in raised gold letters, and inside the card was handwriting in tidy script:

I did my best to find the right words. ♥ *Fabian*

I sprang out of bed and raced to my office down the hall as Tina chased after me, asking what was wrong. I didn't answer; I just sat in front of the computer and pulled up *Nocturnal* with its blinking silver stars. Splashed across the screen was the picture Fabian's photographer had taken last night when I stepped into the tent. My eyes held a hint of surprise, my mouth was slightly open, my hair looked blonder on film than in reality, and the flash had been so bright that it gave me an ethereal glow. It was my best picture ever and I looked completely Photoshopped.

Tina was standing beside me.

"Recent South Carolina transplant Savannah Morgan, daughter of the late media mogul Edward Stone,"

she read off the screen,

"absolutely wowed the Hamptons last night with her Charleston charm. She's a delightful southern belle with beauty that's matched only by her brains, and my opinion is that she's going to be an amazing addition to New York's social scene. Welcome, Savannah . . . we're all so happy you're here."

I exhaled a shaky sigh. There were lots of anonymous comments below the post, and aside from a few lewd ones, most of what had been written was flattering, like

She's beautiful and *What a cute dress* and *Can I get her number?*

"Wow," Tina said, "I hardly even recognized you."

I sat on a lawn chair beside Alex in his grandmother's backyard. It was the first day of August, the sky was clear, the sun was shining, and the air smelled like the burgers roasting on a grill at the other side of the yard. Alex's family was sitting on the patio, strolling in and out of the house, talking and laughing beneath a tree while they gulped Budweiser. Tony was there with Allison and Marjorie, who raced toward me across the grass. Tony chased after his daughter, but she was too quick. She grabbed my knees and lifted herself onto my lap.

"Sorry," Tony said when he reached us.

"No need to be," I told him, stroking Marjorie's red hair as it flowed in the cool breeze. "Go spend some time with your wife . . . I'll take care of this little doll."

He smiled and rejoined Allison on the patio, where he put his arm around her and kissed her cheek. They were even cuter in real life than they were in their wedding picture.

Alex turned toward me. "You want one of these someday?" he asked, tickling Marjorie.

I wasn't sure if that was a rhetorical question or if he was offering to someday give me *one of these*. But I liked it either way. I liked that he was direct. Other than Jamie and Jack, the few guys I'd dated had never asked a more serious question than *Are your boobs real?*

"Sure do," I said, listening to kids jump into a pool next door. "But I'd like to accomplish a few things first. You know . . . simple goals like writing a *New York Times* bestselling novel."

He grinned as the breeze swept through his dark hair. "I'd settle for getting published."

Alex's grandmother crept up behind him and patted his back. She was a frail white-haired lady in her late eighties dressed in a polka-dotted housecoat. "Alex," she said, "I hate to bother you since you've done so much to keep my place up while I was gone . . . but the light in my bathroom isn't working and that electrician did such a shabby job last time. . . ."

"You're not bothering me, Grandma Frances," Alex said. "I'll fix it before I leave."

I smiled as she tousled his hair. Then she headed toward the patio, and I turned to Alex.

"How cute," I said as Marjorie reached down and yanked a dandelion from the grass "The way you call her Grandma Frances, I mean."

Alex shrugged. "I started doing that when I was a kid . . . so I wouldn't get my grandmas mixed up." He turned his eyes to Marjorie, who was offering him the dandelion. He took it, and then gave her a big smile and a soft pinch on her cheek. "Thank you, honey," he said before looking back at me. "So what do people call grandmothers in the South?"

"Mimaw," I said.

He laughed. "That's cute, too."

"I know. But I never got to say it. I didn't have any grand-mothers."

"Oh," Alex said after a moment. "Well . . . then you can share mine."

"Hey," a gravelly voice boomed from across the yard. "The food's ready."

It was Alex's father, who sat opposite me at a crowded picnic table a few minutes later. He was short and stocky, with gray hair and ruddy skin. *USMC* was tattooed on his forearm, a clad-dagh ring circled one of his fingers, and he wore a T-shirt printed with *Adair Plumbing of Staten Island*.

"So you're from the South," he said as I bit into a hamburger.

I swallowed. "Yes, sir . . . I was born and raised in Charleston."

"'Yes, *sir*,'" he echoed, nudging Tony beside him. "You see the good manners people have outside New York? And good looks, too," he said, giving me a wink. "I've never met a real southern belle before."

I'd been getting compliments since Alex and I arrived in his Honda. His family treated me as if I was something different, something special, like a rare antique they admired but didn't dare touch. "I'm not really a southern belle. I'm just an editor's assistant and a wannabe writer."

Mr. Adair wiped mustard off his mouth. "Writing's a nice thing for girls. My wife liked to write. She was a big reader, too . . . we'd go out to Jones Beach during the summer and she'd spend all day under an umbrella, reading those Danielle Steel novels and scrib-bling her own stories into notebooks." His voice trailed off and he gazed into the distance as if he could still see his wife sitting under that umbrella. He blinked and cleared his throat. "Anyway . . . this one right here," he said, pointing toward Alex next to me, "picked up that habit."

"If you don't mind my saying," Tony cut in. "Writing isn't a habit . . . it's a talent."

Mr. Adair took a swig of Budweiser. "It's a talent if it earns you a living. Otherwise it's a waste of time. But the thing is, my wife . . . may she rest in peace," he said, lifting his hand to bless himself, "indulged Alex too much. I wanted him to join the family business, but she was all for him going to college. I would've backed him on that if he'd studied something practical . . . something that'd get him a solid job. But what does he major in? Acting. Writing. It was just money in the garbage."

Alex put down his hamburger. Grandma Frances rubbed his hand.

"Oh, stop it," she said, turning to Mr. Adair. "He's a wonderful boy."

"That's exactly what my wife used to say. Babying him was her biggest mistake."

"At least she supported me," Alex muttered. "Someone had to."

Mr. Adair leaned forward. "*I* never supported you? How much time did I spend with you in the gym? You were a talented fighter. You could've had a future. But what did you do? You quit. You gave up the only thing you're good at."

I heard nothing but bees buzzing over a cluster of dandelions on the lawn. Everyone at the table had stopped talking and eating, and they were all staring at Alex, who kept his eyes on his father before he folded his napkin and tossed it on his plate.

Tony and I looked at each other. I got the feeling that Mr. Adair hadn't meant to blurt so much out, but he'd had a few beers and there it was, echoing in the air. I shifted my attention to Alex, who glanced at his sisters and his brothers and his nieces and nephews, smiling the way Tina did when she was pretending to be made of iron.

"Grandma Frances," he said, standing up, "I think I'll fix that light now."

. . .

The house was quiet except for the racket Alex was making—it sounded like he was rummaging through a toolbox. I followed the noise past the plastic-coated furniture, and then I walked down a narrow hallway and into a bathroom that had pink tiles and smelled of aerosol air freshener. Alex was sitting on the floor below an open window, dissembling a lighting fixture that looked as if it had been around since the Nixon administration.

"It's beyond repair," he said as he fiddled with wires. "I'll have to buy a new one."

I crouched down, thinking that he reminded me of a dedicated doctor in one of those medical shows who keeps shocking a patient's heart even when the patient is graveyard dead. I watched him for a while, and then I gently pulled his fingers from the light.

His hair was rumpled. There was a strip of sunburn across his nose and a smear of barbecue sauce on his chin that I rubbed off with my thumb.

"I'm sure," I said, "fighting isn't the only thing you're good at."

He looked at me, moving his blue eyes around my face—focusing on every part of it like something new he wanted to explore. Then he leaned his forehead against mine and we stayed on the tiles for a while with our arms wrapped around each other, listening to kids giggling and birds chirping and people splashing in the pool next door.

Sixteen

The air-conditioning in Alex's car was busted, so we rode back to Manhattan with the windows open. But that was okay, because it would've been a shame not to feel a night like this. August had broken July's stifling mugginess, bringing a premature hint of fall to the air that caressed my face as I watched the sun dip behind the skyline.

We were back at 15 Central Park West much too soon. I glanced out the window at the entrance, wanting to invite Alex inside but deciding against it. Things were unfolding slowly and it was best to keep it that way, to stretch out all the moments of newness and make them last.

He leaned over from his seat and wrapped his arms around me, resting his hands on the small of my back. My face fit perfectly in the crook of his neck, and his skin felt smooth against my cheek. He smelled like charcoal and fresh air.

"The submission you mentioned," I said, remembering his latest literary letdown, "I'd love to read it."

He leaned backward, keeping his arms around me. "Why?" he asked.

"Tina's always been my best editor," I said. "Maybe I can be yours."

He cocked his head to one side, mulling that over. "Okay," he answered finally, which made me all sorts of happy. He must have trusted me if he'd let me read something that had already been beaten with a red pen. "Text me your e-mail and I'll send it by tomorrow morning."

I nodded, pulled out my phone, and shot him my work address.

"Done," I said, shoving the phone back into my purse as my gaze stuck to his face. I wanted to look at him forever, to absorb all the details I hadn't noticed before—the yellowish-gold ring around his pupils, a tiny mole on his jaw, a thin scar below his right eyebrow that was probably another leftover from his fighting career. Everything was so beautiful that I wanted to feel it, so I reached out, rested my hand against the side of his face, and gently touched his scar with my thumb.

Alex moved my hand toward his mouth. He turned it over and pressed his lips against the center of my palm, giving it a kiss that made me breathe heavier. Then he lifted his head and leaned toward my face, lingering there for a moment as warm waves of anticipation flowed through me. He finally pulled me closer to him and kissed me—a gentle, sweet, slow kiss that tingled everything all the way down to my toes.

"Good night," I whispered afterward.

His forehead was pressed against mine. "*Now* it is," he said.

I had to force myself out of that car. Then I stood on the sidewalk, watched him drive away, and licked my lips in the elevator, still feeling Alex there. A few minutes later I was inside my apartment and I found Tina in the kitchen with a mixing bowl in her hands. I walked toward where she stood by the counter, stepping on an eggshell and crushing it beneath my sandals. Raw noodles were still scattered everywhere, the stove was greasier than ever, and trash spilled from the garbage pail onto the floor.

"Your lipstick is on your chin," she said dryly as she stirred batter. "And your face is red. Just a little hint: Check a mirror after you let a guy ram his tongue down your throat."

I ignored that crude remark. And what had just happened with Alex wasn't cheap and meaningless like she was making it sound, so I decided not to share it with her. "What have you been doing?" I asked as I rubbed my chin.

"Baking for the shelter," she said, pointing to cupcakes in neat rows on the table. "And I thought I'd give some of my delicacies to Tony."

I wasn't sure if she meant the cupcakes. "Don't give him *anything*."

She slammed down her bowl. "Don't boss me. And I was just trying to be productive. How else am I supposed to fill my weekend when you're out with your boyfriend?"

"Oh, I don't know . . . maybe you could start by cleaning this filthy mess."

She put her hands on her hips. "If you want your apartment cleaned, hire a maid. You sure can afford it now, can't you?"

I plopped into a chair at the table, thinking she was right. But it just seemed like wastefulness and sloth to pay somebody for what we could do ourselves. Still, I shouldn't have gotten snippy, especially after she'd been ditched by Kyle and I'd left her alone to think about it.

"Okay, Tina. I'll hire one as soon as I get a chance."

"Fine," she said testily. She crossed the room, pulled out a chair, sat opposite me, and leaned her face on her left palm. She drummed the fingers on her right hand against the table, staring into space like a bored housewife who'd spent all day with measuring cups and flour and had absolutely nothing to say.

"Have you told your dad how much you like your job?" I asked.

"Sure," she said with her eyes on the dishwasher. "He couldn't be more proud."

I was standing in the kitchen at work the next morning, pouring a cup of coffee, when someone poked my back and I turned around to face Ainsley. Her shiny hair was pulled off her face with a headband, and there were pearl studs in her ears.

"Did you enjoy Kitty's party?" she asked, but didn't take a breath to let me answer. "My dad and I thought it was *divine*. Wasn't that band terrific? Most people my age don't even know what jazz is, but I'm wild about it . . . I've got a Duke Ellington collection at home in Indiana. Oh, and did you see Caroline's friend? Or should I say *girl*friend?"

She giggled. I nearly dropped my mug. "Shhh," I said in a scolding whisper as I glanced around the kitchen and into the hallway to make sure nobody was listening. "That's Caroline's personal business. How'd you know, anyway?"

She crossed her arms and shrugged. "I didn't."

I went cold. *She's not nearly as stupid as she seems.* That's what Caroline had told me, and I'd just been outsmarted by a soon-to-be college freshman.

"Don't look so serious," Ainsley said with a disarming smile. "I won't tell anybody. I'm sure Ned wouldn't be happy if I did."

I want to work as an investigative TV news reporter or become a journalist who covers wars, she'd told me. She'd also bragged that Ned had *promised to say the most glowing things* about her when she started her job hunt after college. I didn't worry about her spreading gossip; getting on the bad side of a media empire wouldn't advance her lofty ambitions.

"Make sure you don't," I said, and went back to my cubicle, where Kitty was waiting.

"Do you need help with something?" I said as I sat down at my desk.

She shook her head and adjusted her diamond circle on its chain. "I wanted to ask if you have lunch plans. I'm taking Darcelle to Michael's since it's her last day here, and I thought you might like to come along. She's being transferred to Russia, if you can believe it."

I cleared my throat and crossed my legs and twirled my hair. "I actually do have plans," I said, which wasn't a complete lie. "I mean . . . I'm staying in, but I need to use the time to take care of a few personal things."

"Oh, okay," she said. "You know . . . I was thinking that when I hired you, we discussed the idea of you submitting short fiction for *Femme*. I've kept you so busy that you probably haven't had time to write . . . but I'd love to consider you for our October issue. The deadline is Friday."

I almost busted out in one of my high school cheers. "That'd be fantastic, Kitty," I said. "Thank you so much."

She smiled and headed to her office. I worked all morning, scheduling and researching and updating social media sites, and after Kitty headed out to Michael's I decided to devote my lunch hour to the short story that Alex had sent to my in-box.

Thanks in advance,

he'd written in his e-mail.

Want to have dinner tonight at seven?

I wrote back and accepted the invitation, adding that Tony could drop me off at his building after work. Then I started reading Alex's story, and I'd just finished the first page when my phone rang and the caller ID said *Tina Mae Brandt*.

"Want to grab lunch?" she asked. "I found a nice place near the shelter. I doubt it's as good as the Hominy Grill . . . but we can give it a shot."

I kept my eyes on the computer screen. "I can't. I'm editing a story for Alex, and I want to finish before we have dinner together tonight."

There was a pause. "You're seeing him *again*? That's three days in a row, you know."

I hadn't been keeping track, but *she* obviously had. I sighed, pushing my chair away from my desk. "I'm sorry, Tina. I asked you to come up here, and I don't mean to make you feel like—"

She let out her throaty laugh. "Like what? I feel fine."

I couldn't spend much time wondering if that was true. I had to finish Alex's story and all my work, and I also wanted to buy a new lighting fixture online for Grandma Frances and have it anonymously shipped to her house.

The day went by in a blur, and soon I was sitting beside Tony in the car, asking him to take me to wherever he lived, because I had a date with Alex.

"Well, well . . . ," Tony said in an amused voice, swerving to avoid a bus. "Things are heating up."

Not long after that we were on Staten Island, where Tony parked in front of an unassuming brick building with ten floors and fire escapes painted yellow. Alex was waiting outside, dressed in jeans and a T-shirt. Tony and I got out of the car and surrounded him.

"So where are we going?" I asked.

"Upstairs," Alex said.

Tony gave him a shove. "It's too soon for *that,* my friend."

Alex laughed. "Get it out of the gutter, buddy. I'm cooking dinner for her."

Jack had burned microwave popcorn. Jamie hadn't even known how to properly fry an egg. But Alex was practically a gourmet of Italian cuisine that he served inside his apartment—a small one-bedroom without enough windows that was neat and very clean.

"How'd you learn to cook?" I asked when we sat at a round table in his kitchen.

"My mother's parents were from Italy. They owned a restaurant in the Bronx. She learned how to cook from them, and she passed all of that on to me. She also insisted I make my bed every day and do my own laundry. *I'm not raising a mama's boy*, she used to say."

I swallowed a bite of garlic bread. "I think I would've liked her."

"She would've liked you, too," he said, raking his fingers through his hair. "By the way . . . my grandmother called a while ago. She said I don't need to buy a new light for her bathroom because one showed up at her door via express delivery late this afternoon. She called the store, but they said there was no charge and wouldn't tell her who'd paid for it. You don't know anything about that, do you?"

I played innocent, widening my eyes and shrugging my shoulders. "Why would I?"

"Savannah," he said with a tinge of reproach in his voice, "you can't give me gifts."

I sighed. These Staten Island men were so prideful and stubborn. "You're just like Tony. And I'll tell you what I told him: The gift isn't for *you*. Remember you said you'd share Grandma Frances with me? If she was really my mimaw, I'd buy her gifts non-stop. There's no fun in having money if you can't spread it around."

Alex lifted his arms and locked his fingers behind his head, and I wondered how much working out it took to get biceps that size. "All right," he said after a moment. "And thank you."

"You're welcome. Oh, and I read your story. It's really good."

He raised his eyebrows. "You read it? I thought it'd take a few days for you to—"

"Are you kidding? I know the unspeakable torture of anticipating a verdict, so I wouldn't make a fellow writer wait for long. I have it in my purse . . . do you want to go over it now?"

"Dessert first," he said. "Will I also need a shot of whiskey to numb the pain?"

He was too hard on himself, and I told him so after we'd cleared the table and discussed my editorial suggestions, all of which seemed to impress him. And that flattered me. It was nice to know someone valued my opinion, especially about something so important.

"You think this character needs to be more sympathetic?" he asked.

"Yeah," I said, squinting to see a page. It was still bright outside, but the apartment was dark and the one light in the kitchen ceiling seemed close to burning out.

"I need to fix that," he said, pointing above our heads. "The super here is hopeless."

I nodded. "You should develop this character's background, and . . ." I stopped. Alex was staring at me, which made it hard to talk business. It made me linger on his perfect teeth and his thick hair and his ridiculously handsome face. "Why are you looking at me like that?"

"How can I not?"

Alex cradled my face in his hands, leaned forward, and pressed his lips against mine. His fingers slid from my cheeks to my hair, skimming my scalp and hastening my breath as our kiss deepened and our tongues intertwined. He shifted his hands to my hips and gently pulled me toward him, so close that I felt the warmth of his legs through his jeans. Then my calves were locked around his waist and we were in the same chair. He was at the edge, I was sitting on his thighs, and it couldn't have felt better or sweeter or more right. It didn't matter that we were in a tiny apartment with dishes in the sink, kissing beneath a flickering fluorescent bulb.

It was dark outside when Alex kissed me again, this time inside his Honda parked at 15 Central Park West. "I'm working for the next two nights," he said afterward. "But can I see you on Thursday? I'll make dinner again. Just tell me what you want."

Just tell me what you want. I almost said something dirty after that. But all we'd done tonight was kiss, and I was going to keep it that way for a while—as difficult as it might be.

"That'd be nice," I said, "but I can't let you go to all that trouble again. Why don't we eat out? I can make a reservation at Le Bernardin."

The car behind us honked, because we weren't supposed to be parked there. The noise woke me up and made me remember that Alex had to take care of rent and utilities and probably a car payment and maybe even a student loan on a bartender's salary. Had just a couple of weeks with money made me forget what that was like?

"I mean," I said, "it'll be my treat."

He hung his arm over the frame of the open window. "When I go out with a girl," he said in a taut voice, "*I* pay. I'm not a pauper . . . and I'm not a gigolo, either."

I stared at him, listening to the angry honking behind us. Being mysterious had caused problems with Jack, and now my honesty might ruin everything with Alex. I was so unused to being wealthy that I hadn't realized it could drive a wedge between me and a man who wasn't.

"I never said you were, Alex."

He sighed and wiped his hand from his forehead to his chin. Then he turned his key in the ignition, pulled away from the curb, and parked down the street. "I'm sorry," he said after a moment, staring through the windshield at a group of passing joggers. "I know you didn't say that. But some of the women I've met through my job . . . that's the way they see me . . . or it's what they've wanted to turn me into."

I cupped his chin in my hand and turned his face toward me. "Who's done that?" I asked.

"A few women here in the city . . . I've worked at their parties, and they've made some disgusting offers. But last year I was bartending at a wedding in the Hamptons, and I met a girl . . . she was a bridesmaid . . . and I thought we had something good going."

"You mean the girl Fabian Spader mentioned?" I asked. "The one from the Upper East Side?"

Alex nodded. "She was sort of spoiled and demanding . . . which I overlooked because of how I felt about her. But all along she was engaged to someone else. She was lying, just playing me the whole time. When I found out, she laughed in my face and told me she'd just been having fun."

I'd always known that women could be as mean as men, but until now I'd never seen the effect they could have. I felt as sorry for him as I did for Tina when she got stood up and put down and treated like she wasn't worth anything.

"Alex," I said. "I'm not that kind of girl. And I'll always be honest with you."

He nodded slowly before he took my hands in his. "I will, too."

Seventeen

When I opened my apartment door, I remembered I'd forgotten to hire a maid. Cigarette butts floated in a bowl of melted Cherry Garcia on the coffee table, dust covered the TV, and yesterday's *Daily News* was scattered on the carpet. Tina was in the middle of everything, fast asleep on the couch with her face buried in a cushion.

I couldn't deal with it. I didn't feel like waking her up to tell her off for smoking in the apartment, or breaking out the Windex and a pair of latex cleaning gloves. I just wanted to think about Alex, and I wanted to write. I wanted to write something that would dazzle Kitty and get my name in the October issue of *Femme*. So I went into my office and sat in front of the computer, where I typed until I heard footsteps and Tina yawning in the doorway.

"What time is it?" she asked groggily.

"Midnight," I answered.

She walked into the room and peered over my shoulder at the computer screen. "A new story," she said with a spark of excitement in her tired voice. "When can I read it and give you my brilliant feedback?"

"When it's done," I said.

I finished it on Thursday during my lunch hour. That night, Tony drove me to Staten Island and Alex took me to dinner at a Chinese place two blocks from his apartment where I cracked open a fortune cookie with a slip of paper inside that said: *To the world you might be just one person, but to one person you might be the world.*

I tucked it into a compartment inside my wallet. Then Alex and I held hands while we walked to his building, passing a bakery where we peered through a window at cannoli and tiramisu and rainbow cookies iced with chocolate. "Let's get some," I said, pointing to the cookies, and after a man in the store put them in a box and tied a string around it, I stopped Alex from taking out his money.

He frowned at me. "Savannah," he said, "you know how I feel about—"

"I know how you feel, Alex. And I think it's nice. But I hope you're not too proud to take a gift once in a while . . . because that wouldn't be nice at all."

He scrunched up his mouth for a moment, like he was turning over my words in his mind. "Okay," he said finally. "I guess I can forget my rules every now and then."

A few minutes later, we were at the entrance to Alex's building, where Tony was sitting on the front steps with Allison beside him and Marjorie on his lap. They were people-watching as they ate Italian ice with tiny wooden spoons. We chatted with them for a while, and then Alex and I went inside and stepped into an elevator.

"Tony's such a nice guy," I said. "Smart, too. He's like a walking encyclopedia about the history of this city."

Alex nodded as the elevator doors closed. "I know. Did he tell you he used to go to Columbia? He had a full scholarship there, but he didn't graduate."

"No," I said, surprised. "He's never mentioned it."

Alex hit a button to take us to the fourth floor. "Well, he's not one to brag. And the reason he didn't finish college is that Allison got pregnant with Marjorie and he had to drop out during his sophomore year so he could work full-time. He and his mother pitched in so Allison could finish her nursing degree after the baby was born. He's had it rough . . . but he seems happy anyway."

"Yeah," I said, thinking that Tony was an even nicer guy than I'd thought.

A few minutes later, I was sitting beside Alex on his yellow fire escape with our legs dangling between its metal slats while we nibbled rainbow cookies on paper napkins. We gazed across the street at another brick building where a Siamese cat was trying to scratch through a screen and a man in a turban was watering a jungle of plants on his windowsill. The setting sun washed over the building, turning its bricks into a fiery shade of red.

"How was work today?" Alex asked as he brushed crumbs from his hands.

"Fine," I said, listening to a TV blare in the apartment above us and thinking about the story I'd folded and put inside my purse after lunch. I wanted to show it to Alex, to get his opinion like I'd given mine, but sharing my writing seemed even more personal than kissing at his kitchen table. Still, it was due on Kitty's desk tomorrow, and I valued his opinion. "I finished a new story," I said. "Kitty's going to consider it for the October issue of *Femme*."

"Really?" he said. "I'd love to read it."

I went into the apartment and walked toward my purse, which I'd left in the living room on a black futon that doubled as a couch. I grabbed a pen from atop a sudoku book on the coffee table, and then rested the pen and my story on Alex's lap as he sat on the fire escape.

"This makes me nervous," I told him. "I'll wait inside."

I took a seat on the futon and nibbled my nails for what felt like hours while Alex flipped pages and scribbled notes. When he was done, he sat beside me and said my story was definitely magazine worthy, aside from a few minor things.

We talked about it until the sun disappeared and the sky filled with stars. The story was on a flash drive in my purse, so Alex took out his laptop and I perfected my work while I sat on the futon and he stretched out beside me, watching TV. It was late by the time I finished, but I was in no rush to leave. I curled up next to him, and we watched Letterman and a repeat of *Showbiz Tonight* until we dozed off.

When I woke up, the TV was still on, Alex's right arm was around me, and his left arm was dangling limply off the futon. His T-shirt rode up, exposing the scar that ran straight down his stomach and below the waist of his jeans. I reached over him to grab the remote control and shut off the TV, and he stirred and opened his eyes.

I gently ran my finger down his scar. It was light purple and fading into the same color as his skin. "Does it still hurt?" I asked.

"Yes," he said. "Always."

I pulled his shirt back down. "It's two in the morning. I'll call a cab to take me home."

"You don't have to go home," he said, his voice velvety smooth. "You can sleep here."

I hesitated. That was a tempting offer, but it was too soon.

He gave me a crooked, knowing grin. "Take my bed and I'll sleep here."

I rested my cheek against his chest, listening to his heart beat beneath his soft shirt with *Pace University* printed across the front. As much as I wanted his face to be the first thing I saw when I woke up in the morning, I couldn't let him spend the rest of the night on this flimsy futon. I told him that, and repeated that

I was going to call a cab, but he wouldn't let me. He drove me home and kissed me when we sat beneath a streetlight in his Honda.

"I wish I could see you tomorrow night, Savannah . . . but I have to work all weekend."

I nodded as I laced our fingers together, studied his knuckles and his fingers, and thought about how small and dainty my hand was compared to his.

"Look at me," he said, and I shifted my gaze to his eyes, which were serious all of a sudden. "I want to tell you something important."

Our hands were still connected. I kept them that way and nodded again. "Sure, Alex," I said, leaning toward him. "Go ahead."

His Adam's apple bobbed as he swallowed. He combed his fingers through his hair and rubbed his neck and glanced out the window and then back at me.

"I just wanted to tell you . . . I wish you the best of luck with your story," he said as the grave look in his eyes disappeared and he flashed a stunning smile. "I bet you'll be a published author before you know it."

I flipped on the light in my dark apartment and nearly screamed. Tina was on the couch with her legs crossed and a bottle of beer in her hand.

"Where were you?" she asked. "I left three voice mails and texted you twice."

"For God's sake," I said, tossing my purse onto a chair. "Why are you lurking in the dark? You almost scared me to death."

That didn't seem to matter. She stared at me like an outraged den mother. "I asked where you were, Savannah."

"With Alex," I told her, noticing the room reeked

of cigarettes. It seemed to have seeped into the carpet and the curtains and the furniture. "I guess you've forgotten your promise about not stinking up my apartment."

"*Oh,*" she said. "*That's* interesting. I thought it was *our* apartment. *This is your apartment, too*—those were your *exact* words."

I walked toward her. "And I meant them. But it's so unbelievably rude of you to smoke in here. I don't know how I'll ever get the tobacco stench out of this place."

"Don't change the subject. Why didn't you answer my messages?"

I shrugged. "I told you . . . I was with Alex. I didn't check my phone."

She slammed the bottle onto the coffee table. "And you call *me* rude? Maybe you *should* check your phone. Did you ever think I might be worried about you?"

I rolled my eyes. "I already have a mama, darlin'. I don't need another."

"Yeah, I know you have a mother. But did you forget her number? She called a while ago, just as concerned about you as I was. She said she hasn't heard from you lately."

I'd been so busy that I hadn't given much thought to Mom except when I sent her a portion of my latest check. I looked away, keeping my eyes stuck to an empty pizza box on the love seat. When would I ever remember to hire that maid? Or maybe I just didn't want to.

"By the way," Tina went on, pointing to a clock on the wall, "it's a little soon, isn't it?"

I hated when my own words got thrown back at me, and she'd done it twice tonight. I'd asked her that question after I found Kyle in her bed, but Alex hadn't been in mine and I hadn't been in his and she was the last person in this galaxy who should get judgmental about what time I came home.

"Not that I have to explain anything to you," I said, "but we didn't do anything."

She stood up and turned her attention to a stray white thread on her powder-blue satin robe. "Whatever," she said as she flicked the thread from her fingers. "As you've so clearly pointed out, it's none of my business."

She headed toward her bedroom. I followed behind and caught her arm.

"Tina," I said, "what's the matter with you? Don't you know that if anything serious had happened with Alex, you'd be the first person I'd tell?"

She jerked her head toward me. Her synthetic hair smacked my face, but she didn't apologize. "Do you expect me to believe that? I never see you anymore. You hardly talk to me. You can't even spare an hour for lunch. I think the real question is: What's the matter with *you*?"

Her chin was quivering. I backed up and leaned against the wall, thinking that everything she'd said was right and I was a poor excuse for a best friend.

I reached out and squeezed her shoulder. "I'm sorry," I said. "I'll make it up to you. We'll spend the whole weekend together. We'll shop and I'll treat you to Le Bernardin . . . and we'll do absolutely anything you want."

She thought about that for a moment. Then she nodded and offered to make a reservation for Saturday night, but I wasn't sure if I'd been completely forgiven.

I stood in front of Kitty's desk the next morning and handed her fifteen crisp pages.

"Please be impartial, Kitty. I only want you to publish my work if it's good enough."

Manhattan was outside the window behind her, grayer than

the sky above it. She crossed her legs inside her white pants suit and pointed to a stack of papers beside her computer.

"This is your competition," she said. "I'm choosing three stories for *Femme*'s October issue, and you can be sure that if yours isn't good enough . . . it won't be in it."

I hated wondering if I'd made the cut. I went back to my desk and logged on to my computer, where I found an e-mail from Alex that said: *Can't wait to see you on Monday.*

I smiled as a wave of exhaustion swept over me. I'd only slept a few hours, and I'd been working so hard since Kitty hired me. I deserved one Friday to slack off, didn't I?

I wrote back to Alex, we e-mailed for most of the morning, and I pushed away the list of topics I was supposed to research. Kitty had gone out for meetings that would take up the whole day, so I was sure she wouldn't notice I'd gotten nothing done. I decided I'd just catch up on Monday as I online-shopped for makeup and shoes.

Then I went out at noon, bought new clothes at Bergdorf Goodman, and enjoyed a leisurely lunch at the restaurant inside, which was bright and airy, with oversized chairs covered in mustard-colored leather that looked like something out of *Alice in Wonderland*. I sat in one of them, getting curious stares from a table of well-coiffed women who could have been contestants for the next season of *The Real Housewives of New York City*.

"Are you Savannah Morgan?" one of them asked.

"Yes," I said.

She smiled with a mouth full of veneers. "I thought so. Your picture is all over the blogosphere, but you're even prettier in person. And that dress you had on is *phenomenal*."

People used that adjective much too frequently, but it still felt flattering. Everyone at the table was showering me with the same admiring smile, and I thought they were the Manhattan version of Mount Pleasant girls like Eva Lee who'd never let me in.

Only now they were opening the door, and I couldn't help that it gave me a smug satisfaction.

A few minutes later, I took a cab back to Stone News. I walked past the Stone haters on the sidewalk and headed toward the entrance, where a man wearing a FedEx uniform and carrying a stack of boxes struggled to open the door. I grabbed the handle and held it for him, and just as he walked into the building Caroline and Virginia walked out. Virginia glanced at me in her typical snooty way, and then she tapped her gold watch as Caroline stood behind her and stared from behind her cat's-eye glasses.

"Just returning from lunch at this late hour?" Virginia said. "I doubt my daughter-in-law will appreciate your tardiness."

"Kitty's not here," I answered dully.

Virginia raised a black eyebrow. "Well," she said with a fake smile, "this is one time I'm glad we ran into each other. Now I can let your boss know you're not as honest as she thinks."

She brushed past me with her chin up and her hips swaying slightly beneath her sheath dress. Caroline stayed where she was, looking uncomfortable in a plain taupe suit.

"Thank you," she said finally, and I had a feeling it wasn't just because I'd held the door.

Tina got all dressed up for dinner in a Lilly Pulitzer dress on Saturday night, and she spent lots of time on her hair and her makeup like we were going to an important event. Then she stood in the kitchen, spritzing herself with mango perfume that she tossed into her purse.

"Is Tony picking us up?" she asked.

"No," I said, noticing how snugly her dress fit across her chest. "We'll take a cab."

She widened her eyes. "*Savannah,*" she said in an irritated voice as she walked toward the pantry, where she opened the door and pulled out a cookie-covered dish wrapped in cellophane. "I

baked these for his family. You're not going to deprive his precious little daughter, are you?" she asked, glancing at Marjorie's
thank-you note on the refrigerator.

I studied Marjorie's crayon scribble and stick-figure artwork.
I didn't want to take Tony away from her during his off-hours,
but getting her out of a small apartment was important, too. I
only wished Tony would let me give him some money toward his
house fund, but I knew he'd never take a dime he hadn't earned.

So I called him, and I was relieved that he wasn't at home. He
was working, dropping somebody off a few blocks away, and it
only took a few minutes before the sedan was parked outside and
Tina and I slid onto the backseat, where she leaned into the front
and handed him the dish.

"For your family," she told him in the most syrupy voice.

"Oh," he said. "That's really nice. I'm actually not supposed
to take gifts, but Savannah's convinced me to break the rules. So
thank you."

She smiled. He put the dish on the seat beside him and she
lingered where she was, gazing lovingly in his direction. It was
so embarrassing that I grabbed her arm and yanked her backward as he pulled away from the curb.

A half hour later, we were sipping wine and buttering bread
inside Le Bernardin. Tina kept grinning and bouncing in her
seat like this was her first night of freedom after a lengthy prison
sentence. She also chattered on and on about how much she
loved her job and how rewarding it was, and I was happy for her,
but it was hard to pay attention. My mind kept drifting to Alex.

She put down her fork when we were eating our salads. "Are
you even listening?"

"Of course I am," I said as my cell phone vibrated in my
pocket. I pulled it out and read a text from Alex that said: *I'm at
work. I'm bored. What are you doing?*

This was one of the things about a new boyfriend that

I loved—the warm rush of adrenaline that came whenever I heard from him, even if it was just a message complaining about being bored. And it was good to know somebody cared what I was doing.

I'm at dinner with Tina, I wrote back.

Tina picked up a knife and tapped it against her plate. "Texting at the table is very rude."

I knew that, but it didn't stop me from glancing at the screen again when the phone vibrated in my palm. *Message from Katherine Stone,* I read.

"I need to see this," I said.

Tina threw her hands up. "Don't mind me. I'll just sit here and gossip with the bread."

I read Kitty's message, which said she'd chosen my story as one of the three to be featured in the October issue of *Femme.* She said it was more than good enough.

I let out such a high-pitched squeal that a couple at the table beside us glanced at me like I was insane, but I didn't care. I only cared that I was finally going to be a published author.

"What are you so happy about?" Tina asked as she finished her second glass of wine, and after I told her she seemed to forget my bad manners, because she squealed as loudly as I had. "Congratulations, Savannah," she said, beaming at me. "I'm so happy for you. This is your *dream.*"

"Tell me about it. It's amazing. I have to call Alex and thank him."

Her forehead wrinkled. "Thank him for what?"

"For editing my story. His ideas made it so much better."

I typed a message into my phone and sent it off, and then I looked up at Tina, whose face had gone pale. "This story . . . ," she said slowly, "is it the one you were writing the other night . . . the one you said you'd let me read when it was finished?"

I felt awful. I *had* told her I'd let her read it, but that didn't seem necessary after Alex had. "Well," I began, feeling guilty and trying to find a way to soothe her bruised ego, "you're busy with work, and I didn't want to bother you. . . ."

"Bullshit," she said.

The couple beside us shook their heads. Other than when Tina and I had gotten into that fight back home a few weeks ago, this was the first time I'd heard her swear for real.

"*Tina,*" I said. "Watch your language."

"Screw my language. Who are you to tell me how to act? I've been your only editor since you learned how to put two sentences together, and now you ditch me for a guy you barely even know?"

I didn't feel like I barely knew Alex, and her superior tone annoyed me even though I understood why she was upset.

"I asked for Alex's help," I said, "because he's an aspiring author, too. He's very talented, and he's got a degree in—"

"Oh," she said indignantly, "he's got a *degree.* Well, I guess all the time I've spent editing your work means nothing because I don't have a *degree.*"

That wasn't what I'd meant, but I doubted I could convince her of it. She called the waitress over and ordered something stronger than wine as my phone wiggled in my hand and I looked down at a text from Alex that said: *I'm so proud of you.*

I smiled. Tina glared at me. Our dinners arrived and so did her drink, which she downed quickly, then ordered another.

"Cool it with the booze," I told her.

She tossed her hair. "Don't worry. I'm paying for myself tonight."

"That's not what I meant. This was supposed to be my treat, and I'll take care of the check. You don't make a lot at the shelter."

Her drink arrived—a cocktail with a maraschino cherry at the bottom of the glass. She plucked it out by the stem and stuck it in her mouth. "Well," she said between chews, "we can't all be an editor's assistant and work for media empires and have massive checks delivered to our front door every week. But you seem to have forgotten that *my* daddy has money, too. I'll put my half of the bill on the credit card he gave me."

I sighed. She was so worked up that beads of sweat had broken out on her upper lip. "I know your father has money, Tina. But you can't charge anything on his credit card. He said he'd only support you until you found a job, right?"

She swigged her drink and slammed the empty glass onto the table. "Don't concern yourself with what my daddy says, Savannah. You never gave a damn about it before."

Eighteen

Tina kept her arms folded and her legs crossed as she stared out the window when we were in the back of Tony's car. All I heard was muffled traffic and "WCBS News time is ten seventeen."

Tony seemed to feel the rift between me and Tina. "So," he said cheerfully, like he was trying to smooth over the awkwardness, "Alex called earlier, Savannah . . . and he told me you're going to be published in the magazine you work for. You must be really excited."

"Yes," I said stiffly.

He cleared his throat and turned a corner. "Alex also mentioned he's sorry he has to work all weekend. He really misses seeing you."

Tina's eyes shot toward me. I nearly winced. I was sure Tony had meant to cheer me up, but he couldn't have found a worse thing to say.

"Oh-h," Tina said, lengthening the word, "Alex has to work all weekend. Well, aren't I an idiot? I thought you'd cleared your schedule so we could spend some time together when all along I've been a cheap consolation prize."

"That's not true," I said, but maybe I was wrong.

She leaned forward and stuck her head into the space between the two front seats. "You know something, Tony?" she said, her words slightly slurring. "Savannah and I were best friends once. She loved my cooking . . . but now she won't touch it. And I used to be the first person she'd let read her stories because she didn't trust anybody's opinion except mine. But suddenly she thinks Alex's opinion is more important, which is why she let him edit the story that's going to be in the magazine. She never even let me see it. She thinks I'm useless because I didn't finish college and anybody who doesn't have a degree is *stupid*."

Tony looked at me in the rearview mirror. I remembered Alex saying that Tony hadn't graduated from Columbia, which made me want to vanish. And there was no time to argue with Tina and salvage Tony's opinion of me. We were at 15 Central Park West, and Tina flung open her door with no regard for the passing cars.

"Tina," I said, watching her stumble onto the street. "Be careful."

She slammed the door in my face. Tony turned around.

"Is that true?" he asked.

"Of course it isn't. I don't care if people have a degree or not."

He held up his hand. "No. I mean did you treat her like crap because of Alex?"

I didn't say anything; I just stared at his brown eyes and the fading freckles on his cheeks before I opened my door and stepped onto the sidewalk, where Tina was staggering toward the building. She'd nearly reached the entrance when she slipped out of her shoe. She twisted her ankle, fell to the ground, and scraped her bare knee against the concrete. I raced toward her and tried to help her up, but she shoved me away.

Then Tony was there, crouching beside her. He took a handkerchief out of his blazer, wrapped it around her bloody knee,

and carefully touched her ankle the way he'd examined my
knuckles after I slapped Ned.

"It's probably just sprained. Do you have a compression bandage upstairs?" Tony asked, and when I shook my head he went
back to his car and returned with a first-aid kit.

"I can't stand up," Tina told him.

"I'll help you," I offered.

"Don't bother," she said.

Tony put his arm around her waist and hoisted her up. She
leaned on him, hopping on one foot while he led her through
the lobby and into the elevator as I trailed behind. Then we were
outside my apartment, and I opened the door into such a mess that
I wondered if Tony thought I was like one of those crazy hoarder
people on TV.

"I'm getting a maid soon," I said, inhaling a whiff of air that
smelled like Marlboros and garbage. I let out a chagrined laugh
to cover my embarrassment, but Tony didn't laugh back.

"Where's the bathroom?" he asked.

I pointed the way. Tina tightened her arm around his shoulders and he guided her down the hall while I followed them. I
leaned against the doorframe, watching as he put her on the edge
of the tub, opened his first-aid kit, and cleaned her knee with
cotton soaked in peroxide.

Tina lifted her eyes to mine. "We don't need an audience."

I skulked away and headed to the kitchen, where I stuffed
some trash into a plastic bag, and dumped it into a chute near the
elevator. When I came back into the apartment, I heard Tony
talking in the bathroom.

"Cut it out, Tina. You don't mean that. You're drunk."

She let out a husky laugh. "I do so mean it. I've liked you all
along. Don't you like me?"

"As a friend," he said. "I can be friends with you the way I
am with Savannah."

"Savannah doesn't know how to be anybody's friend. And I want to be more than that to you. It doesn't matter that you're married . . . I can be discreet, and I'd never do anything to hurt your wife and your little Marjorie. I've been with a lot of single guys, you know . . . and not one of them has been as sweet to me as you have. So I'll share you if I have to. I don't mind."

My heart deflated and my temper spiked. I'd never thought she'd go this far, but all the letdowns seemed to have destroyed her pride. I rushed toward the bathroom as she rambled on while Tony spoke to her calmly, like he was trying to talk a nutcase jumper off a ledge.

"Stop it," he was telling her when I reached the doorway. She was still sitting on the tub, and there was a cloth bandage around her ankle and a square piece of gauze taped to her knee. Her arms were locked around Tony's neck and his hands were clamped to her wrists, gently prying her off. "You don't know what you're doing."

"Yes, I do. I also know you don't really want me to stop," she said as she unclasped her hands and slid one of them down to the top of his thigh, skimming the edge of his crotch.

He shoved her away so roughly that she landed in the tight space between the tub and the toilet. Then he sprang up and glared down at her, his face flushing and his fists clenched. "God damn it," he said. "Why'd you do that?"

"Why?" she shouted back. "Because I want you, that's why."

"Yeah?" he said. "Well, that's too bad. I have a wife. I love her. I don't want *you.*"

I don't want you. She'd heard those words so many times and I pitied her for having to hear them again, especially from him. I wavered between hugging her and shaking her for being so selfish and dumb, but I didn't do anything except stand there and watch. Neither of them seemed to notice they weren't alone until Tony rushed past me and into the living room, where he opened the front door and slammed it behind him with a bang that rattled the dirty dishes in my kitchen sink.

Tina sniffed, shuddered, and failed at trying to stand up by leaning one hand against the bathtub and the other on the toilet seat. Her foot slid against the tiles, and her hand plunged into the toilet as she fell back to the floor.

"Damn it," she said, shaking water off her fingers.

I walked over to her and offered my hand. "Get up," I said.

She shot me the most hateful stare and slapped my hand away. I stared down at her—at her disheveled hair and her chicken-pox scar and the streak of pink lip gloss on her chin.

"Don't look at me that way," she said in a hiss as she narrowed her eyes and clenched her teeth. "What do you want to say, Savannah? Do you want to tell me how disgusting I am?"

"What you just did was *beyond* disgusting. I never thought I'd see you stoop so low."

She pushed herself up from the floor, hobbled toward me, and looked ready to spit in my face. "Well," she said, "I guess now you know how it feels."

After that, Tina limped to her bedroom and shut the door behind her, and I didn't have the energy to stay awake and wonder if things between us would ever be the same. So I went to my room and slipped into a nightgown without washing my makeup off.

My lashes were stuck together when I opened my eyes the next morning. Somebody was thumping on the front door and sunlight streamed through my windows, and for a moment I forgot about that ugly scene in my bathroom last night. Then I remembered, and I wanted to shove my head under one of my pillows and keep it there for the rest of the day. But I couldn't, because whoever was knocking just wouldn't stop and it was clear that Tina wasn't going to hop out of bed on her good leg to answer it.

I dragged myself off my mattress, rubbing my eyes as I walked across the apartment in my bare feet. I was still rubbing when I opened the door and saw a blurry image of a man with chestnut hair, dressed in jeans and a button-down shirt.

"It's twelve thirty," he said in a Charleston accent.

No wonder it was so sunny. I blinked and crossed my arms around myself, realizing that he was Sawyer Brandt and yesterday's makeup was probably smudged all over my face and I was standing there in a flimsy gown without a bra underneath. I reached over to the chair where I'd flung my blazer after work one night last week, picked it up, and wriggled into it.

"Mr. Brandt," I said, my voice raspy as I buttoned the jacket across my chest.

His eyes held a mix of scorn and horror when they moved above my head and scanned the apartment. "Where's my daughter?" he asked, brushing past me.

I shut the door. "What are you doing here?"

He was walking around the living room, examining cigarette butts and old newspapers like they were part of a crime scene. "I haven't heard from Tina in days," he said. "Late last night she left me a voice mail, but she was crying so hard I couldn't understand what she was saying. I was out of my mind with worry, so I got on the first flight I could find."

"Oh," I said with a jittery laugh, hoping to cover for her even though she hated me. "You shouldn't have flown all the way up here just because of that . . . she gets so dramatic when she's had a drink or two."

His eyes had been on the empty pizza box that still hadn't moved from the love seat, but he shifted them to me. "What was that? Did you say she was drinking?"

I hadn't been awake long enough for my mind to work right. "No, sir . . . I just meant you shouldn't have been worried. Everything's fine. If Tina hasn't called you, it's only because she's been so busy with her job."

I thought that was a valid explanation, but he didn't seem to agree. He squinted and took a step toward me. "What job are you referring to, Savannah?"

He couldn't be more proud, Tina had said. Was he so worked up that he'd forgotten everything? "You know . . . at the homeless shelter. She loves it there."

"The homeless shelter?" he said in a tone that would've been appropriate if I'd said she was working as a masseuse who gave happy endings. "Tina's supposed to be here on vacation. She kept extending it until I insisted she come home, and then she stopped calling. And I suppose you're going to tell me you're not behind that?"

I swallowed. She'd been lying to me all along, pretending Mr. Brandt approved of her being on her own and working at the shelter. But I knew why. She'd just been trying to keep everyone happy.

"No, Mr. Brandt," I said.

A door creaked open. "Daddy?" Tina called from down the hall.

He yelled back at her to come out, she told him she couldn't walk, and he shot me a furious glare, as if all of this had to be my fault. Then he dashed down the hall and I followed after him, watching Tina as she leaned against her bedroom door in her blue satin robe, trying to wave away the cloud of cigarette smoke behind her.

Mr. Brandt looked at her battered leg. "Tina Mae . . . I don't know what happened, and right now I don't want to know. I just want you to pack your bags because we're leaving."

I couldn't believe how easily she nodded. He put his arm around her and she leaned against him as she limped into her room, and I had to speak up. She'd come too far to go back now.

"Tina," I said, "you can't leave. What about your job?"

"My daughter," Mr. Brandt said, looking at me over his

shoulder, "already has a job in Mount Pleasant where she belongs. *You* might not care about her risking her life around a bunch of worthless junkies and degenerates, but *I* do."

"They aren't like that, Daddy," Tina said.

He ignored her and turned toward me. "Speaking of filth . . . you've made me realize that all the money in the world can't change white trash. This is an impressive address, but I guess somebody like you doesn't know how to treat fine things. You've brought the place right down to your level. But you won't do the same to my daughter, Savannah. I've put up with your influencing Tina for far too long, and this is where it ends."

Air from a vent in the ceiling was blowing down my neck, but that wasn't what had given me a cold shiver. It wasn't even what Mr. Brandt had said. It was that Tina had been standing beside him all along, listening to every word, and she didn't protect me like she had against schoolyard bullies and vicious cliques. She didn't say a thing.

Nineteen

I kneeled on the kitchen floor, polishing the wood to a glossy shine. It was dinnertime, but I wasn't hungry even though I'd been working all day. Everything sparkled and was neat and dust free, and I'd taken five trips to the garbage chute down the hall.

I couldn't find the sense in hiring a maid. Besides, I needed something to keep my mind off the memory of Tina limping out of the apartment with her father and her designer luggage. So I kept polishing while listening to a teaser for a breaking news report on NY1. All I heard was "Edward Stone," "investigation," and "shocking turn of events."

I raced to the living room, where I stood in front of the TV, biting my nails and waiting for commercials to end. Then I listened to an anchorman saying, "New evidence indicates that the late media giant Edward Stone of the Stone News Corporation might have concealed information about a possible link between global conglomerate Amicus Worldwide and cancer at Lake Kolenya because he was romantically linked to New York senator Carys Bowman Caldwell. Caldwell—the wife of Amicus's COO, Jonathan Caldwell, and a member of the U.S. Senate

Committee on Energy and Natural Resources—read a statement for the press at her home in Westchester this afternoon,
denying these allegations."

The screen changed from an anchor behind a desk to a
woman outside a sprawling house surrounded by reporters who
shoved microphones into her face. She was slim and pretty and
had caramel-colored hair and she looked vaguely familiar, but I
didn't figure out who she was until I heard her voice and realized that Senator Carys Bowman Caldwell was the woman
who'd sat beside me at the New York Public Library gala and
told me what a great guy my father was.

"These allegations are false," she said with a plastic politician's smile. "My dealings with Edward Stone were merely professional, and I have never been unfaithful to my husband. If Mr.
Stone violated his ethical principles by not investigating Amicus
Worldwide—which has denied any connection between its plant
in Putnam County and a cancer outbreak in the Lake Kolenya
area—it was of *his* choosing and completely unrelated to me."

I dropped onto the couch, where I sat with my hand over my
mouth as the anchorman came on the screen and said, "Despite
Senator Caldwell's denials, there's mounting evidence that she
was romantically involved with Edward Stone—who, at the
time, was married to socialite Virginia Barlow Stone. Our
sources believe that Stone did not ask his corporation to investigate the Lake Kolenya story as a favor to Caldwell during her
reelection year. This twist in the Stone News controversy brings
additional questions about Edward Stone's untimely death in a
car accident last month, which has been blamed on a drunk
driver who has not yet been found."

The TV cut to a commercial, and I switched to a home-
shopping channel because I had to avoid hearing the Senator's
lies on a continuous loop. I kept thinking about the night we
met, when she said I looked like Edward, when she could barely

tear her eyes away from my face, when it seemed so important to her that I believed only good things about him.

There had to have been something between them, but now that her career was at stake she obviously had no problem smearing his name along with everyone else. But maybe he deserved it, because loyalty stopped being admirable when it resulted in suffering and death. Or maybe he'd been fooled—maybe Senator Caldwell had convinced him that Amicus wasn't responsible. And I supposed Mercedes Rawlings Stark had been wrong when she said Mom was the only woman special enough to make Edward stray from his wife.

I tugged at my hair to stop the flood of scenarios filling my brain. The idea that Edward had been killed by a heartbroken husband or mother was still plausible, but so was the possibility that Senator Caldwell had used him and strung him along and gotten rid of him because he'd somehow become a liability. He could have threatened to tell the truth about Amicus, or maybe he never even knew the truth. Senator Caldwell's husband might have found out about the affair, or she might have eliminated Edward herself to protect her marriage and her career.

It was too much to think about. I turned up the TV to drown out the voices in my head, went back to the kitchen, got down on my hands and knees, and polished the floor until someone said my name. Then I gasped and spun around, landing on my rear end. Alex was standing in the doorway, holding a bag from a restaurant down the street and explaining that he'd unexpectedly gotten the night off.

"What's going on?" he said. "I kept knocking, but there was no answer . . . and when I tried the doorknob, it was unlocked. Why's your TV turned up so loud?"

"It keeps me company," I said, thinking I must have forgotten to lock the door after my last trip to the garbage chute. "It gets too quiet in here."

He glanced around. "Where's Tina?"

I stood up, wiping my hands on my shorts. "She went home. Didn't Tony tell you what happened last night?"

He shook his head, and I wasn't sure why I'd even asked. The majority of men would most likely gossip and brag after being propositioned so boldly by a gorgeous girl. They'd probably snicker and joke and say the cruelest things about how needy and desperate she was. But Tony was such a nice guy that I was sure he'd take the whole thing to his grave.

Alex put the bag on the counter and walked toward me. He was dressed in jeans and a polo shirt, and he smelled like Jamie used to—fresh and clean and minty. I stared at him for a long moment before I took a step forward, pressed my face against his chest, and wrapped my arms around his back. I was glad he didn't ask what was wrong or why I was clinging to him so tightly. He just smoothed my hair as I closed my eyes and felt his warmth seeping through his shirt. I'd tell him the whole story later—but for now, this was everything I needed.

Tony held the car door open when I walked toward it on Monday morning. He looked at anything but me—a UPS truck, a professional dog walker with eight leashes wrapped around her wrist, the limestone on my building. I wasn't sure if he was embarrassed or angry or worried that I was holding a grudge because he'd shoved my best friend onto a bathroom floor. But I wasn't, and I wanted both of us to forget all of it.

"Tina went back to Charleston," I said.

He looked at me. "I'm sorry, Savannah. I shouldn't have yelled at her, and I shouldn't have pushed her. I swear I've never done something like that to a woman before last night. It was just that she—"

"It's okay. You don't need to explain. And we never have to talk about it again."

He nodded and we both got into the car. Soon I was at Stone News, and I checked my cell while I walked toward the kitchen, hoping for a text or a voice mail from Tina telling me she wanted to salvage our nineteen years of friendship, but there was only a message from Alex saying: *Have a good day.*

I smiled over that and sighed about Tina when I stuck my phone in my pocket and walked into the kitchen. Coffee was brewing on the counter, and *The New York Times* was on a table beside a box of doughnuts. Ainsley was there, too, holding her head in her hands as she sat in a chair and bent her neck above the newspaper.

"Good morning," I said, pouring a cup of coffee.

"No . . . it isn't," she replied.

I whirled around, wondering if Ainsley had been replaced by a bad-tempered look-alike. "What's wrong? You're not your usual chipper self."

She didn't answer; she just kept her head down and her attention on the paper. I stared at her until a tear dripped from her eye and splashed onto the front page.

I walked toward her and rested my hand on her shoulder. "What happened?"

She looked at me with bloodshot eyes before grabbing a napkin to dry her cheeks. "Bad weekend," was all she said. Then she pushed her chair back and stormed off.

"That seems to be going around," I muttered when I left the kitchen and headed for my desk, where Kitty stopped by a few minutes later.

"I'm sure you've heard the latest," she said, and I nodded as I sat in my chair. "Virginia's devastated. She hadn't known about Senator Caldwell, and she can't stand that it's all over the news. She's a private person . . . she doesn't like when her dirty laundry is aired. But who does?"

"Nobody," I said, thinking that two affairs were bad enough, but it had to be so much worse when the whole world knew about them. "I hate to say it, but . . . I feel bad for her."

"I have to admit I do, too," Kitty said, and then moved on to business, asking if I'd finished a project she'd given me last week.

I remembered my Friday laziness. "I didn't have time. But I'll finish it today."

"Oh," she said, sounding surprised and a little disappointed. "I guess that's okay, as long as I have it soon. By the way . . . Virginia said something about running into you the other day. She claimed you'd taken a really long lunch."

I rolled my eyes. I should have known my soft feelings for that woman couldn't last. "I'm not surprised she reported me."

"So she wasn't making it up?"

I shook my head. "It was just once."

Kitty touched her hair, twirling it around her index finger until the tip turned white. "Well," she said, "it's fine . . . but don't make it a habit. We don't want the other employees to get the wrong idea . . . and you said you didn't want me to play favorites."

"Right," I said, even though being a favorite had its advantages.

She untangled her hair from her finger and dropped her hand to her side. "Anyway . . . the main reason I stopped by is that Ned and I want to take you to dinner at Café Boulud on Saturday night to celebrate your upcoming publication . . . and you can bring that handsome boyfriend of yours."

She was cheery and smiling, but I wasn't. My stomach turned at the thought of being forced into hours of civil conversation with Ned and possibly another hug.

"What's wrong?" Kitty asked. "If you don't like French cuisine, I assure you the menu is *quite* multicultural."

"It's not the food," I said. "It's just . . ."

Her smile dimmed. "I thought everything was fine with you and Ned now."

The discouragement in her voice killed me, and I had to do something to get rid of it. "It is," I said. "Everything's fine. So what time should we be there?"

That night, I walked out of the elevator at 15 Central Park West and headed toward my apartment. I rounded a corner and saw Alex down the hall, standing in front of my door with a gym bag at his feet and two paper bags stuffed with groceries from Gristedes in his arms. The mere sight of him lifted my spirits, and a wide grin broke out on my face.

"Hey," I said, heading toward him as I jangled my keys in my hand. "I was going to call you later. Want to go on a date Saturday night?"

I was in front of him now, and I almost bounced up and down in my shoes. He looked amazing, with his dark hair and his blue eyes and his strong body dressed in jeans and a T-shirt with sleeves rolled to his biceps. His muscles were bulging even more than usual, like he'd spent the afternoon bench-pressing or whatever it is that guys do to make themselves look so delicious.

"Or maybe I shouldn't call it a *date*," I went on, "since Ned Stone will be there. But Kitty will be, too . . . she invited both of us to dinner at Café Boulud to celebrate my authorhood. Is that even a word?"

He laughed. "I'm not sure. But I'd love to go. And I hope you don't mind me showing up here again, Savannah. I just came from the gym and I have the night off . . . and I thought you might like a home-cooked meal after working all day."

God. He was the whole package: hot and thoughtful and so adorably domestic. I couldn't have come up with anything better if I'd whipped him up from scratch.

"I'd love it," I said, "as long as you'll let me help."

He agreed. We went inside and I slipped into my bedroom,

where I stripped off my suit and changed into shorts and a tank top while he unpacked groceries in the kitchen.

Then I crept into the kitchen in my bare feet. Alex was turned away, standing at the sink and rinsing lettuce under the faucet. I sneaked up behind him, wrapped my arms around his waist, and closed my eyes as I pressed my cheek into his back.

"You smell nice," I told him.

"I'm not wearing cologne or anything," he said.

"I know. It's just you."

He laughed again. I reluctantly let go and moved to his side, where he handed me the lettuce and a knife. We made dinner together—a delectable Italian feast like the one he'd cooked for me at his apartment—and afterward we sat across from each other at the table, talking over a lit candle until it was dark outside.

"You still haven't told me," Alex said, leaning back in his chair, "why Tina isn't around."

I let out a sigh before I spilled the whole story, including the verbal butchering Mr. Brandt had unleashed on me. The bruises were still fresh and sore.

"Because of where I come from," I said, "some people see me as nothing but trash."

I shook my head and stared at my empty plate until I felt Alex's fingers beneath my chin. He lifted my face to meet his eyes.

"*I* don't," he said.

That made me believe nothing else mattered. I reached for his hand and squeezed it gently in mine. "Do you have a toothbrush in there?" I asked, nodding toward his gym bag that sat in a corner across the kitchen.

"Yeah," he said. "Why?"

"Because," I began, "I don't want you to go all the way back to Staten Island in the dark. Because I have an extra bedroom with nobody in it. Because I really want you to stay."

. . .

Moonlight filled my room as my back pressed against my mattress. The bed was soft and the air-conditioning was set at an ideal temperature, but I still couldn't sleep. I just kept staring through the window, at the ceiling, into the darkened hall.

I stayed there until after midnight, when I started fiddling with a loose button on the front of my pink nightie with its spaghetti straps and eyelet trim. I felt thirsty, so I got out of bed and went to the kitchen, where I gingerly opened the fridge and pulled out a Snapple, doing my best to be quiet so I wouldn't wake Alex.

He was asleep in Tina's room, which I passed on my way back down the hall. The door was open a crack and I lingered by it for a moment, just listening to him breathe.

I carefully pushed the door open halfway and saw him lying facedown on the bed. His torso was bare, the rest of him was covered with a sheet, and his arms were spread across the mattress with his fingers dangling off the sides.

His skin looked so smooth and flawless that I wanted to put my hands all over it. I wanted to cuddle up next to him and fall asleep with our legs intertwined. But instead I just pulled the door back to its original position, and cringed when it creaked. Alex didn't move, though—so I tiptoed to my room, got into bed, and closed my eyes.

I fell asleep. But then something woke me—something that sounded like a squeaky floorboard. I opened my eyes, squinted at the clock on my night table, and saw that I hadn't been out for long and Alex was standing beside my bed. He was wearing cotton shorts but was still shirtless, and I had to blink a few times to make sure I wasn't dreaming.

"You were outside my room, weren't you?" he asked, his voice soft but serious.

He must've heard the door. He had to know I'd been ogling him while he slept, but now I didn't even care. "Yeah," I said.

"Why didn't you come in?" he asked.

He waited for an answer, but I didn't have one.

Alex leaned down, resting his right hand beside my head to steady himself as he carefully shifted his body onto the bed, where he straddled me and looked into my face.

"Tell me to leave," he said in a velvet whisper.

I stared at him. My blood was racing through my veins.

"Say you want me to leave, Savannah . . . and I will."

I shook my head. "I've already told you that I want you to stay."

One corner of his mouth lifted into a seductive smile that made my whole body smolder. He put his lips on mine, kissing me gently at first, and then deeper, sliding his hands over the pink fabric that covered my naked chest. His fingers moved to the buttons, undoing each one, and then my nightie was open and off and lying beside me on the bed.

His lips went everywhere—my breasts, my stomach, the insides of my thighs. I bent my legs around his hips and tugged at the waist of his shorts. I tossed them away, and then we were covered only by the glow of the full moon outside my window.

"Alex," I said as I slid my bare heel down the crease in his back. I could hardly get his name out, because he was kissing my neck, sending me into a trance.

"What's wrong?" he asked breathily, glancing down at his muscular body against my thin frame. He lifted himself onto his elbows and suddenly looked worried. "Am I hurting you?"

I almost laughed at that question. I hadn't felt so good in a long, long time. I hadn't cared this much for anyone other than Jamie. "No," I answered, not even sure what I'd meant to say before. "And there's absolutely *nothing* wrong."

He gave me a drowsy grin and slowly ran the tip of his index finger from my throat to my navel as he stared alternately at my face and my body like he was hungry for all of it.

But he couldn't have been hungrier than I was. I draped my arms over his shoulders and pulled him in for a kiss that felt like the coldest drink on the hottest day.

His hands went lower, slipping gently down my thighs and ending up between them, making me squeeze my eyes shut and gnaw on my lower lip. His fingers moved to my underwear, gently pulling until it was at my ankles and finally on the floor.

Then there was nothing separating us and he was moving slowly and skillfully against me, back and forth, his pecs skimming my chest. Our noses touched as we kept our eyes locked, and I thought he was *so* much more than worth the wait.

It was Saturday night, and Tony was picking me up soon to drive me to the Surrey hotel, where Café Boulud was located. I could have taken a cab, but he'd jumped at the chance for overtime when I mentioned I was having dinner with Alex. Tony was going be in Manhattan chauffeuring other clients anyway, he'd said.

I was in a new dress and ready to go as I stood in my guest room. Alex had made the bed before he left on Tuesday morning, and I could still smell his scent, mixed with the fading trace of Tina's mango perfume.

I opened the closet, which I thought was filled with empty hangers until I saw something pink and sparkly all the way in the back—the dress I'd borrowed for Tina's debutante ball. I took it out and admired the lipstick-rose satin and the chiffon, wondering if she'd purposely left it as a cherished gift or if she'd discarded it like a bad memory.

She still hadn't called or texted or e-mailed, and I hadn't, either. I hadn't even told Mom the full story about Tina fleeing from Manhattan—I'd just given her a sanitized version and cut the conversation short. I didn't want to repeat what Sawyer Brandt had said, and I was sure if Mom heard it she'd do something crazy enough to get her locked up in the county pen. She'd probably rush to his house and bang on his door and give him a big dose of attitude along with a swift kick to his most treasured area.

I exhaled a long sigh and put the dress away, shooing Tina out of my mind. I was about to celebrate the achievement of an important goal, and I wouldn't let anybody tarnish it. And I also wouldn't let myself dwell on the fact that Ned was going to be at Café Boulud tonight. Alex would be there, too, and with him beside me, I was sure I could handle anything.

A few minutes later, I sat next to Tony as he drove toward the Upper East Side and I scrolled through text messages that Alex had sent during the week—*Sweet dreams* and *I miss you* and *Got the night again off so let's have dinner.* There were also pictures on my phone that we'd taken of ourselves in Central Park. Some of them were blurry and most were too close-up, but looking at them made me smile.

The phone vibrated in my hand, and it was Alex, and just seeing his name on the screen turned me giddy. "Hey," I said in a bubbly voice, thinking of how dashing he was going to look in the Armani dress shirt I'd bought at Barneys and had delivered to his apartment this afternoon. "Ready for tonight?"

"Savannah," he said, and his tone scared me. It sounded like bad news was on the way. "I'm really sorry, but something came up . . . and I can't make it for dinner."

Something came up. It was such a standard bail-out line, and very unlike Alex. "Are you okay?" I asked as worrisome possibilities swirled through my head. "Did you get into a car accident? Are you sick? Is everything okay with your family?"

"They're fine," he said, "and so am I. It's nothing like that."

I waited for more as Tony drove past old buildings with ornate carvings above their windows, but Alex didn't say a thing. "Then what is it?" I asked. "What's wrong?"

"Nothing," he said. "It's just that I have to go to Queens tonight."

That made no sense. He'd known about this dinner for days. He knew how important it was to me. "You have to go to Queens?" I asked, and Tony glanced at me. "Why?"

"I have to see someone," he said, as if that were enough.

"Can't you see this person tomorrow?" I pressed. "I can go with you. I wouldn't mind seeing Queens again . . . I've only been there once, when I flew in from Charleston."

"No," he said. "It has to be tonight."

What was he talking about? "Who exactly do you have to see?" I asked.

"Just a friend," he said.

I was getting suspicious, imagining another girlfriend or an ex-wife he'd conveniently forgotten to mention. "What kind of friend?" I said while sweat seeped into my armpits and I feared I'd been completely wrong about him.

He seemed to catch my accusation. "Savannah," he said. "Come on . . . it's not like that."

"Then what *is* it like?" I asked as Tony stopped at a red light. "You've been nothing but vague, so please give me an answer I can understand."

Tony hit the gas when the light turned green, and Alex paused before he spoke again. "I've told you everything I can. I promised I'd be there. Please don't ask questions."

My beaded choker was pressing into my clammy flesh; I stuck my finger between the beads and my skin, but I was too rough and the necklace snapped, sending beads tumbling down my dress and onto my feet. "I have every right to ask questions," I said, my temper flaring. "You promised *me*, too . . . and that promise was made first."

"I know," he said. "Don't get mad. I never meant to upset you."

How could I not get mad? It was unforgivable for a guy to let a girl get all fixed up for a night out and then call at the last minute without a reasonable excuse for not showing up, especially after they'd made love for the first time just five days ago and four times since—once in my shower, twice in my bed, Thursday night on his futon because we couldn't keep our hands off each other long enough to make it to his room. This was the sort of ungentlemanly behavior I refused to tolerate, but I'd never expected it from him and that made it so much worse.

"I wouldn't be upset," I said, "if you'd just be straight with me. What's going on?"

Alex exhaled another sigh, and it was long and weary. "Can't you trust me and cut me some slack this one time?"

"Tell me the truth or there won't be another time."

"Jesus Christ," Alex said. "I thought you weren't like all the other spoiled, rich brats who throw a fit when they don't get their way. You told me you weren't one of those girls."

"And you told me you'd always be honest," I shot back. "Is that another broken promise? You've humiliated me, you know. Can you imagine what Ned's going to think when he finds out that you've stood me up? He'll laugh his pompous ass off."

"Since when do you care what Ned thinks? You said you can't stand him."

I also couldn't stand that I'd just yelled at Alex for being dishonest when I hadn't been all that truthful myself. I'd never told him why I detested Ned in private and hugged him in public. Still, I'd told him everything else, so it wasn't fair that he was holding back.

"Don't throw my words in my face. I hate that."

"You know what *I* hate?" Alex asked. "I hate when women with too much money want to dress me up as if I'm their own personal Ken doll. I have a closet full of shirts, Savannah . . . you don't need to send one over like I can't afford my own or I don't have the brains to wear something appropriate for a dinner with your family."

I'd never said he didn't have brains or couldn't afford his own shirt. I'd thought he was smart and talented enough for me to brush Tina aside and let him replace her as my editor. I'd even spent an hour at Barneys, searching for the perfect shade of blue.

"You're taking it the wrong way," I said. "You've got a chip on your shoulder. You're an evolved guy, Alex . . . but right now you're being rigid and old-fashioned and chauvinistic, and you're obviously intimidated because I have money. But there's no reason to be."

He scoffed. "*Intimidated?* Don't flatter yourself."

That stung, but I let it go. "I don't know why you're so angry about a stupid shirt. Didn't you agree to accept a gift once in a while?"

"Yeah," he said. "But not something that probably cost three hundred bucks. Like I told you before . . . I'm not a fucking gigolo."

Did he really say that? Had what happened between us over the past few days made him think I was trying to turn him into my own private hooker? That was absurd and insulting, and I didn't care for his biting tone. He didn't apologize for it, or for anything he'd said, and that was what bothered me most of all.

"Maybe it's the other way around," I said. "Maybe you got what *you* wanted and now you've lost interest."

There was silence. "That isn't true," he said finally. "How can you even *think* that?"

I didn't know what to think. And I could barely talk, because my throat was closing up.

"Well," I forced myself to say as Tony neared The Surrey—a small but elegant hotel in a quiet, residential area. "I'm almost at the restaurant, and I need to end this conversation because it'd be rude to keep Kitty and Ned waiting. I actually *care* how other people feel."

"Me too," he said in a tight voice.

"It sure doesn't seem that way. So I guess we're done."

I heard noise behind him—a TV blaring and birds chirping and kids giggling in the distance. I wondered if he was on his fire escape, looking across the street at the Siamese cat that was always gazing through a window screen.

"Do you mean with this conversation or with everything?" he asked.

I swallowed, seeing his apartment and the kitchen table where we'd had our second kiss. I forced that image out of my head and took a deep breath.

"Alex," I said, "I think you know exactly what I mean."

Twenty

I was looking at the remnants of my broken necklace scattered across my lap when Tony screeched into a spot in front of The Surrey and the car lurched forward.

"What's happened to you?" he asked. "A few weeks in high society and you're blending right in."

I narrowed my eyes, staring at his boyish face. "What's *that* supposed to mean?"

"A few things. First off, why are you worried about Ned's reaction to Alex canceling your date?"

I shifted in my seat. "I'm not."

"It sure sounded that way when you were on the phone. It makes me think you were just using Alex to get a rise out of that guy. You know . . . bring a lowly bartender around to piss off the rich relatives. I suppose it's even more effective when he's their employee."

I'd thought about that when I invited Alex to Kitty's party in the Hamptons. I'd relished breaking Ned's we-do-not-fraternize-with-bartenders rule. But that wasn't why I'd been seeing Alex, and I'd never, ever meant to use him. Still, the way

Tony was looking at me made me feel like I was no better than that girl who'd strung Alex along just because it was fun.

"I didn't *use* him," I said. "I liked him. I wanted to be with him."

Tony nodded. "I believe that. But the rest of it was a bonus, right?"

I couldn't listen to this. I reached for the door handle, but Tony popped the locks, trapping me inside. I stared straight ahead at a homeless man pushing a shopping cart filled with aluminum cans. *That makes me so sad,* Tina used to say.

"My second point," Tony went on, "is that I don't like the way you've changed. You ditch your best friend for your new boyfriend, and then you screw things up with him because he doesn't do exactly what you want. I think you're getting accustomed to being a Stone."

I shook my head. "You don't understand. Alex blew me off tonight because he—"

"Yeah, I heard. He has to go to Queens."

Tony sounded like he understood something I didn't. "Why is that an acceptable excuse? Who's in Queens? His ex-wife? His friend with benefits?"

"Savannah," Tony said, "you're too smart to be a psycho girlfriend with paranoid suspicions . . . none of which are valid."

"Then why is it more important for Alex to go to Queens than to keep his date with me?"

Tony was quiet for a moment as he pinched the bridge of his nose between his fingers. "I don't know exactly what he's doing there tonight, but I'm sure I can guess. And I can't tell you more than that because when you first got together, he asked me not to," he said finally. "What I *can* say is that your mistake was not having any faith in Alex, and his was not being up-front with you. But if you want to do the right thing, call him back and tell him everything's okay."

I couldn't do it. I couldn't call Alex, and I couldn't tell him everything was okay, because it wasn't. I just wouldn't go on caring about someone who'd take offense because I'd bought him a shirt that matched his eyes. And I refused to put myself in danger of falling any further for a man who'd keep a secret from me even though I'd told him most of mine.

Café Boulud's front door was right beside The Surrey's entrance. I walked past small tables on the sidewalk, under an awning, and through a front door that led to a restaurant with subdued, contemporary décor. There were intimate tables, flower arrangements in corners, and paintings of the French countryside on the walls. I struggled to get myself together as I followed a hostess past flickering candles and waiters memorizing orders. I tried not to be angry or sad or shaken, and I refused to unravel just because things with Alex had.

I spotted Kitty and Ned, sitting at a corner table, drinking wine and holding hands and gazing lovingly at each other like they were in one of those TV commercials I'd seen for romantic weekend getaways in the Poconos. They seemed to be the prototype for a blissful marriage, but I knew better and so did Ned. The joke was on Kitty, and being part of that made me lose my appetite before dinner had even started.

You can handle this. That's what I kept hearing when the hostess pulled out my chair and handed me a menu while Kitty smiled at me.

"Is Alex on his way?" she asked.

Ned's pale-green eyes were on mine. I picked up my napkin, flicked it into the air, and spread it across my thighs. "No," I said breezily as my fingers trembled under the table. "Unfortunately, he couldn't make it tonight. He isn't feeling well."

Ned lifted an eyebrow. I opened my menu, and after we placed our orders Kitty had to go and mention Darcelle. "I haven't heard from her since she left for Moscow," she said. "Not even an e-mail. But she was acting weird right before that, anyway . . . sort of distant . . . and I felt like she was giving me the cold shoulder when I took her to lunch on her last day at work. It was so strange."

Ned didn't flinch. He just straightened the lapels on his dark blazer. "I wouldn't dwell on that, Kitty. I always thought she was nothing but a ditzy talking head who loved to barge into my office and brown-nose for a promotion."

And get nailed on your desk.

Kitty's cell rang. "Forgive me," she said, glancing at the phone. "This is work related . . . it might take a while, so please start without me."

She left the table and crossed the restaurant in her simple black dress, holding the phone to her ear as she went through the front door that led to East 76th. Then the waitress brought our dinner, and I stared at my plate after she walked away.

I couldn't have been any less hungry. But eating was a good way to pass the time until Kitty returned, which I hoped would be soon. It was bad enough sitting across the table from Ned when she was here, but her absence made it even more awkward. So I got started, keeping my eyes on my food. It was so quiet in this corner of the restaurant that I could hear a cracking sound inside my jaw when I chewed.

"What happened to Alex?" Ned asked.

I gulped a chunk of Vermont chicken *deux façons.* I would've preferred to listen to my jaw than his voice.

"I already told you. He's sick."

Ned smiled with his mouth closed. "Sick of *you,* probably. He stood you up."

I slammed my left hand on the table. "Why do you have to say that?"

"Because it's true. You wouldn't be so angry otherwise."

He looked at my right hand, which was clenched around a knife. I let it go and sighed.

"You don't know everything," I said.

He leaned forward. "I know more than you think. So I'll stop teasing you and pass on some of the wisdom I've gained during thirty-three years as a Stone. That is . . . if you'll let me."

I groaned. "Do I have a choice?"

"Not really," he said while he pressed his thumb into the cleft in his chin and rubbed it up and down, moving his eyes around the restaurant like he was formulating a speech. "The thing is," he continued as he dropped his hand to the table and shifted his focus back to me, "there's a reason why people with resources shouldn't get involved with people like Alex. I'm afraid that things just can't work between them and us. As I'm sure you've discovered since you've come into money, there are too many differences, and these differences result in problems and arguments and very hurt feelings."

I didn't agree that I shouldn't get involved with people like Alex, but it was painfully true that our differences had caused everything Ned had just said. Much of what Alex and I had fought about never would've been an issue if I didn't have money. Still, I hated to believe Ned was right on any level whatsoever, and I wasn't going to admit he might be.

"That's *your* opinion," I said.

"I think it's *yours,* too. Remember I tried to keep you away from Alex during the gala? I'm sure you see now that it was for your own good." He looked closely at my face. "Go ahead and cry, Savannah . . . you don't have to try so hard to hold those tears back."

I sprang up from my seat, toppling my chair. "I'm leaving," I said.

People were looking at us. Ned glared at me like I was a total embarrassment. "Sit down," he said calmly. "The only reason you're angry is because I'm right about everything, and you know it. And if you leave, Kitty will get suspicious. Can you imagine how upset she'll be if she finds out we aren't as cozy as she thinks?"

I glared back at him. He was right again, and I had to find a way to make it through this dinner without gutting him with my knife. So I picked up my chair and sat down. "Do you know how it feels to hear Kitty talk about Darcelle?" I asked. "I detest you for putting me in this position."

"May I remind you this deal of ours was *your* idea? And this is how it's turned out: a lovely dinner with just the three of us."

"The deal was for Kitty's sake," I said, "so she wouldn't know who you really are."

"Let's not pretend you're Saint Savannah. The deal was also for you . . . so I'd stay out of your way at work and let you keep collecting your inheritance and hold my tongue about whatever asinine decisions you choose to make. And I've kept the bargain. I didn't say a word when you brought Alex to my wife's birthday party—as distasteful as *that* was. I'll do the same thing for the next loser with whom you decide to squander your pre-Botox years. Unless, of course, your heart is so broken from being stood up tonight that you've sworn off men."

He chuckled. I wished he'd stop mentioning Alex, because I wanted to forget him.

"You know what?" I said. "I can't help what Edward did . . . so stop trying to get back at me for it."

That seemed to have blindsided him. His eyes narrowed and his mouth opened like he was about to say something, but he didn't because Kitty slid into her chair, apologizing for taking so long.

"I couldn't get that guy off the phone," she said, spreading her arms across the table to simultaneously squeeze my hand and Ned's. "But I'm glad I was able to give you some time together. So what have you been talking about?"

I felt a stab of nausea mixed with guilt. Ned smiled.

"Savannah confided in me," he said, "that Alex stood her up tonight. She was too embarrassed to admit it at first, but of course I assured her that we can be up-front about anything. I also gave her some brotherly advice, which was that any guy who's callous enough to bail on a dinner to celebrate such an important achievement isn't worthy of her."

How I loathed this man. Kitty squeezed my fingers tightly between hers. "Savannah," she said, "I'm *so* sorry. And what Ned says is true . . . you don't need somebody who'd treat you that way."

"Exactly," Ned agreed. "Savannah's not going to see him again. Isn't that right?"

The braised chicken I'd eaten earlier rose from my stomach into my throat, nearly choking me. I swallowed and clenched my teeth and felt like screaming.

"Right," I said.

I faked friendliness for a while after that, and then I excused myself to the ladies' room and lingered inside, wishing I could escape through a back door. But instead I just left the bathroom and headed toward the table, dragging my feet and keeping my eyes on the floor as I passed two men speaking French.

"Savannah?"

I spun around. Jack was standing there with a chef dressed in white.

"*Sympa de discuter avec vous, Jacques,*" the chef said, shaking Jack's hand.

"*Merci, toi aussi,*" Jack replied with a smile.

Then the man was gone, and Jack turned to me. "You know the chef?" I asked, because I was so surprised to see Jack that I couldn't come up with anything else to say.

"He's the owner," Jack said. "So what are you doing here?"

He smelled the way he usually did—of cologne and Scotch

and cinnamon. His skin was darker and his hair was blonder than the last time I'd seen him. He looked like he'd just returned from a week on the white sand of some exotic island. Or maybe he'd climbed to the top of a snow-peaked mountain like in that picture I'd noticed at his house.

"Having dinner with Ned and Kitty," I said.

"Dinner with Ned? That must mean he's gotten over your deadly right hook."

Jack smiled, but I didn't. There was nothing to smile about, and he had believed Ned over me, and maybe Ned's idea of swearing off men was a good one. I turned around and started walking, but Jack followed me and blocked my way.

"Hey," he said gently, "aren't you ever going to have a real conversation with me again?"

"Probably not."

He let out a chuckle. "You're not still upset about what happened at my house, are you? That was all a big misunderstanding."

I sighed, folding my arms across my chest. "Yes, it was . . . and it was also partly my fault. I should've told you who I was right away . . . but you shouldn't have sided with Ned."

Jack nodded. "You're right, Savannah. I shouldn't have . . . and I'm sorry."

I blinked. This was so unexpected. But if he was trying to win me over, he was wasting his time.

He took a step closer. "I saw you at Kitty's birthday party. You didn't even say hello."

"Oh, didn't I? Neither did you."

"I didn't want to intrude," he said. "You were with your boyfriend. Is he here tonight?"

I shook my head. "He's not my boyfriend anymore."

"Really," Jack said slowly. "What happened?"

"We had a fight because he stood me up. But I don't care," I said, tossing my hair and reminding myself of Tina. I sounded hard and tough even though I didn't feel that way. I was holding back the tears that Ned had been goading me to let out.

Jack lifted his hand and ran his finger down the side of my face. I backed away, because it made me feel something and I didn't want to. But he didn't let me go. He slid his hand to my wrist and kept me close to him.

"I'd never treat you that way," he said as I stared at the amber flecks in his eyes. "But I have to admit I'm not surprised Alex did. He's not exactly squeaky-clean."

I stared at him, waiting for an explanation. "Am I supposed to guess what that means?"

He let go of my wrist and leaned against the wall. "I'm sure you know he's a fighter."

I nodded. "I know. But he quit a while back."

"Yeah," Jack said, "after he paralyzed someone during a cage fight in New Jersey."

Was it freezing in here all of a sudden, or was it just me? And why was my mouth so dry that it was impossible to form words?

"Are you okay?" Jack asked. "You've gone pale. I didn't mean to shock you."

"You did," I said. "But if you have more to tell me . . . I want to hear it."

"Well," he went on, "I mentioned when we met that I'd heard something about him, but I didn't want to spread gossip. Since then I had a source of mine check into it . . . and the rumor is true. He put another fighter in a wheelchair . . . permanently. From what I've heard, it was a pretty vicious brawl . . . Alex ended up losing his spleen, and he broke the other guy's spine."

I swallowed hard. I'd touched Alex's scars, but that was as far as he'd let me in.

"Didn't you ever look him up online?" Jack said.

"I try not to do that. Sometimes it's all lies—"

"This isn't a lie, Savannah. There wasn't much written about it since they were just amateur fighters, but I was able to get the inside story. It was an accident, of course . . . but because you were dating, he should've mentioned it. I'm sorry I had to be the one to tell you."

"Yes," I said, my voice ringing in my ears, "I am, too."

Jack said something about calling me tomorrow before he followed me back to my table to say hello to Ned and Kitty. He stood there for a few minutes, chatting and laughing with them as I stared into space and my body quivered beneath my dress. Then he went back to his table, and I somehow made it through dinner without fainting or throwing up or ripping my hair out of my head. When it was over, I walked out to East 76th, where Tony drove up in the sedan. I opened the door and slid inside before he came to a full stop.

"What are you doing?" he asked.

"Why didn't you tell me why Alex quit fighting?" I said. "Why didn't you tell me he hurt somebody?"

Tony sighed. "Who just couldn't wait to tell you about *that*? Ned Stone?"

"It wasn't Ned, and it doesn't matter. What matters is that Alex kept it from me. He's a liar, and don't you ever lecture me again that I made a mistake by not having faith in him, because he doesn't deserve any."

"Savannah," Tony said, "calm down. Alex never meant to hurt that guy . . . it just happened. Unfortunately, it's an occupational hazard."

One of Tony's library books was under my feet. I kicked it away. "I *know* that. What I *don't* know is why he kept it from me. *I just wasn't interested anymore—that's* what Alex said when I asked why he stopped fighting. Now I can't believe a word that ever came out of his mouth. God only knows what he's *really* doing tonight."

"I talked to him while you were at dinner," Tony said. "And what he's doing . . . it's something important."

"What is it? Tell me."

He shook his head. "It's not my place to do that. You'll just have to trust me."

Trust him? I was starting to think I couldn't trust anyone. "No," I said, "I *don't* trust you. I used to, but not anymore. You were pushing that relationship from the beginning, when all along you were just as deceitful as he was. So do me a favor and stop giving me advice. Maybe it was a mistake for us to be friends. Maybe we've gotten too familiar with each other."

He stared at me with a mix of pain and disappointment and stunned disbelief. As angry as I was, I still couldn't stand it, so I looked through the windshield at a carving on a building near the hotel—an owl staring at me with menacing round eyes.

"You know," Tony said after what seemed like an hour, "the day I met you, I thought you were nothing like the rich people I drive around this city. But now I see you're all the same. And by the way, Ms. Morgan . . . my employers sit in the back."

I threw open the door, slammed it behind me, and slammed it again after I slid onto the backseat. The tires screeched as Tony pulled out from between two cars, nearly grazed the one in front of us, and took off down the street. He hit a button to separate us with a soundproof sheet of glass, and I rode the rest of the way staring out the window at Manhattan and thinking that even though it was overflowing with people, it felt like the loneliest place on earth.

Twenty-one

I couldn't sleep that night. I kept thinking about my argument with Alex and my fight with Tony, and I tossed and turned and ended up on the couch with the remote control. I must have dozed off eventually, because when I opened my eyes it was light outside and my cell was vibrating on the coffee table and the TV was on. I turned it down, answered the phone, and heard Jack's voice.

He'd told me he would call, but I'd been too rattled about Alex's secret past and our sudden breakup to give it a second thought. Jack asked if I wanted to have breakfast—he'd discovered a restaurant in Brooklyn that featured authentic southern cuisine and had nothing but rave reviews.

"Remember you offered me Sunday-morning grits?" he asked. "Well, let me buy some for you. It's the least I can do after ruining your Saturday night."

I held my head in my free hand. It felt sore, and so did every other part of me. I thought something from home might soothe everything that had been battered, but I wasn't itching to get romantic again. I also didn't feel like spending a rainy morning in an apartment that was much too empty.

"I'll go," I said, "as friends."

He didn't answer right away and I thought I'd let him down, but he probably wouldn't have felt that way if he knew how much I needed a friend.

"Okay," he said after a moment, "we can be friends."

An hour later, I hailed a cab outside my apartment instead of calling Tony for a ride. The driver took me to Brooklyn, where he stopped on Smith Street in Carroll Gardens—a simple neighborhood with trees growing in patches of dirt between cement squares. The block was full of stores and restaurants inside old buildings that had two floors of apartments above them.

I got out of the car and saw Jack. He was holding an umbrella over his head and standing against one of the buildings, beside a window with *SEERSUCKER* printed across the glass in capital letters.

I walked toward him. He was dressed all weekend-casual chic in beige pants and a black pullover. His Cartier watch was on his wrist, and his cologne was the spicy one I liked.

"Thanks for coming out in this weather," I said, looking at him through the steady stream of water that poured off my umbrella.

Jack winked. "A little rain couldn't stand in my way."

He turned and opened the door into the restaurant, which smelled deliciously of bacon and biscuits and everything I was used to. I heard southern rock and looked at exposed brick walls, and then Jack and I were sitting at a table beside the window, where he had his first taste of grits while I just picked at mine.

"What's wrong?" he asked at the end of the meal. "Isn't the food up to Charleston standards?"

"It definitely is," I said quickly. "But my manners aren't. This is a great place, and it was thoughtful of you to invite me here. So I'm sorry for being such a drag."

"You're not a drag," he said. "And it's okay. You must have other things on your mind."

I nodded, keeping my eyes on a pat of butter melting into my barely touched grits.

Jack sipped his coffee. "I guess one of those things is Alex?"

It was. And sulking about him right now was rude even though Jack and I were just friends. "I'm sorry for *that*, too," I said as the check came. Jack reached for it, but I got there first. "This isn't a date . . . so let me take care of the bill."

I watched him, wondering if he'd blow up and say he wasn't *a fucking gigolo*. But all he did was stare at me until a smile spread across his lips and creased his dimples into his cheeks.

"That's not my usual policy," he said. "But I won't argue with you."

I liked that he didn't. I supposed someone who owned a multitude of buildings in Manhattan had no need to get defensive about his finances. He probably wouldn't even be insulted if I bought him an Armani shirt.

I hated to take Ned's advice about anything, but maybe he'd been right when he said there was a difference between people who had money and people who didn't and trying to mix those people wouldn't work. Maybe it was true that it would always end in hurt feelings. And maybe I shouldn't try anymore, because I'd had enough of those.

"How's the writing coming along?" Jack asked as I handed the waiter a leather folder filled with cash. "Are you still aspiring?"

"Actually," I said, smiling for the first time today, "I guess I can now be described as semi-accomplished. I wrote a story that's going to be published in *Femme*."

"Kitty's magazine," Jack said. "Ned told me you work there."

"I'm Kitty's assistant . . . but she promised there wasn't any nepotism involved. She said my story really is good enough for the magazine."

"Well, of course it is. She wouldn't risk her reputation."

I needed that. I smiled again, noticing the blond stubble growing into Jack's cheeks and his chin. It glinted under the lights like a million golden specks.

"You should let me take you out to celebrate," he said.

My smile faded. "That's what dinner last night was for. But it didn't work out very well."

He leaned into the booth and kept his eyes on me. "Then let me make it up to you. I'll take you out tonight . . . any restaurant you want."

I thought about that. "We could go to Le Bernardin," I said cautiously, remembering Alex's reaction when I'd suggested the same thing.

"That sounds good. I'll reserve a table for seven o'clock."

How easy and simple and tension-free. I didn't have to worry about fracturing fragile pride. I agreed, thinking that after last night's catastrophe, I deserved another chance at a real celebration. Then we left the restaurant and went outside, where I escaped the weather beneath an awning and Jack stayed under his umbrella as he tried to hail a taxi in the rain that was strangely cold for August. But cabs kept passing by, splashing sooty water onto the curb and his expensive shoes.

"You're as bad at that as I am," I said with a laugh when he joined me under the awning.

He laughed, too. "I give up. And I hate the subway . . . so why don't we call your driver? I've also got an account with his service."

I shivered in the damp air that was seeping into my bones. "My driver?"

Jack nodded. "The one who picked you up from my house . . . what's-his-name . . ."

"Tony," I said flatly.

"Yeah . . . he's driven me around quite a few times. Real nice guy."

He doesn't think the same of you.

I took my cell out of my purse even though I wished I could avoid Tony forever. I couldn't, though, because he'd been assigned as my personal driver and if I requested someone else he might get in trouble or lose his job and I couldn't do that to his family. It wasn't Marjorie's fault that her father hadn't been straight with me.

Tony arrived ten minutes later. I supposed he was in the area and getting his overtime from somebody else, and even though he'd always had other clients, I got the strangest feeling of being cheated on.

His dark eyes filled with surprise when he saw Jack, but Tony forced a tight smile as he held the back door for us. Then we were inside, and Tony slammed the door so hard that I jumped in my seat. But I tried to ignore it like he was ignoring me. He didn't say a word except to ask where we were going, and he turned up the radio while he drove and Jack and I chatted in the backseat. Then we were parked in front of Jack's brownstone on East 70th, where Jack told Tony to charge the ride to Lucas Enterprises, kissed my cheek, and said he'd pick me up for dinner. A minute later, he was gone and the car was quiet except for the traffic report on WCBS and the storm beating down on the roof. I kept my eyes on the fogged-up window and the rain that slid down the glass, and soon the car stopped outside my building.

"You don't waste much time, do you?" Tony said without turning around. His eyes were in the rearview mirror, and they were stern and judgmental and disapproving.

"It's not like that," I said tersely. "We're just friends."

He let out a coarse laugh that annoyed me. "Sure you are."

I tensed up. "How can you tell? You don't know the first

thing about being a friend," I said before I opened the door and stepped onto the sidewalk, where I got under my umbrella and leaned my head into the car. "My personal life is none of your business anymore. So do me a favor and stay out of it."

"Gladly," he said, glancing at me over his shoulder. "As long as you do *me* a favor and don't call during off-hours."

I stared at him. His face looked so different when he was angry—his eyebrows lowered and his nostrils flared. "What about your house?" I asked. "You want my business, don't you? You need the extra money."

He shook his head. "Not *that* much."

I slammed the door. He sped away, and his tires splashed muddy water from a puddle onto my shoes. I shook it off and walked toward my building, trying to pretend he hadn't hurt me as much as he'd wanted to.

The rain stopped before Jack picked me up in a cab, and I was glad I hadn't put on a new dress and spent an hour on my hair and makeup for nothing. I appreciated that he was right on time and whatever else he could have done tonight wasn't more important than me.

A half hour later, we sat across from each other inside Le Bernardin, clinking champagne glasses over our amuse-bouches. I excused myself to the ladies' room after we'd put in our dinner order, and I was touching up my makeup in the mirror when I saw the reflection of a woman walking in the door. She was tall and slender and effortlessly graceful, she had the shiniest black hair, and she started speaking with a French accent.

"We met at the jazz club on Murray Street," she said. "You're Savannah, *oui?*"

"Yes," I said, admiring her pronunciation of my name. She'd accented the wrong syllable, but it sounded more interesting that way. "And you're Angelique."

She nodded and leaned her bony shoulder against the wall. "You were with Jackson Lucas when we met. I just passed his table . . . I guess you're still seeing him?"

That didn't come out catty or nosy, just friendly like she'd been at the club.

"Actually," I began, "we only went out once, and then . . . well, it didn't work out and I was dating somebody else for a while."

"But Jack stole you away from him?"

She sounded intrigued, like I was updating her about the latest episode of a salacious soap opera. "No," I said. "He—"

She chuckled. "You don't have to explain. I know Jack very well . . . and he has ways of getting what he wants."

A gang of women walked into the bathroom, filling it with laughter and conversation and a burst of perfume. Angelique disappeared inside a stall and I went back to my table, where Jack and I stayed until long after he'd paid the bill. Then we caught a cab that took us to my apartment. We stood outside my door, and I noticed he'd shaved since this morning. The stubble was gone and his bronzed skin was smooth.

"I enjoyed tonight," I said as we lingered in the hallway and my key chain dangled from my fingers. Jack kept looking at it like he expected me to open up and let him in. But I couldn't flit from one man to another as if neither meant anything. So when he leaned forward and tried to kiss me, I turned my head and his lips landed on my cheek.

"Ouch," he said. "You know how to hurt a guy."

"And you know how to treat a girl. I really needed somebody today, and I appreciate that you were there for me. The last thing I want to do is hurt you, Jack . . . which is why we should just be friends like I said before."

He gave me a wry smirk. "I guess that decision has nothing to do with Alex?"

"It does," I admitted. "I can't get over a man overnight. I guess I haven't become as sophisticated as I'd led myself to believe. I'll never be one of those types."

"*That*," he said with a laugh as he tweaked my nose, "is what I love about you."

Tony and I didn't say a word to each other when he picked me up for work the next morning. He held the door and turned up the radio and acted like he was my employee just as I'd requested. It felt so lonely inside the car that I rushed out of it when we reached Stone News.

Then I was at work, where I walked past the front desk and the white wall with *Femme* splashed across it in purple paint. Everyone was looking at me strangely while I strolled through the lobby and down the hall leading to my desk like I was the star of a freak show.

I wanted to ask what was wrong, but I feared I was imagining things and Kitty's office was empty, so I couldn't get the scoop from her. I tried to ignore the stares as I settled into my chair and logged on to my computer, where I found an e-mail from Kitty that had been sent last night, inviting me to another Stone News black-tie banquet. This one was on Friday night at The Plaza, and she suggested I bring Jack. *I ran into him today,* she wrote. *He's got it bad for you.*

"Bitch," said someone behind me in a flat voice, like that was my name. Bitch Morgan.

I spun around in my chair and there was Caroline in a drab suit with her chest heaving and her fists clenched. She wasn't wearing her glasses, and the thick kohl around her eyes made her look like a deranged raccoon, ready to sink its pointy teeth into my throat.

"Caroline," I said, clueless as to what was making her breathe so heavily that I could hear it from a few feet away. I was under the impression we'd reached a mutual tolerance. "What's the matter?"

Her mouth scrunched into a bluish-white line. "Like you don't know," she said, coming closer and speaking in a low growl. "*I won't tell a soul*—that's what you promised. Was it so I'd keep my guard down while you plotted against me?"

I hadn't told anyone. I'd kept my word. I just stared at her with my mouth half-open.

"If you wanted to hurt me," Caroline went on, "you could've told my mother directly. You didn't need to broadcast it all over the Internet. We've had our fill of that with Dad."

I gulped, thinking of the Senator. "I didn't do anything on the Internet. What are you—"

"You posted my personal business on *Femme*'s social media sites. Kitty deleted the posts when she found them this morning, but it was too late. *Caroline Stone is Out in Manhattan* is such a catchy caption that it's been picked up by just about every celebrity gossip blog in town, especially the ones that like to crucify people for keeping their private lives quiet. The only one who didn't glom on to the story was Fabian Spader, and that's just because he's in my family's back pocket. Tell me . . . how'd you happen to snap a picture of me and my girlfriend holding hands at the High Line? Did you hire a private investigator with my father's money to follow us around, or were you hiding in the bushes?"

My ears were buzzing. "I swear, Caroline . . . I'd never do that to you."

"Why?" she asked. "Because we've been such good friends?"

I shook my head. "I wouldn't do it to anyone."

"Well," she said, folding her arms, "we both know that's a fucking lie, because you're the only one who updates those sites . . . and other than Kitty, nobody else has the password."

The password was *jessamine* . . . *The state flower of South*

Carolina, Ainsley had said—which was probably why it had been so easy for her to remember. I knew she'd figured out Caroline, but I'd convinced myself that she had no reason to spread the dirt around.

"I didn't do it," was all I could say.

Caroline glared at me. "Then who was it . . . my sister-in-law?"

"Of course not," I said. "Sites get hacked all the time. It could've been anybody. Considering all the enemies that Edward had—"

She scoffed. "I'm not interested in a conspiracy theory. I doubt my father's enemies would waste time on something so small."

"It isn't small to you," I said.

"And that's why you did it. Bravo, Savannah. My mother won't return my calls, and she probably never will. I guess you thought you hadn't taken enough from me."

I tried to tell her that wasn't true, but she just held up her hand and stormed off, paying little attention to Kitty as she passed by and gave her a pat on the shoulder.

"It wasn't me," I told Kitty the second she stepped into my cubicle.

"I know," she said, leaning against the calendar on my wall like she was exhausted even though it was only a few minutes after nine. "But Caroline doesn't . . . and I doubt either of us will be able to convince her otherwise, since all the evidence is against you."

Not all of it. "Well, even though I had nothing to do with this . . . I'm sorry."

Her red hair was twisted into a side bun; she fiddled with it, pulling out bobby pins and sticking them back. "It isn't really all that shocking. Ned knew, and I never pushed him on the subject, but I suspected. Virginia, however, clearly didn't . . . and she doesn't take kindly to being kept in the dark or having her family business in the press." She sighed and stared at a sprinkler in the ceiling. "What a day so far. I've got two meetings this morning and a doctor's appointment at noon . . . he's going to do some tests to make sure I'm okay for another round of IVF."

Oh, no. No way. You simply can't reproduce with someone like Ned. "You're doing that again so soon?" I said. "Wasn't the plan to focus on work for a while?"

"It was . . . but things are so good between me and Ned right now that I'm willing to multitask and give the pregnancy thing another try. I'm just aching for a little Edward Stone the Third. Or an Edwina . . . that's an elegant name . . . very British and *Masterpiece Theatre*–esque. Don't you think?"

I thought she should call a divorce lawyer. But I'd kept the cover-up going so long that I was in too deep, and she seemed so excited that all I could do was nod and pretend Edwina wasn't the most hideous name I'd ever heard.

After Kitty left for her meetings, I bolted out of my chair and searched for Ainsley. I finally tracked her down inside a conference room in the corporate division, where she was sitting at a polished table with stacks of documents. She was surrounded by mahogany walls and file folders and colored tabs, and she didn't notice I was there until I shut the door behind me.

"Hi," she said perkily, her dark bob bouncing around her face when she lifted her head. "Did you know it's my last day? Purdue doesn't start for a couple of weeks, but some professors have posted their reading lists, and I want to get started. I just came in to finish some things . . . I'm flying back to Indiana later this morning."

"That's convenient," I said as I walked toward her.

She twisted a pearl stud in her ear. "I'm leaving in a few minutes."

I pulled out a chair opposite her and sat down. "I'm sure you know what happened to Caroline."

She nodded as she picked up a *Sign Here* tab. "It'll all blow over soon. The news cycle is so fleeting these days that people will forget by tomorrow."

"Caroline won't. And she thinks it's *my* fault."

Ainsley stuck the tab on a document, grabbed a silver pen, and tapped it against the table. "I heard about that . . . but I didn't believe it. Social media sites get hacked quite often, so there's no way to tell who did it . . . but I'm sure whoever it was, he or she has nothing against you. He or she might even consider you a very lovely person."

I paused. "If that's so . . . then why would he or she do something that could only work against me?"

"Well," she said as she twirled the pen between her fingers, "the person probably figured that because you want to keep your job, it wouldn't make sense for you to be vindictive toward Caroline . . . thereby deflecting suspicion onto an anonymous hacker."

I crossed my legs. "I suppose he or she never considered that Caroline hates my guts and would accordingly consider me the prime suspect?"

"He or she probably gave it some thought . . . but with all the scandal surrounding Stone News, and considering the shoddy way Caroline treats people, there could be a number of suspects. As I'm sure you've noticed, she isn't exactly a ray of sunshine."

"True. So is your point that such behavior could provoke retaliation?"

She wouldn't stop goofing around with that pen, twirling it and doodling on a notepad while she kept her eyes on me. "That might've played a role . . . but only a minor one. You see, some people believe the best way to get back at someone is to hurt a person they love . . . like their child, their spouse . . . or maybe even their sister."

She started tapping the pen against the table again, and the noise irked me. I grabbed it out of her hand, and I noticed it wasn't a regular pen. It was a fancy one with *Visconti* engraved on the handle. My eyes shot to her face.

"This belongs to Ned, doesn't it?"

"Gosh, I'm not sure," she said. "He might've left it lying around the office and I accidentally picked it up. He really should be more careful about how he treats valuable things. He should also learn to be considerate toward trustful people who are new to certain intimate experiences."

I raised an eyebrow. "*What* did you say?"

She didn't answer. She just fiddled with her earring again and kept talking. "It's dangerous," she said, "for a man to string a girl along and pretend to care about her, only to abruptly end everything at a Pinkberry on a Saturday afternoon and then rush off to pick up his wife from a hair appointment."

I remembered Ainsley's teardrop splashing onto *The New York Times* and her telling me that Ned was *a little grumpy in the morning.* "Ainsley," I said, "I can't believe you had an affair with Ned . . . and that you'd hurt Caroline to get back at him because he ended it."

She let out a faint laugh. "I did no such thing, Savannah. We're just speaking hypothetically. I didn't do anything wrong . . . and you won't go around telling people otherwise. Unfounded rumors about mistakes I allegedly made at eighteen could trash my reputation in the news industry, and you have too much character to cause something like that."

She really had me pegged. She stood up and headed toward the door, and I watched her stroll out of the room, leaving the scent of baby powder behind. And then I just sat there for a while, deciding that her cheerleader costume was lined with steel.

Twenty-two

I barged into Ned's office. He was sitting behind his desk with his head bent over a thick document and his fingers pressed against his temples. He didn't look up, even when I closed the door and sat in a chair across from him.

"I'm furious about what happened to Caroline," he said.

I nodded. "I am, too."

"And I'd blame *you* for it," he went on, keeping his eyes on the document. "But like Kitty, I don't think you're responsible. You're so desperate to hang on to your inheritance that I doubt you're stupid enough to give me such a good reason to kick you the hell out of here."

"Well," I said, "I wouldn't use the word *desperate*. But you're right about the rest of it."

He turned a page. "I think it was a disgruntled secretary or somebody in the newsroom with unfulfilled aspirations of anchor-person stardom." He looked at me. "You can be sure that when I find out who did this . . . the penalty will be swift and severe."

I had no doubt about that. I swallowed hard and forced myself to nod again.

Ned looked back at his papers. "The truth doesn't matter right now, though . . . Caroline's convinced it was you, and so is my mother. Virginia loathed you before, but now you've shot to number one on her shit list."

"I don't care. And I came here to talk about your breach of our agreement."

"Our *agreement*?" he said as he flipped a page. "If you're referring to your blackmailing me . . . you know I've complied and Darcelle is in Moscow."

"Yes, I know. But you've been unfaithful with someone else."

I pulled the Visconti pen from my pocket and dropped it in front of him. He picked it up and stared at me.

"Where'd you get this?" he asked.

"Ainsley had it," I said.

He stuck the pen inside his jacket and began searching for loose threads on his lapel. "Did she really? Well, I probably left it somewhere around the office and she picked it up."

I shook my head. "That was her explanation, but I don't buy it. Since you made such a point of telling me that a Visconti pen isn't a toy, you wouldn't be so careless as to leave it lying around here. She must've found it somewhere else . . . like . . . oh, I don't know . . . maybe in your bedroom."

He pulled a thread off his jacket and cast it into the air. "Is *that* what she told you?" he said with a hearty laugh. "It's just a teenage fantasy, Savannah. In case you haven't noticed, the girl's got a raging crush on me. She's been following me around like a lovesick puppy all summer. Pay no attention to what she says."

I shook my head and folded my arms. I couldn't spoil the glowing reference that Ned had promised Ainsley—especially considering what she'd done to earn it. "She didn't say anything. And I know you broke our deal."

He tapped his fingers on his desk, glancing out his window at the blue sky over Manhattan. "Let's just pretend I *did* have something going with Ainsley," he said after a moment. "I still didn't violate our so-called contract. As I recall, you told me it would be null and void if there were any illicit activities between me and any woman who isn't my wife."

"I'm glad you remember."

He wagged his finger at me. "If you ever want a decent position here, you need to learn about business. And one of the most important things to know is that you have to be careful with the fine print. Ainsley isn't a *woman,* Savannah . . . she's an annoying kid who rambles on and on about vapid bullshit like state flowers and whoever the fuck was the President of the United States in 1851. Now why would a man like *me* involve himself with a tiresome girl like *that?*"

I shook my head. "You're right . . . she *is* a kid, which makes what you did with her even more disgusting."

"I object to your insinuation that I'm a pervert. The age of consent in New York is seventeen, and she turned eighteen in May. Not that it matters, though. I didn't touch her."

"Sure you didn't," I said.

He leaned back in his chair and stretched out his legs. "But even if I did . . . you wouldn't tell Kitty. I'm sure she's mentioned our plans to try again for a baby . . . and there's no way you'd be vicious enough to ruin that. You simply don't have it in you."

Maybe he'd rubbed off on Ainsley instead of just rubbing up against her. She'd been as good at predicting my next move as he was. I supposed his implication that I was too considerate to wreck Kitty's life was a compliment, but I doubted he saw it that way. He clearly viewed kindness and weakness as the same thing.

"Besides," he went on, "Darcelle is gone, and Ainsley's on her way back to the Midwest. All threats have been relocated."

"Not if you count the entire female population of the tri-state area."

He laughed, plopped his feet on his desk, and adjusted his Rolex. "From what I've heard, it seems you've gotten over your little heartbreak with that bartender and you've gone back to my best friend. So how about this: You keep out of my marriage, I'll put up with your dating Jack, and we'll all be one big happy family . . . just like my father wanted."

I could've thrown up. "You don't have a clue about what *our* father wanted."

I left his office and went to my desk, where I couldn't concentrate on work because all I could think about was Caroline and Ainsley and Kitty, who came back from her doctor's appointment a few hours later with a big smile on her face.

"How'd it go?" I asked, trying not to sound too eager for bad news.

"Fine, I think . . . I'll have the test results soon." She glanced at my computer. "Did you get my e-mail about the party this weekend at The Plaza?"

"Yes," I said, "but I'll have to pass. I assume Caroline and Virginia will be there, and after what happened this morning—"

"Caroline's already canceled," Kitty said. "Virginia will definitely be there, but that's all the more reason for you to attend. I know you're innocent, and so does Ned . . . but if you don't show up on Friday, my dear mother-in-law will take it as evidence of guilt. And you have nothing to hide, Savannah . . . so go to that dinner with your head held high. Besides . . . I need you there. I can't deal with Virginia by myself."

She needed me. That meant something. I nodded, thinking of the gown that Tina had left in my closet. "I have a dress I've worn only once, so I guess I should get some use out of it."

Kitty dragged her diamond circle back and forth on its chain. "What kind of dress?"

"It's strapless and sparkly. The color is called lipstick rose."

"Well," she said, "that sounds beautiful. But this event is

rather subdued . . . so you'd probably be better off with something black and simple."

On Friday night, I stared at the clothes stretched out on my bed—the pink ball gown from Charleston and the formal black dress I'd bought at Bergdorf Goodman.

The black dress was safe and unassuming. It would make me blend into an orchard of upper-class clones. But I didn't want to be an assembly-line cutout, a carbon copy of every woman I'd seen at high-end stores on Fifth Avenue. I wanted to be me, and I wanted to wear Tina's dress with its full chiffon skirt and flowers made of hand-sewn sequins, and what was wrong with that? The dress I'd worn to the Hamptons had been a smash in the blogosphere even though it violated Manhattan's fashion code, so maybe I knew more than Kitty did. Maybe New York's high society needed a dash of southern-style glamour.

By the time Jack knocked on my front door, my hair was curled and my makeup was done and I was wrapping a lipstick-rose shawl around my shoulders.

"Well," he said, eyeing my dress after I opened the door, "that's unique."

I couldn't imagine he meant it in a negative way. "Yes," I agreed as I admired his tux. "And as I recall from our first date, unique is what you've been looking for."

I sounded flirty, like I'd changed my mind about being just friends—and maybe I was starting to. He'd been so sweet all week, calling every night and sending bouquets to my desk and doing his best to make me feel better about the Caroline controversy and to sew up the gaping wound that Alex had left.

"I think I've found it," he said, sliding his hand around my waist and leaning in to give me a peck on the cheek. But this time I turned my mouth toward him instead of away. Our lips met, and when they parted his dimples sprang into his cheeks as he smiled and kept his arms around me. "So you're okay with this, Savannah? I don't want to rush you."

"You haven't," I said. "That's why it's okay."

I took his hand and we left the apartment and walked down the hall as my hem swept the carpet. Then we went downstairs and headed outside, and I stopped in my tracks when I saw Tony at the curb. He was opening the back door of the black sedan to let out a smartly dressed couple who walked past us arm in arm on their way into the building.

I caught Tony's eye. He looked away, and Jack spoke up.

"Hey," Jack said, giving Tony a wave as he kept his other hand in mine and led me toward the car. "Since you're here, do you mind giving us a ride to The Plaza? You can charge it to my account."

"Jack," I said, turning my head toward him and keeping my voice low, "it's Friday night. He wants to go home."

"No I don't," Tony said, probably just to spite me.

"Of course you do," I insisted. "Think of Allison and Marjorie."

His jaw tensed up. "I *always* think of them, Ms. Morgan. That's why I'll be happy to drive you to The Plaza."

Jack chuckled, eyeing me and Tony quizzically. "What *is* this? A brother-sister spat?"

I made myself laugh that off. "Don't be silly," I said as Tony held the back door open for me and Jack. We slid onto the seat and then Tony pulled away from the curb, and I kept looking at his key chain dangling from the ignition and the picture of Marjorie. I almost asked how she was doing, and I nearly drowned inside a wave of sadness after I remembered that I couldn't.

"Are you all right? You're so quiet," Jack said a few minutes later, when we were stuck in traffic and The Plaza was visible in the distance. It was twenty stories high and had a majestic entrance with steps covered in red carpet. He leaned toward me and nodded in Tony's direction as he spoke into my ear. "I made a joke of it, but I didn't like the attitude this guy had with you. Are you upset about it? I'm on good terms with the owner of the car service . . . one word from me and he'll deal with Tony."

"*No,*" I said quickly. "Don't you dare do that, Jack. I'm fine."

It took a moment for him to nod. Then Tony veered around a limousine and sped up, which made something slide across the floor and land against my foot. I reached down and picked up a hardcover book coated in transparent plastic that had a sticker on its spine printed with *New York Public Library*. I leafed through a chapter, and a laminated card fell out.

I put down the book and examined the card. A prayer was printed on one side, and on the other was the name Michael Neill and last Wednesday's date. *Foster Funeral Home* was written across the bottom. *Elmhurst, New York.*

I glanced at Tony, hoping Michael Neill wasn't his uncle or his cousin or one of his best friends, and wondering if he'd wanted to talk to me about him but thought he couldn't.

I leaned over to Jack and whispered in his ear. "Where's Elmhurst?" I asked.

"Queens," he said.

Tony stopped in front of The Plaza. Jack slid to the edge of the backseat, opened the door, and stepped onto the sidewalk. Then he leaned inside and offered me his hand.

I didn't take it. "Can you please give me a minute, Jack? I'd like to speak with Tony."

Jack seemed confused as he moved his eyes between me and the front seat. "All right," he said finally. "I'll be waiting by the entrance."

He shut the door. I bent toward Tony, holding the funeral card under his chin.

"Who's Michael Neill?" I asked.

He stared at the card for a long moment. Then he let out a heavy breath and turned around. "He's the reason Alex quit fighting . . . and the reason he stood you up last week."

I checked the card, focusing this time on the birth and death dates written in small print that I hadn't noticed before. "But this says he died on Sunday. . . ."

Tony sighed again. "He'd been doing badly for a while . . . paralysis can cause a lot of other complications. He went into the hospital late Saturday afternoon, right before Alex was supposed to meet you. Mike and Alex were close friends for a few years before that fight. . . . Alex was devastated about what happened, but he did everything he could to help Mike and his family. Alex promised he'd be there for him, and he wasn't going back on that promise at the end."

The card slipped from my fingers and fell next to Tony. I held my hands over my mouth and sank into the backseat, wishing I could rewind to last Saturday and do it all over again.

"Why didn't he tell me?" I said through my fingers. "Why didn't he tell me any of it?"

Tony shrugged one shoulder. "It isn't easy to admit you've put somebody in a wheelchair, even if it was an accident. He kept searching for the right time to tell you . . . but he couldn't find it."

I recalled an early morning when Alex and I had sat in his car in front of my building. *I want to tell you something important,* he'd said. But he didn't. And I hadn't caught on when I asked him if the scar on his stomach still hurt. *Always,* he'd told me.

"And then *this* happened," Tony went on. "The only reason he kept Mike a secret is that he didn't want you to think badly of him."

I shook my head. "I never would have."

Tony looked at me the way he used to, like he could see who I truly was instead of who I'd been lately. "I know that."

I held my head in my palms. "Why didn't *you* tell me? You were my friend."

"Yeah," he said. "But I'm his, too."

I looked up and into his face, and I was sorry for telling him that he didn't know the first thing about being a friend. He knew so much more than I ever had.

Tony drove away, and I held my hem above the steps as I headed toward The Plaza. Jack was waiting for me at the entrance, which had three gold doors with flags above them that sagged in the still air. When I reached him, he bent his elbow to form a right angle like gentlemen do at weddings and in old movies.

"Ready?" he said with a smile that would've seemed captivating to anyone but me.

I shook my head, glancing at people swerving around us as they headed into the hotel. Jack seemed confused again, his arm dropped to his side, and I led him to a corner where we were out of everyone's way.

"Jack," I began, "when you checked into that rumor you'd heard about Alex . . . did you do it because you wanted to help *me* or because you wanted to hurt *him*? And were you truly sorry to be the one to tell me?"

He stuffed his hand into his pocket and jangled the change inside. "What do you mean?"

"You know what I mean. And since your sources are so reliable, I have a feeling you also know Mike Neill died on Sunday."

He gazed out at the street. "Yes," he said. "I do."

"Did you know he was the reason Alex didn't show up for our date last Saturday?"

"Not until later," he said, looking at me again.

I shook my head and crossed my arms. "But you still didn't tell me."

He stared at my face for a moment before he caressed my

shoulder through my shawl. "Don't get yourself worked up, honey . . . especially when you're looking so beautiful. And please don't be angry with me. Everything I did was for your own good."

For my own good. That gave me a chill. It was something Ned would say.

"Savannah," Jack went on, "the reason I had Alex investigated is because I saw you with him at Kitty's party and I was worried. He isn't the type of man you should be involved with. You're miles above him . . . and he just isn't good enough for you."

"You're wrong," I said. "I'm no better than he is."

Jack slid his hand from my shoulder to my wrist, which he held gently between his fingers. "It's sweet of you to think that way . . . but it's also naïve. As smart as you are, you're still very young . . . and inexperienced with men."

I wondered if he'd sent a detective down south to interrogate Jamie and round up every guy I'd gone out with to find out exactly how inexperienced I was. Or maybe someone had been watching 15 Central Park West with binoculars and reported that Alex came to my apartment at night but didn't leave until morning and Jack just couldn't let it go on.

"Well," I said, "did you investigate *that,* too?"

He shook his head. "I figured it out when you were in my bedroom."

My lips tightened. I was sorry I'd ever set foot in his bedroom.

"And," Jack continued, "it's one of the reasons I was looking out for you. I couldn't just stand around and let you get dragged down by a guy like Alex. He's going nowhere."

I shook my head. "That isn't true. He wants to be—"

"I know," Jack said with a roll of his eyes. "He wants to be an actor and a writer. But all he's accomplished is putting a man in his grave."

"That was an *accident,*" I said.

Jack shrugged. "It doesn't change the fact that he ended someone's life."

Jack said that so smugly, so self-righteously. "You misled me," I said. "You used the accident against Alex and let me go on believing he stood me up for no good reason."

"Because," Jack said in an irritatingly calm voice, "I thought the truth might hurt you more. I was trying to protect you."

I scoffed. "*Protect* me? You can't be serious," I said so loudly that guests filing into The Plaza were beginning to stare.

Jack glanced at them and back at me. "I'm *very* serious," he said, pushing a stray lock of hair away from my eyes. "If Alex can paralyze a fighter with his bare hands, imagine what he might do to you if you ever made him mad. And judging from that fiery temper of yours, you could set him off quite easily."

Jack chuckled and tweaked my nose. That had seemed cute when he did it at my apartment door, but not now. Now it was infuriating, and I had to get out of there before I committed my second act of battery.

"I'm finished with you," I said, turning toward the entrance.

Jack caught my arm, and I whirled around. "Okay," he said, sounding close to running out of patience. "All right. You've made your point. I understand why you're upset. Maybe I should've been more honest with you. But other than that, I didn't do anything wrong."

I just stared at him, amazed that he thought he hadn't done anything wrong. He seemed to believe it was perfectly acceptable to use a tragedy to beat out the competition, especially if the competition wasn't in his tax bracket. He'd eliminated Alex just as easily as he would have made Tony lose his job, and he'd given as little thought to their feelings as Ned had given to Kitty and Ainsley.

"Do you mean," I said, "that you think it's okay to step on people to get what you want?"

His features hardened. "I don't look at it that way, Savannah.

And I don't like being judged, either. As you get older and spend more time working at your father's company . . . you'll understand why the rules need to be bent once in a while to protect what you care about."

He was so disgustingly like Ned, giving me a lesson in Business 101. But maybe that shouldn't have surprised me, since they were best friends. *I doubt he's any better than Ned,* Tony had told me. I wished I'd taken that into consideration earlier, and I shouldn't have let Ned convince me to stick with men who had money. It didn't make things easier at all.

I folded my arms across my chest. "What happened," I said, "wasn't *business.* I'm not one of your real estate deals, Jack."

"Of course you aren't," he said smoothly, like he wanted to relax me, but it didn't work. I was livid, and I remembered Tony telling me that Jack had given him *a shady vibe* and Tina saying, *I wouldn't think too highly of a man who's so easily swayed. It's a bad indication of his character.* If I'd only listened. "Let's not make a big thing out of this, okay? It's so unimportant. Besides, we're here for a party. We should forget what happened and move on." He offered me his arm again. "Let's just go inside."

I backed up. "You have ways of getting what you want. Isn't that right? That's what Angelique told me when I ran into her at Le Bernardin. She said she knows you well, and I guess that's true. I wonder if it's the reason she didn't accept that expensive engagement ring."

I lifted my hem and headed toward the door, but he got in the way.

"Take it easy," he said in that gentle, soothing voice he'd been using on me all along. "You're blowing this way out of proportion. Come on, now . . . you know I'm a nice guy."

He smiled. Maybe he thought his looks and his charm and those dimples in his cheeks would make me melt into his arms and forget everything, but they didn't.

I peered into his hazel eyes. Tonight was the first time I'd been able to see through them.

"You know something, Jack? I've finally realized *you're* the one who just isn't good enough for me."

I left Jack on the steps and rushed into The Plaza, beneath chandeliers and past gilded walls toward the Grand Ballroom, which had arched windows and tables with gorgeous centerpieces made of flowers and lit candles, and everything was awash in rose-tinted light. I glanced around, hoping to spot Alex standing behind a bar in his black shirt and white tie just the way I'd found him. But he wasn't there, and I stood alone in the middle of the room while people veered around me, my body so limp that my shawl fell to the floor and stayed there until Fabian Spader picked it up.

"Bold choice," he said, draping the shawl around my shoulders. "But I already know how daring you are. Word on the street is that *you're* the one who outed Caroline Stone."

He'd halfway complied with tradition tonight. He was in a tux, but his cummerbund and bow tie had a loud zebra print. "That isn't true," I said.

He tossed his hair. "Maybe not . . . but since you and Caroline were whispering all sorts of secrets at Kitty's last birthday, I can't imagine you didn't know everything before it hit the Net. Yet for some odd reason, you chose not to tell me. And you continue to keep things from me, even after I gave you that smashing write-up on my blog. I didn't get a word of thanks."

He was wearing the most pungent cologne, which sparked a pain at the back of my head.

"Thank you," I made myself say.

He shrugged. "I'm afraid it's too late for that . . . and you don't seem to understand how things work around here. When I give *you* something, you're supposed to give *me* something. I made you famous, and you need to pay me back with information about the Stones. Everyone's sick of hearing about all the shenanigans Edward was up to before he expired, Caroline's fifteen minutes are done . . . and I suspect there's more salaciousness in your family to entertain the masses." He took a step closer and rubbed his knuckles beneath his pointy chin. "You see, Savannah . . . I've had my fill of kissing Virginia's regal ass. If you agree to give me a steady supply of accurate information, it would advance my career and keep your reputation pristine."

I shook my head. "I said thank you for the write-up. That's all you're going to get."

I whirled around and walked away, and then I saw Kitty coming toward me with Ned. He was in a tux and she wore a black dress, and she seemed surprised that I hadn't worn one too. But she didn't say anything—she just glanced around and asked about Jack.

"He told me you invited him," she said.

"And then I uninvited him. It's complicated, Kitty . . . I'll explain later."

A woman passing by with a champagne glass in her hand caught Kitty's arm and started gabbing in her ear. They headed toward a table where waiters were serving salads, and Ned looked down at me as we trailed behind.

"Did you get dumped *again*?" he asked.

I didn't answer. And I couldn't stand the sound of his highbrow accent, especially when I was sitting at a round table with him and Kitty and Virginia and a few other guests. Virginia kept looking at my gown like it was one of those trashion dresses made from cut-up credit cards or used condom wrappers, but nobody seemed to notice her snooty stares—not even Kitty, who was caught up in Ned. She kept rubbing his back and squeezing his hand and it nearly made me retch, thinking about where that hand had been.

"Savannah," Kitty said, leaning toward me when we were in the middle of the main course. She sat beside me, and Ned was next to her, and Virginia was on my left, cozying up to a man who seemed to be some sort of dignitary. "Good news: My doctor cleared me for IVF."

My head snapped toward her. Virginia abandoned her conversation and looked at us.

"What was that?" she asked in her saccharine voice. "Something about IVF?"

Kitty cleared her throat. "I wasn't planning to tell you for a while, Virginia, but—"

"You weren't planning to tell me for a while? Yet you told Susannah, and—"

"Savannah," I said, staring at my plate.

"—I can't imagine why you'd reveal that information to a *stranger* before *me*."

"Savannah isn't a stranger," Kitty said. "She's Ned and Caroline's sister."

Virginia ignored that and adjusted her sapphire necklace. "Let's return to a more important topic: You're going to make another attempt at giving me a grandchild."

"I'd phrase it differently," Kitty said. "But that's the idea."

Virginia stroked her wavy hair. "Well, that's good news," she said with a phony smile. "Make sure you start soon, though . . . I know women wait forever to have babies these days, but I'd hate for you to be mistaken for a grandmother at your child's high school graduation."

Kitty stiffened beside me as Virginia went back to chatting with the man next to her. Then Kitty guzzled a glass of wine while she dragged her circle of diamonds back and forth on its chain and started talking to Ned about turning a guest room into a nursery.

This was unbearable. I couldn't take it anymore. I couldn't

allow Kitty to stay trapped between a lying, cheating husband and an abusive monster-in-law. So I mustered my courage, clamped my fingers around Kitty's wrist, and led her to a quiet corner away from all the tables.

"What are you doing?" she asked.

I decided to spit it out before I lost my nerve. "You can't have a baby with Ned."

She looked at me blankly, like she wasn't sure whether that statement was an order or a premonition. She seemed not to know if she should laugh or panic. "What are you talking about?" she asked with a jittery titter. "Why would you say such a thing?"

My breath was coming in shaky spurts and my knees felt close to buckling, but I made myself keep going. "Because he cheated on you," I said, "with Ainsley and Darcelle . . . and probably other women . . . I don't know for sure."

It was a relief to get those words out, but now that they rang in the air between me and Kitty I felt like my burden had been shifted to her shoulders, where it was infinitely heavier. Her throat moved like she was swallowing and her left eyelid twitched and she opened her mouth a little, but all that came out was half a gasp.

"You just found out about this?" she asked, her voice halting.

I shook my head. I couldn't pretend anymore. "I've known about Ainsley since Monday, and I know Ned broke up with her recently . . . on a Saturday afternoon while you were at a hair appointment. She told me he picked you up afterward," I said, and her eyes darted around the room as if it were covered in clues she hadn't seen until now. "I caught him in the act with Darcelle a while ago. I made him send her to Moscow."

Kitty's brown eyes narrowed. "I brought you in. I helped you. I thought we were friends. . . ."

"We *are*," I said as the stricken look on her face pierced my heart.

She shook her head. "A friend wouldn't have kept this from me. Now I'm wondering if you were just trying to get on my good side so I'd ignore things that I wouldn't with my other employees. The slacking off, the two-hour lunches—"

Maybe I *had* taken advantage. But it had nothing to do with this. "That isn't true, Kitty. The reason I didn't tell you about Ned is that I know you love him . . . or at least, who you thought he was. I didn't want to ruin your marriage, and that's why I tried to fix everything."

"*Fix* everything?" she said with a harsh laugh. "How? By turning me into a *fool*?!"

She'd said that loudly enough for people to hear, including Ned. He pushed back his chair and crossed the room, and then he was standing beside us, asking what was wrong. Kitty didn't answer—instead she shoved him with both hands, but it only made him stumble slightly backward and skid on the slippery floor.

"Kitty," he said in a controlled voice as he straightened up and smoothed his jacket and glanced at the growing audience. It included Fabian Spader, who was dangling his arm over the back of his chair while he sat beside his photographer. "I have no idea what's going on, but please don't make a scene. You know my family's had enough bad press lately."

"Maybe," she said as she tried to twist her wedding ring off her finger. "But I'm not part of your family anymore. That ended when you betrayed me with my former friend and some little teenage intern. Savannah told me *everything*."

His eyes burned with anger when they struck mine. He reached for Kitty's hands, but she jerked them away as her ring came loose. She threw it at him; it bounced against his lapel, dropped to the floor, and skidded across the polished surface, spinning on its side. Then she yanked off her necklace, breaking the lock, and tossed it into a nearby trash can overflowing with soiled cocktail napkins.

Ned glanced at the diamonds sinking into a glob of ranch dressing. "Kitty," he said, "what Savannah told you isn't true . . . and surely you're not going to take a stranger's word over mine."

She shook her head as her face reddened. "For the first time in a long time, I actually *do* know what I'm doing. I'd thought the way you treated Savannah wasn't who you really are, but obviously I was wrong. I guess I don't know you at all, and if anybody's a stranger . . . it's *you*."

Tears welled in her eyes. She turned to walk away; he reached out and grasped her hand.

"Kitty," he said again. "Don't leave. Please."

His voice was pleading, and I hadn't expected that. Kitty sniffed and hardened her jaw. "You can find someplace else to sleep tonight," she said. "I'm sure that'll be easy for you."

She stormed out of the ballroom and into the lobby, and Ned and I just stood there, watching the door slowly close and click into place.

He turned toward me. I detected something sad in his eyes that I'd never seen there before. It surprised me, and maybe it did the same to him. I wondered if he'd just figured out that he wasn't as cold as we'd both thought. Maybe he knew the brownstone on East 70th wasn't the only thing that had just slipped away. And I would've rubbed that in his face if he didn't suddenly look like a wounded little boy who'd lost what mattered most.

He caught me staring at him. He drew in his cheeks and lifted his chin.

"Satisfied?" he said from between clenched teeth.

I shook my head, seeing Fabian from the corners of my eyes. He was out of his seat and picking Kitty's necklace from the trash, wiping the dressing off with a tissue. "If you think I enjoyed what just happened, you're dead wrong. *I've* lost something, too."

Ned disregarded that and headed toward the door with Fabian following after him, holding the necklace in one hand and Kitty's wedding ring in the other.

"Don't you want these?" Fabian asked.

Ned ignored him and kicked the door open on his way out. Fabian stuffed the jewelry into his jacket as the door closed, and then he turned around and looked at me.

He wasn't the only one. I realized I was being watched, like I was alone onstage without a script. It was embarrassing and uncomfortable and I wanted to escape, so I headed for the door but didn't get far. As soon as I touched the knob, nails dug into my shoulders and hands spun me around, and I was inches from Virginia. The ivory skin on her forehead was bulging with ropy veins.

"What's wrong with you?" she screeched. "Is it your goal to ruin my family?"

Her voice was shaking and so was everything else—her chin, her fingers, the sapphires around her throat. I couldn't help but understand why she hated me, and even though none of this was my fault, she'd never believe it, so there was no point in trying to explain.

"Mrs. Stone," I said calmly, feeling eyes on me from every direction, "this hasn't been a pleasant night for either of us. So I'm going to say good night to you and walk out that door."

"Where are you planning to go?" she asked, lowering her voice so only I could hear. "Back to that trailer-park trollop you call your mother?"

She was trying to get at me, to hit a spot that would set me off, and it was working, but I refused to give her what she wanted—public evidence that I was ill-bred and bad mannered and *all the money in the world can't change white trash.*

"I'm sure you don't mean to say such cruel things," I said.

"It's merely the truth. You know . . . recently I've been wondering why Edward would stray to a low-rent beautician like your mother. The only reason I can come up with is that women of her class are appealing to powerful men merely because they agree to do things that are typically reserved for paying customers."

My chest tightened like it was about to cut off my blood supply. "Well," I said in a steady voice, "if that's what he was looking for . . . then how can you explain the Senator?"

Virginia's jaw clenched. "Excuse me?" she said after a moment.

I knew she'd heard every syllable. I hated to be so awful—even to her—but she'd given me no choice. "I mean," I continued, "if he was only after what you're implying, he *could* have just paid for it. But I think he was looking for something else . . . something more valuable that he wasn't getting from *you.*"

She looked like I'd just socked her in the stomach and I felt sort of bad about that, but only until she opened her mouth again. "Do you know what you are?" she said after a moment of thought. "You're a hustler. You're nothing but a crafty little hustler who thinks carrying a designer bag and accepting invitations to exclusive parties and sleeping with a rich man like Jackson Lucas will get you into *my* world. But trust me . . . no matter how hard you try, or what you buy, or who you get on your knees for . . . you'll *never* fit in here."

She gave me a contented smile. I shook my head and held it high.

"You've got your facts all wrong, Virginia. But you *are* right about one thing: If I live to be a hundred, there's no way I'd ever fit in with people like *you.*"

I turned around and headed for the door, but she grabbed my arm to stop me.

"I'm not finished. Don't you dare turn your back on me," she said in a caustic whisper, pressing her nails into my flesh and nearly wrenching my arm out of its socket.

I grabbed her hand and pried it off of me, and when we separated she slipped in her high heels and landed on her back, skidding across the floor.

I hadn't meant for that to happen. Everything was spiraling out of control. "I'm sorry," I said, but nobody seemed to hear. The photographer snapped pictures and Fabian rushed toward us with a crowd of people who helped Virginia up while she put on a big I'm-the-victim act. She limped between two men as they led her back to her table, and everybody else glared at me, shaking their heads and whispering while I struggled to see through colored splotches that the photographer's flashes had burned into my eyes. Then there was Fabian's zebra tie—dizzying, zigzagging stripes of black and white that he straightened as he gave me a smug smile.

"You should go now, Savannah," he said. "I think you've lost your place here."

Twenty-three

I dialed Tony's number as I raced down The Plaza's front steps, catching my heel in my skirt and ripping the hem. It dragged behind me while I paced Fifth Avenue, pretending I didn't see the reproachful glances of guests leaving the party. They all stared at me like I was something to be picked up by the Department of Sanitation in the morning.

I dove into the back of the car when Tony arrived, slammed the door, and was grateful for the tinted windows that shielded me from scowls and stares. "Please get me out of here," I said, and Tony took off, glancing at me over his shoulder when we were halfway down the street.

"What happened?" he asked.

"What *didn't*?" I said. "I told Kitty that Ned's been cheating on her, she hates me for not telling her sooner, I accidentally knocked Virginia Stone on her ass, but everybody thinks I did it on purpose, and unless you've forgiven me for all the idiotic things I said to you, I don't have a single friend in this entire city."

Tony stopped for a red light and twisted in his seat to face me. "Nobody's immune from being a jerk once in a while . . .

including me. So let's forgive each other and stop all this back-seat crap. I can't stand it anymore."

He started driving again, and I gathered up my skirt and squeezed through the space between the two front seats. The skirt filled up my entire side and looked like an explosion of chiffon. I tried to push it down, and when I was shifting around I felt something underneath me that turned out to be Tony's iPhone.

"Can I use this?" I asked, fearing what might be inside.

Tony nodded. I knew better than to look, but curiosity beat common sense and soon I was staring at a high-resolution shot that Fabian had already posted on *Nocturnal*—Virginia in mid-fall, openmouthed guests halfway out of their chairs, Kitty's wedding band glimmering beneath a table leg. Then there was me, caught in a blend of grimace and sneer. The gentle lighting that had looked magical in person turned menacing in its digitized form, and I resembled a comically clad party crasher in the midst of an attempted mugging.

I should have listened to Kitty's advice about simple and black. My dress looked awful, and each of the constantly multiplying comments stung as if they were scratching off my skin, one little nick at a time. I read things like

Just because you have money doesn't mean you have taste; She's nothing but trailer trash with cash; The last time I saw that shade of pink I was puking it up; Bitch needs somebody to fix her makeup; That hair is pure southern ghetto; I'm not surprised the daughter of Edward Stone would lay out somebody's mom; Hasn't Virginia Stone suffered enough?

and

Savannah Morgan, do us a favor and disappear.

Tony yanked the iPhone from my hand, tossed it into the glove compartment, and slammed the door shut. "What happened to the good old days when it was impossible to find out what people thought about you unless you heard it directly from their mouths?"

A lump popped into my throat; I tried to swallow it as I spotted my building in the distance and slumped in my seat. "I don't remember those days," I said.

Tony parked at 15 Central Park West. "Savannah," he said, "what people think about you isn't your business . . . and it isn't your problem. Don't waste time worrying about it."

He was right, but it was hard not to worry. The meanest words always stuck for so much longer than the sweetest ones. I nodded and said good night, and then I went to my apartment, where I sat on the couch in my dress with its wayward hem, picked up the phone to call Mom, and told her everything as tears welled in my eyes.

"Oh, darlin'," she said when I was done. "Just come home."

I looked around at the expensive furniture and the shiny floors and Central Park outside my window, thinking about how hard I'd fought and how much I'd lose if I surrendered. *I have no plans to leave Stone News,* I'd told Ned, and the thought of eating my words sickened me. But there just didn't seem to be another choice.

"What about the money?" I asked.

"Savannah," Mom said, "I'm sure now you see how little it means."

Monday morning was soaked in a gray haze that hovered over the Manhattan skyline when Tony drove past. "Are you sure you want to do this?" he asked.

We were on a bridge heading to JFK. The car rattled over the same grates as the day I arrived, when Tony was driving me in the opposite direction. I wasn't sure about anything, so I shrugged as I reached into my purse for the itinerary I'd printed from the computer at my apartment—a one-way flight to Charleston International. "You'll tell that lawyer I've left?"

"Ms. Stark will get the message," he said. "Should I pass along any others?"

I was sure he was asking if I had any last words for Alex. I did, but they were in such a confusing jumble that they couldn't be untangled. In the stark light of day, I knew fixing what had happened to us wasn't simple and even if it could be fixed it didn't make any difference, because I was going home.

"No," I said.

A few minutes later, Tony and I were at JFK, where he took my bags out of the trunk and lined them up at the curbside check-in. People were getting out of cars and kissing each other good-bye, and Tony stood beside my luggage, staring at me as he jammed his hands into his pockets and rocked back and forth on his heels.

"Well," he said, "I guess this is it."

I could tell he wasn't the type who'd say all the gooey things I was feeling, but I couldn't leave with a handshake. He'd been too important for that. So I took a step forward, put my arms around him, and hugged his slender frame.

"I'll miss you," I said.

He didn't say anything, but he held on for longer than I'd expected. He waited on the curb until my bags had been checked and I was inside JFK, and then he got into his shiny black car and drove away.

After Mom met me at the airport, we sat inside her old Toyota, watching our neighborhood whiz by as we neared home—the one-story houses, the carports, the Buicks on blocks. Everything seemed so much smaller and dingier than it used to, like it had all faded and shrunk since I'd left.

It was the same at our place, where I couldn't even look at my rusted old bike when I headed toward the front door. The slats on the porch creaked more loudly than usual, the furniture seemed to have aged years, and the smell of fried chicken didn't make my mouth water like it once did. Still, Mom had worked hard on my welcome-home lunch and I was happy to eat it while I sat across from her in our kitchen and a breeze rustled our gingham curtains.

"I forgot the best part," Mom said, popping up from her chair. Her auburn curls bounced around her head and her hips swayed beneath her jeans as she walked to the refrigerator and returned carrying a plate of Ritz crackers smeared with pimento cheese. "I made it with chopped pecans . . . just the way you and Tina always loved it."

My eyes fell to the linoleum floor, remembering all the things Tina and I used to love.

Mom reached across the table to give my wrist a squeeze. "You two will make up the way you always do . . . you girls have never been able to stay apart for long. Everything will be fine . . . just like it was before."

"Mom," I said after thinking for a while, "was everything *really* fine before?"

She leaned back into her chair and sighed. We finished lunch, and afterward I went to my room with plans to unpack, but instead I wandered around looking at Charleston High pom-poms, a ninth-grade fiction award, and stacks of college papers marked with A or B+.

I plopped down on my bed, remembering what I'd dreamed about in this room while staring at a water stain on the ceiling. I'd wanted to use my talents and live somewhere exciting and be with a man who cared about me so much that he wouldn't stand in the way of those things. I'd found all that in New York, but it had gotten messed up enough to make me run back here.

Now I felt like I was caught someplace in the middle and didn't belong anywhere at all.

Two weeks later, I sat in the living room and searched classified ads online while Mom did a blow-out in her salon at the other side of the house. The dryer hummed and the customer gossiped, and I scratched a rash that had popped up on the inside of my wrist the day after I came home. I was still scratching when Mom mentioned needing more conditioner for her next appointment.

I sprang off the couch, eager for a break from the drudgery of reading job descriptions and sending out résumés. I'd saved enough money that we'd be fine for a while—so I didn't have to rush into a minimum-wage mall job—but the cash wouldn't last forever, and I couldn't spend the rest of my life watching reality TV and helping to sweep up hair.

I left the house and jumped into my old car, which Mom had picked up from the shop while I was gone. I drove it through a scorching day to a strip mall and went into Sally Beauty Supply, where I lingered in the aisles, browsing for so long that the salesgirl got suspicious and started following me around. I went to the cashier and paid for the conditioner, and then I stepped outside into the blazing sunshine where I put on my Chanel sunglasses and walked toward the car, thinking about what I'd be doing if I were in New York. It was Monday and just after two, so I'd be at *Femme*, scheduling and researching and maybe chatting with Kitty. But I'd ruined things with her just like I'd trashed everything else.

"Savannah?"

I nearly plowed over Raylene Brandt. She was standing outside a store with a *Back to School* banner in its front window, chewing a gumball that had turned her tongue green. Her blond hair was tied into braids and she flashed her gap-toothed smile, and before I could say a word she wrapped her arms around my waist the way she always did to Tina.

That really did feel nice. I hugged her back as a bell jingled and a door opened, and then Tina was there, dressed in shorts and a T-shirt and holding a stack of notebooks and folders.

"Raylene," she said, pulling her keys from her pocket, "go wait in the car . . . and make sure you blast the air. It has to be a hundred degrees out here."

Raylene took the keys and everything else from Tina's hands and skipped toward the BMW in the parking lot, and Tina and I stared at each other. She looked different, better, more natural without extensions and heaps of eyeliner. Her brown hair was straight and it fell to her shoulders, and her face was prettier than ever with just a dab of dewy makeup on her tan skin.

"What are you doing here?" she asked. "Visiting your mama?"

I couldn't explain that I'd been defeated and I'd crawled back here to hide. "What are *you* doing here?" I asked, noticing that her lips were back to their natural size and she'd switched perfumes. She smelled like freesia instead of mango. "At the mall, I mean."

"We were shopping for school supplies. Summer's almost over."

I nodded, thinking about how painful it was to make small talk with someone who'd once shared the big things, the important things, the secret things I'd never tell anyone else. "You aren't working at the firm today?"

Her face glistened with perspiration that had seeped from her skin since she left the air-conditioned store, and a tiny pool of sweat was forming inside the chicken-pox scar at the edge of her left eye. "I don't work there anymore. I got a job at a homeless shelter downtown."

I hung somewhere between not surprised and totally shocked. "That's great, Tina. I mean, it's . . . it's fantastic. But your father—"

She held up her hand. "He wants the best for me . . . but I've figured out that what *he* thinks is best isn't always. I worked at his office when I came back and I felt like I was suffocating, sitting there answering phones. It was even worse at home with Crystal. I quit the firm. . . . and Daddy wasn't happy about that, but he's getting used to it. He's also dealing with my moving into an apartment next month. I'll be roommates with a co-worker . . . a girl I met at the shelter."

My smile broadened with every word. "That's great news," I said. "I mean it, Tina."

She nodded. "I'm also thinking about applying to college part-time next year. Being away from here helped me figure out that I can do more than I was before. I'm thinking about majoring in social work . . . I know I'm old to be a freshman again and I might be thirty by the time I graduate . . . but it's better late than never."

"You'll be thirty anyway. And I've always said you could do more."

She ran her hands through her hair, pushing it off her face. "Yeah, you did. I want to thank you for that . . . and for the time we spent in New York. It wasn't exactly good . . . but it turned out to be good for me."

I nodded and felt ready to cry. "Tina . . . I'm so sorry about everything . . . for how I treated you, and the way I ditched you for Alex. That wasn't right. It wasn't right at all."

"No," she said. "It wasn't. But I always thought he was a sweet guy."

"He was," I said, glancing at the sidewalk. "We're not together anymore, though."

Tina was quiet, and I wondered if she was coming up with the responses I deserved—things like *It serves you right* and *What goes around comes around.* I braced myself as I stared at cracked concrete, but all I heard was a sigh and, "I'm sorry to hear that, Savannah."

She knew me well enough not to push, not to ask questions, to just let me be. I shifted my gaze from the ground to her face. "You know what?" I couldn't help but say. "Friends like you don't come along every day . . . sometimes they *never* do . . . and I forgot that for a while."

She stared at me, taking everything in. "I'm glad you finally remembered. I accept your apology, but I owe you one, too . . . I shouldn't have let my father speak to you the way he did. I was so angry about everything that I let him. It won't happen again, though."

I smiled, feeling a gleeful rush of forgiveness. Mom was right when she said Tina and I could never stay apart for long. "Does that mean we're back to being friends?"

"Yeah," she said, "if you want to be."

"Of course I do. And I'm not visiting, Tina. I moved back because some horrible things happened, and . . ." I stopped. I couldn't even talk about it.

Tina took a step forward and squeezed my hand. "You don't have to explain. I read the celebrity gossip blogs, remember? By the way . . . I think my dress looked fabulous on you. Yankees have no damn taste."

Damn. Not GD or dang or darn. She'd really made progress. I laughed, she slung her arm around my shoulders, and we took Raylene with us to Wholly Cow across the road, where we escaped the heat with peppermint stick ice cream and lemon twist sorbet as we talked for hours. Then it was dinnertime and Tina had to take Raylene home, so we walked back to the strip mall and our cars.

Raylene slid into the BMW and Tina was just about to when I clutched her wrist to stop her. Everything had been mended and I didn't want to risk ripping the stitches apart, but there was something I needed to say.

"Tina," I began, "I want you to know you shouldn't share

any man. You're too good for that. And there's a wonderful guy out there somewhere who'll treat you right. You just have to be patient until he comes along."

The parking lot was bright and the asphalt was hot beneath our feet, but I saw in her eyes that she remembered a dark night and cold bathroom tiles, when she'd put herself in a position far beneath her. Tony wasn't a concern anymore, but Charleston was filled with men who made me worry just as much.

"Yeah," she said with a nod. "I know. It took a push— *literally*—for me to figure that out, but I have. As much as it hurt, I'm glad it happened. And I'll find the patience to wait."

She ducked into the BMW and promised to call me tomorrow. I stood there and waved as she drove away, wondering if saying that had felt as good as hearing it and thinking the simplest words sometimes mean the most.

When I walked across my porch, I heard voices in the house and followed the noise to the kitchen, where Mom was sitting at the table with a plate of fried chicken and Kitty Stone.

My jaw dropped. I stood frozen in the doorway. They didn't see me at first—they just kept chatting while Mom swigged lemonade and Kitty nibbled a drumstick. The floor creaked beneath my feet, and Kitty and Mom glanced at me.

"Hey, darlin'," Mom said, rising from her chair. She draped her arm around my shoulders and led me to the table, where she sat down and plunked me into the seat beside her. "We were just having some girl talk about a few things . . . including our experience with Stone men."

"We've found that certain tendencies seem to be in their genes," Kitty said, and she and Mom smirked at each other like they were members of an exclusive club. It was utterly surreal yet sort of poetic. "But like you, Joan, I won't tolerate those tendencies. And I have Savannah to thank for bringing them to my attention. That's why I'm here."

Thank me? I thought she hated me. I shook my head, baffled. "But you said—"

"I know." Kitty looked guiltily at the floor. "I know what I said, and I regret it. I was caught off-guard, Savannah. What you told me was a total shock . . . and people say things they don't mean when they're upset."

That was true, but I was still surprised she'd come all this way just to see me. And she looked good, so much better than she had when she stormed out of The Plaza's ballroom. She seemed relaxed and refreshed, dressed in white Capri pants and a sleeveless red top.

"You were trying to be a friend," she said. "Ned put you in an impossible position, and you didn't deserve any blame for it. It took some time for me realize that . . . but as soon as I did, I asked my father's pilot to fly me down here. I couldn't wait to tell you that I'm sorry."

I sighed, feeling as relieved as I had when Tina and I patched things up. "I'm sorry, too. I never meant to take advantage of you at work. I just got wrapped up in so many new things that I wasn't myself."

She nodded, touching her left hand where her wedding ring used to be. "I understand," she said. "And it's all forgiven. So when are you coming back to *Femme*?"

I was surprised again. "Are you still working there? I mean . . . you and Ned . . ."

". . . are getting divorced. But we're ironing things out maturely. I'll still have *Femme,* and you know I can't keep it going without the best assistant I've ever had."

Mom's eyes moved between me and Kitty, and I didn't know what to say. I'd thought New York wasn't an option anymore, but Kitty had lit a tiny spark of hope. It made me think I actually did have something left in that city. But then I remembered everything that was wrong, the things Kitty couldn't fix, and that little spark fizzled out.

"You'll have to," I said. "I can't afford New York anymore. As you know, I broke the deal. The inheritance was contingent on my staying there, and I didn't. All the money is gone."

"No, Savannah," she said. "It isn't."

I lifted an eyebrow, perplexed. "Of course it is. What are you talking about?"

Kitty leaned forward, clasping her hands against Mom's vinyl tablecloth. "After I found out that you left, I called Ned to salvage the situation. I convinced him that I sent you down here on assignment for an unspecified period of time. So as far as he knows, you're still an employee of Stone News . . . and you haven't broken the deal."

My mouth fell open and stayed there for a moment—not only because I hadn't lost my inheritance but also because Kitty had still been looking out for me in spite of what happened between us. But even though the cash was back, there was no way I could show my face in New York. "I still can't go back, Kitty. I've been publicly humiliated."

"Oh, come on," Kitty said. "Are you going to let that blog nonsense get the better of you? I'm sure you're not the type to hide from this sort of thing."

I thought of junior high, Eva Lee, my story on the Internet. I'd locked myself in a bathroom stall while my classmates laughed, but I didn't stay inside forever. I'd crawled away for a while, but then I got right back on that football field and cheered.

"Is that your biggest reason for not coming back?" Kitty asked.

"No," I said, glancing at Mom. "It's the smallest."

Mom didn't say anything. She just got up from the table and

started washing dishes at the sink. Kitty sighed and sat back in her chair.

"Well," she said, "as much as I wish you'd reconsider, I can't pretend I don't understand why you want to stay here. And I respect you for it, Savannah."

I smiled. Kitty reached for her purse and stood up from her chair.

"Even so," she went on, "I'll get a temporary assistant and hold your spot open for a while. It'll be there until the end of September . . . in case you change your mind."

Before Kitty left, she put something on the kitchen table—an advance copy of *Femme*'s October issue that I couldn't bring myself to open. It reminded me of everything I'd abandoned—including Alex, who wasn't easy to forget. So I just left it there, and even though I didn't explain anything to Mom, her maternal radar must have kicked in, because the magazine was gone in the morning.

That night, I sat with her and Tina inside a booth near the front door of Melvin's Legendary Bar-B-Q—a restaurant that had been around forever and served the most delicious chopped-pork sandwiches and fried okra. I normally would've devoured my dinner, but tonight I just pushed it around my plate. I wasn't hungry, and my rash was flaring up. It was bumpy and warm and spreading toward my elbow.

"Want to share some banana pudding for dessert?" Tina asked.

Mom rubbed her hands together. *"Share?"* she said with a laugh. "I want my own."

"None for me," I said as I glanced across the restaurant and saw Eva Lee. She was holding a grease-stained doggie bag and heading in my direction with her usual Mount Pleasant entourage.

I looked away and stared at the remnants of Tina's sweet potato soufflé, but it was too late. Eva Lee had spotted me, and she stopped at my booth on her way to the door and put on her very best Melanie Hamilton Wilkes act. She asked her friends to wait outside, and she was all sweet and polite and innocent when she stuck out her hand to show off the gold band that matched her engagement ring.

"We've been newlyweds for three weeks," she told us.

"Congratulations," I made myself say, keeping my eyes on Tina's plate. I could barely stand Eva Lee's flowing red hair and her cute freckles and the giddily prideful smile on her face.

"I heard you fell into some luck and moved to New York. How's it going up there?"

I looked at her. Her smile had turned into a smirk. She'd probably also heard that I was back for good, and I was sure she'd seen my online bashing and couldn't have loved it more. But that probably wasn't enough. She seemed to be aching for me to admit I'd lost in every possible way. *Oh, things just didn't work out and it's all for the best.* That's what I'd always been afraid of, what I'd never wanted to say, and I couldn't say it now. I couldn't say anything. All I did was scratch my rash.

"Savannah's doing just fine," Mom answered, glancing at my nails clawing my wrist.

"She couldn't be better," Tina added.

I was grateful for that, but my guardian angels couldn't shadow me forever to protect me from Eva Lee and her kind. The thought of dodging nosy questions for the rest of my life made everything feel like it was closing in on me—the walls, the booth, Charleston in general.

I made it through dinner, collapsed into bed early that night, and slept late the next morning. When I woke up, the house was quiet except for the sound of birds chirping and our porch swing creaking. I went outside in my nightgown and my bare feet and found Mom sitting on the swing, staring across the street through the hazy air. I plopped down beside her.

"What are you doing?" I asked. "Don't you have any customers today?"

"I canceled all my appointments," she said, and turned toward me. Her curls framed her face, and the lines in her forehead creased as she stared into my eyes. "Last night, I told Eva Lee that you're doing fine. But the thing is . . . you're not. You're not fine at all."

"Of course I am," I said, scratching my wrist.

She grabbed my arm. "Savannah, when have you ever had a rash like this?"

"I don't know . . . maybe when—"

"*Never*, that's when. This is a nervous condition caused by anxiety and depression and stress," she said assuredly, like she was a dermatologist with a bonus psychology degree. But I didn't argue, because she was probably right. I shrugged, and she moved closer to me. "You're pretending you're okay to make me feel better . . . and to make yourself feel better. The truth is you're in the same spot you were before you left . . . only now it's worse because you've had a taste of something more."

I wasn't sure how to answer, but I didn't have to. She sprang off the swing and went into the house, slamming the screen door behind her. She came back a moment later with the October *Femme* in her hand.

"I always knew you could do this, Savannah."

I sighed and looked across the street at one of our neighbors hosing down her driveway. I didn't take my eyes off her until Mom sat next to me and put the magazine in my lap.

"I've always told you not to settle," she said. "And that's exactly what you're doing now. It's partially my fault, but I'm going to fix that by telling you to go back to New York. You'll never have an opportunity like this again."

"I know," I admitted, staring at Spanish moss hanging from a tree branch. "But I can't."

"You only think you can't. You think you have to stay here with me because I didn't approve of you going up there in the first place. But I was wrong about that. I was selfish and stubborn and completely wrong."

I couldn't believe what I was hearing. I shifted my eyes from the moss to Mom.

She sat up straight. "I've been thinking about it, and it seems to me that Edward felt you'd bring some fresh blood into his company and turn it around. I know you've started off small and his other kids are in charge, but that could change. You've got a whole lifetime ahead of you for things to change. And maybe by leaving you his money and bringing you to New York, he was trying to make amends. He wanted to do the right thing . . . and *I* do, too. I think you should let us."

It was the first time my parents had done something together, something especially for me, and that meant something.

"I know you won't let all that Internet stupidity keep you down," Mom went on. "You're gutsier than that. You're stronger than I ever was . . . I never had enough courage to even *visit* New York. I should've admired you for going the first time . . . but at least I do now. I called Kitty, and she's arranging for her father's plane to pick you up tomorrow. So go back up to that city and show everybody what you're made of. Let them see that a Morgan is stronger than a Stone."

She was right. I couldn't let anything keep me down. I had to go back.

I nodded, Mom squeezed my hand, and we sat quietly for a few minutes, staring across the street and rocking the swing together as mourning doves cooed in the trees. A young boy sped past on a bicycle and I remembered when I used to zip around

Charleston like that, on my bike that had been left for so long in its lonely corner.

"Mom," I said finally. "Did Aunt Primrose *really* have a good heart?"

She stopped rocking and stared blankly at the boy disappearing down the street. Then she turned toward me, and her lips spread into a wistful smile. "Yes," she said. "*He* did."

I was relieved to hear that from someone who knew for sure. "When Kitty was here," I went on, "you were laughing about what Stone men are like."

She reached out and gently pushed my hair behind my shoulders. "It's a choice, darlin'. We can laugh or we can cry."

That was so true. "But your relationship with Edward wasn't a joke," I said cautiously, feeling like I was digging into a part of her life she'd never wanted me to touch. "Was it?"

Her face turned serious, but she didn't get angry or storm off like I'd feared. "No, Savannah," she answered after a moment. "It wasn't. I loved your father. He was just . . . so real."

My throat tightened. *Your father.* She'd loved him. I'd never heard those words come out of her mouth until now, and they sounded like the prettiest song.

"That's what he said about *you,*" I said, and she gave me a quizzical look, deepening the lines in her forehead. "At least . . . that's what his lawyer told me."

"Really," Mom said. "Well . . . then maybe it's time *I* told you a few things, too."

I wasn't sure if I should be excited or terrified. "Okay . . . like what?"

"Oh," she said, moving her eyes toward the thin white clouds that streaked the blue sky. "Like how many good times Edward and I had together . . . and that before or since I met him, I've never felt happier with anyone . . . except you." She looked at me again and smiled. "He and I were both looking for something . . . and I hadn't expected to find it in a *bar,* of all places. . . ."

I laughed. "Did he give you a smooth come-on line or something?"

She shook her head. "He wasn't that way. It was very innocent, actually. He was in Charleston on business and I was having a girls' night out with some friends from cosmetology school . . . and he just stopped in for a drink. We started talking, and he was respectful and funny and *so* interesting . . . and that gorgeous hair didn't hurt," she said, touching mine again. "Letting him go was one of the hardest things I've ever done, Savannah. But I couldn't turn against everything I believed in just to hold on to that man. I wouldn't do that for anyone."

"Yeah," I said slowly. "I know what you mean."

She smiled and rested her hand on mine. "I guess I was wrong to keep him from you. But he was so busy with his work—it was like an addiction—and I thought it would be better for you to have no father at all than to have half of one. I didn't want him coming in and out of your life, splitting what little time he had to spare between two families. I thought it wouldn't be good for you, but . . . maybe I made a bad choice."

I shook my head. Who was I to judge her choices? She'd been a few years younger than me when everything happened, and she'd probably been confused and scared and it would have been tempting to take the easy way out. And if she'd done what Edward had wanted and moved with me to New York, I would've grown up with everything that money could buy, but I might have turned out as screwed up as Jack and Ned.

"You didn't," I said, putting my free hand over hers.

Mom breathed a long, relieved sigh. "Edward," she said after a moment, "was an imperfect man. He made a lot of mistakes. But like I said . . . he had a good heart. And I'm so lucky that he left me with the best of him."

She ran her knuckles across my cheek and smiled. I smiled back, thinking that maybe, in his own way, my father had tried to give me the best of him, too.

A car stopped in front of our house—Tina's BMW with the top down and Dierks Bentley blasting loud enough for me to hear him all the way on the porch.

"What's she doing here?" I asked.

Mom rocked the swing again. "I gave her a call after I talked to Kitty. Tina agrees it's best for you to go back up north, and she wanted to come by to help me convince you to go. She even offered to drive you to the airport tomorrow." She smiled and sifted my hair through her fingers. "You're lucky, Savannah . . . those are some real good friends you've got there."

I clutched Mom's hand, watching Tina head toward the house. It would be so much easier to go back to New York now, because even though most of Team Savannah were staying in Charleston, they'd be on my side no matter where I was.

"You didn't have the courage to visit New York years ago," I said, "but you've changed since then, Mom. I'm sure you can do it now . . . and I've heard there's no place like Manhattan for Christmas."

She gave me a wink. "I've heard the same. And I sure would like to see for myself."

"Hey," Tina said, walking across the porch. She was in shorts and a loose tank top, and there was a white square taped to her arm. She noticed me looking at it and smiled. "It's a nicotine patch. I'm finally taking your advice."

"*Finally* is right," I said. "And my next bit of advice is if you're considering college, you should think about schools in New York. I do believe Manhattan owes you another chance."

She mulled that over as the sun washed across her face.

"Well," she said, "I reckon I'll give it some thought."

Twenty-four

Kitty picked me up in a limousine from a small airport on Long Island and said she had a surprise: We were going to a resort spa in the Hamptons, because after everything we'd been through we deserved two full days of pampering.

Not long after that, I was inside an elegant hotel room with a king-size bed, a private terrace, and a view of the water. Kitty's room was across the hall and she knocked on my door a few minutes later, saying we'd better hurry because we were scheduled for massages and facials and hairstyling.

I was so blissfully relaxed after having my back rubbed and my skin exfoliated that I thought I might doze off when my hair was being washed. I closed my eyes while a beautician slathered me with conditioner and kneaded my scalp.

"Savannah," Kitty said. "How'd you like a change?"

I glanced to my left, where she was sitting in a chair identical to mine with her head bent backward into a sink. "I think I've had a lot of changes lately," I told her.

"True . . . and that's why your new life deserves a fresh look. I'd love to see your hair a few shades lighter . . . and a little shorter."

I used to be against changing the superficial, but after what had happened at The Plaza I wasn't going to ignore Kitty's fashion advice. Maybe I could fit in and still stand out as an enhanced version of me. So I took a deep breath and agreed, and soon I'd changed from golden wheat to sunflower blond—which matched my natural shade from my younger years—and my hair fell just below my shoulders and framed my face with razor-cut layers that accented my features in the most flattering way. Several inches of hair had fallen to the salon floor, but I didn't miss them at all. I felt lighter, like I'd let go of something I didn't need anymore and was ready to move on to better things.

I felt the same way that afternoon when I walked beside Kitty into an airy restaurant with lots of natural light in the town's village.

"Lessard, party of three for lunch," Kitty told a woman at the front desk, and I gave her a quizzical look that made her smile. "The reinstatement of my maiden name isn't official yet. But I'm using it anyway."

I nodded and we followed a hostess carrying menus. "I don't blame you. But that's not why I'm surprised. Who's the third party?"

Kitty bent her elbow tightly around mine as we neared our table, like I might bolt if she didn't. Then she gestured toward a petite woman with light-brown hair cut to her chin, wearing a white blouse and beige pants. "It's Caroline," Kitty whispered in my ear.

I never would have known. She looked so much better and a lot less sour without the harsh makeup and the glasses and the jagged black bangs. Her complexion had improved, and I thought she'd probably taken Virginia's advice about seeing a doctor to help her skin. I also thought she was surprisingly pretty without that disguise she'd been lugging around.

Kitty had clearly decided to be a fairy godmother again and

to give both of us a makeover, but that was the only thing that made sense. Nobody was holding a gun to Caroline's head, so why had she agreed to have lunch with me?

Kitty spoke into my ear. "Caroline and I are still friends. As devastating as Ned's philandering was, I won't let myself stay angry, because he isn't worth it. But *she's* furious."

That didn't explain everything. Kitty pulled me toward the table, where I sat beside her and opposite Caroline while a ceiling fan spun above our heads.

I stared at her over a small arrangement of hydrangeas. "You look nice," I said.

Caroline's olive-green eyes widened and she touched the ends of her hair. She didn't thank me, and she seemed surprised, and I wasn't sure if it was because she was shocked that a compliment had come from me or if she wasn't used to flattery in general.

"I guess you weren't expecting to see me," she said.

I shook my head. "I thought you were mad because of—"

"I was. But I had it all wrong. And you knew that."

I looked between her and Kitty. "I already swore I didn't post that picture of you."

"Right," Kitty said, lifting a glass of water. "What you didn't tell us was who did."

I swallowed. "Nobody knows. It was probably a hacker."

Caroline raised a freshly plucked eyebrow. "A hacker named Ainsley Greenleaf. You're too smart not to have figured that out."

My pulse sped up and I started to sweat inside the cool restaurant. "I don't know what—"

"Savannah," Kitty said, cutting me off as she reached into her purse and pulled out a sheet of paper. "After the dust settled, I remembered I'd asked Ainsley to show you how to access *Femme's* social media sites. When I put that together with Ned dumping her, she became our main suspect. I contacted her father, and he got her to confess that she was the one who spread the picture of Caroline through your account at work. Mr. Greenleaf wasn't exactly pleased, considering what good friends he and Edward were. I must say I was merciful . . . I spared him the part about his daughter sleeping with my husband. He only knows what she did to Caroline, and he made her write an apology to both of you."

Kitty put the paper down in front of me, but I didn't need to read it. The relief of vindication was enough. "Other than telling her father, you're not going to do anything to her because of this, are you?" I asked. "She did a terrible thing, but she's young and foolish and she has such high aspirations—"

"Is that why you didn't tell us it was her?" Caroline said.

I heard forks scraping dishes and glasses clinking. A waiter came to take our drink orders, and when he left Caroline was staring at me, waiting for an answer.

I sighed. There was no way out. "Yes," I admitted. "It was."

Caroline nodded slowly. "Well," she said after a long pause, "I guess I have to admire you for that . . . and for keeping my personal life private when I'd given you every reason not to."

The waiter returned with Coke and sparkling water and a glass of wine that Caroline swigged and plunked down on the table before she started talking again. "I'm glad you told Kitty about Ned. Just because he's my brother doesn't mean I'll excuse that misogynistic playboy shit. And to answer your question about Ainsley . . . I'm settling for the apology. Her father's disappointment in her is enough payback for me."

I agreed, watching her sip wine. "I'm glad you've accepted her apology. I don't condone what she did . . . but you really should be more careful what you say to people."

She stopped drinking and stared at me over her glass. "Point taken," she said finally. "Looking on the bright side . . . Ainsley did me a favor. Now that my mother knows, she's starting to deal with it. I think what she was most upset about was that I kept the truth from her. Maybe I didn't give her enough credit to begin with. But we're talking again, and . . . I'm just happy I don't have to pretend anymore."

I nodded. "I'm with you on that one. I hate pretending, too."

She smiled in a different way than usual. Her smiles were usually the smug, sarcastic, condescending kind. But this was a genuine smile, and she was looking me right in the eye like we'd actually connected about something.

A cell beeped. Caroline reached into her pocket, pulled out her phone, and read a text.

"Oh my God. It's from my mother. The driver who hit Dad's car has been found. She wants me to go back to the city and meet her and Ned at the office."

"The limo will take you," Kitty said as Caroline rose from her seat.

"It'll take both of us," Caroline said, nodding toward me.

I shifted in my chair. "But if Ned and Virginia will be there . . . I really don't belong."

Caroline grabbed her purse. "You *do* belong. Mom and Ned will just have to learn to deal with that. After all, Edward was your father, too."

When Caroline and I sat beside each other in the backseat of a limousine that headed toward Manhattan, we discovered that Edward's name was, once again, everywhere. Caroline scrolled through Web sites on her iPhone, reading out loud.

"Halstead Simms," she said, *"was forty-nine years old and lived in a basement apartment in Bensonhurst, where he was found dead this morning. Neighbors say Simms had battled alcoholism for most of his adult life."*

She kept researching and reading until the limo pulled up in front of Stone News. It was quitting time, people flooded from the building, and the latest turn of events had affected the mob of protesters who were always outside. There were more than I'd ever seen.

"Ignore them," Caroline said as she slipped out of the car.

I followed after her but didn't get far. A hand caught my arm, and I looked up at a man with a gray goatee and a Mets baseball cap. I recognized him and the birthmark between his eyes from weeks earlier, when he'd told me that I should rethink where I got my paycheck.

"I thought you just worked here," he said. "Now I know better."

I thought I might be in danger, but I stayed where I was. I glanced down at his left hand clamped around my arm and noticed the tip of his index finger was missing.

"You're right, sir. I'm Edward Stone's daughter. But he might not deserve the blame for what y'all are protesting about. We don't know if he's guilty."

He let go of my arm and adjusted his hat. "Sometimes," he said, "people get blamed for things whether they're guilty or not. People suffer when they shouldn't."

What exactly did *that* mean? He backed away from me and walked off, and I watched him vanish into a crowd until Caroline called my name from the entrance of Stone News. I caught up to her and we rode the elevator to the corporate division, where Ned and Virginia were standing in that conference room with the brass lamps and mahogany walls. They were so blown away by New Caroline that they didn't seem to notice I was there.

"My God," fell from Ned's lips.

"Caroline," Virginia said. She was in a mauve dress, and her mouth hung open. "You look . . . you're just . . . beautiful."

She was clearly unaccustomed to using that adjective to describe her daughter, and Caroline seemed equally unfamiliar

with hearing it. But she didn't have time to respond, because
Virginia quickly snapped out of her trance and switched her attention to me.

"What are *you* doing here?" she demanded, stepping in my
direction. "This meeting has nothing to do with you."

Caroline got between us. "Please don't take that attitude,
Mother. You know Savannah's innocent of leaking anything to
the media about me, and she's more than paid for what happened
between the two of you at The Plaza. We all have to stop blam-
ing her for Dad's decisions . . . and we also have to include her in
family business because she *is* part of the family."

Virginia's cheeks indented like she was gnawing the insides.
She folded her arms and stared at a lamp across the room as Ned
scoffed.

"What about what she did to *me*?" he asked, walking toward
Caroline in his dark suit and leather loafers. "She ruined my
marriage."

Caroline shook her head. "You ruined it yourself. If you had
just kept your pants zipped, you'd still have Kitty. But you didn't
want her anyway."

He tightened his Rolex. "That isn't true," he said with his
eyes on diamonds that circled the current time.

Caroline studied him for a moment. "Maybe not. Maybe you
regret how you treated Kitty and you'll do better if you ever get
married again. But you acted like a single man when you
weren't, and now you can do it legitimately. You should thank
Savannah for that."

"All right," Ned said sharply, rubbing his temples. "I've heard
enough."

"Not quite," Virginia cut in. "I was never a fan of Kitty's, but
that doesn't mean I condone your behavior, Ned. I'd hoped
you'd inherit many of your father's traits . . . but infidelity isn't
one of them."

Ned's eyes fell to the carpet. He was quiet for a moment as he massaged his forehead and then let out a heavy sigh. "Understood," he said, raising his eyes to Virginia's. "But we're not here to talk about me . . . the issue at hand is Halstead Simms and whether we believe he was really the driver of the car that hit Dad. So why don't we all sit down and discuss it?"

"*All* of us?" Caroline said, tapping her foot.

Ned looked at me and then back at her. "*Yes*, Caroline," he said tersely.

We settled into cushy leather seats around the polished table, where I stayed quiet while Ned and Virginia and Caroline debated whether they would accept the case being closed if the NYPD determined that Halstead Simms was responsible for Edward's death.

"The detective with whom I spoke," Virginia said, "thinks there's enough evidence to prove Simms is responsible. He also thinks the forensics will show this man died from alcoholism . . . or alcohol poisoning . . . I can't quite remember what he said."

Ned pulled his silver pen out of his blazer and began scribbling on a legal pad. "It just seems too easy. There are so many other suspects . . . and I hate to bring up Senator Caldwell in your presence, Mother . . . but she and her husband might be two of them."

Caroline nodded. "So might any family members of the Lake Kolenya victims."

I thought about the man downstairs. I hadn't been sure what he was trying to tell me, but it concerned me enough to bring it up. "You're right," I said, and everyone but Caroline looked at me like they were surprised that I was really going to involve myself in this conversation. "There was a man outside tonight . . . one of the protesters . . . he knew who I was, and he said something strange."

Ned tapped his pen against the pad. "And what was that?"

"He said *people get blamed for things whether they're guilty or not.*

I'm not sure what he was referring to, and it could mean nothing. But he might've been talking about Edward or Simms . . . maybe he knows something we don't."

Ned stared at me, his forehead furrowing as if he couldn't believe my input wasn't utterly useless. "What did this person look like?" he asked finally, poising his pen against a thin blue line on yellow paper.

"He's probably in his early fifties. He had a goatee and a Mets hat."

Ned dropped the pen. "A middle-aged Mets fan," he said dryly. "That narrows it down."

I grabbed the pen and the pad. "Reddish-purple birthmark between his eyes shaped like Spain," I said as I wrote it down. "Tip of left index finger missing."

I slid the pad toward Ned, who drummed his fingertips against it for a moment. "That might help. You never know. Thank you," he said finally, which was more than shocking. "I'll give this to the detective. But if the NYPD closes the case with Simms, we'll hire a private investigator to keep looking. Are we all in agreement?"

He glanced around the table. Virginia and Caroline nodded, and I considered it a major victory when everybody looked at me as if my vote counted.

I stood on the curb outside Stone News a few minutes later, waiting for Tony to pick me up. Summer was dwindling, the sun was setting, and the rash on my arm was starting to heal. A cool breeze flowed through my brand-new hair and I stroked it, feeling a surge of excitement as I listened to familiar city sounds—cars honking, sirens wailing, vendors on corners hawking chintzy souvenirs. *You can handle this*, I'd told myself on my first day here, and I felt a familiar urge to break into a touchdown cheer when I realized I'd been right.

There was a tap on my shoulder. I whirled around, looked at flowing black hair and olive-green eyes, and caught a whiff of tasteful perfume.

"We're not friends," Virginia said. "We're not anything. But I appreciate that you gave Ned the information about the man you spoke with tonight. Even though Edward and I were divorced and he did things that have given me a steady flow of grief, he was still my children's father . . . and if his death wasn't an accident, I want the right person to pay."

That was a lot, coming from her. It had probably been hard for her to say. I nodded, she turned to walk off, and I remembered something she should know. So I chased after her, calling her name. She turned around, and the breeze blew her dark hair across her face.

"Don't trust Fabian Spader," I blurted out. "He acts like he's on your family's side, but he isn't. He tried to manipulate me into giving him information to trash y'all in the press."

Virginia cocked an eyebrow and stared at me. "That can't be. Fabian's very loyal."

The air was getting cooler; I wrapped my arms around myself as we stood beside a traffic light on a corner where people were waiting to cross. I stared back at Virginia, thinking she might dash away in her designer heels when the light changed, but she didn't.

"No," I said. "He's only pretending to be."

She was quiet for a moment. "Well," she said finally, "I'll keep that in mind."

Then she was gone and I went back to the curb, where Tony pulled up in the sedan. I opened the front door and stuck my head into the passenger's side.

"I knew you'd be back," he said with a laugh.

"How?" I asked.

A wide smile spread across his boyish face. "That's just the kind of girl you are."

Twenty-five

It was Halloween, and gray clouds loomed over the Manhattan skyline. I saw them through a window when I walked into Kitty's office at five on a Friday, asking if she needed anything else before I left. She leaned back in her chair, locking her fingers behind her head and giving me a smile.

"You've been doing so well since you came back from Charleston," she said.

I'd been trying. I hadn't taken long lunches or online-shopped at the office, and there were no romantic interests to distract me from my work. There also hadn't been any attempted humiliation or sabotage. Since that day at the spa, Caroline and I hadn't gone to dinner together or even shared a coffee break. But we'd been cordial, which was what I'd asked for when we first met. And Ned hadn't been troublesome, either. He kept his distance up there in the stuffy corporate division, probably so he could avoid both Kitty and me—and that was fine, too.

"Do you have plans tonight?" Kitty asked.

My social calendar had been sparse since my return, but Mom

and Tina tried to keep me from feeling alone. I'd bought web-cams for me and for them, and not a day went by when I didn't see and speak to one or the other. I'd also bought them plane tickets to come here for Christmas, and counting down the days helped. But most of the time, I felt alone.

"Maybe I'll do some writing," I said, thinking of my story in the October issue of *Femme* that I'd framed and hung on the wall in my home office. "I'm outlining a novel . . . and I have an idea for a new short story. I might try to convince a certain editor that it's worth publishing."

"I doubt it'll take much convincing," she said as I glanced at a business card on her desk, which was for an adoption agency on East 92nd. I thought it might be a leftover from her marriage, so I quickly shifted my gaze, but I wasn't fast enough. She caught my eye, picked up the card, and tacked it to a corkboard on the wall. "I can be a mother on my own," she said with a serene smile, "if I want to be. But even if I decide not to, that'll be okay, too. I'm taking all steps toward my future slowly . . . I think there are a lot of options out there for me."

I nodded, smiling back. "I think so, too, Kitty."

Her e-mail beeped. She clicked on a message, read it, and twisted the monitor around for me to see. The e-mail was from Caroline, and it said the NYPD had made a final determination about who had hit Edward's car: It was Halstead Simms, it was an accident, and the toxicology reports showed that Simms's death had resulted from alcohol poisoning. *We'll see,* Caroline had written at the end. *Ned just called our PI.*

"Senator Caldwell and her husband are still being investigated," Kitty said. "I'm sure they both knew Amicus was indirectly killing people. But . . . do you think Edward did?"

I'd thought a lot about that, and I still hadn't come up with an answer. "I don't know," I said. "But I like to believe he didn't."

. . .

I left the Stone News building and headed for the black sedan. But before I could reach it, the front door swung open and Marjorie rushed out, dressed in a bumble bee costume with antennae and wings. She jumped into my arms and I carried her back to the car, reaching into my purse to pull out a bag of candy I'd bought during lunch. "I was going to have your daddy give this to you . . . but since you're here, I'll do it myself."

She thanked me and gave me a hug, pressing her soft cheek into my neck. I smiled, brought her into the backseat with me, and slammed the door.

Tony turned around. "I thought you weren't going to sit in the back anymore."

"I will when I'm with *her*. I like her better than you," I said, giving him a wink.

He laughed, pulled into traffic, and not long after that we were at 15 Central Park West, where Marjorie gave me a good-bye hug and Tony turned around again.

"See you on Monday?" he asked.

"Absolutely," I said.

Marjorie waved at me through a half-open window when I was on the sidewalk and Tony was driving away. When they were gone, I stayed where I was, watching a small group of kids in costumes holding trick-or treat bags as their parents escorted them into buildings. It was getting dark and the cold air smelled of leaves burning somewhere—maybe upstate. Tony had told me that a scent could travel all the way down the Hudson River.

"Happy Halloween, Savannah."

I glanced to my right, startled. Alex was standing there, dressed in jeans and a leather jacket with a black turtleneck underneath. I didn't smell leaves anymore—the air had filled with something fresh and minty. And I couldn't say anything. I just stared like he was a ghost.

His blue eyes moved between me and the sidewalk, which was littered with squashed candy corn and crinkled gum wrappers. "You look different."

I was so surprised to see him that it took me a moment to figure out what he meant. My hand rose to my head and my sunflower-blond locks. "I suppose I do."

He nodded. "I didn't think you could be more beautiful . . . but I was wrong."

You're beautiful, too, I almost said, but only, "Thank you," came out.

He raked his fingers through his dark hair, staying a few steps away. "Remember my story you edited during the summer? The one that had been rejected, I mean."

I didn't need clarification. Did he really think I could have forgotten the summer?

"Sure," I said.

"It was accepted by a literary journal. It'll be out in December."

I felt as excited for him as when I'd achieved authordom myself. "That's fantastic, Alex. I'm so happy for you."

"You had a lot to do with it. That story would've stayed buried inside my laptop if you hadn't worked your magic on it," he said, jamming his hands in his pockets. "I'm happy for you, too, by the way. I saw your story when it was published . . . I'm generally not a reader of women's magazines, but I bought a copy when it came out."

I imagined him wearing a disguise as he covertly picked up the October *Femme* from a newsstand in a neighborhood far from his own. I nearly laughed, but it was more touching than funny. "You did?" I asked.

"Yeah," he said in his deep, smooth voice. "You should be proud of yourself."

I shrugged, remembering all the help he'd given me on that warm night in his cramped apartment. "I couldn't have done it without you, though."

"Well," he said after a moment, "I guess we were a good team."

I nodded, kicking a candy corn toward the sewer.

"Savannah," he said. "Tony told me you went to South Carolina, and he told me when you came back. I should've come by here sooner . . . I've been thinking about it for weeks . . . but I wasn't sure if you'd want to see me."

I stepped on another piece of candy, grinding it beneath my shoe. "Then that's the second thing you were wrong about," I said, staring at yellow dust on the ground. "I've spent lots of time thinking about going to see you, too, but I haven't . . . for the same reason."

I looked up; there was stunned hope in his eyes. "I also know," he said, "Tony filled you in about Mike. But he shouldn't have had to. I shouldn't have kept it from you."

I shook my head. "It's not your fault. At first I thought it was, but I've changed my mind. We hadn't known each other for long . . . maybe I was expecting too much."

He took his hands out of his pockets. "You weren't. You told me so much about yourself . . . about your father . . . and you deserved to know more about me. But I thought you wouldn't want me if you did," he said as sadness crossed his face. He absorbed it like the fighter he was and squared his shoulders.

I couldn't let him accept that pain and endure it forever like an incurable ache. I took a step toward him and squeezed his arm through his jacket. "Don't blame yourself for what happened to Mike. It was an accident. Now get that through your thick skull and don't you dare ever think otherwise, okay?"

His mouth tightened and his jaw clenched, but after a moment he gave me a slight nod. Then he wiped his hand down his face like he was washing something off. "You know," he said, shifting his eyes to the glowing streetlights and the traffic passing by, "this city is filled with people . . . but so few of them matter to me. And I matter to so few of them."

I nodded, remembering a dinner we'd eaten at a Chinese restaurant and a fortune I'd slipped out of a cookie: *To the world you might be just one person, but to one person you might be the world.* It was still inside my wallet, and I was sure it was exactly what Alex meant.

"I've missed you," he said, his eyes on the gum wrappers at his feet.

I felt the way I did whenever I lost something and thought I'd never find it again, and then out of nowhere there it was—at the bottom of a drawer or zipped into a secret pocket inside a purse I hadn't used in months—and even though I'd gotten along without it, everything seemed so much brighter now that it was back again.

"I've missed you, too," I said.

He stopped staring at the sidewalk and looked at me. "I'm sorry for everything."

I nodded again. "So am I."

His lips parted into a small, cautious smile. "Does that mean we can . . ."

It was getting colder; I reached toward the top buttons on my coat and closed them. "Yeah," I said, "we can give it another try . . . providing there are no foolish hard feelings about how much money is in my bank account. I can't help that, and I won't apologize for it, and you can't hold it against me if I want to share some of what I have with you."

I supposed I sounded as bossy as I had when I was dealing with delinquent teenagers at the library in Charleston, but everything I'd said was what he needed to hear. We couldn't move forward unless we fixed what had broken.

He laughed as if my schoolmarm tone amused him. "Yes, ma'am," he said, mixing southern manners with his Staten Island accent. "No more hard feelings. You were right when you said I had a chip on my shoulder . . . but I'll do my best to take it off."

I crossed my arms. "You certainly will, sir. And *you* were right when you said I was spoiled. At least, I was becoming that way . . . but I think I've put a stop to it."

"Well," he said, coming closer. "Since that's settled . . . what should we do now?"

Butterflies whirled in my stomach like they had the night we met. I glanced around at the kids on the sidewalk and the pumpkins at the buildings' entrances and the blinking orange lights that framed a window across the street, and all I wanted was to stay outside with Alex and the October air.

"We can start by going for a walk," I said, holding out my hand.

He laced his fingers into mine and smiled when I looked into his face. We started walking and I wasn't sure where we were going, but it felt like we were headed in the right direction. As we strolled under streetlights and past doormen in uniform, I remembered once thinking that Manhattan seemed like the loneliest place on earth. But right now, it didn't feel that way at all.